I0659888

HEATHER CARTER

Ellie and the King's Pandemonium Candle

First published by Heather Carter 2023

Copyright © 2023 by Heather Carter

All rights reserved. No part of this publication may be reproduced, stored or transmitted in any form or by any means, electronic, mechanical, photocopying, recording, scanning, or otherwise without written permission from the publisher. It is illegal to copy this book, post it to a website, or distribute it by any other means without permission.

This novel is entirely a work of fiction. The names, characters and incidents portrayed in it are the work of the author's imagination. Any resemblance to actual persons, living or dead, events or localities is entirely coincidental.

Heather Carter asserts the moral right to be identified as the author of this work.

Heather Carter has no responsibility for the persistence or accuracy of URLs for external or third-party Internet Websites referred to in this publication and does not guarantee that any content on such Websites is, or will remain, accurate or appropriate.

First edition

ISBN: 978-0-578-27860-5

*This book was professionally typeset on Reedsy.
Find out more at reedsy.com*

To all those who look at the stars and dream.

Contents

Acknowledgement

I would like to acknowledge all of my alpha and beta readers that helped me shape this story! A big shout out to my family for their patience while I wrote this, and to my cat Smokey for being the best writing buddy EVER.

Note: Ellie and the King's Pandemonium was previously published on Kindle Vella.

Chapter 1

Black.

Sprayed with flecks of silver and swirls of green.

Lifetimes above me, a white dot streaked over the dark canvas, stirring that familiar bubbling in my chest. An echo of eons past, when our kind once rode those same stars. When our people were strong and proud and light was more abundant.

A memory that none of the living held in our minds, but still imprinted on our life forces—the glowing, white-blue gem buried within our chests, under our shimmering skin and ribs. It is said that we are part stardust—said by those that still dream of old ways.

I framed a circle of stars within my long, thin, azure fingers as I peered with one eye as if observing through a spyglass. Manne used to challenge me to count all the stars I could frame. No matter how much I counted, I was never successful. But I improved my counting skills as a young child.

"*Ellie,*" Manne would say, her violet eyes bright, "*do you know that whoever can call the stars into order will rule them?*"

"*Rule the stars? But only a soul paver could do such a thing, and Panne says they don't exist?*" Even my bright, youngling mind was hard to convince of such a far-fetched fairy tale.

"*Panne is wise, but he doesn't know everything,*" she replied with a wink.

I still remembered the way her eyes lit up like those very stars when she spun her magical tales for me. We were opposite in many ways: I was a skeptic; she was a dreamer of impossible things. Same silvery purple hair, violet eyes, deep blue skin—people said I had grown up to be her very image.

1

But her soul burned so much brighter than mine ever could. The day it returned to the stars, I felt mine dim. I felt the whole world dim.

Clanging bells rang out in the distance, marking the oncoming starset. Sitting up, I smoothed the rebellious hairs from my face and let my gaze follow the glow of Silis, the towering, silver city to the west. Glistening buildings that pricked the sky within the circle of the glowing amber moat stood as a reminder that life awaited me. Safety awaited.

Sure enough, the edges of the horizon were slowly closing in with the blackness, consuming the beautiful stars. I'd stayed out a bit later than intended, but one advantage of my long legs is that I was faster than most of my peers.

Standing on the large flat surface of the rock, I approached the long sheer drop that surrounded it. A vast waving field of tall white grass stood between the Tower Rocks and the moat bridge. Wildions wouldn't be out until the last star was consumed, but it would not be long now. Panne would die of fear if I got caught out after the guards raised the bridges. The ugly scar down my back reminded me never to let it happen again.

I backed away several paces and then charged ahead before sailing through the air. The instant my bare feet left the ground is when I felt most free. For just a moment, I was flying. Every time, I willed myself to rise instead of fall. To ascend and disappear with the stars, to wherever they go. Wherever Manne was. But the ground met my feet every time.

Bounding high, I sprang from the ground three times, legs pumping on the third descent as I met the ground running. My waist-length hair, both loose and mixed with small braids, trailed behind me like wakes on water. A stark, colorful contrast to the pale grass, I was a vulnerable target for the ravenous beasts that awoke soon after the final bells.

The remaining stars fueled my energy, and I pushed forward at a rapid pace before it waned. Celestials rely on starlight for strength as much as food and water. Outside of the safety of the city, our survival was slim in the complete darkness.

Just as the last stars were fading, I reached the drawbridge and sprinted across, barely crossing the threshold as it raised behind me with the closing bells. Icy stares of the gatekeepers burned into my cheeks as I quickly blended in with the flow of work-weary people making their way to their assigned homes.

Even in total darkness, it was never truly dark in Silis. Buildings emanated light. The streets glowed softly. Even the ambient light of the acidic moat reached the top of the shining city walls. We were a star in the darkness, the only city around for leagues. Three star-rises travel to the next. Only special armored carriages could make the trip, and ours were only questionably sufficient.

Walking among a crowd of fellow Celestials, it was hard to blend in. Worn brown trousers under a sleeveless, worn dress of the same color, no shoes—I looked like someone far below my station. My station was hardly low. Panne was commanding chief of the King's guard, in direct service to Premier Diltron, ruler of our city.

Our living quarters were larger than most. It was not really fair to even refer to them as "quarters" when they took up the entire top half of a massive tower. Craning my neck, I could see it now—smooth, metallic and stone sides that soared to the sky, capped with a spiked peak. Every bedchamber had exquisite views of the shadow-bathed landscape and the city below. Though we entertained guests and employed staff, only Panne and I lived in our quarters. It was lonely.

As I stepped through the soft disc of light, the gentle, upward stream of air caught and whisked to the entrance of our home. Upon coming through the exit disc, my ears were assaulted by a loud screaming match. Groaning, I rubbed my temples and stalked toward the receiving room to temper the flames again.

"You have cost me my lost cryst, Humett!" screamed Advisor Braxton as he exploded an arrow of red-hot light in Panne's direction.

Panne dodged the assault, leaping to the opposite wall with ease and scaling up to the corner above the door. His boots lay carelessly at my feet.

"Come now, Braxton! Can we never have a civilized conversation about this?" coaxed Panne through thinning patience.

Silver skin reddening in contrast to his long black robes, Braxton raised his stun blaster again, poised to strike. His long, silver hair was slicked back and bound, which usually meant he'd come expecting a battle. Sneering up at his opponent, he ground a reply through clenched teeth.

"You're the uncivilized one! You viper!"

"I will not force her! Oh," said Panne upon catching sight of me leaning on the door frame with my arms crossed. "Ellette! I didn't see you come in, dear." His pale blue face shifted into a bright smile as he leaped to the floor.

Braxton whirled my direction, embarrassment replacing his rage. Holstering his blaster, he parked his hands on his hips, unable to look me in the eye. "Ellette," he offered in greeting with a terse nod.

Unamused, I rolled my eyes. "The answer is still *no*, Advisor," I said dryly, like every other time before.

Face crumpling in defeat, Braxton's shoulders slumped with a sigh. "But he loves you! I don't want to have to match him with that Rierdly girl!"

Narrowing my eyes, I glared at the mention of my friend. "Agatha is a perfectly lovely young woman and would make anyone a wonderful wife!"

"Yes, yes, I'm sure she is, but—"

"As I said before," I boldly interrupted, taking a step toward the desperate politician, "when and *if* I decide to marry someone, it will be on my *own* terms. Not *anyone* else's."

Features hardening, Braxton glared at me with steely blue eyes before turning once again to Panne, shoving him roughly. "You ought to get a better hold on your daughter! Wild and uncivilized, just like you!"

Fire reignited as they began screaming and chasing each other once more. Had the walls not been burnished silver, the room would be in absolute tatters. As it was, the furniture had to be replaced regularly because of the heated arguments between two men who had been like brothers since childhood.

Throwing my hands in the air, I stalked out of the door. "You know what? Fine! Kill each other."

Sounds of the match dulled when I disappeared into the dim outer stairwell. There was an air lift nearby, but there *was* something wild beating in me. My eyes traveled to the first landing, lit only by the glow of the city through a small window. I bit my lower lip briefly in anticipation as I reared a few paces until my back met the wall. Arms pumping, I lunged at the bottom step, pushed off with my feet, and flew up and forward, landing on the first landing with barely a thud. Another swift movement, using the wall as leverage, and I sprang up to the next landing.

My heart pounded in my ears, air bursting in and out of my lungs as I took entire sections with single, flying bounds. Up, up, up—almost to the top floor.

Upon exiting into the hallway of my destination, I stopped to catch my breath, leaning on the wall next to the stairwell door. It was always a rush, coming close to flying. Blessed with Panne's agility, I liked to imagine that I'd come closer than anyone else of my generation. But the achievement was as rare as black crystals. It had faded into the world of legend.

Down the short hallway, I entered the set of frosted glass doors into my large, vaulted bedchamber. A soaring, black ceiling of stars, walls depicting the beautiful, pale landscape surrounding our city, and a soft, white, circular bed set into the center of the floor, so I could immerse myself in it all when true escape was impossible. It was my own indoor haven. I'd painted it myself, with Manne, many years ago when I was young.

With a yawn, I trudged into the adjoining bathroom for a quick bath, scrubbing the dirt from my feet, and cleansing the sweat from my hair. Afterward, I changed into my favorite long, violet nightgown and sat out on my balcony to comb my wet tresses.

The air was fresh and cool, with the scent of field grasses and flowers wafting on the gentle breeze. Our set skies were dark, but the land remained awake.

Wildions should've be out of their burrows by then, roaming those fields in their predatory state. Long, gleaming teeth below silvery whiskers and green eyes, knife-like talons hidden in paws the size of my head—they were deadly sentinels that reminded us who this land *truly* belonged to. Kings and premieres could make any claim they wanted, but it was the dark and beautiful wild creatures that ruled our world. Mutual respect kept us alive. Following the rules of *nature* kept us alive.

I was so entranced in my thoughts that I almost didn't hear the soft thud of feet as they landed on the balcony. By now, I was so used to this occurrence that it wasn't even necessary to look.

"Are they still at each other's throats?"

Gillion Braxton plopped down in the chair next to me, drawing a deep breath, just as he always did after scaling the side of the building from his balcony to mine. His long, silver arms draped over the armrests as his exhausted, crystal blue eyes fixated on the black sky above us. Without the stars out, we had only the residual glow of the city to draw from. Yet he came to my balcony more nights than naught.

"I think they've finally settled down for drinks now."

Grinning, I shook my head. "I swear our pannes fight like an old married couple."

"I guess since our mannes are gone, there's not much to tame them." A hint of sadness tinged my best friend's voice. His manne had only been gone two years, and it still felt as fresh as the day it happened.

Casting him a sympathetic glance, my hand found his, interlacing our fingers, causing a familiar soft, white glow that ebbed at the point of contact. The corner of his mouth tipped up in appreciation as he lifted my hand and planted a kiss on the back of my palm. It stirred that same curious rush I felt every time he did that, but I restrained myself from allowing my thoughts to wander any further.

Gil was like a brother to me, and I like his sister. Living above and below each other, we'd spent our days together as children, chasing away the boredom and loneliness that came with being the children of high-stationed officials.

Looking at him now, hip-length, silver hair draped loosely over the back of the white chair; long, muscular legs stretched out in exhaustion... he was no longer a child, any more than I was. Yet we still spent our time together when he wasn't working as his father's apprentice, learning the ins and outs of the government and all the boring politics thereof.

I longed to enlist as a guard or even a king's soldier, but my duty was to learn how to be a lady and run a household. To be a good wife to whomever

I was matched. They wanted me in gowns and jewels. *I* wanted to feel the wind through my hair and touch the stars one day. Braxton was right: I *was* a wild thing.

"I've invited Agatha over tomorrow," I grinned, squeezing his hand.

Gil immediately perked up, tired eyes sparking with new life. Though he tried to remain casual, I could see this was welcome news. "Well, that's interesting, since I'd also planned on spontaneously dropping by since it's my day off."

Laughing, I stood and leaned back against the wide stone railing with crossed arms. "Well, you can *'spontaneously drop by'* about midrise and we'll have our meal together. Then perhaps I can get sleepy and need a nap."

A broad smile stretched across his beautiful, argentine face as he rose to his full, towering height and quickly closed the space between us, pulling me tightly into his arms. The glow enveloped us instantly. "You are the best, you know that?"

Straining for breath, I patted his back with my free hand and forced a smile. "You're welcome."

He quickly released me and took a step back with an apologetic wince. He often forgot his own strength, so extraordinary, even after starset. Drawing in air freely and deeply, I waved dismissively as I smiled.

"I'm fine."

Sighing deeply, Gil's smile softened. I hated it when he smiled at me like this. Tipping my lips up briefly, I fiddled with my comb and averted my eyes to the city below.

"You'll find your match someday, Ellie. They'll never deserve you, but you'll be happy. I know it."

Words meant to uplift and comfort only caused a sting. I wanted him to be happy. I wanted happiness for myself. But that would mean parting from him forever. At least in the way we were now. I hated that thought, and I hated growing up.

"I'm going to turn in for the night," I announced with a fabricated yawn. "See you tomorrow?"

Gil was already sitting on the ledge, legs dangling over. He shot me an excited grin. "Wouldn't miss it!" And then he was gone with a whoosh.

I rolled my eyes and shouted after him, "You can use my door, you know!" Retreating laughter reached my ears in response.

Chapter 2

"Do you think the yellow is too much?"

Sitting up in the lounge chair, I rested my chin in between my fingers and drew the corners of my lips downward with the wag of my head. "No! It looks radiant against your skin."

Agatha beamed and smoothed the flowing yellow gown as she turned from side to side in the mirror. She really did look lovely—icy, light-green complexion, long emerald curls, and large jade eyes. We'd just finished applying cosmetics from my rarely used collection to complement her new dress. Her brilliant white smile could light up the entire city right now. Our morning shopping trip was well worth the crysts it cost me.

"I hope he likes it," she sighed dreamily.

"He will, believe me!" I assured, rising to wrap an arm around her shoulders. "Gil loves yellow."

We stood in stark contrast to each other. Agatha looked like royalty, while I looked ready to crawl into a comfy chair with a book in my long, unadorned black tunic and loose black trousers. This is how I wanted it though—for my friend to shine even brighter, as if she possibly could.

Many suitors had offered themselves to Agatha Rierdly, but so far she'd turned down every single one, holding out hope for Gil. She hoped that one day, his father would consent to the match, and that Gil would formally declare his intentions. It was frustrating, watching them dance around each other like this, but like a good friend, all I could do was choreograph the steps.

"You're so good to me, Ellie," Agatha mused with a smile as her hand reached behind to close over mine, setting off a cherry glow.

Grinning in response, I squeezed her shoulders. "That's what friends are for. Now—"

There was a knock at the bedroom door. Agatha stiffened and blanched. Passing her a reassuring look in the mirror, I pried myself from her grip and went to see who it was.

"Mr. Braxton is here to see you, Ma'am," informed Teli, our housekeeper.

My eyes widened. "Really? I wasn't expecting him this rise."

She arched a brow in suspicion. "Shall I turn him away, then?"

"No!" cried Agatha from across the room.

I shot her a warning glare before turning back to Teli with a sweet smile.

"Of course not. We wouldn't want to be rude. Show him to the tearoom and we'll be down in a moment. He can dine with us if you'd be so kind as to pass along instructions for another place setting?"

Teli nodded and left to do my bidding. From the look on her age-worn blue face, she could see through my charade, but was kind enough to play along.

It wasn't long before we entered the flower-filled tearoom. A tall, broad-shouldered vision of a man stood with his back to us, bedecked in black, with a thick silver braid trailing down his back. When he turned around, my heart fluttered in that annoying fashion that it sometimes did.

Gil's eyes were bright when they met mine and then quickly swept to Agatha, a cheery smile slashing his face. The whole room glowed brighter when they saw each other. Satisfied at my success, I hooked my arm through Agatha's and tugged her forward.

"Gil! How nice of you to drop by," I exaggerated with a wink.

"Oh, you know, I was just in the building."

Taking seats in the fragrant atmosphere, I did my best to blend into the background, only prodding along the conversation when either of them grew quiet. Both of my friends had an unfortunate propensity for shyness. Lucky for them, I was a wise matchmaker and much more confident.

Appetizers were served along with the strong petal tea that I knew Gil adored. I watched in anticipation of Agatha's coming comment about the sweetness of the brew, but I was sorely disappointed to only see her face twisted in disgust as she discreetly set it back on the saucer. She caught my furrowed brows and merely shrugged before pasting on her sweet smile once more for the man of her dreams.

"Lovely rise, isn't it?"

Gil affirmed with a smile as his gaze traveled out the window to the canvas of color-swathed stars beyond the eternal glow of the city. "It is! Though I hear we are expecting rains this set."

A shadow of disappointment cast over her features. The rains sometimes stayed for several rises at a time. "Oh. I had not heard that."

After a reprimanding look from me, Gil hurried to redeem himself of the negativity. "But of course, without rains, we would not have such beautiful flowers," he added, raising his teacup with a smile before taking a generous sip.

Giving up on that vein, I merely forced a chuckle and drank the rest of my tea in one gulp. Getting these two to relax and generate a strong flow of conversation was proving a challenge. Facilitating the atmosphere was only half the battle.

Mealtime in the dining room was not any better. They cast bright smiles and twinkled gazes at each other, but hardly any independent conversation. I felt like a chattering fool, throwing conversation back and forth between my two good friends on either side of the table. It was giving me a genuine headache.

"Well, this has been a wonderful visit, but I'm getting an ache in my head," I announced, rubbing my throbbing temples. "You two are more than welcome to stay and visit in the tearoom. My panne will be out until starset. I'm going to lie down for a little while."

We rose from the table, but I noticed Agatha practically cling to my side, blanching. This was not part of the plan she was privy to. She glanced at me with wide terror in her eyes, and I sensed her trepidation.

Smiling, I squeezed her hand in reassurance before nodding toward Gil. He offered her his arm, ever the perfect gentleman.

11

"Shall we?"

Gulping, Agatha accepted and smiled tightly as he whisked her off toward the tearoom again. Crossing my arms, I peered down the hallway at their retreating forms down. Too stiff. Not what I'd expect from potential star-crossed lovers. Wrenching my lips in disappointment, I turned and made my way to my room with a sigh.

***

Sobbing awoke me from my blissful slumber. Through bleary eyes, I found Agatha sitting on the step at my bedside, face buried in her hands. Glancing outside, it was still rise. Not terribly long after I'd fallen asleep. Pain still lanced through my head, but I sat up and reached a hand to her arm, only to quickly snatch it back when the light flashed in my eyes with her intense emotions.

"Agatha? Did something happen?"

She merely sobbed louder. My stomach clenched. Something was very wrong, and terrifying possibilities were floating in my head.

"Agatha," I repeated, unsure if I was ready for an answer, "did Gil upset you?"

Sniffling, Agatha wiped her black-streaked cheeks. "He's going to Star City."

I froze. Star City: our kingdom's heart. Five star-rises travel, by one of the most dangerous routes. This meant that not only would Gil be at grave risk, but so would Panne, as he would be required to attend to them.

"Are you sure of this?" I questioned sternly.

Agatha nodded through renewing tears. "He said they'll be gone a month, starting two rises from now."

Blankets were flying as I leaped out of bed and flew to the door, face twisted in grief.

"Wait!" Agatha called, "Gil isn't here—he went home before I came up here—hey! What are you doing? Ellie!"

I barely registered her panicked cries as I was running full speed to the balcony, leaping upon the rail before diving off with outstretched arms. Her shouts faded to the back of my mind as I flipped mid-air and bounded down from balcony to balcony at a rapid pace, swinging myself inward, diving out, like a tumbling drop of rain. It was still star-rise, and people were out to see me, but I didn't care. Let them talk. Let them whisper about how scandalous and wild that Humett girl was behaving again. Only one mission burned clear in my mind.

Landing with a thud on my bare feet, I found Gil's balcony door's thankfully ajar, not that it would've stopped me, anyway. I burst in with blazing determination, only to find a very surprised Gil, stepping out of his bathroom in a state of undress.

"Whoa! Ellie! What—"

I was already throwing his robe in his face, not affording him a moment of modesty by averting my eyes. Instead, I launched into my interrogation. "When were you going to tell me?"

Quickly, he slipped the black robe over himself and tied the belt, squaring his jaw. He was annoyed at my intrusion, but I stepped up to him, not backing down. He had some answers for me I wasn't about to leave without obtaining.

"Well?" I pressed.

His features hardened and his tone was surprisingly cold. "I thought it would be best if you heard it from your panne at starset. Now, would you please excuse me?" He tried to sidestep me, but I was just as quick, grabbing his forearm with a blazing iron grip and pulling him back. Groaning in frustration, he tried to shove my hand away, but I step in front of him and firmly grasped both of his shoulders, pinning him back against the wall. Light burst from the point of contact.

"Gil," I ground out through clenched teeth, *"Talk. Now."*

He met my intense glare, and I felt the determination finally ebb from his iron muscles. Losing a long breath, Gil finally confessed. "Okay, yes, we are leaving."

Confirmation hit me like a blow to the gut. I struggled to keep up my angry demeanor. Fear was seeping in through the cracks. "Why?" The word came out shaky to my ears.

"The king has called. I don't know any more than that. And that's the *truth*."

Stilling the quaking in my jaw, I clenched it. This was horrible. No, *horrifying*. The risk of death to make the journey in person, even with the armored carriage, was high. Star City had better carriages, resources they could trade out for the journey home… if they ever made it there in the first place.

"But in person? That's just…" My resolve cracked. Just as my hands slipped from his shoulders, Gil pulled me to his chest and his tight arms wrapped around me. My tears slid onto the silky fabric of his robe as I tried to wrap my brain around the truth. Shutting my eyes tightly to block out the light, I welcomed the warmth.

"Hey…" he coaxed quietly, "your panne will come back safe and sound. I'll make sure of it. *He'll* make sure of it. He's the best we've got."

The thought of losing panne was enough to send me into a rare torrent of sobs. I hadn't cried much since the day manne died, but my anxiety took hold. Panne had only been to Star City once, and Gil had never even left Silis. It was as good as signing their execution orders to demand they come now, without bringing new carriages first. The wildions and panteours and all manner of beasts, growing progressively more in number and violence along the way, would tear them to shreds, slicing through the insufficient metal shields.

And here, my best friend, a man still in his prime years, was about to head in for the slaughter to obey the orders of a king who cared little for his future. To imagine his smile slashed to bits by long, deadly talons made my stomach roil. No matter how I tried, I could not force the horrific images from my mind.

"Why do *you* have to go?" I cried, shoving away from him. I stalked toward the balcony with my hands grasping my scalp, desperate for some fresh air.

Footsteps rapidly caught up to me, and in a whoosh of air, Gil was suddenly in front of me, blocking the exit. Startled, I stumbled back, sprawling to the floor. Kneeling before me, unbound hair slipping around his shoulders to frame his sad face, Gil calmly held out his hand. I took it and he pulled me to where I could sit on my heels in front of him, knee to knee.

"Ellie," he sighed, "There's a good chance that I'm going to take my father's place soon. The Premier has ordered I attend. I cannot disobey. Besides, I'd volunteer in a heartbeat to keep our pannes safe, anyway."

My heart broke. "I don't want to lose you, Gil," I confessed through tears. "I *can't* lose you."

A hand rested on the side of my face as his thumb brushed away a stream of tears from my cheek. My hand closed over his and I held it with dear life as if it would keep him there forever. He brought my other hand to his lips and softly kissed my inner palm, sending a curious wave through me from the point of contact. Opening my eyes, I met Gil's. They were soft, but in a strange, intense way.

Something in me felt warm and rushed all at once. That heart flip. Suddenly, the world around us felt different and faded. I was crying, but not as hard as before. Beautiful, crystal blue held me in a trance. Watery, but brilliant. I wasn't sure what was happening, but I knew I wasn't afraid of it.

Slowly, Gil leaned in. The moment his lips captured mine, I lost all concept of space and time. And, oh, the light… soft, brilliant, just like his lips. Rising to meet him, I wrapped my arms around his neck and let myself become lost with him. Lost in his arms as they pulled me close.

Pulling away for a moment, Gil's forehead rested on mine as one of his hands threaded in my hair. Breathing deeply, we drank each other in.

"Ellie… I—"

A thought crashed through the haze of desire and I suddenly leaped back with a gasp, breaking the spell. What was I doing? "No… no! We—we can't…" I rose to my feet and hugged my arms as I paced the floor, racked with guilt.

Frowning, Gil rose and approached me with an outstretched arm. "Ellie? What's wrong?"

I leaped away as if he were on fire. Hurt flashed across his face. Tearing my eyes to the floor, I hunched my shoulders, as if to protect my confused heart.

"Gil... *Agatha!*"

Raking a hand down his face, Gil groaned in frustration as realization dawned on him. We'd just betrayed a friend. So easily, she'd slipped from our minds in that moment of heightened emotions. I'd worked hard to arrange meetings for them and now I'd gone and undermined everything.

"This is all my fault," I said in a panic, stalking toward the balcony door. "I shouldn't have come here! Oh, Stars..."

"Stars be damned, Ellette!" Gil snapped.

I ceased my retreat and whirled around in surprise at the sound of my full first name. Gil had never called me that before. I found him with his back to the wall and his forehead braced in his palm.

Tears threatened to flood my eyes, but I steeled them away. I wanted to go to him and put my arms around him, like any old time, but that was too dangerous now. Everything was ruined.

"We're the ones who are damned, Gil."

My name caught my ears, but I was already bounding away, back to my own balcony, just as the thunder rumbled far in the distance.

Chapter 3

That set, I had to sit and listen to an overly positive Panne tell me about all the wonderful gifts he would bring back for me on his journey. Promises of jewels, trinkets, gowns—everything short of a star itself.

Every word was torture. I wanted to shake Panne, beg him to stay, to defy the king. But that would only land him in a den of beasts, and a grisly public death. In the end, all I could do was humor him with nods and the slightest of smiles. I had nothing else to say. No tears left to cry. I'd expelled them all after fleeing Gil.

Numbly, I lay in my bed later that set, hugging my pillows. Rain streamed down the windows like tears. The sound should've been calming, but I barely registered it. Everything I loved was about to be taken from me, and I was cold.

Manne would have the perfect words to say. She would react the right way. She would know what to do. I still remember how she cradled me to sleep every night for a year when I had a nasty streak of nightmares after my first wildion sighting.

After my "incident", when one nearly killed me, Manne was no longer there to cradle me. It was Gil that slept by my side for days and days until I was healed enough to be deemed "surviving". He'd snuck through my balcony several times until Panne gave up and just let him come through the front entrance. Though mostly unconscious, I could remember clearly sensing his presence. His warmth at my side. The comfort of him merely being nearby. I craved it even now, deep down under the stones I'd erected around myself.

Agatha did not know what happened between Gil and me. I aimed to keep it that way. Her heart was far purer than mine. She had not sullied herself with someone else's intended. Or intended to be intended, rather. Everything was so confusing now. Gil loved Agatha, and she loved him. Why would he kiss me? And why would I kiss him? It wasn't one-sided, that's for sure. That's the worst part of it all: I'd been the biggest hypocrite.

None of that mattered much now. Gil was as good as dead. As were our pannes. Soon, I would be alone. With no panne to arrange a match, no man in his right mind would offer one. It was just as well. My heartbreak may very well do me in.

As I lay moping, I didn't hear my bedroom door open or softly click shut. It wasn't until I felt the depression on the bed behind me that I registered that someone else was in the room. A familiar scent surprised me, but I didn't protest. Closing my eyes, I snuggled back into the wall of warmth as I lifted the blanket for him to cover up. When the strong, silver arm wrapped around my waist, I breathed deeply.

"I don't want us to end like that, Ellie."

"I'm sorry," I whispered into the soft blue glow enveloping us like a glove. "I just don't know what to do."

He gently stroked my hair and planted a soft kiss on my temple as he lay his cheek against mine, fully enveloping me. "Just sleep, then."

It was an intimate act, one that wouldn't have been thought of so deeply before our previous encounter that rise, but now it *was* something deep. Solidifying. Hesitantly, I rested my hand over his and hugged him closer, never wanting to let go. He responded by splaying his fingers to interlace with mine as he planted another slow kiss on my cheek.

"Goodset, Ellie," he whispered in my ear.

Stars, help me...

I was in love with Gil.

***

Star-rise came, but the only indication was the clanging of the rise bells. The rains still blanketed the sky in darkness. Feeling rested, I stretched and rolled over, still enveloped in Gil's arms. He hummed in his sleep and tucked me in close to his chest. Wrapping my arm around his waist, I savored the moment. Before any wakefulness brought regret. Fire may consume us in the afterlife, but I didn't want to leave his side. Not yet.

Lifting my head, I took in his angelic, sleeping face. Long, dark eyelashes rested on glowing, shimmering cheeks. A straight nose over perfect, silvery-pink lips. I couldn't help but fixate on those lips now. Just yester, they were pressing against my own. The last thing I remember before falling asleep was how they whispered in my ear. Life was in those lips. For how long? How long would this body hold its warmth? Its glow?

Before I had given it full thought, my thumb was grazing his lower lip. Gil's eyes fluttered open and held mine. We lay and just watched each other for a long time, eyes full of things unsaid. I knew what I wanted to say, but I found I couldn't say anything. Speechless, I lay there like a willing captive. We were sad, but filled with longing. And contentment. It was a heavy weight to bear.

Gil raised his hand and tucked a stray violet tendril of hair behind my ear. I lost a shuddering breath at his touch. Taking the cue, his fingers wove in my hair as he dipped his head down and I felt those warm lips just grazing mine...

There was a knock at the bedroom door. Wide-eyed, I rolled away from Gil and the light disappeared. It had been near-blinding, filling the entire room. I could still see the spots in my vision.

"Um, yes?" I called, trying to sound sleepy, praying the door was locked.

"Ellie," Panne's voice called through the door. My eyes snapped to Gil's as the color drained from my face. Panne continued, "I have to head to the palace for the day, but I'll be back before starset."

"Okay, Panne! Good rise to you!"

"You too, dear... and to you, Gillion."

I nearly fainted, but Panne merely walked off down the hall without another word. Releasing my breath, I buried my head under the blanket. My blue cheeks were burning scarlet.

Gil found me under there. He was biting back laughter. "You think he'll feed me to a wildion?"

Shoving him, I sat up, pressing my palms to my eyes. Gil pulled up next to me and rubbed a hand on my back.

"Are you all right?"

Fighting back sudden tears, I shook my head. "Gil, what if you don't come back?"

"We *will* come back," he corrected.

"But what if you don't?"

"And what if I do?"

Groaning in frustration, I started to rise from the bed, only to be caught by the wrist.

"I'm serious, Gil!" I cried, resisting his hold.

"So am I."

Immediately, my attempts to flee his side ceased when I caught the look in his eyes. He was indeed serious. With a sigh, I slumped back down and cast him an apologetic glance as I wrapped my arms around my knees.

"I'm sorry for being so negative, Gil. I don't want to put any more stress on you than you're already under. That's very inconsiderate of me."

Wrapping his arm around my back, he squeezed me. "It's okay. I think a little stress is expected right now," he said with a nervous chuckle.

Regarding him somberly, we grew quiet for a time, the air thick with what lie ahead. Gil was so capable—more so than anyone I knew, next to Panne. He was built to be a warrior, yet had followed in his panne's chosen path of politics. No military training, so only instinct and his strength to rely on if and when danger came. I could imagine him trying to take on a beast and outlasting most, but not ultimately succeeding. Perhaps my lack of faith in him would be his ultimate downfall. My skeptic nature was nearly impossible to control at times like those. Manne would uplift him with brightest blessings.

20

Eventually, Gill stood and went into the bathroom. While he was in there, I changed for the day and tried to rack my brain of ways to make the day better. To turn things around. There had to be *something* I could do. Something that didn't involve uncharted territory that perhaps we weren't quite ready for. Gil meant the world to me. I couldn't let him go without that brightest blessing.

I finished changing and turned to find Gil standing in the bathroom doorway, arms crossed, leaning against the doorframe with an amused smile and bright eyes. Blushing from head to toe, I froze in place.

"H-how long have you been standing there?"

He quirked a brow as his gaze dragged over me from head to toe, making me blush even brighter. "Long enough."

Just when I thought I would faint, he broke into laughter. "I'm joking, Ellie! I just came out."

Shooting him a glare, I threw my comb in his direction and stalked off to make my bed. Only moments later, I yelped as he scooped me up and tossed me on the bed like a child. Gil pounced over me and began tickling me in my worst spots that only he knew, making me howl with laughter until I couldn't breathe.

"Hey, that's what you get for walking in on me yesterday!" he teased.

Pleading for mercy, I attempted to grab hold of his wrists, but he flipped his hands and in a flash, he had mine pinned down on either side of my head. Still giggling, I was staring up at him, curtains of his silver hair on either side. Gil's eyes were bright above his soft smile as his laughter died down.

"I love your laugh."

My brows shot up, biting back further giggles behind a smile. "You love torturing me, that's what!"

Pausing, Gil held my gaze. "I'm going to come back to you, Ellie."

Laughter ceased. There was no hint of jest in his expression, only admiration. A strange feeling stirred in my chest again. I felt increasingly warm, and sort of like I was floating in mid-air. Like *we* were floating in mid-air.

To *me*. Those were his words. Words that gave me hope. If only a shred.

I wanted to confess my love for him right then and there, to pull him into my arms and give myself to him, propriety be damned. But I knew the hour was growing later, and he was expected at the palace with his panne. Not showing up was not an option.

Pulling my wrists free, I wrapped my arms around his neck and pulled him down for a tight embrace. "You'd better."

***

Later that rise, I sat uncomfortably in a public tea house across from Agatha. She'd shown up at my door, out of sorts, after Gil left. Despite my massive guilt and desire to run, she was still my friend.

The third berry mini cake was just entering her mouth and her shoulders slouched as her elbows and forearm rested on the table. She'd had something stronger than tea before showing up at my door, but I didn't fault her for her uncharacteristic behavior. I would've downed an entire bottle of bulb wine myself if it were placed in front of me.

"I don't understand why Gil has to go!" she lamented, words slurring slightly through her cake-filled cheeks.

Sipping my tea from the translucent, lavender teacup, my eyes swept the shimmering room, filled with flowers in crystal vases and cheerful, upper-station patrons. I dared any of them to turn their noses up at us right now. At Agatha, and her tear-stained, thrice-mended blue dress. My dear friend was as heartbroken as I was, only she was inebriated enough to show it.

It was in this very tea house that I met Agatha. Panne brought me one rise several years ago, and a lovely, emerald-haired young lady was serving us. She accidentally spilled an entire tray of tea and pastries all over my new dress. Agatha lost her job but gained a friend.

Now, as her patroness, I saw she was able to finish her education in the respectable art of hairdressing without having to balance jobs she hated to survive. Coming from a low-station family, her prospects of pursuing a preferred career were slim. I knew how it felt to be tied down, so if I could help one young woman to achieve her dreams, it was well-worth the crysts I had little use for.

Agatha moped over her untouched tea. It was a tea she preferred, but it had grown cold during her cake-binging session. She was ordinarily a bubble of life, and it was sad to see her so... sad.

"Gil has been ordered to go by the premier, unfortunately," I said with a sigh.

Her eyes snapped to mine as she straightened. "So, you talked to him last set? What else did he say?"

Shifting awkwardly in my seat, I nodded and cleared my tightening throat. My eyes could not fixate anywhere near hers. She would see straight through me, and it would all be over.

"He just told me it's mandatory. The king has called."

Face falling, Agatha resumed her slumping, "Oh."

Pained to see her grief, my hand reached out to cover hers. "Don't fear, Agatha. They will return before we know it."

"Yes, perhaps," she said, before raising her red-rimmed eyes, "but will it be in one piece?"

Anger flashed through me at her gruesome suggestion. My hand slammed down on the table next to hers, startling her and drawing the attention of the other patrons. Staring daggers at her, I spoke in low, gritted words. "That's enough!" I hissed. "Have you forgotten that Gil is not the only one going on this journey? That *my panne* is risking his life as well? Or are you too selfish to consider anyone else that doesn't affect you?"

Agatha stilled, gaping at me. Hurt leached into her features as they drooped. Then indignation. Reaching into her bag, she pulled out a fifty cryst piece and tossed it on the table before rising. I grabbed it and handed it back to her, but she shook her head. "No. I'll pay for it today. After all, I wouldn't want to be *selfish*." She spat that last word with venom before stalking off out the door.

Cursing under my breath, I grasped my scalp and closed my eyes. Whispers were floating through the air, burning my ears. A hand touched my shoulder, and I flinched. "What?" I turned to see a wide-eyed server backing away with her tray.

"I'm sorry, Miss, I just wanted to know if you needed a refill?" she said, voice shaking as she pointed to the teapot in the center of the table.

I shook my head and tried to gather my composure. "Sorry. No, I'm all right, thank you."

She nodded and backed away slowly. The moment she turned, I grabbed my things and fled the tea house, hurrying toward home, not bothering to open my umbrella or hail a ride in the pouring rain.

Chapter 4

Rain ran down my face and soaked my clothes as I ran across the field. Though the stars were hidden, the wildions still obeyed the time and remained in their burrows. It was miserable outside, but it was safe. Energy wasn't as abundant this far from the city with no starshine, but I had enough for what I needed.

Soon, I was climbing the face of one of the tallest Tower Rocks. Ordinarily, I would bound up in seconds, but my muscles enjoyed the current challenge. The rocks were slippery in the rain, and I slipped multiple times, but eventually, I reached the top and laid flat on my back, letting the cool rain hit my face in large, splashing drops.

Panne was still gone for the rise, and I couldn't bear to sit around in that large house, imagining what it would be like to be there alone. Agatha was angry with me, and I with her. I was a terrible friend, but she was insensitive as well. And she loved Gil. That hurt more than I'd like to admit.

I lay there in the pouring rain, letting every thought I'd been avoiding come rolling through my mind. Manne's death... Panne's upcoming demise... my stupidity at rejecting Advisor Braxton's offer of Gil's hand all these years. We could've been married and had a family by now. Then again, that would leave fatherless children after this suicide journey.

I was so caught up in my thoughts and the soothing sounds of the rain that I initially failed to notice the first warning bells of starset. Sleep was tugging at my eyes even through the chill and soaking wet clothing. There, away from the rest of the world, I was safe to rest for a while.

Suddenly, I registered what I had heard, and bolted upright in a panic. How much time had passed since that bell? Scrambling to my feet, I ran for the ledge, ready to bound to the ground, knowing it would take all my energy to reach the drawbridge at that rate. Just as my feet reached the ledge, however, I slipped on the wet rock and tumbled off the side with a scream. I was free-falling to my death; the ground rapidly growing closer to me. This high up, if I hit the ground on a non-bound, I was doomed.

I was able to tuck myself in and straighten a thin moment before impacting the ground with my feet. It was a partial bound, but not an even one, and not good enough to spare me completely. I cried out in agony as a sharp pain shot through my left ankle. Hitting the ground once more, on my side this time, I bounced slightly and rolled to a stop. Gasping for breath and paralyzed by pain, I blinked the stars away from my vision and tried to assess whether I was, in fact, still alive.

Just when I finally drew a full breath into my lungs, my death knell rang out through the land. The last bell screamed through the air. Starset had come, and I was still a good distance from the drawbridge, which would be raising that very moment.

"No... No! No!" I cried, pulling myself to my feet. As soon as the weight hit my ankle, I cried and nearly crumpled again. I could never bound high enough to get back up to the top of the rock in that state. I had made the gravest of mistakes.

I was easy prey for wildions, and I knew I had no chance. But I wasn't about to lie down and let them take me. Recalling every iota of strength I had left, I bounded as high and as far as I could. And it *hurt*. Badly. As hard as I tried, I could not contain the scream that tore from my throat on the second bound. The pain was nearly blinding, and my head felt like air.

Out of the corner of my eye, I detected rapid movements in the grass, coming from multiple directions. Growls pierced the darkness, and I knew exactly what they belonged to. The memory was imprinted on my soul like the sound of my Manne's voice. Still, I refused to resign myself yet. I would rather die in the moat than face the talons of these beasts ever again. A dive headfirst into the acidic liquid would end things in a mere moment. The suffering would be minimal.

Again and again, I made pathetic bounds, quickly draining of energy and losing strength in my ankle, despite my determination. Bound, stumble, bound, stumble. Over the tall grass, I could see a long-haired, orange tail moving toward me rapidly, with more behind. It was over.

With one last cry, I bent my knees and pushed off the ground, just as the green eyes and bared teeth of the wildion came flying toward me from my left. I braced for the impact, but it came from a different direction.

A wall of silver and black collided with me from the front, pushing me backwards in an explosion of light. Strong arms banded around me as the wildion roared and missed us by a hair's breadth. I could feel the brush of its fur against my bare feet as they trailed behind my savior.

Hardly had we missed one wildion when another leaped. With fast and furious bounds, we dodged them right and left as the skies rumbled and the beasts roared. Faster, faster we went until a mighty bound sent us soaring straight upward. I felt the rock against my back briefly as we launched against a small ledge and up against another foothold.

At last, I tumbled across the flat surface of the Tower Rock, encased in arms, with my head tucked in close to a warm sweat and rain-soaked chest. We hit a large rock, and separated, with my savior stopping short as I flew a bit further before rolling to a stop on my side.

Clenching my eyes shut from the pain, I stiffened, trying to remember how to breathe. Ringing filled my ears, and my teeth sang. But I was alive.

I heard groaning nearby. When I could breathe again, I opened my eyes to find Gil sprawled out on his back, trying to catch his breath. Eyes widening, I pushed myself up to a half-sitting position.

"Gil!" I cried in alarm.

Gil shot up, eyes snapping to mine. He immediately crawled over and crushed me to his chest, his hand grasping the back of my head like a child. "Stars in hell, Ellie! What were you thinking? Didn't you hear the bells?"

I shook violently as I clung to him. "I dozed off, and then I slipped and fell, and my ankle…" Dizziness nearly overcame me, and I clenched my eyes shut, burying my face in his soaked shirt as I regained my bearings.

Wildions still growled on the ground below, stalking at the base of the tower. They couldn't reach us, but up there, on barren rock, exposed to the elements, they knew we couldn't last forever.

"How did you find me?" I asked through chattering teeth.

"I was just at your house. When Teli said she saw you leave with no shoes, and you weren't back yet... Ellie, why are you even out here?"

"I-I just needed to get a-away for a bit."

Gil scoffed and swept his gaze over the rock. "Here? In the pouring rain?"

Nodding, I couldn't think of a clever excuse. It was as stupid as it sounded. I was a fool for taking the risk of coming out here in that weather.

"I'm so sorry, Gil. Thank you for coming after me. I'm afraid it might be in vain, though."

Squeezing me closer, Gil did his best to warm me, but there wasn't much to go around. The air was rapidly getting colder with the set. "We've got to get off this rock."

"I don't know where we could go."

Gently, Gil laid me down. "I'll think of something."

He stood and walked around the rock, surveying for any clues. The wildions followed his every movement from below. I could hear their gruffs and growls. Each noise sent a shock of terror shooting through me.

Gil wasn't gone for long before he trotted back to my side and scooped me up. We were stalking toward one of the other edges. Panicked, I gripped his arms with white knuckles.

"What are you doing?" I demanded.

Readjusting, Gil got a firmer hold on me and stared downward in anticipation. "Just hold on." I moved my arms to hug his neck and squeezed my eyes shut as he leaped off the side of the rock.

Falling, my stomach dropped and my lungs drew in a sharp gasp. One bound, then two. After the third, shorter bound, we came to a stop. Branches brushed my arms as Gil stepped forward.

Opening my eyes, I found we were in a small cave. Brush grew over half the opening, but across from it I could see the sheer wall of the other rock tower.

"We're high enough that we should be safe for the set," remarked Gil as he gently sat me on the dry ground.

The air was still humid and chilly, but not nearly as bad as it was on the exposed surface outside. Relieved, I laid down and hugged my arms. Right now, that cave may as well have been a palace. Guilt drowned out my relief.

"I'm so sorry... I'm... sorry..." I repeated, shaking with tears and cold.

Concern stole over his face when he turned back to me. "Ellie, you're pale."

Glancing down at my arms, they were indeed at least two shades paler than normal. Cold. Pain. Sleepiness. Even in my weary state, I knew it wasn't a great sign.

Without a word, Gil kneeled by my side and carefully sat me up, holding my face in his hands and looking me directly in the eye. "Ellie, I have to get a fire going somehow. And we have to get you out of those wet clothes before you freeze to death."

Holding his gaze, I tried to focus on his words, and not on what lay ahead, or that I was about to fall asleep. "It's okay. I trust you, Gil."

Nodding, Gil held my eyes steadily as he peeled off my top, followed by my trousers, which were painful to remove with my swollen ankle. He paused over my undergarments. Closing his eyes, his throat bobbed as he slowly removed them and tossed them in the pile of wet clothing.

Averting his gaze, Gil helped me turn toward the wall before laying me down. He jumped up and began wrestling with the brush covering the cave entrance. For a short while, I heard snapping twigs and cursing. Finally, the growing crackling of flames. Gil's breath blew in a slow, steady rhythm until I felt the warmth. But my shaking wouldn't subside.

A firm hand shook me awake again.

"Ellie! Stay awake!"

I nodded and pried my eyes open.

"Turn toward the fire."

With help, I rolled slowly to my other side, haphazardly attempting to protect my modesty with my shivering arms.

"Stars, Ellie, you're just about as pale as me," fretted Gil, taking my face in his hands. "I think your body is jolted from your injury."

My eyes met his, noting his furrowed brows over genuinely terrified eyes. I felt his concern leaking into me.

"H-how do w-we—"

"I need to get you warm, Ellie... with myself. Do you still trust me?" he asked insistently, thumbs brushing my cheeks. I nodded, and he released me.

When I looked back up, Gil was stripping off his clothes. Had I not been so tired, my eyes would've widened to the size of saucers. I had briefly glanced at him when I'd burst into his room the previous star-rise, but I hadn't even registered what I was seeing. Now I couldn't take my eyes off him—off every perfect inch. Long, lean, strong... everything I imagined he would be. My cheeks flushed when my eyes traveled downward. Quickly, I averted my eyes when he caught me looking at him.

When he was bare, Gil made quick work of laying out our wet clothing near the fire. He then stepped behind me and laid down. Two strong arms banded around me—one around my upper chest and the other around my waist. He tucked me in close and molded his body around mine. Skin to skin, we slowly warmed. At least, I certainly did.

I wondered if he could feel my heart pounding through my back, or perhaps through his arms. Could he feel the blush on my cheeks or the deepening of my breath? Could he feel... me?

"Ellie?" he whispered in my ear. The brush of his breath against me sent a rush of warmth through my belly.

"Yeah, Gil?"

"Are you warm enough?"

I nearly said yes, but quickly thought better of it. I wasn't about to spoil this. "No."

His fingers lightly trailed up and down my upper arm, sending a shudder through me. "Your skin is looking better."

Hard swallow. "Oh? That's good."

"How's your ankle?"

Wincing, I remembered the throbbing pain still afflicting my lower left leg. "Not great, I'm afraid."

Gil patted me on the arm before releasing me and sitting up. "I need to look at it."

Gasping, I folded up and covered myself with my arms. "Gil!" I hissed, turning scarlet.

With a sigh, Gil ignored my protest and scooted down, gently lifting my ankle and resting it on his thigh. I gritted my teeth and cried out in pain at the movement.

"I'm sorry," he apologized, "but I need the light to see it."

Squeezing my eyes shut, I tried not to focus on the pain or my embarrassment. Gil's touch was gentle, but it was still agonizing. What I may have once fantasized as a romantic gesture was, in reality, torture. When he turned it slightly to check the joint, I screamed out a very un-ladylike word.

"I can't believe you bounded on this," he remarked with a scoff. "It looks like you've probably broken it."

I heard ripping fabric, and I lifted my head enough to look down and find Gil tearing his wet shirt. "What are you doing?"

His eyes found mine in the dim glow. "Wrapping your ankle."

"But your shirt?"

Smiling briefly, Gil gently laid a hand on my knee and brushed it with his thumb. "It's only a shirt, Ellie. Now, I need you on your back."

My eyebrows could not have raised any higher.

"To wrap your ankle," he stressed.

I hesitated, blinking at him. Moving would mean...

Ellie, said Gil, sighing in frustration, "we've been snuggling alone, naked, in a cave. I don't think the awkwardness can get any worse at this point."

Slowly, I lowered my arms and complied, carefully turning from my side to my back while Gil supported my smarting ankle. He made quick work of wrapping it. I bit down on my lower lip to keep from crying out in pain. The fabric was cold and wet, and the wrappings snug, but the extra support provided a measure of immediate relief.

When my ankle was taken care of, Gil crawled back to my side as I quickly rolled over. His arm wrapped around my waist and tucked me in close once more.

"How do you feel now?"

The question felt weighted. It wasn't intended to be, but I was feeling so many things at once. This was our last set together. Time for confessions was at hand. We'd kissed, so clearly, he felt *something* for me. But why didn't he say it? Why didn't I?

Perhaps this was for the best. He was leaving. There was no hope for us anyway. But laying in his arms, feeling his body pressed up against mine, was like brushing the stars with my fingertips.

Intertwining my fingers with his across my stomach, I smiled, even as a tear broke loose down my cheek. "Wonderful."

Chapter 5

When I awoke, the rains had ceased. I was relaxed but surprised to find my head laying on a warm chest, with an arm wrapped around me. Gil's heartbeat was like music in my ear. His steady breathing nearly soothed me back to sleep. I didn't know how we ended up in this position, but I didn't want to move. Not just yet.

Memories of the set before replayed themselves like a dream. The terror of the wildions… the chill of the rain… the feel of Gil's warm body against mine… A wild, lovely dream.

Gil took a deep breath as he awoke, and suddenly, he was leaping up and away from me, leaving me slumped to the ground. Frowning, I looked up to find him with his back turned, quickly shoving on his undergarments and trousers by the now-cold fire.

"Gil? Are you all right?" I dared to ask as I sat up, hugging my arms to my chest. Suddenly, I felt cold and exposed.

"Yes, I'm all right, um." Without looking at me, he grabbed my clothing and tossed them at me. "Your clothes are only damp now."

"Gil—"

"Just get dressed, Ellie!" he snapped.

Flinching at his harsh tone, I snatched my clothing to my chest and leaned away. Gil had never spoken to me that way. It hurt to the core. Feeling none of the previous warmth and sweetness from him was a dagger to my heart. Steeling my features, I quickly and quietly slipped on my clothing, biting back tears of agony as I worked around my swollen ankle.

When I was just barely dressed, the first devastating bells of star-rise split the quiet air. Our time was at an end. And not the end I'd hoped for.

"We have to return. Travel to Star City is supposed to begin soon after first bells," Gil explained as he returned to my side to help me to my feet. No eye contact, no emotion.

When I put weight on my ankle, I flinched. "I can't—"

"I know. You'll ride on my back."

Quickly, he hoisted me up into position. As Gil approached the edge of the cave, I tightly wrapped my arms around his bare shoulders, burying my face in the back of his neck and clenching my eyes shut. Gil gripped my thighs and took a deep breath before leaping without further warning.

Soon, we were out of the maze of Tower Rocks and bounding across the field under the blankets of stars and soft, undulating ribbons of color. It was a beautiful rise, but the silence between us, and Gil's speedy determination to return spoiled any sense of awe.

Holding him tightly, I savored each passing moment we had. The fragrant wind blew through our hair, but it was the scent of him I treasured. If only he knew just how much I treasured him. If only I had known sooner.

I wanted nothing more than to turn us around, go back to that cave, and find the nerve to tell him. But onward, we flew, the city rapidly growing closer. Too fast.

"Ellette!"

Lifting my head, I peered around Gil to find a large group of people, mostly guards, running toward us. Panne was leading the pack, half-bounding, half-sprinting in desperation. Advisor Braxton wasn't far behind.

My heart leaped at the sight of my Panne. Relief and joy washed over me. The moment we reach them, Gil skidded to a stop. I slid off his back, but crumpled to the ground, forgetting my injury. Gil whirled around and helped me up, just as Panne appeared at my other side, arms wrapping tightly around me.

Panne kissed my cheeks and my forehead over and over as he held my face in his hands and then crushed me to his chest.

"Ellette! Oh, thank stars! I thought you were dead!"

Burying my cheek in his jacket, I felt his shaking as his tears wet my hair. "I'm okay, Panne."

"Mind explaining just what in the hellfire you were doing out here?" Advisor Braxton spat in my direction.

Lifting my head, I saw him standing nearby with crossed arms and hardened features. Gil stood next to him with an unreadable expression, eyes fixated on the ground. I willed him to say something, but he kept his silence.

Panne tensed up and shot a glare at his sometimes-friend. "Braxton, now there's no need for—"

"No need?" he hissed, stepping forward with a squared jaw. "No *need? My son* may have been killed coming after her! She violated the law—*again!*"

I clung to Panne's arm as he straightened his shoulders and faced him fully. "What are you trying to suggest, Braxton?" His dark tone was aggressive and ready for battle. Here, in the open field, nothing was holding them back from real damage.

"I'm suggesting that it's time she faces real consequences for her actions. You coddle her, Humett, and see what's happened? It was only a matter of time before she put lives at risk again!"

Panne was growing hot—literally. The warmth was leaking through his sleeve. I was afraid of being this close. They were on the cusp on destruction.

"I will deal with my daughter as I see fit," said Panne through clenched teeth.

Braxton crossed his arms and glared directly at me. "Ellette Humett, as highest rank under the Premier, I sentence you to a punishment of twenty-five lashes, followed by a thirty-rise confinement of house arrest."

"No!" protested Panne, "I forbid it!"

Gil's fists clenched at his side as the muscles of his jaw feathered. I could only gape at Braxton in horror. I've never been lashed before, and my legs felt weak at the thought of the whip slicing through my flesh, creating more brutal, painful scars. And so many... Panne caught me as I slipped.

Pointing a finger my way, Braxton sneered. "She is a grown woman, though she acts like a foolish child. She will take her punishment—"

"I'll take it."

Our eyes jumped to Gil as he dared to defy his panne. Braxton's jaw fell open as he reddened and stumbled over his words.

"You will do no such thing!"

"*Yes, I will,*" Gil insisted, turning his hardened gaze to his panne. "Twenty-five lashes will kill her, but I can take it. I have also violated the law, in case you've forgotten. Or am I above it somehow?"

The air grew thick with silence as panne and son stared each other down. I could only look on in utter shock and terror at the thought of the outcome. His challenge was entirely unexpected, and I hoped his panne would reject it. I would take a thousand lashes if it meant sparing Gil pain. I was the reckless wildling, not him.

Just as I was about to speak out in protest, Braxton turned to me with a new sentence.

"Ellette, I sentence you to fifteen rises in the black pit, starting immediately after our departure. You will remain house-bound until then."

This sentence was worse than death for many. Not violent, but torturous, nonetheless. Panne did not protest, but gathered me close to his chest protectively. It was the best I could hope for, given the situation and Braxton's resolve.

Braxton walked away, but stopped and turned to give one last, damning sentence…

"Oh, and Humett?" Panne and I both responded with wary looks before he continued, "We permanently withdraw our offer of marriage. If that wasn't obvious enough."

Worse than the dark pit. Than a hundred thousand lashes. More painful than death by wildion. My love, ripped away. Any chance of a life with him had just been squashed by my foolishness.

Meeting my eyes at last, Gil matched my shock. So many things I wanted to scream across that small patch of land between us, that patch that might as well have been an endless chasm. I wanted to cry, beg, throw myself at the feet of his panne and plead for anything else—*anything* but that. For it was the worst punishment of all.

After Braxton walked away, tugging a reluctant Gil behind him, guards surrounded us and reached out toward me. With a mighty roar, Panne got them to back off. "I'll take her myself! Don't touch her!"

Respectful of their commander, the guards backed off. Panne lifted me, cradling me in his arms, and bounded high, soaring right over the heads of Gil and his spiteful panne, ahead of all others, before barely touching the ground and bounding again. We reached the town in lightning time, and he whisked me away from prying eyes to the safety of our home.

* * *

Numbness set in as the doctor worked to examine and set my ankle. His miraculous care would aid in speeding my healing, but only in the physical sense. My heart was a different matter entirely. If he could have removed it, I would've gladly accepted.

Departure was put off for a few hours, considering the circumstances, but they could not delay things any more than that, under threat of the gravest of punishments. One did not dare disobey the king. Even in the event of a loved one's death.

When I was laid up on the couch in my bedroom, sufficiently bathed and tended to, Panne came in with a somber countenance. Sitting at my side, he grasped my hand in his own and kissed my fingers. The red in the whites of his eyes suggested he was not quite so numb. I regarded his tear-streaked blue cheeks with a frown. So much pain I'd caused him when he had more to face. His reputation was tainted.

"I'm sorry, Panne. I never meant for this to happen." I hoped he heard the sincerity in my voice. Pain medicine was making me sleepy, but I couldn't have slept if I tried.

"No," he said, shaking his head and squeezing my hand, "I'm sorry that I couldn't protect you. From any of this. It's my job, as your panne, to keep you safe. And I've failed."

Seeing fresh tears brimming, I forced a slight smile. "It's not your fault. None of this is. Braxton is right—I'm reckless. If it wasn't for Gil, I'd be dead."

"Gillion," Panne began, eyes averting, "I owe him a great debt. To go against his own panne like that…"

Taking a deep breath, I tried to fight off the sudden wave of emotion that threatened to crash over the barriers I'd erected. Yes, Gillion. My savior. My love. My friend. Now, he had to be nothing. Yet my mouth blurted out the words my mind fought so hard to contain.

"I love him, Panne."

Panne's eyes jumped to mine in surprise, and then they faded into the heartbreak reflected in my own. With a sigh, he gently gathered me up in his arms and let me soak his jacket as the dam involuntarily burst. Stroking my hair, he held me and let me blubber and moan like a child. When at last I'd quieted down to sniffles, Panne spoke.

"I will right this when we return," he declared evenly.

Sitting up, I wiped my cheeks under wide eyes. "But, Panne—"

"I will right this. For you."

I threw my arms around him again. "You just return to me, all right?" My voice broke. "That's all I ask."

***

Time went by too fast. Too many words left unsaid to my panne. Too many questions about his life, about Manne, about everything. But I couldn't fit them all in during the short time we had together. Why did time move so quickly when it was all I wanted?

They graciously allowed me to be wheeled down in a wheelchair to the convoy to bid goodbye a final time before being taken away to serve my punishment. One last time to glimpse their faces. To glimpse the stars before they were shut away from me.

It seemed the entire city had gathered near the bridge to bid our representatives good luck. Five large, rectangular, black, armored boxes sat waiting with thick doors open for their occupants. Two turrets were attached at the top of each one for the defenders. They loomed in the glow of rise, like spots of shadow that didn't belong. They were too old, with armor that was not strong enough. As oppressive as they looked, they weren't oppressive enough.

Guards surrounding me kept a respectable distance when Panne was at my side. I couldn't run, so there wasn't much point in physically trying to hold me down. Not that I would've run, anyway. My days as a wildling were over. The cost was too great.

People continually came up to Panne and greeted him, even as he gave instructions to the guards staying behind and consulted with the other passengers. He always had one hand on my shoulder, as if to keep me from being snatched away from him. I appreciated the gesture; however, it was Panne I wanted to keep hold of.

Premier Diltron was hanging nearby, with his own posse of guards and advisors, including Advisor Braxton, who would go as his personal representative. I hated Braxton now. There he stood, in his finery and intricately braided hair, laughing with the premier as if he were going off on some pleasurable excursion for the rise. Meanwhile, the other men were consoling their sobbing families. *Cruel. All of it.*

The breath left my lungs. Gil entered through the crowd, joining his father across the courtyard. Outfitted in a tailored, deep blue coat with the glittering red crest of our city pinned to his chest, hair gathered back in braids, he was strong and beautiful. To think that just under that jacket, and under the crisp shirt below, was the same chest I'd awoken upon that very rise. I'd kissed those same lips that were now pressed into a tight, somber line as he gazed at the ground. His eyes looked... lost. Perhaps he felt as lost as I did.

"Gil!"

I turned at the cheery voice coming from behind me and saw Agatha pushing through the crowd, clothed in her yellow gown. Makeup slightly askew around her eyes, it was clear she'd been crying, but now, she put on a brave face. Ignoring me entirely, Agatha pushed past my chair and made a straight line for Gil. He watched her approach with a tired smile. It wasn't his usual bright-eyed one, but not unpleasant in the least. Jealousy instantly bubbled up in my chest. Had I not been guarded, I would've wheeled myself over and planted my chair in between the two.

With eyes glued to them, I watched the scene unfold. I couldn't hear the conversation Agatha was having between Advisor Braxton and Gil, but Braxton and Agatha wore ever-brightening smiles as the conversation went on. Gil nervously glanced between the two, a smile pasted on his lips. A pit formed in my stomach. His panne had never spoken to Agatha with any measure of the enthusiasm he now showed.

Suddenly, Agatha was nodding and squealing with joy. She leaped and threw her arms around a very surprised Gil. After a moment, he returned the embrace. There they stood, hugging each other in plain view of the public. The message was sealed. Even more so when she leaned back and planted her lips on his in a long but chaste kiss.

Whispers and chatter erupted from around me. I did not know whether it was shock or approval. My vision tunneled on the heartbreaking scene. Gil was no longer mine in any sense or hope. I'd lost them both.

Panne's other hand came to rest on my other shoulder, and he gave me a firm, but gentle squeeze. He sensed my pain and stood quietly behind me. I could cry no tears. The world was too much for them. Everything I loved was being taken from me.

"Take me to the pit." My throat bobbed as I gripped the armrests.

"Ellie..." Panne said quietly.

I finally ripped my eyes away from the scene. "Please, Panne. I want you to be the one to do it. I want to see your face last."

After a long hesitation, Panne patted my shoulders and complied with my request. With a nod from the guards, we turned and made our way through the crowd, who were thankfully too enamored with what was going on with the rest of the party to notice our departure. They had no interest in the young woman in the wheelchair when there was an engagement happening before their eyes.

When we reached the prison in the quiet section of the city, built against the wall, the guards quickly admitted us through the gates. Panne lifted me from my chair and carried me the rest of the way, down the meandering halls and staircases.

It was a dark stone building with very little glow. Artificial lights illuminated our path, but did little for strength. The halls were narrow, and not large enough for bounding. Everything was designed to encase a Celestial and subdue our natural abilities.

At last, we came to a dusty, long-forgotten, dead-end hallway with a black hatch in the floor. A tall ladder hung on the wall nearby. One guard opened the hatch, while the other removed the ladder, which was then placed down into the pit. Only six rungs were exposed above the void.

Whimpering from the sudden, visceral fear that gripped me, I clung to Panne and buried my face in his chest. Shaking, I worried I might fall from his arms. He gripped me closer to him and tucked my head under his chin.

"Shh, it's going to be all right, dear," he tried to reassure. I could hear from the hitch in his voice that he wasn't entirely convinced either.

The guards held the ladder steady as Panne slowly, but deftly, stepped us down into the inky pit. The chill and the thick darkness greeted us, oppressive even with the dim light coming from the opening above. With white knuckles, I held on, fearing to lose even one moment with him.

At the bottom, he gently lowered me onto a small cot against the stone wall. It filled the width of the cramped pit, truly only made for one person to be abandoned.

For as long as we could steal, Panne and I sat, holding each other. His tears soaked my hair, even as he tried to soothe me, to reassure me that all would be righted, and we'd reunite in the starlight the moment he returned. He assured me that the guards would take care of me. Knowing what I knew about this punishment, that was little comfort, and possibly even a lie. But I didn't contradict.

Finally, we bid our final, painful goodbyes, and Panne ascended the ladder, pausing midway up to look back at me. "I love you, Ellette."

"I love you too, Panne," I replied, giving him the best smile I could muster.

The moment he was on the surface, the guards pulled the ladder away. I heard an insistent conversation between them and Panne, and then I heard my name being called from a distance. It grew nearer, and the lowering hatch was paused mid-way.

Gil's face appeared in the space of light. He was out of breath, as if he'd been running at full speed. Blue eyes locked on mine, and I felt a jolt of both pain and joy. I waited for him to say something, but he just stared at me. There was much to say, and nothing at all. Slowly, the latch closed again.

"Goodbye, Gil…" I bid quietly, before the darkness consumed me. His face was now imprinted clearly in my mind.

Chapter 6

Black.

Only black. Not a single star. Only the ever-so-faint glow under my ribs, shining from under my skin. It's something that I never noticed or saw, but there, in the complete darkness, it was the only thing that stood out. I clung to the sight as my only source of comfort in the hellish pit.

How did I end up there? I went from a free thing, bounding to the stars, to a prisoner in the deepest pit. How did life take such a wrong turn? How did I?

Perhaps that was the purpose of this pit? To force reflection on one's misdeeds; on one's life. Or was it to slowly drive one insane? With close walls, stuffy air, no light… It was the absence of the light that was the worst of all. That's what fueled the bad dreams.

Time was impossible to keep track of, except for that glorious moment when the hatch opened to pass down food, collect empty trays, or the chamber pot. At that moment, even the dim light of the hallway above felt blinding. I longed to bound up into it. But my energy was already draining like a sieve, away from the starlight.

Exhausted, I took to laying on the cot. My ankle was getting better as time went by, possibly rise by rise. But it was still noticeably sore. Every time I felt the twinge of pain, it took me back to that moment of the long fall off the rock. Time slowed down to a crawl as I slipped through the air. Raindrops ceased their descent around me, and it was just me—falling through diamonds, brushing them aside as I went. As the ground came close to greet me, only then did everything speed up. Only then did the pain come.

Gil's face shone brightly in my mind. If I looked up, I could still see it clearly in my mind's eye, peering down at me through the hatch. Why did he have to come? Why *did* he come? It should've been Panne's face I remembered so vividly, not Gil's, dancing around in my brightest visions. But I loved Gil's face, hurt or not. As I lay there, if I tried hard enough, I could imagine his body pressed up behind me, arm tucking me in close. Although I knew I shouldn't, sometimes I even replayed our kiss over and over in my mind's eye, thinking about how different things would be if I hadn't stopped it short—if I'd just thrown aside any objections and let things progress. Perhaps I'd be the one intended for him now.

An indeterminate amount of time passed until I first heard it—the voice. "You think louder than most."

High in timber, almost snake-like, yet small and frail, like an old woman. It startled me out of my reveries, and I shrieked. Cuddling against the wall, my eyes darted around the room as if I'd be able to see anything in front of my face. I clenched my eyes as I shook, trying to grasp hold of my sanity. There was no one there. I was alone in the darkness.

"In the darkness, you may be, but alone, you are not," the voice spoke once more.

Heart pounding, I ducked my head between my knees, slamming my hands over my ears. Rocking slightly, I concentrated on the rhythm, reassuring myself that I was okay, and that it was just my imagination. The solitude was getting to me.

"Curious thing, you are. You trust your eyes, but not your ears." The voice sounded as if it were only an arm's length in front of me.

"Go! Go away!" I cried, my voice hoarse in my ears.

"Go away? Why? You're in my home," the voice replied, smoother, like a snake slithering over rock. "I like the company, though."

I looked upward and listened for any signs of life beyond the hatch. A guard should have been posted nearby.

"Help! Help!" I screamed.

Again and again, I called until finally I heard pounding footsteps above me. A patch of light appeared, nearly blinding me, as a violet male face appeared through the opening.

"Ms. Humett?"

Scrambling from the cot, I whirled around. "There's someone down here!" Even as I said those words, my heart dropped.

I was completely alone.

"Ma'am," the guard replied slowly. Turning my eyes up to meet his face, he wore a look of concern. "You're the only one down there."

Looking in the mysterious voice's direction, I sighed sharply, shaking my head. "No, I can't be! They were right here! I heard them, clearer than I hear you now."

"Well, there's no one there now. I'm going to shut the door."

Panicked, I snapped my eyes upward. "No! Please leave it open! At least for a while?"

Wincing apologetically, the guard shook his head and slowly lowered the hatch back into place, the clang of heavy metal sealing me back into darkness. My thoughts and my terror swallowed me once more.

Half-whimpering, half-growling, I felt for my cot and retreated under the blanket, hugging myself into a ball. This was too much. Too much to bear for my already-fragile mind.

I'm going mad!

Things took a turn for the worse. Through the blanket, an icy hand wrapped over my shoulder. A primal scream tore from my throat as I leaped up, shoving the hand away, and backed up to the wall, hitting my head. Slumping back down to the bed, I clutched my head, feeling a warm trickle of blood run down my temple. Crying, I sat holding the blanket to my head.

"You seem a bit stressed. Here, have some tea."

To my astonishment, I heard the distinct sound of liquid being poured into a cup. A hard, cool object gently brushed the backs of my fingers, causing me to flinch. Hot liquid splashed onto my hand. I yelped.

"Forgive me. I forget your eyes don't work well down here. How about you hold out your hand, and I'll help you grasp it?" the voice offered politely.

Peering in the voice's direction, I held my hands close to my body in clenched fists. "Who are you?"

"My name is not important. But if you must call me something, you may call me… Mara."

Mara. It sounded like such an ordinary name, something you might call a person. But whatever it was in my presence was no person. And it was offering me *tea.* The spot on my hand where the tea had spilled still smarted. I rubbed it and brought it to my nose. It smelled faintly of petal tea. *Could it be real?*

Shifting to a more relaxed, but wary position, I continued conversing with this 'Mara'.

"What are you, then? A spirit?"

"In a way."

The answer was not exactly comforting. "Why couldn't I see you in the light?"

"I'm not visible in the light. Just as you are not visible in the dark. At least not to Celestial eyes. So strange, considering you are children of the night."

Furrowing my brows in her direction, I pondered her strange answer. "Night?"

Mara laughed and gently took my hand with her icy fingers. I flinched, but didn't pull away. She wrapped them around a warm teacup and patted my hand, encouraging me to drink. Hesitantly, I brought the cup up close and inhaled first. It definitely had the aroma of petal tea. My stomach growled. And my chilled body ached for the warmth it would bring. After a deep breath, I took a small sip and was relieved to find that it *was* tea. The soothing warmth ran down my throat and into my stomach, bringing a long sigh of relief. It wasn't long before I'd finished the entire cup.

"Better?"

I nodded. "Yes, thank you."

"Would you care for more?"

"Yes, please." Holding out the cup, it soon grew heavier with the weight of more carefully poured tea. I began to feel more relaxed, sitting with my hands wrapped around the teacup.

"You called us 'children of the *night*'. What does that mean?" I asked. If I were going to be haunted by a spirit, I might as well take advantage of having someone to talk to.

"*Night* is like your *set*, on other worlds. The night is when the stars come out to shine."

Twisting my mouth, I set the teacup at my side. "I'm not sure what you mean. Set is when there are no stars."

Mara was silent for a moment. I wasn't sure if she was even there, but then she spoke again.

"Think of the brightest star you've ever seen—no, the brightest light. Would you believe me if I told you that there are worlds where there are stars so big and so bright that they light up the whole sky and everything below?"

Eyes widening, I considered this possibility. The brightest light I'd ever seen was when Gil and I... No. I couldn't think about that now. Thinking about that was becoming slow torture.

"I've never heard of such a thing."

"Perhaps someday you will see the sun for yourself."

She spoke as if it were something familiar to her, perhaps from a lifetime ago. Such a curious thing, this *being*, or whatever she was. The more I spoke to her, the less afraid I became.

"Have you been down here long?" I asked, finding my tea again.

"Well..." mused Mara, "I suppose you could say that. Time matters little to me."

How could time matter little to anyone? All I wanted was more time—more time with my panne. Even more time with... others. But it was stolen from me. From them.

"Why do you live down here?" I ventured to ask.

"You ask a lot of questions."

Okay, so not a question I'd be getting an answer to. I shifted.

"I'm curious. And I have no one else to talk to."

"Most are content with screaming rude things at me until their mind snaps. I've never understood why."

I averted my gaze to the ground, assuming she could see me clearly. It did suddenly feel very rude to scream at her the way I did. Especially when she was kind enough to give me tea and keep her patience.

"I suppose it's because you're... *unexpected.*"

"Hmm. So very strange to be unexpected in your own home."

"I don't think anyone knows about you," I reasoned. "They throw people down here to be alone."

"Alone? Whatever for?"

My stomach fluttered. I would have to confess. Perhaps it wouldn't be so bad to talk to someone about it in the end.

"As punishment for crimes."

A long silence hung in the air. I had the sense that Mara was still there, but I feared I'd made *her* uncomfortable somehow. She could be a hideous monster for all I knew, but I was still her guest, even if unwillingly.

At last, she spoke. "I will not ask your story if you do not wish to tell it. But I do not believe you are a criminal."

"Really?" I asked, surprised. "And why is that?"

"Because you drank the tea I offered. No one has ever been that polite."

Smiling, my hand found the teacup at my side. I ran my fingers over the cool crystal rim. I imagined it was purple, or blue, like the cups at the teahouse.

"That's a shame. It is excellent tea. It's actually my... it's the favorite of someone I know. Or knew."

Try as I might, I couldn't stop the stubborn liquid from pooling in my eyes. Gil may have been fighting off a pack of wildions at that very moment. His face was still staring at me through that hatch, looking like he wanted so badly to say something.

"Do you have someone up there?" Mara quietly asked. "Someone who shines brightly?"

Nodding, I wiped my cheeks. "I did. But not anymore."

"Perhaps they will shine for you again, dear Ellie. Don't lose hope just yet."

The sound of my name snapped my attention and caused my heart to speed up. "Wait, how did you—"

A loud metallic sound from above interrupted my words. Light poured into the pit, and I found myself alone once more.

"Ms. Humett, we are coming down momentarily to fetch you."

Panic crash through my chest. "Why? Has something happened?"

"No," replied the guard, confused, "your sentence has been served. You are being released."

Blinking, I slumped back on my cot. *Impossible!* It had not yet been fifteen rises ... or had it? My hand then brushed against something hard beside me. I looked down to see a single purple teacup.

Chapter 7

Starlight never looked so beautiful as it did there, on my balcony. A reclining armchair had been moved out there so I could rest and breathe in the fresh air as much as I liked. I couldn't bear to be confined.

Teli coddled me like a child. The doctor said I needed to resume activity slowly and do daily exercises as my energy restored. It felt hard to do much of anything.

I had no desire to run or bound. The great unknown held nothing but fear for me now. I could still feel the fur of the wildion, brushing against my feet. Being reckless only brought suffering. And darkness. So much darkness...

Even then, resting comfortably in my home, I was afraid of the dark. Afraid to be alone at set. They set up an extra bed near mine, and Teli or one of the other servants would sleep there. They slept, though I did not.

Frightening and heartbreaking dreams plagued me. I dreamed of unnatural things, reaching out through the dark, of my loved ones dying... and of Gil choosing Agatha.

Why did it still bother me so much? Had I not set things up in their favor? Was it not my own fault? My blindness all those years cost me greatly. And yet I knew I would've still said "No". An arranged match was just not within me. But stars, I loved him now, more every time his face crossed my thoughts. It was my punishment to love. It was my darkness.

"Time for your meal," bubbled Teli, setting a tray on the small table beside me.

Looking upward, it was already mid-rise. The stars had just barely taken to the sky when I'd settled out there on my chair and gotten lost in my musings. Assigned exercises still awaited. Feeling suddenly lazy and sheepish, I smiled in gratitude and ate my meal quickly. The warm, home-cooked food was a boon, and after ten days of freedom, I was finally putting some weight back on. If I wasn't careful, that's all I would put on. Not that I minded. Agatha had plenty of curve to her and look what she...

No! Stop thinking of them!

Rising slowly, I picked up my tray of empty plates and made my way into my room and toward the door. Teli was humming a cheery tune as she made the bed, but stopped when she caught me. Running over, she started to take the tray from my hands.

"Oh, let me get that, dear!"

I kept a firm hold on it. "No, Teli, it's all right. You are working yourself to death, and I don't mind. I need to walk more."

Frowning, Teli released the tray with a nod. "All right, I suppose, if you are feeling up to it."

"I am. My ankle really doesn't hurt much at all anymore. I'm tired, that's all," I assured with a bright smile, ignoring the ache in my muscles.

Patting my shoulder, Teli reluctantly turned back to her task, releasing me to make my way down to the kitchens. Down the hall, I took the air lift down to my destination and deposited the dishes by the large sinks. With no one around, I pulled up the sleeves of my dusty-pink robe and washed them myself.

It became painfully obvious how inexperienced I was at simple things when I ended up soaked with water all down my front. The surrounding mess was embarrassing, but I finally found the tools I needed and washed the dishes until they shined. I scrubbed them all, humming a tune just like Teli would. Proudly, I stacked the last dried dish in the cabinet and made my way back to the air lift.

Just when I was about to step through the disk, I remembered something: exercises. The doctor had told me to do repetitive exercises, like lifting my knees high in the air and lunging low to the ground, working across the room. Boring things, over and over. I'd begrudgingly complied, but it felt fruitless. Or was it?

Turning from the air lift, I eyed the door to the stairs and debated. It felt like an eternity since I'd really felt my lungs working. Sitting and looking up at the stars was all my broken heart wanted to do. Time was winding down, and I was still wasting away.

With a sigh, I entered the door to the stairwell. The moment it clicked shut behind me, I pressed my back to the wall nearby and listened carefully for any signs of life above. When I heard nothing stirring, I braced myself into a partial crouch, one foot pressed behind me against the wall.

Before I could change my mind, I launched ahead and bounded. Up, up, and up, until I reached the first landing. Briefly, I stumbled, but caught myself against the wall ahead and skidded to a stop when I bounced off. With a laugh of disbelief, my cheeks stretched into a smile.

Now that a successful bound was under my feet, the first vestiges of adrenaline hit my veins like petal nectar. The memory of why I loved bounding. The rushing of wind in my hair, the feeling of flying freely… it was better than the best medicine.

Backing up to the wall opposite the next landing, I bit my lip and eyed the next target. Again, I flew up through the air, until I found the ground again. Giddy, I hardly waited before bounding again, up, up, and up. To the next floor, and the next. By the time I reached the upper floors, I was bounding without ceasing, feet hitting the wall corners, and shooting up to the next. I was back.

Just as I was flying through the air and reaching the very last landing, a figure appeared, and in a flash, I crashed into them. We landed hard on the floor, heads nearly hitting the wall in the small space. The breath left my lungs.

Groaning, I pushed myself up enough to get a look at the person I was sprawled out on top of. A cry tore from my throat. Had I not already been on top of them, I would've pounced.

Gil. Dirty, bloody, wild-eyed. But my Gil.

Before I could speak a word, his hand clamped over my mouth as his other wrapped around the back of my head and held me steady. My brows knitted in confusion as he quickly sat us up and looked around.

"Shh! Don't let anyone hear us," Gil whispered harshly.

Sensing his fear, an icy feeling sank in my stomach. I nodded and tried to steady my pounding heart. Slowly, Gil released his hand from my mouth.

"Gil!" I whispered, leaning back to inspect him. "What's going on? Are you hurt?" Blood seeped from a gash on his right arm and his right side. My eyes widened. "You're bleeding—"

Jerking me close, Gil shushed me once more and then clenched his eyes closed in pain. "I'll be okay, but I need your help. You're the only one I trust right now."

Hairs on the back of my neck stood. "Gil, you're frightening me."

Silently, he stared back at me. I wasn't the only one who was frightened. Throat bobbing, I tried to steady my shaking limbs. "What do you need?"

"We need to get to your room."

Glancing at the door, I stood and helped him up, wincing at the pain etched across his face. I put a palm on his chest. "Wait here. I need to be sure that no one is in there."

To my surprise, Gil took my hand in his and opened the door, pulling me along behind him. "I was just there, it's clear," he whispered, barely loud enough for me to hear.

Carefully, we darted down the hall and slipped into my room. After searching to be sure that it was empty of life, I locked the door and let out a long breath. Teli must've gone to finish her other duties.

Gil went to my wardrobe and began sorting through my clothes. I ran up beside him as he tossed me clothing. "Hey! What are you doing?"

Barely glancing at me, he stalked to the bathroom. "Get dressed," he ordered over his shoulder.

I held the bundle of clothing to my chest and followed him in. He was already carefully peeling off his shirt, groaning in pain. Setting my clothes on the counter, I caught the hem and helped him. When the shirt was off, I saw the long gash over his ribs and gasped. Grabbing a towel, I wet it and gently pressed it over the wound.

"Gil, will you please tell me what is going on? What did this to you?"

Avoiding my gaze, Gil took over, putting pressure on the gash. "Wildions."

Something snapped to attention within me. He was lying. Something he'd never done before. Angry, I snatched his chin in my fingers and forced him to meet my glare.

"Gillion Braxton, you are lying! Now, either tell me the truth, or I will alert the entire damn household that you are in my bathroom right now!" I hissed my threat, but even to my own ears, it was unconvincing. I could never betray him, but I was beyond dancing around my need for answers.

To my surprise, tears leaped to his eyes. "They attacked us, Ellie. It was a trap."

My grip dissipated and my hand fell. "What? Attacked where? In Star City?"

Gil shook his head. "Ellie... there is no Star City. Not anymore."

Panic rose within me. His words made no sense. "I don't understand."

Letting the towel drop to the floor, Gil gently grasped me by the shoulders. "We have to get out of here. The king has been deposed. There is a new king in his place, and he is mad. And he is coming for me. For us."

"Gil..." I began with a trembling lip. This was not a question I wanted to ask. "Where is Panne?"

Pain lanced his features as the tears escaped their bounds. My heart crashed into my stomach. His expression said it all.

The air in the room grew too thin. My head was too light. Strong arms caught me as the floor suddenly rose. Gil's warm chest muffled the screams and sobs that tore from deep inside. It couldn't be true. My Gil made it back, so my panne should be back too. Panne was the best, the strongest. He was supposed to watch over everyone. *How?*

Gil tucked me under his chin as he grasped me close and soaked my hair with silent tears. The light was soft blue, like Panne. Even wrapped in Gil's warm arms, I shook violently. Flashing back through memories of losing Manne, my pain doubled. They were both gone. Into the stars.

When at last my wails subsided, Gil whispered into my hair. "I'm the only one who made it out."

I sat up, wide-eyed. "Your panne…"

Nodding, Gil dropped his head and his throat bobbed. "He fought them off long enough for me to escape."

Grasping his face, I lifted it to find him fighting off his emotions. Capturing his watery gaze, I spoke as clearly as I could manage with my shaking voice. "Your panne loved you very much, Gil. He was a brave man."

Catching my hand, Gil pressed a firm kiss to my inner wrist and stifled a sob. He held it there for a few moments and then pulled away, forcing deep breaths. With renewed determination, he squared his jaw and averted his gaze to the ground.

"We will grieve later, Ellie. There's no more time to waste. How is your ankle?" He stood and pulled me to my feet.

Glancing down at it, I tapped my foot. Still good. "Mostly healed."

Picking up my clothes, Gil handed them to me before stripping off his trousers without warning. My eyes widened, and I whirled around, turning my back to him. He didn't seem to notice.

"You need to change quickly. Then bound down to my room and grab me a change of clothes as fast as you can. We have to get out of here. Out of the city."

I started to open the door, but Gil caught me by the shoulder and reached his other hand around me to keep it shut. When he whispered in my ear, I felt a shudder run through me.

"In here. I don't want you out of my sight a moment longer than you have to be."

Drawing a hitched breath, I nodded. When he backed off, I quickly stripped off my robe and nightgown. Looking from my peripheral vision, I grabbed my clothes and slipped them on, memories of the cave dancing unbidden through my mind. *Time, if only we had more time.*

To my surprise, the bathwater started pouring from the tap behind me.

"I have to wash these wounds or they'll become angry before we've barely traveled," he explained, seeing me flinch. "It won't take long. Go and hurry back." With a nod, I opened the door, and he arrested me once more, this time, his arm banding around my shoulders and pulling me close.

"Be careful, Ellie," he whispered.

My heart was screaming at me to turn around and kiss him, to tell him how I felt before another moment slipped away. But my level-headed mind took over, and I merely nodded before exiting the room and hurrying for the balcony. He was still intended for Agatha.

Climbing up on the railing, I took a deep breath and steadied my nerves. I eyed my first target below and tested the spring in my ankles. All good. Taking that first leap sent a familiar rush of adrenaline coursing through me that I hadn't felt in a long time. It was like the first time I'd ever dared to bound downward along the massive tower. Now, my motivation wasn't merely to impress my best friend, it was to save him. I bounded down in record time.

Chapter 8

It felt like an invasion, rifling through Gil's things. However, I knew that I only had one chance at this. If things were as pressing as he made it sound, we needed to be out of here in a hurry.

Gil knew my room better than I knew his. His wardrobe was not quite as well-organized. I found a rucksack and began shoving clothing in it. My mind was still reeling from all the terrible news there was to absorb, but I forced myself onward, knowing that my new mission was to keep Gil from meeting the same fate.

Once satisfied that I'd grabbed what he needed, I fastened the cover of the rucksack and darted toward the balcony door. Something on the bureau, however, arrested my attention. There, in a frosted, crystal dish, lay his manne's necklace. It was a simple silver chain, with a teardrop-shaped amethyst on the end. It meant the world to Gil. Without a second thought, I grabbed it and slipped it into the bag, carefully tucking it down into the bottom under the clothing. If we never saw our home again, Gil would have that to hold on to.

It took longer to ascend to my balcony than expected. By the time I reached it, my ankle was smarting again. Ignoring the pain, I hauled myself and the bag over the railing and fell on the floor, panting. The swelling in my flex shoes was going to be a problem.

After allowing myself a brief moment to catch my breath, I pushed to my feet and jogged to the bathroom. Quietly, I slipped into the room. At first, I didn't see Gil. There was no greeting. Then my heart froze.

His arm hung loosely over the edge of the bathtub. He lay slumped back, his head lolling to the side, eyes closed. The bathwater was tinged pink.

Stifling a cry, I dropped the sack and rushed to the bathtub. Grabbing his face, I firmly patted his cheek.

"Gil? Gil! Wake up!" I commanded harshly, raising my volume, but trying to keep my senses under control.

His eyes fluttered but wouldn't open all the way. A soft groan escaped his lips. I shook him, which only elicited another small reaction. Now I was really panicking. I needed to get him out of the tub.

Slipping my arms down into the water, I wrapped them around his back, under his shoulders, and hauled with all my strength until I lifted him. At last, he regained consciousness as he slumped over my shoulder and I was about to fall backward. Gil's knees buckled, and he caught himself on the edge of the tub with the hand of his good arm, while the other wrapped around my back.

Bracing my feet, I regained control, and we stabilized. With my help, Gil stepped out of the tub and over to the counter, where he leaned heavily, one hand clamped onto my shoulder. Groaning in pain, he clenched his other fist, eyes rolling back in his head. He was going downhill fast.

"Gil, you're still bleeding," I noted, staring, horrified, at the wound over his ribs.

His eyes traveled down to his wound. "They tipped their blades with poison that makes wounds keep flowing over time," he explained hoarsely. "It's getting worse, instead of better."

Ice flooded through my veins. At this rate, he would die before long. "Gil, we have to get the doctor. I need to get help—"

"No!" he growled, as another wave of pain flashed over him. His tone was enough to freeze me in my tracks. "No," he repeated, less harshly. "We cannot involve anyone else in this. The more people involved with me, the more will die. They're already at risk as it is."

Grabbing a clean towel, I firmly pressed it against his wound, ignoring the whimper it caused. When at last he settled, I dipped my head under his and caught eye contact. "Gil. You need to tell me what I need to do. What is the antidote?"

Breathing shallow, Gil swallowed hard. "Bells root."

My eyes widened. Bells root was outlawed in our city, only sold on the illicit market. Desired for the temporary boost of adrenaline it gave, it was also dangerous and known for being easily overdosed and highly addictive.

"H-how do I get it?"

Gil averted his gaze. "My father's study. He keeps it in his desk. I've seen it."

Shock was not the word. The great Advisor Braxton? A bells addict? He, the most vocal proponent of harsh punishment for offenders caught with the substance, a captive of it himself.

"Ow! Hey!"

I snatched the towel back as Gil practically doubled over. I hadn't realized that I'd been pressing harder and harder in my growing disparity at the news. Gently, I moved my hand back to the wound. Gil placed his hand over mine and nodded, indicating that he would take over.

"Just get my underpants and trousers. No point in putting my shirt on yet. I'll just bleed all over it. You need to change again, though. You're soaking wet." His eyes flicked to mine, twisting with both guilt and gratitude.

Quickly, we re-dressed, with me aiding Gil the best I could, ever mindful of his wound. I was vaguely aware of his nakedness the whole time, but did my best to keep my eyes averted from the most private areas and focus on the tasks at hand. It seemed we were forever doomed to deal with this vein of awkwardness between us.

When we were decent at last, I helped Gil over to a chair in the bedroom. He slumped back in it and took a deep breath. His silver skin was losing its shimmery properties. We were running short on time.

"Listen, my father's study is on the fourth floor. If you come out of the lift, you make a right turn and—"

"Whoa!" I protested, raising my palms. "I am not leaving you by yourself again."

Gil growled in frustration, "Ellie, I can't walk down there, if you haven't noticed."

Stalking to the corner of the room, I rolled my eyes and grabbed the wheelchair. Pushing it over in front of Gil's seat, I motioned to it with a nod of the head as I crossed my arms. "Get in."

Arching an eyebrow, Gil regarded it warily. "You seriously think you're going to push me around in this, unnoticed?"

"I don't think we're going to do anything unnoticed, but I'm not leaving you here, only to come back and find you half-dead again. Get in the chair before I throw you in it!" I demanded, mustering as much ferocity as I could find in my weariness.

Unaffected by my display, Gil rolled his eyes. But he complied. I slung the rucksack over the back of the chair and quickly pushed him toward the door.

I looked several times up and down the hallway before wheeling him out. We rushed quickly and quietly toward the main air lift, knowing the service lift would be the only one in use today. Down we went, all the way to the first floor of my home.

Upon coming out of the exit disc, we locked eyes with Teli, just entering the hall from the opposite doorway. She gasped and sprinted our way. With no way to hide, I racked my brain for some sort of excuse as to why I had the half-naked, injured son of Advisor Braxton in our home.

"Ellie! What is going on?"

I silenced her with a finger to my lips and wide eyes. Teli stopped short and glared at us. I glared right back.

"You'd better explain yourself right now!" she hissed.

Sighing, I could think of no good explanation. Nothing that would soften the blow of our current situation.

"Teli, the less you know, the better."

Not satisfied, Teli came over and grabbed me roughly by the upper arm, ready to drag me away. I gripped the wheelchair handles and shoved her back. Shocked at my defiance, Teli gaped at me. She parked her hands on her hips like a manne who's child had just barked curses at her.

Taking a deep breath to still my irritation, I began again. "Teli, we need to get to Gil's house right away. We need something there, or else he will die.

You cannot tell a single soul that you saw Gil, either."

Eyes shifting to Gil, Teli realized his full state for the first time. Her gaze dropped to the bloody towel and widened. Hand raising to her mouth, Teli reached for the towel, but Gil stopped her with a quickly upraised palm.

"No, please. The less evidence on you that you've encountered us, the better," Gil insisted, attempting to sound authoritative, but only sounding desperate. My hand went to his shoulder. It was growing warmer by the moment.

Teli's eyes met mine, something sad stealing over them. "You're leaving, aren't you?"

Nodding, I fought tears. "Panne is dead, Teli. Both of our pannes. Now, we're in danger. You have to let us go."

For a long while, Teli just stood, staring at me, debating. I could see the internal struggle warring within her. Like a manne, she wanted to keep me home and keep me safe, like she'd promised panne. But like a friend, she wanted to trust me. I prayed to the heavens she would trust me.

At last, she spoke. "Wait here. Just for a moment." Before I could question, Teli turned and hurried off down the hall, disappearing through a doorway.

Gil patted my hand on his shoulder. "Okay, now's our chance. Head for the—"

"No."

Taken aback by my refusal, Gil scowled at me under a sweat-beaded brow. "What? Come on, Ellie! We have to go!"

"Just wait!" I hissed back.

Sure enough, Teli came scrambling out the doorway again, arms full of bundles. When she reached us, she fell to her knees next to me and nodded to the rucksack, trying to catch her breath. "Open the bag. I've got food."

Raising my eyebrows, I briefly met Gil's surprised expression before quickly complying. Teli shoved bundles of food, tied up in dish towels and cloth napkins, into the sack, along with a leather water sack. The moment the bag was secured, she leaped to her feet and crushed me in her arms.

"I don't know where you're going, but run fast and take care of yourself, do you hear?"

I wrapped my arms around her and nodded. "Thank you, Teli."

Teli slipped away without another word and hurried off down the hallway, stifling her sobs in her sleeve. Guilt lanced me, but I obeyed Gil's renewed insistence and we sped off toward the other lift.

* * *

Getting through Gil's house was much easier than mine. Since no one was left in residence, the only people that ever entered were cleaners for weekly tidying, to keep the dust at bay. All the other servants had gone to visit family and enjoy an extended break. We found ourselves alone, breaking the lock on Advisor Braxton's study room door.

Once inside, we found the room dark and cold, with the set bells having just rung. Feeling along the wall, I found a switch, and the fireplace sprang to life with a roar. Squealing, I jumped back, my hand flying to my chest. I'd forgotten that Advisor Braxton had all sorts of updated conveniences installed recently, at Premier Diltron's insistence. Woodless fireplaces being one of them.

My hand reached for the other switch, but Gil's hand batted it back down. Laboring for breath, he shook his head in the dim light. "No, please. We can't draw any more attention. Let's just look through the desk."

Nodding, I pushed him over and we began pulling open drawers and rustling through contents. Gil got through one and a half drawers before he just about collapsed off the wheelchair. Alarmed, I left my task and pushed him back, where his head slumped back with a groan. His forehead was blazing. He needed the root urgently.

Turning back to the desk, I began tossing out contents right and left. I rummaged through every single drawer and dumped them out on the floor, scrambling through the mess on my hands and knees to find the drug that would save Gil's life. Papers, writing utensils, coins, gems, random things of both great and no value, but not the thing I desperately needed.

Crying out in frustration, I threw a drawer across the room. "Where is it?"

The drawer hit a marble pillar and busted. Slumping to the floor, I grasped my hair and fought back tears. Gil was barely conscious, his blood soaking through the towel now. Perhaps it was too late, anyway. I was on the verge of losing him all over again, and I couldn't bear...

Something caught my eye from across the room. Something *white*—stark in the firelight. Scrambling across the room, my hand closed over the pale, gnarled root with a joyous laugh. The broken drawer nearby revealed an extra compartment in the back, now snapped open. My rage had been beneficial, after all.

Rushing to Gil's side, I found him laboring for breath, eyes rolling back into his head. Quickly, my hand slipped behind his neck, and I pulled him upright, shaking him as I did.

"Hey—hey! Wake up, Gil! I've got it!"

Gil's eyes fluttered and finally opened to a half-lidded state. His words were quiet and slurred. "Just a... small..." He lost consciousness again, but I shook him violently.

"No! Stay awake! How small, Gil? Do you swallow it? Put it on the wound? What?"

I was shouting, but he barely responded, except by swallowing hard. That was the only response I would get from him in his growing daze. The only thing I knew about it was that it was potent. They arrested people for having even a pinky-nail-size's worth.

Peering down at my pinky nail, I racked my brain for an answer. The worst that could happen is that I could overdose him, and he would die. If I gave him too little, he would also die, and soon. So, I did the only thing I could do... I guessed.

Grabbing the letter opener nearby, I shaved off a tiny amount the size of my pinky nail. Carefully, I coaxed his mouth open and slipped the root on his tongue.

"Gil, you have to help me. I need you to swallow."

It took a lot of repeating, and shaking, but at last, his throat bobbed, and when I checked again, the root piece was gone. Pulling up the desk chair in front of him, I pulled Gil forward into an embrace, and let his head rest on my shoulder, waiting and praying for the medicine to work its magic.

"Come on, Gil... Come on... Stay with me..."

We sat there for what felt like hours. Gil was still as death, but warm on my shoulder. My back screamed in agony under the weight and from sitting in that position for so long, but I wasn't about to move for all the stars in the heavens. I needed to feel him. To feel his breathing and his heartbeat.

As I sat, hoping for a miracle, I couldn't help but think about how I could possibly go on without him and Panne. I keenly felt Panne's loss and felt Gil's all over again before he'd even gone. Once again, I'd had my chance, and circumstances had stolen it out from under me. Stolen it from him. But if he went, he would not be alone when he did. So, I would sit with him until that time.

Tears slipping down my cheeks, I could hold it in no longer. I dipped my head down and gently kissed his cheek before pulling him in closer. Softly, I whispered in his ear.

"I love you."

There was no response. I didn't expect one. I wasn't even sure he could hear me. So, I just sat, holding him close, until somehow, I fell asleep too.

Chapter 9

When I awoke, I found myself on the floor. Confused, I tried to remember how I'd gotten there. This wasn't how I fell asleep. How *we* were sleeping.

Then I saw him. Gil sat with his back against my legs, hugging his knees, and gazing into the fireplace. The bloodied towel lay in the now-empty wheelchair. He was alive and awake at last.

Gasping, I sat up, drawing his attention. Bloodshot eyes snapped to mine, and I immediately ceased my pursuit. Gil was alive, but not entirely well. I'd only heard rumors of what the drug did to people, but he was clearly under the influence.

Averting my gaze, I bit back a nervous smile. "You're alive."

"I am."

Gil's voice was steady but slower, and a bit lower in timbre. Almost... sultry. Something pressed in the back of my mind, but I couldn't quite put my finger on it. He was acting strange.

A warm hand closed over my knee and his thumb caressed the inner part where it met my thigh. My eyes widened when I felt it, and I looked up to find him heavy-lidded, lips tipped up in a lopsided grin.

Oh no...

I remembered. Bells root: adrenaline booster... and aphrodisiac. A *powerful* aphrodisiac. Eyes sweeping over him, I caught sight of confirmation that it was indeed having that effect.

Burning scarlet from head to toe, I pressed my hands over my eyes and shook my head, trying to remember that it was just the root. This was not real. The pounding of my heart was from embarrassment, not… desire. I didn't desire him, not when his thumb was… brushing my leg… and he was looking at me like that…

Taking a deep breath, I pushed myself to standing and walked across the room, turning my back to him. I had to keep control of myself. And think of something else, *anything* else. Like picking flowers, or vomiting, or something completely not related to Gil and—

"Ellie."

I whirled around and found Gil directly behind me. His hungry blue eyes drilled into mine. They were beautiful and wild in the dancing firelight. The shimmer had fully returned to his skin, and I'd never seen him so glorious.

Gulping, I backed away as he stepped toward me, like a wildion stalking its prey. I had to distract him somehow. "Your wound looks much better already," I commented, glancing down at his wound. Judging by his body's reaction, I wish I'd kept my eyes trained ahead.

Gil let out a low, quiet laugh. "It's okay, Ellie. I won't bite. Unless you want me to."

Definitely not the Gil I know!

Placing a hand to his chest, I ceased his pursuit as my back hit the wall. "Gil, you are not yourself right now."

Grasping my wrist, Gil pinned it to the wall by my head. He pressed himself against me, his hips pinning against mine. Immediately, heat coursed through me, and my thoughts scattered. The feeling of his hard body against mine in this state drove me mad.

Gil smiled when he picked up on the effect he was having. Dipping his head down, his warm breath grazed my lips, eliciting a shuddered gasp.

"Maybe I'm more myself than I've ever been?"

Before I could respond, if I ever could respond, his lips were devouring mine with unbridled passion. I whimpered in surprise at first, but my sound only drove him deeper into his frenzy. His hands found my hair and my back before traveling all over me.

I tried to form a cohesive thought, to put a stop to this, but I was completely drunk on him. I wanted him so badly I could taste it. So, when his lips explored my neck, moving down toward my curves, I welcomed them. He lifted the hem of my shirt, and his fingers found the waistband of my trousers, teasing just beneath it in lazy strokes between my hips.

"I dream about you, Ellie," he purred, voice thick. "I dream about us." He tugged my neckline down and dragged his lips and tongue over the swell of my breast as his fingers dipped lower down my trousers until they found their mark.

I gasped and bit my lip as I gripped his shoulders. I was losing control fast. His touch sent a strong, aching pull to my core. He was turning me into a puddle under his stroking fingertips, and I couldn't stop the moan that slipped from my throat.

He chuckled against my skin. "I think you dream of me, too."

Just when I thought for sure things would go further, Gil stopped and abruptly released me. He turned, falling to his knees, and vomited violently. The spell was broken, and my senses slowly returned.

Kneeling at his side, I sighed, burying my face in his back as I held his hair. I'd let myself fail and forget. Guilt clenched me like a vise. How could I have been so weak? How was I going to explain to him what happened?

When he finished vomiting, Gil crawled and slumped to the floor nearby, catching his breath. I quickly straightened my shirt and came to his side. Brushing the sweat-soaked hair from his face, I watched as he slipped off into a deep sleep. Even in his wreck of a state, he still looked beautiful. Vulnerable, but glorious. I felt the overwhelming urge to protect him in any way I could. Even if that meant from me.

Gil slept for hours. Every passing moment, I was watching out the window, or listening by the door. Watching his breathing, feeling his forehead. It was risky to stay, and I knew we were in danger. But I had nowhere to go at set. No way to leave the city. I only hoped that we would be safe until rise.

* * *

"Ellie? Ellie! Wake up!"

Opening my eyes, I found a no-longer-shirtless Gil hovering over me, eyes darting around. The soft colors of rise were already filtering into the room. In a panic, I sat up, nearly head-butting him. He jerked back at the last moment, grasping my shoulders.

Judging by the dizzy feeling that washed through my head, I hadn't been sleeping nearly long enough to be rested. I didn't remember falling asleep. Still next to the door, I must've dozed off while listening for signs of intruders.

Gil helped me to my feet and rushed over to the wheelchair to grab the rucksack. It was then that it finally registered—the booms and the distant sounds of shouts and screams. Horror sent ice flooding through me.

"We have to get out of here *now*!" Gil urged, grabbing me roughly by the hand and tugging me across the room toward the balcony.

Briefly noting how remarkably well he'd recovered, I still had major reservations about his choice of escape. One wrong move, and he was incapacitated again. Tugging against him, I tried to get him to cease course, but he dragged me along.

"Gil! Wait! Maybe the balcony isn't the best way?"

He barely looked at me. "We're not taking the balcony."

To my astonishment, he went to the bookcase that butted up to the corner nearest the balcony and yanked on the curtain cord that hung next to it. There was a clicking sound, and a section of the bookcase swung inward. Beyond was a dark corridor that led downward in a spiral staircase.

My jaw dropped. I didn't even have time to comprehend what I was seeing. Deciding to trust his judgment, I followed Gil into the corridor as we plunged into darkness at rapid speed. Grasping tightly to Gil's hand, we used our light to guide us as best we could. Awful sounds were still echoing somewhere beyond the thick walls.

Down and down we went. And then down deeper still, until I was sure we were below the level of the entrance to the building. My heart thrashed against my ribs, remembering the black pit. I somehow doubted there would be a friendly Mara down here to help us.

Finally, we came to a halt. Out of breath, I leaned heavily on the cold, damp wall as Gil let go of my hand, plunging us into darkness.

"Gil, where are we?"

I could hear what sounded like his hands moving over the stone nearby, searching for something.

"Secret exit. My father uses it when he needs to slip out unseen."

"Unseen? Why would he…"

My sentence trailed off as I realized the answer to my question. *Bells root.* Gil couldn't see me, but I was burning with embarrassment. "Oh."

Growling in frustration, Gil reached out and found my arm. He yanked me to him and held me tightly from behind. The light burst forth and lit up the small, cave-like room. At last, he could see what he was looking for and promptly reached out and pressed a slightly off-colored stone. A section of the wall recessed and slid aside, revealing a large cave beyond, glowing with amber light.

Dripping through cracks in the ceiling into a river winding through the cave, the acidic liquid was everywhere, like a deadly rain. What was once a clear path ahead had now eroded into patches. Holes in the ground revealed a current of glowing acid only inches below.

Arms slackening to his sides, Gil stood beside me, gaping at the nightmarish sight.

"The explosions must've breached the moat."

"We have to turn around," I said, tugging his shirt back toward the stairs. Gil gripped me by the hand and followed, but the ground shook violently beneath our feet as an explosion rocked the building above.

Rocks rained down the stairwell as chaos broke forth. We leaped back to the doorway and braced ourselves. Dust was quickly building up as more and more debris came down from the dark. Terror had me by the throat, but my feet still moved. Latching onto Gil's arm with an iron grip, I yanked him into the flooding room and slammed the door shut.

"What are you doing?" he hollered over the din, glaring at me.

I pointed across the cave, into the shadows on the other side that held a pinprick of light in the center. "We have to get out! Now!"

Gil swept his hands across the quickly deteriorating room. "Are you insane?"

"Well, we can't go back the other way! Now, follow me!"

"Ellie—"

"*Gil!*" I yelled, silencing his protest as I glared at him. "There is no other way! Please, trust me!"

Growling in frustration, Gil debated for a moment, glancing between the way ahead and the door behind us that was thudding violently against its hinges as debris hit it from the other side. Making his choice at last, he plunged ahead, motioning his head for me to follow.

"Fine, but I'm leading!"

I wanted to roll my eyes, but I needed to focus on survival, so I carefully followed Gil's lead.

Gingerly, we stepped from stone to stone—left, right, left, left again, right by two stones. Things were crumbling around us, carried off by the rising stream. The room was hot and growing hotter. Sweat leaked from every pore.

One step ahead had Gil plunging downward as the stone below his foot gave way. With a shriek, I grabbed his hand and hauled with all my might. His foot came within a hair's breadth of the acid before I pulled him to safety. We fell backward onto the hard stone, Gil landing on top of me and pushing the breath from my lungs.

Pain sang through my bones as I gasped for air. He scrambled off me and helped me to my feet. Clinging to him, we surveyed with dropped hearts the eroding stone before us, washing away in the stream. The gulf between us and the exit was ever-widening. Backing up continuously, we avoided the acid as it ate the stone at our feet like a hungry monster, hell-bent on consuming us.

Whirling around, we discovered the ground being eroded from the other direction. Trapped. Our island of stone was shrinking. *Fast.*

"We have to bound!" I yelled over the noise of explosions and crashes.

"It's too far, Ellie!"

"Well, we're bounding anyway!" I reared up, focusing on the other side of the deadly river.

A hand slipped in mine as Gil stood at my side and took position. "Then we do it together!"

Briefly, I glanced at him with a nod. We either survive together or die together. And I had every intention of surviving.

"Are you ready?" I called.

Gil nodded. On a three-count, we bounded with every bit of strength we possessed. As we sailed high through the air, time slowed. A new stream of acid broke through from above a split second after we passed under it. I felt the hair on top of my head brush the rock of the cave ceiling, as we barely cleared it below. Everything was *just barely*.

When our feet finally touched the ground on the other side, there was more quaking, sending us stumbling and rolling along. But we made it. Quickly, we jumped to our feet and bolted for the exit, down a long tunnel, and through a door that now lay on one hinge. Gil ripped the door out of the way, and we burst forth into the open air.

Falling to our knees, we gasped for breath, recovering from the fumes that had filled the enclosed space. Shaking, it dawned on me just how close we were to landing in acid and dissolving into nothing. Everything was utter chaos, and we weren't completely safe yet.

Taking in our surroundings, I found in astonishment that we were no longer inside the city, but beyond the moat on the far western side, in the fire forest, so named for the bright red trees.

"How did we end up here?" I asked in astonishment as I whirled around the scarlet thicket. The fire forest had always terrified me. No one ever dared venture here.

The ground shook again as violent collisions ripped the air behind us. I looked up through the trees, and a scream tore from me as the towers, including our own home, imploded and fell, one by one. They were smashing into other buildings and crashing over the city.

Debris and clouds of dust blew outward and shot up high into the air. Trees around us began to crash as large stones and jagged sheets of metal came raining down.

Screams mixed in with the overwhelming roar of destruction. Specks were dropping from towers among the debris, and to my horror, I realized they were people. People, *my people*, were dying before my eyes.

I was so hysterical that I hardly registered Gil's arms binding around my waist and yanking me off my feet. He ran like lightning, dodging trees and deadly projectiles as the wave of destruction barreled our way.

I was still screaming when he threw me in the small, black carriage and leaped in behind me, narrowly missing a smoldering piece of roofing that cut into the ground. The door slammed shut, momentarily plunging us into darkness.

A glowing sphere leaped to life when Gil placed his hand next to it as he jumped into the driver's seat. The view in front of the carriage appeared. With a few swipes of his fingers, the carriage roared to life and lifted off the ground. Gil grabbed the steering handles, pressed forward, and we shot off through the forest.

Scrambling to the small slit of a window at the rear, I watched the glow of fire and the last structures crumbling.

"Gil, we have to go back! People might need help!" I cried, turning to find him gripping the steering columns.

"It's too late for them," he replied grimly, voice choked.

"What? What are you talking about? Turn around!"

"They're already gone, Ellie." Gil's shoulders shook. "Just like Star City."

Our city… our home…

The breath caught in my throat as I turned back to the window with glazed eyes. We'd just witnessed the death of everyone we knew.

Silis had fallen.

Chapter 10

I don't know how long I sat, shaking and curled up in the corner of the bench as Gil sped us far away. Far from the destruction, and the enemy that was surely hunting through the rubble for him… hunting through the remains of the once-proud people of Silis.

Shock. Fear. Grief. Anger. Lots and *lots* of anger. Anger at the premier for ever sending Gil. Anger at the enemy for what they'd done. Anger at Gil for coming back and leading them to our home.

When at last Gil brought the carriage to a halt, he landed it gently and exhaled a long breath, slumping back in his seat. I stared daggers at the back of his head. I'd never in my life wanted to strike Gil, but at that moment, he was safest at a distance.

"We're all right for now." Gil dared to turn and look at me. *Dared* to meet my eyes. Almost immediately, his eyebrows rose. He started to say something when I leaped up and shoved my way out the door.

Stalking through the unfamiliar fire forest, I picked a direction and moved forward at a furious pace. There wasn't much of a plan in my mind except to just go. I wanted to put as much space behind me as possible.

"Ellie!" Gil called, jogging to catch up. "Where are you going?"

"Far away from you!" I replied angrily over my shoulder as I picked up my pace.

"Why?" He sounded annoyed, which only infuriated me further. What right did *he* have to be annoyed with *me*?

Finally catching up to me, I felt his fingers brush the back of my shoulder.

Fire raged through me at the audacity, and I bounded high and far, nearly hitting a tree. A branch caught my arm, slicing through my shirt and the skin just below my shoulder. Crying out in agony, I barely landed the bound before tumbling across the forest floor. Gil was at my side in a flash.

"Ellie! Are you all right?"

He was no longer annoyed, but I was. The moment his hand touched my arm again, I snatched myself away and then shoved him to the ground with all my strength as I hauled myself to my feet.

"Don't touch me, Gillion!" I shouted, backing away. I tripped over a tree root and landed on my backside with a painful thud.

Gaping at me from the ground nearby, Gil made no move to come near. "What in the hell is wrong with you, Ellie?"

"Me?" I spat, sitting up straight. "*Me?* You," I pointed at him, "have blood on your hands, Gillion Braxton! An entire city's worth!"

His jaw tensed, and hurt washed over him like the encroaching of set. His eyes were still trained on mine, but something within them broke. It threatened to break me, but I held fast to my anger as images of the destruction played over and over in the back of my mind.

"Is that what you think?" he asked, barely loud enough for me to hear.

Tears filled my eyes as I tried to keep my composure. "You led them there, Gil! You led them to our home! Teli, Agatha—they're all gone! Because those monsters were looking for you. *You*, Gil!"

Rising to my feet, I swallowed the lump in my throat and turned my back to him. I couldn't even look at him anymore. To be so careless…

"No, Ellie," Gil replied sternly, rising from the forest floor. "They were looking for *you*."

I froze. Perhaps I'd just misheard? Slowly turning around, I found Gil standing with his arms crossed, and a newfound agitation.

"What are you talking about?" I asked, with hesitation.

Tearing his eyes from mine and fixating on the forest floor, Gil sighed sharply. "They couldn't care less about what happens to me. I found out they were coming for you, so I stole one of their fastest carriages after I escaped the bloodbath and got here first."

My body felt as if it were going numb. "You're lying."

His eyes flicked to mine with a burning intensity. "You know I'm not."

He wasn't. I braced myself against the tree behind me with shaking hands. "W-why? Why? Why would they want me?" I was panicking. My hands. *My* hands, not his.

"How much do you know about your manne, Ellie?"

His words hit me like a heavy stone. Slumping to the ground, I buried my hands in my hair. Whatever he had to say next, I wasn't sure I was prepared to hear. Not about my precious Manne…

Gil changed course and gathered me off the ground, gently looping his arm around my waist. "Set is coming soon. We'll talk more in the carriage."

Nodding, I let him lead me back without protest. It was a longer trek than I realized, and blood had seeped through my sleeve by the time we reached our destination. The light was changing with the disappearing stars beyond the treetops, so we quickly shut ourselves inside and bolted the door.

Somehow, the rucksack had made it there with us through all the running and nearly dying it took to get out of the city. Gil dug through it, looking for anything useful.

I kept staring at my right hand, now physically covered with blood after touching my wound. My blood. My hands… Slaughter was on my hands…

This was all my fault. It was me they wanted. Not Gil. And they destroyed thousands of lives before our eyes.

The room grew smaller. Blood was crying out. The blood of my people. The blood of my panne. They were screaming in my ears. It was a roar, like thunder. Growing louder… My ears began to ache until my head felt like it would split wide open.

Scrambling to my feet, I pulled off my shirt and began frantically wiping the blood with it. It kept dripping down my arm. I worked myself into a frenzy trying to get it all off.

My own voice was wailing and screaming in my ears, an otherworldly pain I haven't experienced in years. They were all gone. Panne was gone.

I had to get the blood off. I had to get clean.

Gil snatched the shirt from my hand and quickly wrapped it around my wound. Using water from the sack, he rinsed and scrubbed until the blood was barely visible. He then firmly gathered me in his arms.

As my tears soaked his shirt, the screaming slowly faded. The only sound was my own anguished cries and his steady, strong heartbeat. It was his heartbeat that I latched onto, focusing my energy on it until the world slowly calmed again.

Drawing in a shuddered breath, I clung to him. "Why is this happening?"

There was a space of silence as Gil stroked my hair. I could sense that he knew, but was hesitant to tell me. As fragile as I felt, however, I knew I needed the truth.

"Please, Gil?"

Relenting at last, he spoke softly into my hair. "They're searching for something. An object that can control... everything. Unleash something awful."

"I don't understand." Sitting up, I wiped my eyes. "You said they were looking for me?"

"They believe you can help use it. Perhaps only you."

Twisting my face in confusion, I watched him for any betrayal of jest or deception. I found none. Gil regarded me with steady eyes. This frightened me more than anything.

"What is this... object?"

"I only know what I overheard. They referred to it as a candle... a *Pandemonium Candle*. It's hidden somewhere and has been for a millennium. The flame is lit, all is well; the flame is extinguished, all is... hell."

Shivers ran through me. "A candle? That's all that's standing between life and destruction? None of this makes sense! Are they mad or something?"

"Ellie, this is serious," said Gil, catching my good arm as I stood. I caught the stern look in his eye and sank back down as he continued. "They won't rest until they've gotten what they want. Until they've gotten you and the candle."

"Who are these people, anyway?" I asked, exasperated.

"Invaders from another world. They've conquered other worlds in search of this candle until they finally traced the origins of the legend back to ours.

And then to you—to your lineage."

Other worlds? He was making little sense, but he was scaring me. And he still wasn't lying.

"Gil, why did you ask about my manne earlier?" I asked, swallowing past the lump in my throat. A sick feeling was forming in my stomach.

Sadness twisted Gil's features. He took my hands and tread softly with his words. "I didn't want to tell you this, but I saw them... with your father. Interrogating him while they..." his gaze flicked away as he pressed his lips in a tight line.

Then my panne had not died a quick death with the rest of them. I bit down bile and steeled myself. "Go on."

"Your manne was not an ordinary woman, Ellie. They believe she was the descendent of a Star Child, and not in the sense that we all are. She—*you*—come from a line of the ones who birthed this world. It was one of your ancestors who formed the candle at the moment the world was breathed into life. The moment many, many worlds were breathed into life. The first king, ever."

My jaw dropped. The tales manne told me as a child. All the fantastical stories... Somehow, these people had heard the same stories. The story of...

"The soul paver." The words rushed out on a breath. "But it's just a story. A myth!"

"They don't seem to believe that."

I stood and paced the small carriage interior, only a few steps available in each direction. "This doesn't make any sense! If that's true, then why would they destroy the city and try to kill me? How could I blow out some mystical candle if I have no breath? This is madness, Gil!"

"It is. But it's all we have to go on. And we have to find a way to stop them."

"No," I pointed a finger to my chest, "I do. If it's me they want, then I know exactly how to stop them—"

"Don't even think it!" snapped Gil, rising to meet me. "See, this is why I didn't tell you the truth at first—because I knew you'd be rash about this."

Narrowing my eyes, I swept my hand toward the door. "Rash? Gil, they just murdered an entire city! What is one life compared to the thousands and millions more that will be lost? Seriously? Do you even hear yourself?"

"Ellie, they would've destroyed that city regardless, just as they've destroyed countless others. The destruction will continue, with or without you. And, besides, if there's even the slightest chance that what they say about you is true, then you may be the only hope this world has. You could be our damnation... or theirs."

Pausing, I considered his words. What if they were true? What if...

"Gil," I stopped my pacing and approached him with determination, "If this is true—*if*—then merely running away will not solve anything. And you running with me is only putting you at risk. You have nothing to do with any of this if it's me they want."

Scoffing, Gil crossed his arms. "How can you say that? Ellie, you're forgetting these people just murdered my people too, *my panne!* You think I'm just going to run and hide while they get away with it? While they take you from me, too?"

Through my anxiety and frustration, those last words caused that familiar flutter in my chest. They were possessive. As much as I longed to ponder about his meaning, it was not the time to let myself slip into such thoughts.

"Okay, fine. We'll stick together—for now. But we have to come up with a plan. We can't just run without one. There's too much at stake."

Relenting, Gil nodded. "We'll think of something-"

A low growl froze us in place, followed by several more surrounding the carriage. The sound of claws scraping metal grated our ears.

Wide-eyed, we looked at each other and confirmed in unison,

"Wildions."

Chapter 11

Surrounded by hungry beasts, we huddled in the carriage's interior, wide eyes following the sounds outside. The carriage rocked slightly as something butted up against it. Shrieking, I clutched the edge of the bench that ran along the walls.

Gil cursed and flew to the control panel. Bringing up the front view, we were greeted by the sight of at least two dozen wildions prowling around us. And those were the ones we could see.

"They're everywhere," whispered Gil as he flipped off the lights. He joined me on the floor and put his finger to his lips. Catching the worried look on his face did nothing to allay my fear.

Scooting close, I whispered in his ear. "Is there a defense system on this carriage?"

"Yes," he whispered back, barely loud enough for me to hear, "but there are too many. We'll never fight them all off with a one-gunner."

My eyes grew wide. Now I really felt the rush of panic. The scar on my back ached.

Memories of running across the field toward Manne's outstretched arms, wildions at my heels, played vividly in my mind. The feeling of the claw tearing the flesh on my back just as I was landing in her arms... the way she threw herself over me as a shield... the light that blinded me from the horror that came next...

Arms wrapped around me now, enveloping us in soft light. I hadn't realized how badly I was shaking until I was met with Gil's steadiness. Or how much I needed it. Burying my face in the crook of his neck, I tried to focus on him and not the rocking of the carriage and the growling that grew louder as the pack grew in number. Perhaps this is where it would end for us. Maybe this would be the end of our dilemma.

"Gil, I'm scared," I confessed quietly.

"I know." His lips pressed to the top of my head. "We just have to wait them out."

Lifting my head, I met his eyes. They were etched with worry under weighted brows. But they were still beautiful. Blue like jewels. Perfectly complementary to his silvery hair, which now fell on either side of his face like a curtain as he looked down at me. I reached up and gently brushed a wild lock into place before tracing the contour of his jaw with my fingers. It was a bold thing to do, but I wanted to remember every detail of his face if indeed we failed to make it out of this. Just like I remember the last time I saw Manne's face. I knew what I had to do.

"I just want to let you know, in case we don't make it out—"

A loud roar that filled our ears to nearly bursting cut my words off. I screamed, but my mouth was suddenly covered in a kiss as Gil snatched my chin and pulled me close. No sooner had I comprehended it when there was another roar and another kiss.

Perhaps he was only trying to distract me, but I found my arms hooking around the back of his neck as I kissed him back. The light grew brighter and brighter as our kisses deepened, Gil's arms snaking around my waist and settling me to face him in his lap. Thoughts of the hungry wildions faded away as we got lost in each other instead.

Brighter, brighter, the light grew. The roaring became desperate; pained. I barely heard them over the pounding of my heartbeat in my ears. Heat coursed through me in a pulse, and I only had one focus. Gil's lips tasted like heaven. He was heaven. Again and again, we sought each other amid death.

Gil lifted me and laid me down on the floor. The moment his body came into contact with mine, a light burst forth that was so bright, we were both forced to clench our eyes shut.

Howls of agony sounded outside and grew more and more distant as the wildions retreated. He lay on top of me until the air grew silent, and the light faded to a strong glow. When we opened our eyes, the room was still alight, and he was more radiant than ever.

In awe, I glanced toward the door. "I think they're gone!"

Smiling, Gil nodded. "I hoped this might work."

A pang of disappointment eked in. Of course, it was part of a plan. The light dimmed, and Gil's fingers caught my chin again. He peered down at me with eyes that were both soft and intense. "You are amazing, Ellie."

As his eyes fell to my lips, his thumb brushed them softly, and the light grew again. There was nothing to stop us. Nothing holding us back from this moment. And I was more than ready for it.

Just when I thought he would kiss me again, he cleared his throat and smiled awkwardly, patting my arm. "We'd better get going."

He was off me in a flash and returning to the driver's seat, leaving me to gather my wits on the floor. Burying my face in my hands, I bit back a groan of frustration. He was right, but I was ready to throw something. Ready to leap on him and finish what we started. Still, I restrained myself and grabbed the rucksack as the carriage rumbled to life.

"Where are we going?"

"Basillian."

I stilled and stared at the back of his head. "Basillian? That's ten rises away!"

"Eleven, actually. If we make good time."

Scoffing, I dropped the sack and ran my fingers over my scalp. We'd never make that. We'd be lucky to make it through the set at that rate.

"Why are we going there?"

Gil glanced over his shoulder solemnly. "It's where your manne was born."

The mention of manne brought up a flood of emotion. Manne told me stories of her early childhood in Basillian many years ago. The fact that she had made the journey to Silis and survived at all was legendary. It did not come without cost.

"It's our best hope to find answers," continued Gil, "about the candle, about

81

your lineage. The more we know, the better chance we have of stopping them."

Hugging my arms, I sank onto the bench. "What we need is an army."

Gil was silent. Unspoken words hung thick in the air. One thing was clear: we were in extreme danger and would be for quite some time.

Not pressing the matter further, I grabbed the sack and dug through until I found one of Gil's extra shirts I'd managed to grab. It was long on me, nearly a dress, with buttons down the front and long sleeves. Black. Fitting for the occasion. Better than running around in a brassiere, though. With a sigh, I rolled up the sleeves and tucked the hem in my pants before taking a seat next to Gil in the passenger seat. I considered hiding away in the gunnery above, but even that was too dangerous at set.

It wasn't long before I felt a hand rest on my knee. There was a slight quiver to it. When I looked over, I found his eyes misty, but trained on the screen ahead. A set jaw told me he was determined to be a pillar of strength, but I knew Gil. He was not okay. Still, I didn't dare stop our journey. We had no choice but to press on, and press on quickly. So, I took his hand in mine, interlacing our fingers as we'd done so many times before, and was just... there.

* * *

The glow was soft and familiar when I woke up. My hand, connected to his. When I followed his arm, I was startled to find him fast asleep in his seat, head lolling to the side. We were stopped.

Unlacing my aching fingers from his, I shook him by the arm. Gil shot up with a gasp, eyes darting around.

"It's okay," I assured, hoping I was correct.

He buried his face in his hands and groaned. "Sorry. Bad dreams."

"Where are we?"

With a few taps on the glass panel, the screen projection bloomed to life.

A map of the entire kingdom spread before us. Gil pointed to a single blue dot on the brink of a sea of red.

"There. On the edge of the fire forest. I stopped as soon as the rise was high enough. With no rising bells, I wanted to be sure we were safe."

Safe. As if we were remotely such a thing.

Leaning over the screen, I peered over the massive rendering. I only recognized a few areas from my school lessons. Our people rarely traveled. Even our food was cultivated close to the city and only tended during strict rise hours. Now I kicked myself for not having been a better student. Gil always had much better marks. All I ever wanted to do was bound through the fields.

"Where is Basillian?"

A series of movements brought up a meandering, pulsing line from our dot connected to another, ages away. Through dangers abound. My heart sank. We still had so far to go.

"We'll never make that," I breathed, slumping back in my seat.

Gil regarded me wearily. "We *will*. But for right now, let's eat and rest while we have the chance." He rose and fetched the rucksack before heading for the door. My heart seized.

"Gil, do you really think—"

"Ellie, we've been through hellfire. I'm starving, and I'll be damned if I don't get a break from this stuffy carriage. Now, come on."

I was taken aback by his tone, but I could not fault him. Nodding, I dragged myself from my safety zone and climbed out of the carriage after him.

The stars were brilliant, there on the edge of the forest. Wild fields of tall, turquoise grass waved in the breeze before us. Images of wildions, stalking through unseen conjured up in my mind's eye. With a shudder, I joined Gil, who was just sitting down under a broad, red-leaved tree.

A bundle of bread and cheese was untied and rationed between us. As we ate our meager portion, I took in the dark circles under Gil's eyes, and the faraway look—a look in the direction of Silis. He was grim, unlike I'd ever known him to be.

"How's your wound?" I asked, searching for any way to break the awful silence weighing in the air.

Snapping from his daze, Gil finally looked me in the eye. "My what? Oh." He glanced down at his shirt. "Sore. Better than it was though, thanks to you." A brief, weak smile flashed across his lips.

Unbidden images of our encounter after the bells root danced through my memory. A flush of heat rushed through me, and I quickly diverted.

"Well, I'm afraid we don't have any bandages right now. When we get to a town, we should probably take care of that."

After taking a sip from the water sack, Gil offered it to me. "We'll stick to outlying villages. And *only* when necessary. They're more likely to hit the cities first."

My stomach had soured by the time the cool water hit it. "Do you think they'll do what they did to Silis?"

"I don't know. We can only hope not."

His words were not encouraging.

My eyes traveled over the field before us. Such a long distance to go. And somewhere out there was an enemy. *My* enemy. Would they kill me when they found me? Or simply force me to commit atrocities unlike the universe has ever seen? It all seemed so unfair. I was only a single woman—why should a kingdom be uprooted for the likes of me? Lives lost. My panne… lost.

Glow caught my attention as a hand closed over mine. I looked over to see Gil now sitting closer to me, eying me in concern. "You're shaking."

As I looked down at our hands, a tear slid down my cheek. "So are you."

Gil slipped his arm around my shoulders and pulled me close to his side. Together, we grieved silently, lost in heavy thoughts.

Chapter 12

When I awoke, it was dark, save for the glow of Gil's arm wrapped around my waist from behind. The contact of his body melded with mine, even through clothing, was warm and bright in the confining space of the carriage.

The alarm Gil set had not gone off yet, so I knew it was still rise. There was no obligation to move from that spot. Truth be told, I don't even know how we ended up in that position. We fell asleep separated, with me curled up on the bench and Gil on the floor. But there we lay—warm and secure.

Gil shifted behind me and yawned. His arm retracted from its blessed position as he sat up. Disappointed, I rolled over to find him rubbing the sleep from his eyes.

"How did I end up on the floor?" I asked quietly.

"You were pacing and crying in your sleep." He looked at me with pity.

"Oh." Averting my gaze, I sat up and hugged my knees. "I'm sorry."

Gil furrowed his brows. "You don't need to apologize. It's not a surprise after what you've been through."

"*We've* been through," I corrected, rising to my feet and dusting off my pants.

There was no argument. Still, I stood over him with an outstretched hand and a sincere gaze. "Thank you. For helping me."

He stared at me with an indiscernible expression for a moment before accepting my hand and rising from the floor. He hissed in pain as he stood, hand pressing over his wound. Immediately, I was tugging at the hem of his shirt.

"Here, let me look at that."

Though he rolled his eyes, Gil complied and pulled his shirt off. Dried blood was splattered over the angry gash. I winced, observing the spreading redness.

"We need to find a doctor for this, Gil."

"I'll be fine," he assured, putting his shirt back on with a grimace. I followed him over to the driver's seat, where he was already firing up the screens and getting the engines going.

"*Gil!* I'm serious! You need medicine for that!"

"Well, we still have the bells root."

My jaw dropped. "What?"

He cracked a smile over his shoulder. "I'm joking."

Narrowing my eyes, I plopped down in the passenger seat with my arms crossed. "Not funny."

"Well, technically, I'm *not* joking. I did grab it, but it won't help me now."

Starflies fluttered up in my stomach as I turned with wide eyes to the rucksack. He must've slipped it in before we fled his panne's study. We'd been traveling with an illicit drug this entire time. A highly addictive one. One that Gil had just had a healthy dose of...

"Gil, be honest with me. Why did you bring the root?"

He glanced at me with raised brows. "To be prepared?"

Challenging him, I glared at his cheek. "We should burn it."

"Burn the antidote to the poison, yes, wise idea," he shot sarcastically as we took off with a lurch.

"There's no need to have that tone with me. I'm serious, Gil."

"As am I."

I was flabbergasted. "Do you have any memory of the other set? After I gave you the root?"

"No. I was out," he responded, confused.

My eyes drilled into his cheek. There was no way—no way he didn't remember. He was too intense—too *everything*. How could he not remember the way he kissed me, and how his hands...

Shaking the thoughts from my mind, I decided it was best not to press that point. An ache built in my head, so I propped my temple on my fingers and sighed in frustration.

"Are you all right?" asked Gil, glancing at me.

Smiling tightly, I stood. "Yes. I'm fine."

He caught my hand. "No, you're not. Sit and talk to me… please?"

I considered his request, his pleading eyes. He knew just how to work my heartstrings and had since we were children. It was hard to say no to him. But now, it meant so much more than just a chat. His thumb caressed the side of my hand, sending warm shivers down my spine. If only he knew what he was doing to me. But now was not the time for any of this. Not when my heart was hurting so badly. Not when we were *both* hurting so badly.

Retrieving my hand, I shook my head. "No, I think I'll lie down for a bit if that's okay."

Pressing his lips in a tight line, Gil accepted defeat, but I knew he didn't quite buy my answer. That's part of the trouble growing up with your best friend—you know each other too well. We almost always knew when one of us was lying.

* * *

Curled up on the bench, I stared silently into the space before me. We whizzed along our path at max speeds now. Wildions and pantheours would be harder pressed to attack a moving target. Not impossible, but the best defense we had. It was on the brink of set, and we'd already been traveling for hours. The plan: drive straight through set without stopping at all costs.

We'd been lost in our own thoughts. I kept seeing Silis fall, over and over. Kept hearing Panne's last words to me. My last words to him. *I love you.* Agatha's face, and Teli's, and every other soul I knew in that city appeared before me. Everything cycled through my mind like a great whirlwind, incapacitating me from doing anything else but lay there, with fat tears continuously rolling down over the bridge of my nose and splashing on the seat cushion. The quiet roar was all-consuming.

Anger crept in like a slow-rising flood. Manne never told me about the Pandemonium Candle. Did she know about it? Of all the legends she told me, why exclude that one? Leave me completely helpless? If there was even a small chance I was a "soul paver", then why keep it from me? Was Manne a soul paver herself? So many questions peppering my dark thoughts. So many things I wanted to scream at the stars. But I couldn't. There was only the dark metal roof of the carriage above me. Beyond that, the stars were disappearing one by one, slipping away like cowards.

I must've made a sound when I drew a ragged breath. Gil's hand rested on my foot and gave it a gentle squeeze. It took all my strength to keep myself together at the feel of his touch. I couldn't tell if I wanted to scream at him or crawl into his lap. So, I just lay there, balancing on the edge of the precipice of hate and love.

To Gil's credit, he remained silent, his hand resting on me, casting a gentle glow. That's how we stayed for some time until he cursed loudly and grasped the other steering column in a flash. The entire carriage banked sharply to the right, sending me crashing to the floor and into the opposite wall. Before I knew it, we were swinging around in a half-circle and coming to an abrupt halt.

Grabbing my head where it'd met the wall, I pulled myself to my feet just as Gil was flying out the door. In a panic, I ran after him through the meadow.

"Gil! What the hell are you doing?" I screamed after him, noting how few stars were left in the sky.

He bounded high and landed next to something white and crumpled on the ground. Bounding after him, I barely missed him as he was lifting it into his arms. I caught a hint of long, blonde hair hanging nearly to the ground before he was bounding again, back toward the carriage.

"Come on!" he hollered mid-air.

I ignored the pounding in my head and took off in a sprint before launching into the air. Gil was just disappearing into the carriage as I landed. Immediately, I ducked in and slammed the door shut.

"Gil! What is going on?"

He grabbed my hand and yanked me toward the bench. "Hold on to her, we have to go! Now!"

Her?

I practically fell on top of an unconscious young woman. She had long, flowing blonde hair—stained with blood near the temple, and beautiful, delicate features. Her skin was a deathly peachy-pale I'd never seen before. With a gasp, I recoiled. She nearly rolled off the bench, so I quickly reached out and grasped her arm to hold her steady. Warm skin. Chest moving steadily. *Alive.*

There was not much time to ponder our new passenger when a roar shuddered the walls of the carriage. Gil swung us around before slamming forward on the steering handles. We shot forward like a shooting star.

A crash rocked the carriage from the left side, nearly sending us into a tailspin. Gil counter-corrected and we sped along. Growls resounded from just on the other side of the wall from where we sat. They were keeping pace. Another hit.

"Faster, Gil!" I cried.

"I'm going as fast as I can without overheating us!"

We took yet another hit, and this time I screamed as several dents in the formation of claws appeared on the wall. This was getting too close for comfort. Without further delay, I wrapped my arms around the woman and dragged her to the floor. I then leaped up and grabbed the bottom of the ladder leading to the turret.

"What are you doing?" Gil cried.

"Saving our tails!"

Before he could protest further, I was up in the gunnery seat, sliding the shields up from the windows and slamming down on the button to extend the guns. Panne had shown me gunneries before when I was a kid, just for fun. I now racked through my brain trying to recall all the basics that he

89

taught me. So many switches and handles. One of the first I flipped on was the full-round lights that illuminated the area all around the carriage. It devastated me to find at least ten wildions keeping pace around us.

"What do you see?" Gil called up.

"We're almost surrounded!"

Gil cursed again. "Black handles turn! Red buttons fire!"

There was no time to think. Grasping the forking handles, I swung the turret around and pulled the red buttons. Flashes of light exploded from the end of the long guns. This drew the attention of the creatures, and they made running leaps toward the roof of the carriage.

With all the focus I could muster, I aimed and fired. One down in a howling crash. And then another.

A wildion broke through the pack and landed on the roof. I shrieked as it pounced toward the window, cracking the glass. Gil called my name from below.

"Don't stop!" I screamed back.

The yellow-eyed creature stared me down with bared, drooling teeth from the other side of the insufficient glass. It wouldn't hold it long at all. And it was too close to be shot. I gulped.

Just as it was raising its paw to smash through the glass, I had a burst of angry energy. With a yell, I swung the gun around as fast as I could, colliding the barrel with the wildion and sending it flying off into the darkness. I quickly shot off the rest as best as I could, but more kept appearing in the light's wake. Still, I refused to give up.

One after another fell. They flew, I fired. My hands were cramping up from constantly pulling the trigger. We couldn't keep this up all night.

"Gil, I hope you have a plan that doesn't involve stopping!"

"I do! Just hold on! We're almost there!"

"Where?"

"The lake!"

"The what?"

He didn't respond. I kept taking out wildions until at last there was a shift and a spray of water droplets appeared on the front window. The beasts were suddenly no longer behind us, and all I could see were dark waves in the light. Swinging the turret around, I found we were flying over a vast body of water. I clutched the handles as I gasped, accidentally firing the gun.

"What is this?" I asked in disbelief.

"It's a lake. It's just water."

My hand reached out and gingerly touched the glass. Wide-eyed with both wonder and fear, I took in the amazing sight in the limited view available. I'd never seen so much water. And we were...

"Will we drown?"

"No," Gil replied below, breathing a sigh of relief, "the carriage will go right over it. We'll hit land again on the rise."

Half-laughing, half-crying, I grasped my mouth and nodded, slumping back in the seat. We'd found salvation, if only for the set.

Our speed slowed slightly. "Come down, Ellie. I've got it on self-drive now. There's nothing to run into. We're safe." Gil sounded exhausted.

Suddenly, I remembered the woman. With frantic speed, I flew down the ladder into the cabin interior, where Gil was just lifting her back onto the bench. I joined him, taking over her care. Kneeling at her side, I examined her wounded head. Strange skin, but she still bled the same color as we do.

"Did we hit her?"

"No," said Gil, "We nearly ran over her, but she was already unconscious. Our engine heat would've killed her."

I took in her nearly pristine, sleeveless, white dress, made of fine, soft material, and her neatly manicured fingers. Ten fingers, just like us. She was missing a white shoe, and I counted five toes on her unusually small feet. Same number as us, though how she could possibly bound was a mystery.

"However she got there, she must not have been there for very long. Beyond her injury, there's hardly a speck of dirt on her. As if she were just... dropped there, or something."

Gil brushed a lock of hair from her face and twisted his mouth in thought. "You're right. Very odd. In any case, she would be dead if we hadn't stopped."

"She needs a doctor. How long until we reach our next stop?"

He hesitated. "Two rises."

Disappointment dampened my spirits. Another set of wildions.

"Ellie, are you hurt?"

I hadn't even noticed the way I was cradling the back of my head. Waving my hand, I tried to dismiss him, but he turned me around and removed my hand. He searched under my hair for signs of outward injury.

"It's fine, Gil. I just bumped my head when we turned really fast."

I felt his lips press gently to the back of my head as he banded his arms around my shoulders and waist from behind.

"I'm sorry," he whispered into my hair.

Grasping his forearm, I took a deep, stabilizing breath as my eyes slid shut. I relished in his embrace. Now more than ever.

"It's okay. I'm glad you stopped."

For a long while, we just stood there, decompressing after everything that had just happened. If I kept my eyes closed, I could almost imagine we were anywhere but in a speeding carriage, in constant danger, with another passenger aboard. I could almost imagine that we were back home, possibly in a house of our own. Tucked away somewhere safe and sound. No worries, no rush. Just the two of us, basking in each other.

"Um, wow, Ellie, you're really glowing!"

I opened my eyes to find the carriage full of nearly blinding light. Shrugging out of his arms, the light faded to a soft glow. I turned to find him still blinking hard. In shock, my hand flew to my mouth.

"I'm... I'm sorry, I don't know what happened."

Gil smiled softly. "It's okay. I don't mind it."

Our eyes met and my heart fluttered. Surely this was a sign, a moment of meaning. I should just tell him how I felt, just get it off my chest and—

A sharp gasp behind us immediately drew our attention. The young woman was just sitting up and backing into the corner in a panic. Her wide blue eyes settled on us.

"Where am I? Who are you people?"

Chapter 13

Gingerly, I reached out. "It's okay, we're friends," I assured with a smile.

She stared at my hand as if it were an explosive object, ready to tear her to bits. When I took a step closer, she recoiled, hugging her arms. I looked to Gil for help. He crouched down and smiled.

"I'm sure you're confused. My name is Gil, and this is Ellie. You're in our carriage right now."

The woman blinked at him and was silent for a long time, as if trying to make sense of his words. "How did I get here?" she asked at last.

"We found you laying on the ground as we were passing," Gil explained gently.

"Oh..." She clutched her head.

Gil looked at me with his lips pressed into a tight line. The situation was delicate, especially with a head injury.

"What's your name?" I asked.

Her eyes flicked to mine. "Um... Lydia."

"Here." Gil offered the water sack. "It's all the water we have, but take a few sips."

After a moment's hesitation, she accepted it and took a few dainty sips, keeping her eyes on us warily. I couldn't blame her for not trusting us. Waking up in a dark cabin with complete strangers is not the best way to inspire confidence.

Lydia returned the sack and wiped her lips on the back of her hand. "Thank you for saving me. I won't impose on you any more than I have to, though. If you'll drop me off at the next town, I'd be very grateful."

Gil stood. "Unfortunately, that will take a couple of rises."

A dark cloud passed over her. With glistening eyes, she nodded and shifted in her seat. Instantly, my heart pricked. I saw the shadow of trauma. Taking a chance, I sat next to her on the bench. To my surprise, she didn't retreat again.

"Do you know how you ended up in the field?"

Lydia's brows lowered. "No. Not exactly. The last thing I remember was hiding with my mother in a closet and the soldiers found us."

I wasn't exactly sure what a 'mother' was, but did not want to press. "Where was that?"

"Um," she gripped the bridge of her nose and winced, "it was the city, the capital, um, what was it?"

"Star City," Gil finished solemnly.

Nodding, Lydia took in a sharp breath. "Yeah. That's it. I'm sorry. I think I need to lie down."

After she was settled, Lydia fell asleep almost immediately. We stood, watching her wordlessly for some time, both lost in our own thoughts. How was she in Star City after the destruction and suddenly here? It was not an easy or quick journey. None of it made sense. And even the mention of Star City brought up a host of painful feelings for both of us.

There was so much we had yet to discuss concerning what happened there. So much I wasn't sure I was ready to hear. Imaginings were enough to haunt me in the darkest recesses of my mind. Panne's loss haunted me.

Gil tugged my elbow, and we stepped over to the opposite corner. I could tell by his face that he was just as affected by the mention of Star City. He avoided my direct gaze and glanced over his shoulder at Lydia.

"It's okay, she's sleeping," I assured.

Lowering his voice to barely above a whisper, Gil swallowed hard. "I don't like this, Ellie."

"I know it's another mouth to feed, but it's only for a couple of rises—"

"No," he said, leaning even closer. "I mean, the way she showed up seemingly out of nowhere. *From Star City."*

There it was. My eyes traveled past his arm to the sleeping form across the room. "It is a bit strange."

"Ellie, I barely made it out alive, and most certainly *not* unscathed. Those soldiers were *everywhere.* They showed no mercy." His eyes were wild with renewed fear, even though his jaw was set.

My stomach felt weighted. "Wh-what are you suggesting? We can't just abandon her in the middle of nowhere, Gil!"

"Of course not. I just think we need to be careful."

"Define 'careful'."

He drew closer still until his lips were next to my ear. "We're just travelers, selling bells root. We say nothing about who you are, the candle—*anything."*

I yanked back with huge eyes and mouthed the words, *"Bells root?"*

Gil rolled his eyes and whispered in my ear again. "It's only until we drop her off. Although it's not a bad cover story, considering the fact we have more than we could ever need."

A pounding was building in my head. This was not exactly the direction I was hoping we'd end up in. Selling drugs was something my panne would haunt me for.

He wrapped his arms around me and pulled me close. "Just trust me?"

His voice in my ear and the quiet rush of his breath that leaked over my neck held me captive. I could never say no to him. I trusted Gil more than I'd ever trusted anyone. Slipping my arms around his waist, I sighed and tucked my chin in the crook of his neck.

"I trust you."

* * *

We spent that set in silence, with Gil watching the front view screens and me dozing off in the chair or on the floor. Lydia kept sleeping, and I was starting to wonder if perhaps we should've kept her awake with her head being injured. Her breathing was steady, so I didn't disturb her. Although I wished I could've talked to Gil more without waking her up. As stressful as things were, I was bored as hellfire.

When the stars came out at last, I was up in the turret at the perfect time. The lake lit up in a blaze of blue under the soft light. My heart soared at the sight. We were still moving at high speeds. It felt like I was flying.

"Gil! You've got to come see this," I called down.

He laughed. "Come down here. I'll show you something even better."

As much as I didn't want to leave my post, I reluctantly made my way down the ladder. When I reached the bottom, I was shocked to find the carriage door wide open, with Gil standing next to it, smiling. My jaw dropped as I took several steps back and hit the wall. He chuckled and waved me over.

After gathering my nerves, I slowly crossed the carriage and stood on the opposite side of the door frame. I found a handhold and clung to it with dear life. Gil smiled and nodded toward the open expanse.

"Take a look. Just hold on."

Adjusting my grip, I poked my head out of the doorway. The cool wind caught and whipped through my hair. A bit braver, I stuck my entire head out. I could feel the spray of the water. Smiling ear to ear, I looked back at Gil, who was already looking at me.

There was that heart flip again. His eyes were the color of the lake. When he reached out his hand, I accepted it, and carefully crossed to the other side of the doorway. With one hand gripping the handhold above, he pulled me to him and wrapped his other around the small of my back. I looked up to meet his deep gaze. There was nothing else in the universe but the two of us.

Slowly, he dipped his head down and pressed his lips to mine. Heartbreaking tenderness was in his kiss. When we parted at last, he kissed my forehead and looked into my eyes.

"I love you, Ellie," he whispered.

I was just about to respond when suddenly he shook me. "Ellie? Ellie, wake up."

Then I was no longer in his arms, but back in the turret. I felt a tug on my pant leg and found Gil standing on the ladder. Sitting up quickly, I glanced around and found that we were stopped on dry land, with the lake behind us. Disappointment was not even the word for what I felt.

Wiping the sleep from my eyes with a groan, I looked over to find Gil had already disappeared down the ladder. Voices from below told me Lydia had awoken at last. I begrudgingly closed the window shields before climbing down.

The carriage door was wide open, and Gil was just slinging the rucksack over his shoulder. Lydia was eyeing the outside world with caution, but was poised to follow him. When my feet hit the floor, she retreated to my side.

"He says we're going out there," she observed nervously.

Patting her shoulder, I smiled. "It's okay. It's safe during rise."

The half-truth was better than scaring her. She looked like she was on the brink of a full-on breakdown. I pitied her.

When at last we were outside, we sat on the gravel shores of the bright blue lake and shared bits of a fruit tart and more bread. It wasn't nearly enough to quell the raging hunger I felt. I could devour the entire contents of the bag ten times over and still be ravenous.

Lydia was so quiet, I kept glancing over at her to make sure she hadn't fallen asleep again. Her eyes were weary but trained on the watery horizon as she mindlessly chewed her food.

So many questions I wanted to ask her. Who was she? *What* was she? She spoke our language, but her pronunciation was slightly strange. Just barely, but enough that I could tell it wasn't her native tongue.

At last, she spoke. "I know you have questions. It's okay to ask them."

Surprised at her ability to pick up on my thoughts, I froze. Glancing at Gil, he shrugged. Cheeks flushing, I flashed a crooked smile at her.

"Sorry, I suppose we are a bit curious."

Lydia tossed a pebble into the water and sighed. "What do you want to know?"

"Okay... where are you from?"

"Not from here, I'm sure you've gathered." Her lips tipped up in a brief smile. "I'm from a planet called P-T2. We just call it Terra, though."

Another planet? I looked at Gil with twisted brows and he mirrored my expression. He shifted from my side to better face her.

"So, you're not—"

"No, I'm not a Celestial. I'm human."

In shock, I eyed her from head to toe. I was sitting next to an extraterrestrial being. She looked so similar to us in many ways, but also so starkly different. It was slightly unnerving, but entirely curious.

Gil found immediate interest. "Can you bound?"

"Bound? Oh! The leap-thing. No, I'm afraid I can't jump more than a couple of inches off the ground. Your gravity is slightly different from ours, but we're just not built for bounding, I'm afraid."

"We're practically born bounding," said Gil with a laugh, "my panne said manne used to tire herself out chasing me around the house, dragging me down from the chandeliers."

Lydia chuckled, "I would lose my mind if I had to put up with that! If my daughter had…" Her face fell.

"You have a daughter?" I asked gently, unsure if I should even be asking. She looked like she was about to burst into tears.

"I…" There was a long pause as she drew a shuddered breath. "Her name is Katie. She was four years old."

Was. My heart broke. There was that look again. That faraway look of longing. She was retreating into herself again. Not sure of what else to do, I was about to change the subject when she spoke again.

"She had blonde hair, you know. But brown eyes, like her father. Even at four, she could sing very well." A smile lit her sad face. "We used to have little concerts in the family room back home. We'd dress her up with jewels and feathers, and all of that. And she'd just sing her little heart out without a care in the world. It was like the entire world was her stage, and she had no fear. I wish I could be like that. Not be afraid…" The shadow fell again.

When tears slipped down her cheeks, I hesitantly slipped an arm around her shoulders. There was no glow at the contact. Still, she leaned into me and buried her face in her hands. We sat there on the shore, letting her silently empty her heart. We'd all experienced great loss, and she was another kindred soul, different or not.

Chapter 14

It was the next rise, nearly set, when we showed up in Kersi Village. None of us had slept very well, and the carriage was battered from more wildion attacks. I was proudly getting the hang of the gun though, and we fared much better than we had the first time. Still, when we were waved through the gates and beyond the high wall, I wanted to cry tears of joy.

The village was a mixture of old buildings and tent homes. Crumbling stone and wood joined in funny angles, communal fires and wells, and a general sense of being close to one another. Livestock lumbered through the streets in a herd, being driven by little boys with sticks.

We drove through cautiously, receiving awkward stares. It wasn't until we reached the outskirts of the village, on the other side where there was more open land between the village proper and the wall, that we finally stopped. The moment the door opened, I stepped out into the cool breeze.

It had been a particularly confining stretch through shadowed forest. Gil had to navigate in a weaving path through the trees. It took longer, and the constantly turning made my stomach hurt. But we made it.

Lydia poked her head out and wrinkled her nose. "What's that smell?"

Gil grinned as he threw the sack over his shoulder. "Cows."

The air was pungent, but at least it was fresh.

Gil turned to us, and his smile slid into a more nervous expression. "Wait here."

Knitting my brows, I tilted my head. "Why? Where are you going?"

He didn't look me in the eye as he turned and walked away. "Business," he said over his shoulder.

My gut twisted. *Bells business. I hate, hate, hate this!*

"Where's he going?" asked Lydia, entirely confused.

Staring daggers at his retreating back, I bit my bottom lip. This was supposed to be a cover story, but apparently, it was going to be more than that now. Turning to Lydia, I motioned for her to step closer and whispered.

"We're, um, *sellers.*"

She blinked at me. "Of what?"

"Something not entirely... legal." I cringed as that last word left my lips.

I watched as her expression remained entirely unchanged. She nodded and returned her gaze to the village. "Oh."

It was hard to tell just how damaged our reputation was, but it mattered little now. She was going to be staying here, and we'd go on our way. I felt awful all the same.

We waited for well over an hour, and the stars were gone by the time Gil reappeared. His face was alight with a bright smile.

"Come on, I've found both food and accommodations for us."

Lydia was ecstatic. I was cautiously optimistic. Still, I was looking forward to sleeping somewhere other than on the carriage floor.

Gil led us through the winding streets to the far southern side of the village, where a small, blue house lay in wait. When he knocked on the door, it took a moment for the old, lilac-skinned woman to answer. She smiled a scant-toothed grin and shuffled aside to invite us in.

"Ah, there you are! Come in out of the chill!"

I greeted her pleasantly as we passed, and Lydia just about threw her arms around her. The woman seemed more than happy to see us, especially when I saw Gil slip her a sizable cryst. I tried not to think about how he'd gotten it.

"Ladies, this is Mrs. Lunace," said Gil. We exchanged our nods and hellos. "And Mrs. Lunace this is my..." his eyes flitted to me, "uh, Ellie, and this is Lydia, our travel companion."

An awkward way to introduce me. But he didn't say *friend.* A bit surprised,

I bit back a blush. A little smidgen of hope had just been handed to me.

After initial introductions and pleasantries were out of the way, Mrs. Lunace led us to a back room where a large table lie in wait. She poured us all tea and told us stories of her life while she worked away at the stove across the room. It wasn't long before she'd filled the table with steaming food.

We wasted no time in digging in and stuffing ourselves to the brim. I'd never tasted stew that good in my entire life. After nothing but bits of bread, tarts, and cheese for three rises, I was a starved woman. And I loved the cozy atmosphere of her home.

After a while, she left us to our own devices to go tidy up the tents out back. Gil explained she was essentially the village hotel, though they rarely had visitors. Considering what we went through to get there, it was no surprise.

"Lydia, Mrs. Lunace said she is looking for help around the house as well if you are going to be staying here for a while," said Gil before taking a long sip of tea.

Lydia's face fell slightly, but she pulled up another smile. "I'll consider it. Thank you, Gil."

Gil and I glanced at each other. Not the answer we were expecting, considering how happy she seemed to be there. The subject was dropped for now.

At last, the rooms were ready, and Mrs. Lunace led us out back with a proud smile. Two octagonal faded yellow tents, tall enough to stand up in, stood at the top of the hill. Beyond were the fields of crops that led to the border wall. It was nice to see that their people didn't have risk leaving the refuge of the wall just to grow food. In Silis, it was always a race against time.

Mrs. Lunace handed a bundle of clothing and a pair of blue boots to Lydia, who accepted them graciously. The old woman smiled and patted her shoulder. "You'll be much more comfortable in these, my dear."

Beaming, Lydia hugged them to her chest. "Thank you."

Gil stretched his arms over his head and yawned. "You two can share a tent if that's all right. I'm going to turn in for the set."

Mrs. Lunace bid us goodset and shuffled back into the house. Lydia made her way into one tent without another word. I stared after her, concerned. I caught Gil's arm as he was about to head to the other tent.

"Gil, do you think Lydia's all right?" I whispered.

He looked at the tent with a furrowed brow. "Probably not. She hasn't seemed right this whole time. Happy one minute, in tears the next."

"I feel bad leaving her," I confessed.

"So do I. But she's safer here. The fewer people involved with us, the better. We've got to get to Basillian as soon as possible."

Stepping closer to him, I glanced around to be sure we were alone. "What if what we're looking for isn't even in Basillian?"

"Then we'll keep looking." He lifted my chin and looked me in the eye. "We'll find a way through this, Ellie. I promise."

My face warmed. He was close. Even closer when he pulled me into a hug. Our glow felt warm.

He planted a chaste kiss on my temple, and released me far too soon.

"Goodset, Ellie. We'll leave early on the rise."

And with that, he slipped away, disappearing into his tent. My arms felt empty, and the chill crept in without him.

"Goodset..." I whispered to the air.

* * *

It was dark. *Exceedingly* dark. Except for a single source of light, small and flickering. I walked slowly across the expanse of stone, terrified, but drawn to it.

It then called to me by name.

"*Ellie...*" The voice was familiar, comforting. Manne.

The closer I drew, the brighter and steadier the light became. It was a single flame atop a black, carved candle. Its base blended in with the night atop the pillar.

Again, I heard my name. *"Ellie..."*

It knew me, just as I knew it. A soul, trapped in flame. As I approached, I could feel a tingling thrum of power spread over my body from head to toe. My spirit was bursting to leave its cage and tangle with the universe.

Music played softly, coming from all around. It was the most beautiful sound I'd ever heard. My eyes were too drawn to the candle to care about the source.

"Manne?" I asked timidly, afraid to extinguish the beautiful fire.

Something brushed my cheek, like a phantom hand. Tears leaped to my eyes as I reached up to grab it, only to find it was already gone. But she was here. I felt her keenly.

Again, I gazed into the flame. In the center, I saw the silhouette of a woman. The figure was small and steady. It looked like... *her.*

My manne was one with the light. A child of star and fire. Though I could not see her face, I felt her power and her presence. My glow was rising.

"Oh, Manne..."

She reached a hand out to me.

Slowly, carefully, I reached out to the flame. Just as I was meant to. I'd been *destined* to do.

Just as my fingers grazed the heat, the tiny flicker erupted into a raging inferno, shooting up into the dark sky. The fire became a blazing creature with great wings, a long neck, and fangs. It roared as the ground shook.

I screamed and started to run away, only to find the wax from the candle rapidly melting and climbing up my arm, holding me captive. I felt my skin sear under the heat.

"Manne!"

There was no reply. She was gone, and I was trapped. I watched in horror as more gigantic creatures rose from their slumber in the shadows. The light from the beast lit up the whole mountain top and the monsters descended to the lands below—down to my home. More and more creatures kept rising, shooting off into the sky, clambering down the mountain, into the unknown destinations. The creature of fire lifted off the candle at last, leaving a dark mound of hot wax that continued to consume me.

I'd awoken the sleeping evil. And everything and everyone was about to die.

In the distance, I heard Gil's voice calling my name. He was next. They were coming for him, but I was trapped in a shell of wax, which was, at last, filling my mouth and stealing away the last, precious threads of air.

This was the end. I'd failed.

* * *

"Ellie!"

I was shaken violently, and my own screams filled my ears. Flailing, I fought off the hands on my arms as my eyes flew open and I sucked in air.

"Ellie! It's okay! It's me!"

At last, my vision focused, and I looked up to find Gil hunched over me, terrified. Lydia sat on the other side, looking equally frazzled. I sat up and found that I was safely in the tent, laying on the pallet of furs where I'd fallen asleep.

"I'm so sorry, I was just… it was all so real… I…" Choking sobs caught my words away and I leaned into Gil's arms.

"It's all right," he said, "it was just a dream."

"Is there anything I can do?" asked Lydia, suppressing a yawn.

"No, I've got it from here," said Gil as he stroked my hair. "I'll take her back to my tent. You go back to sleep."

I wanted to apologize to Lydia. I must've scared the wits out of her, but my emotions were too high-strung to form proper words. I rose and followed Gil to his tent.

Once inside, Gil switched on a lantern and fastened the door flap. He motioned toward the two fur pallets in the middle. I stared at them. One was unused.

Seeing my hesitation, Gil climbed in the unmade one and patted the space next to him. I didn't have to sleep alone. Relieved, I crawled next to him, and he tucked the soft, heavy blanket over us.

Instantly, I relaxed. We lay facing each other in the dim lantern light. Gil eyed me with worry as he reached up and stroked the hair from my face.

"Do you want to talk about it?"

The tears came again. I kept my focus on his eyes. If I could look into his eyes, then I knew he was alive. Swallowing hard, I explained what I could.

"I saw it, Gil," I whispered. "The candle."

He paused. "The—"

"The Pandemonium Candle." Even saying the words out loud made my blood run cold. "It called to me. I felt it. *Heard* it. I still hear it." I choked on a sob. "And it destroyed everything, including me, a-and you, and—"

That was the end of trying to explain. I was shaking too much, and the panic was rising all over again. Gil worked me through deep breaths and held me to his chest. His shirt became soaked with tears.

After a while, the sound of his heartbeat, his scent, and the familiar soft glow chased away the monsters that still plagued me. I clung to him like life itself. He was all I had left.

"You're safe now, Ellie."

I didn't respond. I knew that wasn't true. None of us were safe, not really. But at least there, at that moment, I could pretend I was.

Chapter 15

When I awoke, I was still wrapped up in Gil's arms. I had slept without a single bad dream.

Gil shifted behind me and yawned. His hold on me then tightened into a hug.

"Goodrise."

"Goodrise."

His thumb gently brushed my upper arm. "How do you feel?"

"Better."

We just lay there quietly for a bit before reluctantly crawling from our warm blanket haven. I wanted nothing more than to hop back into bed and never leave his arms. But reality was calling. And it came calling fast.

Gil was just tying the rucksack when the walls of the tent began to shake. The ground was vibrating. Shouts and screams rose from the village. We looked at each other gravely before bolting from the tent.

The stars were gone. No, not all. In the distance, we saw the stars, but over the village, they had vanished in large patches. Wind was rushing down from the darkness.

"Ellie!"

I turned to find Lydia scrambling toward us from her tent, which was half-collapsed. Her long hair was wildly whipping about in the wind. Eyes wide with fear, she reached us and practically burst into tears.

"We have to go!" she screamed over the din.

"What's happening?" asked Gil.

Lydia's eyes flitted to the sky. "They're here!"

Gil and I locked horrified gazes before looking at the sky. The dark masses began to take shape and form, as if a drop cloth was slipping away. Huge, shining, black vessels, floating up in the sky. Longer than they were wide, with spindly gun barrels twice the size of our entire carriage. The underneath was gradually growing closer as they moved to hover over the inner fields.

"Gil, why didn't you tell me they could fly?" I called nervously as we began backing toward the house.

"It didn't exactly come up! Go!" He grabbed each of our hands and yanked us along toward the side of the house.

We followed as he darted down an alley and into the throngs of panicked villagers. It was absolute chaos, and we were moving against the flow. The carriage was parked at the far end of the settlement. If we were going to have any hope of survival, we had to reach it, and reach it fast.

My heart felt as if it was going to pound out of my chest. All I could hear was a roar of noise around me. People were fleeing for the wall exits, hoping to hide in the fields and woods. *The monsters! ... Hellfire! ... The end!"* Their panicked cries rang out around us. All this destruction was about to rain down, and we were powerless to help them. My panic was as high as Lydia's, but I stuffed it down so deep that by all appearances, I was calm as glass.

Once we reached the end of the road, we ran around the perimeter to avoid most of the crush. Jolts on the ground nearly knocked us off our feet as the vessels found their landing spots, one by one. I grabbed the arm of a screaming Lydia, yanked her up, and hollered in her face, "Keep moving!"

The unmistakable sounds of gunfire erupted as the screaming from the villagers became more intense. Slaughter had begun. Memories of Silis immediately rushed in, unbidden. My resolve was threatening to crumble. I was frightened. And *angry*.

We'd finally reached the carriage when the sound of screaming had filled my ears to bursting. I whirled around and screamed back to the hell, "Here I am! Take me, you bastards! You can have me! Here I—"

A vise-like band snatched me by the waist and someone threw me mercilessly into the carriage. Gil slammed the door shut and hopped in the driver's seat. He gave me a hellfire look over his shoulder.

"Don't you dare do anything like that ever again!" The venom in his words was enough to shut my mouth.

The carriage fired up and roared to life. I jumped in the passenger seat as Lydia cowered in the corner with her hands planted firmly over her ears. As much as I pitied her, I was tempted to join her. We had to focus.

"Do you want me in the turret?"

Gil nodded as he scuttled his fingers over the controls. Without hesitation, I was up the ladder and strapping in. When I opened the shields, I saw a flood of black invading the muted tones of the village. Men and women in shining dark armor I'd never seen, their faces shielded, wielding their guns and knives without mercy.

"What's the plan?" I called down to Gil.

"I drive, you shoot."

With that, the carriage lifted and whipped around before jolting forward. The streets were overrun with both the living and the dead. People attempted in vain to fight back with whatever insufficient weapons they owned, but it was no match for the impenetrable black armor. Defenseless men, women, and children were eliminated like mere vermin.

Shots rang off the carriage armor. I tried not to think about how we were making it through the sea of people. It made me sick. I extended the gun, found clusters of soldiers, and fired. They were raising their guns as they lined up a group of elderly against a wall. I raised mine first, showing no mercy to the invaders. Deep down, I knew I was snuffing out life, but I kept firing, turning off that part of me that shuddered at the thought. I thought of Silis. I thought of my panne.

Eventually, we made it to the gate. We drew more and more attention to ourselves. I was taking out *a lot* of their troops. Shots were pinging off the windows from all directions. I thanked the stars they were reinforced, but chips started to form. It wouldn't hold forever. If it didn't, this would all be over quickly.

Any hope of an easy escape vanished the moment we crossed the threshold.

There, with cannons aimed straight at us, sat one of the vessels. Ground troops quickly filled in to surround us, with their guns drawn. We were utterly trapped.

"Gil…"

"I know! I know."

Lydia wailed hysterically below. Gil shouted at her to be quiet so he could think.

My back ached. I thought of Manne. How she would be covering me right now, the way she covered me from the wildions. I wished I could've covered everyone in that village and taken it all myself.

A hatch opened on the side of the enemy vessel, and a ramp extended. Four guards marched out, followed by a lone figure: a man, clothed in black to match his short, set-black hair. Even from the gunnery, I could see his striking eyes contrast his abnormally pale skin. As he reached the ground and turned toward us, his emerald stare immediately locked onto mine across the distance. An icy chill ran through me from head to toe.

Slowly, he reached up to his ear and touched a small black object. His voice boomed as he spoke, as if coming from all around.

"Ellette Humett, I know you're there."

I nearly fainted. He knew me by name. But I remained frozen to the spot—transfixed by those unworldly eyes.

"Ellie." Gil's hand appeared on my lower leg, but I hardly felt it. "Get down here."

Again, the man spoke, his voice poised, almost gentle. "I know you can hear me. I want to talk to you."

"Don't listen to him, Ellie," said Gil, climbing higher up the ladder and grasping my elbow. "You need to come down now."

"He's looking right at me," I muttered.

"Come out now and you and your friends will not be harmed, I assure you," the man said.

Considering his request, I glanced over at Gil, who was now propped next to me in the turret. He was afraid. I could see it in his eyes. I was afraid for him. Not so much for myself. But I couldn't lose Gil.

If only there was a way to weigh the truth to the man's offer. Me in exchange for their safety. But there was no guarantee that the second I stepped out of the carriage that it wouldn't be invaded for the slaughter. The man was watching me patiently, waiting for a response. I thought I detected a slight lift to the corner of his lips.

"Ellie," pleaded Gil, tugging my arm, "please, look at me?"

His fingers gently found my chin and directed my gaze away from the enemy. I blinked hard and Gil's face came into focus. I was tired. So very tired. And confused.

"I don't know what to do, Gil."

He pulled me close and wiped my tears. "Let your light shine."

Suddenly, I understood. I called down, "Lydia! Cover your eyes!"

Only a moment later, I wrapped my hands around Gil's face and kissed him deeply, releasing every bit of love I held for him. The wave of white burst forth from where we were joined. I felt it surge through my body in a wild burst of energy and expand outward.

Outside, we heard shouts and cries of agony. The shooting stopped. Everything was upended.

Quickly, Gil pulled away and was down the ladder in a flash. The carriage banked left and shot forward. I heard the sickening thuds of bodies slamming into the front as we sped away parallel to the wall, toward the northern forest.

Still blinking spots from my vision and recovering from the warmth, I spun the turret. To my shock, we weren't being followed. Soldiers were laying on the ground, hands to their eyes... except for one lone figure who stood watching us.

As we sped away, I heard him shout in the distance, "Ellie!"

We drove at high speeds for a long time. I could hardly move. Every single emotion was whirling through in an overwhelming maelstrom. Up in the turret, I kept my hands glued to the trigger handles, ready to fire at whatever obstacle flew up before me. Lips pursed, silent tears rolling down my quivering chin... I was a hairpin trigger.

At last, we stopped.

"Ellie—"

I screamed at the sound of my name and fired the gun. Gil was up the ladder in the flash. He yanked my hands from the handles and spun me around to face him. His eyes were hardened as he held my wrist.

"Look at me! Get it together! You may have just let them know where we are!"

Wrenching myself from his hold, I pointed back in the other direction.

"That man *knew* me, Gil! Knew me by name! He killed those people for *me*!"

"Ellie, I know it seems that way, but that's why we—"

"Who is that man?"

"Look, why don't you come down—"

"*Who is he?*"

"He's the king!" Gil shouted. I jumped. Guilt flashed across his face as he ducked his head and sighed.

I couldn't have been more taken aback than if he'd just told me it was a wildion in a suit. "He's the *what*?"

Gil pinched the bridge of his nose between two fingers and grimaced. "He's the new king. The invader. Kromer, I believe. I barely had time to make introductions, of course."

Scoffing, I began angrily unbuckling the straps. "He's no king. He's a godsdamned exterminator!"

Taking my cue, Gil descended the ladder, and I came down after him in a fury, narrowly avoiding stepping on his fingers.

Lydia was waiting near the bottom. "What are you guys talking about? What's going on?"

I glared at her. "I'm a weapon. King wants to use me. There. Now you know. If you'll excuse me."

Slamming the door button, I marched out the moment it was open, with Gil in tow. He pleaded with me to stop and talk. I didn't want to talk. I wanted to bound. I found the tallest tree, reared up, and leaped to the highest branch that would hold my weight.

"Oh, come on, Ellie!" Gil whined below. "That's not fair, and you know it!"

I crossed my arms and leaned my back against the trunk, straddling the branch. "Leave me alone, Gil. I need to think. Is it a crime for me to think now, too?"

With a frustrated sigh, Gil plopped down at the base of the tree and ran his hands through his hair. As much as I didn't want to admit it, I'm glad he didn't go far. But he respected my request enough not to bound up after me, so I was satisfied. I needed to be away from everyone. If only for a few moments. I felt... toxic.

The stars were shining brightly through the treetops. Up there, in the canopy, I could see them better in the thinning gaps. I breathed deeply, and my eyes filled up with tears as I stared into them. Somewhere, out there in the great big unknown, Manne and Panne must've been waiting for me. Watching me. I wished they would give me some sort of sign for what it was I was supposed to do, how to handle this. There was so much I needed to ask. I felt like I didn't know anything about anything anymore. Gil was my only constant.

Looking down, I saw him now, head in his hands, like he did when he was stressed. Our love had saved us. But it was also damning him in the process.

I had to find a way to save everyone. A universe of Mannes and Pannes, Gils, and Ellies. There were a multitude of Silises and Kersis and every other kind of city and village just waiting out there for their turn to be slaughtered. Our world was small but precious. And it sat on my shoulders.

The *universe* sat on my shoulders.

There, under the colorful spray of rise, I let my eyes slide shut. I could feel Manne's arms around me, beaming through my deepest memories. I missed her so much.

Suddenly, the branch jolted. I sighed in annoyance.

"Gil, I said—"

I froze the moment I opened my eyes. Two glowing yellow eyes bore into mine. My heart about leaped out of my chest.

There, not more than three arms-length away, stood a giant, sleek, black pantheour.

Chapter 16

The beast stared me down. Nearly three times my size, I was no match for it. Gleaming white fangs hung down from its mouth like knives, ready to slice through my flesh and bone.

Too terrified to move, I gripped the branch with my thighs and clung to the trunk at my back. At any moment, it could leap, and it would all be over.

My expectation of a quick ending evaporated. It just stood... and then laid down. There it lay, with its head raised, still staring at me.

The leaves from the adjoining branches and twigs were rattling with my shaking. I'd never seen a pantheour, only in illustrations. Nothing prepared me for the sheer size of the animal. Wildions were enormous. Pantheours dwarfed them. Yet somehow, this branch was holding the both of us.

Why wasn't it eating me? Was it intelligent enough to taunt me first? Get my blood pumping?

Suddenly, it came to me: the stars. Stealing a glance upward, I noticed the stars were still out in full blaze. It was still rise. The pantheour was respecting the laws of nature. But why was it here?

The more I stared at the beast, the more I realized how relaxed it was. Its eyes were more curious than hungry. We sat, looking at each other. The longer we did, the less my heart slammed against my chest.

Deep breaths, Ellie...

Glancing downward, I saw Gil still sitting on the ground, oblivious to what was happening. I could scream, get his attention, but it might change the pantheour's mind about being passive.

Returning my attention to the pantheour, I smiled nervously. It blinked slowly in response. Then it finally broke eye contact and began licking its paw before rubbing it over its head and ears. I watched in awe as it sat there, grooming itself casually as if its prey were not sitting right in front of it.

"I guess you're not going to eat me, huh?" My voice shook as I murmured. The pantheour only glanced at me and continued to groom.

A low sound rumbled down the branch. Not a growl... it was *purring*. My brows shot up to my forehead. This beast was acting as if it were a content house cat.

I don't know what came over me. Perhaps it was the emotional exhaustion or the constant expectation of death. Slowly, I lifted my hand and gingerly reached out. At first, the pantheour didn't even acknowledge me. And then it paused.

Holding my breath, I sat still as stone, with my hand outstretched. Certainly, I was about to get my arm bitten clean off. It was too late to turn back now.

Its amber eyes stared at my hand, and then at me. I could feel its warm breath puff across the space between us. Slowly, the pantheour stretched its neck and sniffed my hand. The wetness of its nose brushed against my palm. Fangs were only a breath away from piercing my flesh.

And then, it opened its mouth... and licked me. An enormous, rough, pink tongue slid over my hand and lower arm repeatedly. I lifted my hand and ran it gently over the long bridge of its nose as it continued to lap at my arm.

Laughing in disbelief, I continued to pet the pantheour cautiously. It leaned its head down and nuzzled into my strokes and ear scratches as it purred loudly. Its fur was black, soft, and thick—softer than silk.

When the pantheour finally returned to grooming itself, I sat back in awe. Wiping the slime and fur off on my shirt, I felt incalculably better. Pantheours were supposed to be bloodthirsty beasts who killed without discrimination, not... cats.

"Ellie! Stay still!"

I looked down to find Gil standing below, face white as a sheet, prepared to bound.

"It's okay! Its—"

Suddenly, the pantheour snapped its attention to Gil. Before I could react, it was leaping from the tree and landing on the ground with teeth bared. Gil immediately backed into the tree, defenseless.

I swung my leg around and dropped to the ground, landing between them. Gil grabbed me by the arm and started to pull me behind him. The moment he made contact with me, the pantheour roared, drilling its menacing eyes into Gil's.

Shrugging Gil off me, I reached a staying hand out toward the pantheour.

"Ellie! What are you doing? Get back now!"

Without taking my eyes off the pantheour, I spoke gently. "It's okay. He's okay."

The pantheour's eyes broke in confusion as he darted back and forth between us. Slowly, I lowered into a crouch, pasting a smile on my face. We watched each other for a moment before the pantheour gruffed and stepped forward. I heard Gil gasp, but my other hand shot out behind me and stopped him from attempting to intervene.

Once again, the pantheour relaxed and nuzzled my hand. My smile stretched further as I brought my other hand around and scratched it behind the ears.

"See? It's all right, big girl!"

Gil slowly crouched down next to me. "Ellie, mind explaining why in the hell you're petting a pantheour?"

I shrugged. "She likes me."

"She?"

Looking into the pantheour's slowly blinking eyes, I smiled. "Yes. I think it's a 'she'. I'm not sure why, but I just have a feeling."

Gil's brows raised. "Well, I'm not checking, so I guess I'll take your word for it. I just can't believe that thing hasn't eaten you yet."

I frowned at him. "She's not a *thing*!" Turning back to the pantheour with a smile, "Her name is… Shade."

"Oh, no no. You are *not* naming that th—*pantheour!*"

"Gillion Braxton, you are being very ruuude," I chided in a singsong voice

116

as Shade nuzzled up against my chest.

He stood and crossed his arms with a frustrated sigh. "You don't need to name something you're not keeping. It's *not* a pet, Ellie." Ignoring him, I continued to coo and play with her. Then he leaned down and spoke again quietly. "And what do you think's going to happen as soon as the stars disappear?"

I froze. *Natural laws.* Looking now at the gentle, affectionate giant in my arms, I couldn't imagine being attacked by her... but would she? Was she just playing with her food? Was I being naïve?

My instinct told me no. Something within me felt a strange connection to this beast. When I looked into her eyes, I saw intelligence looking back. I saw respect. Something changed the first moment we connected. But Gil was wise and looking out for my safety.

Shade plopped down and stretched her large chin over my legs, knocking me to the ground. A big yawn briefly displayed her razor-like teeth, sending my nerves skittering about. But then her jaw was closed again, and her eyes slid shut as she purred loudly. Her breathing grew steady, and I realized she was fast asleep. Stroking along her head and long neck, I watched her peaceful slumber.

Gil's hands gently laid on my shoulders. He was kneeling behind me. "I'm not trying to frighten you, Ellie."

"Good, because I'm frightened enough as it is. All the time."

"I know. I'm sorry."

Biting back tears, I swallowed hard. "I know you think I'm out of my mind, Gil, but please, just let me have this moment. Let me have... this. We'll leave soon, but I just need to... I need to..." I couldn't finish my sentence without crying. I couldn't even explain what I needed. All I knew was I'd just been given a gift, and I didn't want it taken away so quickly. After all the slaughter we'd witnessed, and the fear, the universe had sent me something. Even though it was something as unheard of as a tame pantheour, I wanted to keep hold of it.

Clutching Shade's fur, I bent over and touched my cheek to the top of her head. It was a bold, foolhardy thing to do. But I did it anyway. And I began to glow.

Soft, yellow light spread from me to Shade, enveloping us both, even taking over the glow from Gil's contact. Immediately, Gil released his hands and watched in awe.

"But… this is impossible," he said, rising to his feet and circling us. "It's a pantheour, not a Celestial!"

Wide-eyed, I took in the strange aura. The glow continued, even after I lifted my head. It felt natural—as natural as any embrace.

"Gil, I don't think this is any ordinary pantheour."

"Then what is it?"

I looked up at him with a laugh. "I don't know! But maybe it's a sign?"

We both sat there in stunned silence, just observing the unwavering glow. Shade was completely relaxed; trusting. Why was this enormous animal laying in my lap right now? Why was this happening? I couldn't explain any of it. All I knew was that I didn't want her to leave.

"Oh my God, what is that?"

A terrified Lydia stood in the carriage's doorway, clinging to the door frame with wild eyes. Shade's eyes immediately popped open and her head jerked Lydia's direction. She was shifting, about to get up, but I quickly put my hands around her neck and pulled her close again.

"It's okay, girl. She's a friend…"

Somehow, Shade understood. Or seemed to. She rose to her feet, and the glow faded away, but she did not leave my side. Still, she kept a curious eye on Lydia. Gil was poised between them, ready to intervene, as if it would've been possible.

I rose to my feet and dusted myself off. "Lydia, this is Shade. She's a pantheour."

Shade lumbered lazily forward, pushing past Gil, and went straight up to Lydia, who turned white as a bell's root. I followed close behind, hoping beyond hope that there wasn't about to be a bloody confrontation. To my relief, however, Shade merely sniffed at Lydia, nudging her in the stomach. Lydia shook like a leaf, her mouth frozen open in horror.

"Ellie, can you get Shade to back off now?" asked Gil sternly.

"Why? She's not going to—"

"Ellie, she's terrified!"

Taken aback by Gil's anger, I blinked at him. Then I looked at Lydia, who had tears streaming down her cheeks. With a sigh, I patted my thighs. "Shade! Come on, girl!" To my surprise, she actually obeyed, turning from Lydia with indifference and returning to my side.

Gil stepped into the carriage just as Lydia swooned. He caught her in his arms and scooped her up in one swift motion. His eyes snapped to mine and I could tell that he was not pleased with me.

"We leave in one hour." With that, he disappeared into the darkness of the cabin, and the door shut behind him.

My heart pinched. Gil rarely got angry with me. And I still wasn't completely sure what I'd done wrong.

Despondently, I returned to the tree and sank down to the ground. Shade lay at my side, resting her head on my lap again. I couldn't explain why this animal was so attached to me, but I knew it was going to have to end soon and we'd leave her behind. Why couldn't Gil understand? Why couldn't he see that *she* chose *me*?

We were under an inordinate amount of stress. It was enough to crack anyone. I only hoped whatever we possibly had would be enough to survive it.

An hour flew by fast. When Gil found me, I was still sitting at the base of the tree but had fallen fast asleep, my hand resting on Shade's neck. I felt a hand gently shake my upper arm. My eyes opened and met his. He was no longer angry, but full of exhaustion and regret.

"I'm sorry, Ellie, but we have to go."

My eyes moistened as I nodded and slowly shifted underneath Shade's massive head. She woke, looking up at me with sleepy eyes. I smiled and petted her before rising to my feet. Shade followed suit, staying near my side.

"I've got to go now, girl."

She responded by nudging my hand for another pet. I gladly obliged. When I was done, Gil's hand slipped into mine.

"Come on, El."

The moment I stepped away from Shade, she began to follow me back to the carriage. I stopped and turned, pointing to the woods.

"No, Shade. You have to go now." Shade whimpered, nudging my hip. I shook my head and again pointed to the woods. "Go on, girl!"

Turning, I walked quickly with Gil back to the carriage, fighting tears. We made it to the door, and I heard a whine behind me. I looked to find her sitting in the same spot, eying me with the most pathetic look a pantheour can muster.

"Oh, Gil..."

"I know. But she wouldn't fit inside the carriage even if we wanted to bring her."

My eyes searched his. "I know you think all of this is ridiculous, but—"

"Ridiculous?" His brows twitched down. "Of course it's not ridiculous." He brought his hands up to cup my jaw. "Ellie, you are a phenomenon. I may not understand everything that's happening, but you are not, and never will be, ridiculous to me."

He pulled me close and briefly wrapped me in his arms. "I'm sorry I was cross with you earlier."

"It's all right." I was still smarting inside, but I let it go.

Casting one last, sad look back at Shade, I whispered goodbye and then found the strength to step inside the carriage and shut the door.

Chapter 17

It was a long two rises. The wildions were curiously and blessedly scarce. The land changed, with the trees also growing sparse. Grass gave way to hard-packed dirt and sand. We found ourselves on a massive, flat plain, surrounded in the distance by hills and mountains.

The stars blazed brightly, brighter than I'd ever seen them before. We'd been driving for ages, with Gil refusing to stop and sleep since the previous rise. I barely got him to eat. Up there, in the turret, I had finally given up on urging him to take a break. So I lay slumped back in the seat, watching the stars.

"Wow!"

I looked over to find Lydia coming up the ladder with wide-eyed wonder. She made it to the top, just high enough to look out of the windows. This was the first time she'd been brave enough to climb it. Clinging to the armrest, she took in the colorful sight with a bright smile.

I fought back a yawn. "It's something, isn't it?"

"It's amazing out here! I've never seen them like this."

"Do you see the stars where you come from?"

Lydia shrugged. "Some. The city lights are so bright, you don't see them much. We have to drive a couple of hours to get a good look. Even then, it's nothing like this."

I frowned. "How do you get your energy?"

"Energy? Eating, I suppose. If you're talking about power, we get it lots of ways: water, the wind, the sun—"

"The sun?" I shot up and grasped her arm with wide eyes. "You've seen the sun?"

She blinked at me. "Well, yeah. Everyone on my planet has. It's the center of our solar system."

My heart pounded. So Mara *wasn't* a figment of my imagination. And she was telling the truth. Here I was, face to face with someone from a world of light.

"How did you come to Celeste?"

The color drained from Lydia's face. Her eyes averted from mine. "I… well… I, um…" she began to descend the ladder again when I groaned in frustration.

"Lydia, please just talk to me?"

She paused and pursed her lips. Hesitating, she then swept her hair over one shoulder, revealing a small, black, angular tattoo on the back of her neck. I squinted and leaned closer to look at it.

"What is that?"

"It's their mark. We all got them when they took us."

My heart dropped. "You mean, you're a—"

"Slave. Yes." The words were barely audible from her trembling lips.

"Oh, Lydia…"

She steeled herself and continued. "I am—*was*—part of a breeding program. They took all the females in my city. In *every* city. Young, old—we all had some sort of purpose. Scattered us all over the universe on their ships, ready to settle each new world they conquer."

I could hardly believe my ears. It all made sense now—why she was so jumpy and terrified all the time. I almost said, *"You're safe now."* But that would've been a lie. And a terrible one, at that.

"I'm so sorry." It was all I could think of.

Nodding, Lydia stretched her mouth into a brief smile before descending the ladder again. I watched her disappear down the hatch and wondered to myself how she bore the pain.

* * *

Set was rapidly drawing near when something appeared in the distance, at the base of the first lumbering hill beyond the desert. I sat up in my seat and squinted. Whatever it was, it had lights. "Gil, what is that?"

"Uh, I don't know. It's not on the map."

Immediately, alarm bells went off in my mind. I shut the window shields and scrambled down the ladder, where I found Lydia hunched over Gil's shoulder as they tried to make out what was ahead. I joined them and we watched as the object drew closer and closer.

"Shouldn't we flip off the lights?"

Gil shook his head. "They've already seen us by now."

At last, we had a better view: a small town, surrounded by a high, white stone wall. Curved roofs peeked above it, as did towers with large guns aimed from them. The armored gates opened and several small vehicles came pouring out like insects, guns drawn.

"Gil—"

"I know. It's too late to outrun them."

Lydia and I looked at each other gravely. I reached over and grasped her arm. She covered my hand with hers and bit her quivering lip.

Soon, they surrounded us, but they merely followed, escorting us the rest of the way to the city. Still, it was not exactly a friendly reception.

When we entered the city gates, we found groups of men and women watching us closely. Every single one of them was armed. They made way for us and the other vehicles as we came to a stop on the dirt road in the small city square.

"Exit the vehicle!" a voice boomed over a loudspeaker.

Gil sighed and stood. He turned to us and spoke quietly. "Don't give your real names. Follow my lead."

"Are we really going out there?" said Lydia in a panic.

I pulled her to my side and looped my arm through hers. "Just keep quiet."

The moment the door opened, we were greeted with the sight of gun barrels. Men and women in old, patched up armor and utilitarian clothing stared us down. They backed up as we stepped out but didn't take an eye off us for a second. One tall man with deep red skin and dark eyes stepped forward from the troop. He peered at us from under the hood of his tan jacket.

"Who are you?" His request was not a polite one.

Gil put on his best diplomatic smile and held out his hand. "Petra Riller."

The man didn't acknowledge his hand. His eyes then danced between me and Lydia, briefly dragging us up and down. "And the women?"

I was about to open my mouth and answer when Gil stepped back and broke between us, looping an arm around each of our waists. "This is Melba," he said, nodding toward me, "and Dahlia, my wives."

The blood drained from my face, and I had to force myself to keep my expression neutral. I was fine with being "Melba", but one of two wives? Still, I decided I would trust now, holler at Gil later.

The man was unimpressed. "Explain your purpose here."

"Well, we're just passing through—"

"Hunter!" I turned around to see a woman emerging from our carriage with the rucksack. I hadn't even noticed her slip in. She held up the bells root. He held out his hand, and the woman threw the root over our heads, where it landed perfectly in his palm. Carefully, he studied it, and then looked at Gil with a gleam in his eye.

"Just passing through, eh?"

Gil grinned. "Traveling salesman."

Then, to my shock, he tossed the root back to Gil and motioned for the guns to be lowered. "Better keep a close eye on that. Welcome to Stone City."

We were ushered through town, led by Hunter. Stares permeated us every step we took. Distrust, curiosity. Some leers. Lydia clung to me as we stayed close behind Gil.

At last, we came to a large, brown building with open doors. Music poured out into the street, mingling with rowdy laughter. The second we entered the dimly lit hall, all the laughter stopped, and the music died down to a minimum. All eyes were on Hunter.

He led us to a table at the head of the room, where he took the center seat. Gil sat next to him as directed, but when I went to sit next to Gil, Hunter caught me by the wrist. My eyes snapped to his, ready to punch him with my free hand, but I caught a glint in his eye that told me he was not to be trifled with. He smiled, which was slightly more terrifying.

"You look like you are good for conversation. Come, sit next to me. I'm sure your husband won't mind." He sounded jovial, but there was also an edge to his voice, challenging Gil to defy him.

There was a flash of murder in Gil's eyes, but I quickly pasted on a smile and patted his shoulder. "Of course not, will you, darling?"

Gil quickly melted right back into his carefree persona and smiled before taking my hand and kissing it. I was released to go sit next to Hunter, who sat a little taller upon his victory.

Servants brought food and drinks to us as the rowdy activity returned to normal. Greasy meats and stewed vegetables with an endless supply of confections chasing after. I only picked at my food as people continually came to the table and quietly give reports to Hunter, crowding my space.

At last, Hunter turned to me and smiled. He wasn't altogether unpleasant looking when he wasn't glaring, but there was a dark edge to that smile that I couldn't quite put my finger on. I questioned his motive and discreetly slipped the dinner knife under the table to keep gripped in my palm.

"So, Melba, isn't it?"

His voice was quieter; directed. I shifted away ever-so-slightly but smiled pleasantly.

"Yes, that's right."

"That's a lovely name. Where do you hail from?"

Gil coughed forcefully on the other side of him, but Hunter didn't even seem to notice. Inwardly, I panicked, but kept my calm exterior.

"Oh, you know, here and there. My family moved a lot. My panne was a, um, *salesperson*. Like my husband."

Hunter's brows raised to his forehead as he took a swig of his drink. "Was he, now? Dangerous business to conduct with a family around."

My heart pounded. "Yes. Not exactly an easy life... but that's how I met my husband, so not all bad." I added with a bright smile as I leaned forward to beam lovingly at Gil, who was struggling to maintain his own facade.

Hunter's attention remained glued to me. "How long have you been married?"

I raked my brain for an answer. *Any* answer. But I was coming up blank, with his eyes drilling into mine. It was beginning to feel like an interrogation.

"Three years." The answer just popped out of my mouth. I hoped it was loud enough for Gil to hear so we could keep our story straight.

"Three years..." the words rolled out curiously as his eyes drifted over me. "And no younglings yet?"

Color filled my cheeks at the way he was looking at me, as if I were a choice cut of meat. I kept my eyes trained on his as my hand clutched the knife.

"No. Not exactly a family friendly business."

Hunter leaned closer, his voice so low only I could hear. "Tell me, do you partake of the root yourself?"

I trained my eyes straight ahead, resisting the urge to plunge the knife into his neck. "We don't use what we sell."

His warm breath brushed over my cheek. "Would you like to try it?"

The thickness of his words as he made the bold invitation sent me into a flurry of panic. I couldn't respond. With shaking hands, I just sat there, staring blankly ahead, waiting for him to go away.

He chuckled. "Your silence tells me perhaps you're undecided. It's all right. I don't bite."

His words brought back memories of that set when Gil was on the root. *"It's okay, Ellie. I won't bite. Unless you want me to."*

Instantly, I blazed. When Gil spoke to me like that, I glowed with desire. Now it was with fury. A red aura of light lifted from my skin, though I was not in physical contact with anyone. Warmth spread through my shaking limbs. A curious rush began creeping in, and at any moment, I would explode. I could feel it.

Hunter's brow furrowed as backed away.

"What the hell—"

"Darling!" Gil leaped to his feet and was behind me in an instant. The moment his hands contacted my shoulders, the light flashed to a soft, white glow. I took a sharp breath as the feeling dissipated. "You look tired. Perhaps it's time we get some sleep."

I felt Hunter's burning stare on my cheek. The atmosphere was tense, like a tightly wound wire. It was unclear if he was about to murder me then and there or take me for further interrogation first. Gil's grip on my shoulders was firm and possessive. At that rate, I wasn't entirely sure I was the one who needed protection.

At last, Hunter snapped his fingers, and a stout blue man was quickly at his side. "Get them a pair of rooms."

Finally, I dared to look at him and found his eyes hardened with suspicion. And fear. Just a tiny tinge of terror. I cracked a satisfied smile and carefully slipped the knife up my sleeve before standing and taking Gil's arm.

"Thank you. I am feeling a bit tired."

Hunter rose and nodded to us before stalking away. I watched him meander through the crowds and disappear through a back door, but not before he paused and said something to one of his henchmen, glancing back at me across the room. I tightened my hold on Gil's tense arm.

"I don't like this, *darling!*" I whispered tersely in his ear.

Gil tenderly ran his knuckles down the side of my cheek and smiled before putting his lips next to my ear. "Just play your part and we'll be out of here first rise."

Play the part. It sounded so cold. Detached. Now I was frustrated. I was exhausted, and scared, and angry. The last thing I felt like doing was putting on an act. And yet that's how Gil was treating me—as an *act.* Luckily for him, I didn't need to act much.

Giggling flirtatiously, I unlooped my arm from his, grabbed the front of his shirt, and yanked him close before planting a long, seductive kiss on his lips. When I pulled back, he looked at me, surprised. I grinned and winked before tapping him on the nose.

The blue man cleared his throat nearby. "If you're ready, I'll take you to your rooms now."

Smiling, I side-stepped Gil and reached for Lydia's hand. "Come on, Dahlia. Time for bed." She accepted my hand, fair cheeks blushing crimson as her eyes darted between me and Gil.

Everyone's eyes were on me. The room had gone quiet.

I was still glowing.

Chapter 18

We followed the man out of the tavern hall and up two flights of stairs to a long hallway littered with doors. My heart was still pounding, though the glow had vanished the moment I realized everyone was staring at us. Glowing was normal for a Celestial, but my glows as of late had been particularly... unusual.

At the end of the hall, we came to a stop. The man handed Gil two silver keys. "These rooms adjoin, but I highly recommend you keep the outer doors locked. This town isn't used to strangers." He glanced beyond us down the hall as he gave his dark warning. Gil thanked him and he went on his way.

The two rooms were next to each other, both small and nondescript. A bed, a table with two chairs, a dresser, and a small bathroom... they were simple. But the prospect of finally having a bed to sleep on was heaven, even if I had to share it with Lydia.

She wasted no time in crawling under the covers and falling fast asleep. As tired as I was, I knew I couldn't sleep until I'd had a bath. I felt absolutely *filthy*. And beyond stressed.

So I shut myself in the bathroom, peeled off my clothes, and started the steaming water. The moment I slipped below the warm surface, I felt my tension melt away.

It was a while that I lay there, just soaking. Thinking. There was nothing more that I wanted than to be back home in my own bathtub. With Panne down in his study, arguing with Advisor Braxton.

I missed Panne so much it physically hurt. And Teli, and Agatha. It killed me inside that Agatha and I had parted on bad terms. I couldn't blame her for loving Gil. Especially not with the part I'd played in throwing them together. None of it mattered now. Agatha was gone, and it was because of me. They were all gone because of me.

My tears mingled with the bathwater. I had to crush my hand over my mouth to stifle my sobs. They came on fiercely. As did the violet glow.

It grew until it illuminated the entire room. As shocked as I was, it did nothing but frustrate me.

"Just stop… just stop!" I pleaded with no one in particular.

Still, it lingered. I knew I had to calm down. Whatever was happening was tied to my emotional state. Taking deep breaths, I closed my eyes and tried to think of happy times. Times when things were all as they should be.

I went back to when I was a youngling and Manne had me curled up to her side, listening to her stories. When Panne would take me shopping and spoil me with sweets. And when Gil and I would play in the fields and come home covered in mud…

Slowly, I relaxed again as the fond memories flowed. When I opened my eyes, the glow was extremely faint. My hand hovered over my heart, and I took another deep breath. Finally, the glow disappeared completely.

I couldn't explain what was happening—why my body was reacting this way. It scared me. But it served as confirmation that there was indeed something strange about me. Whether or not I was this mythical "soul paver", I had to find answers. And soon.

After finishing my bath, I reluctantly put my dirty clothes back on and finger-combed through my long hair before braiding it. I still looked like hell from lack of sleeping and eating, but at least I smelled better.

Lydia was still out cold when I came out of the bathroom. I paused, staring at the adjoining door. Gil would welcome me into his bed without question. We'd shared a bed many times growing up. But it was getting harder and harder to do so and pretend it didn't mean more. Stars above, I wanted so much more! But we were walking a tightrope between friends and lovers in a time when the world was completely upended. It was hard to decipher his actual feelings for me, and I didn't want to get it wrong. My heart couldn't take getting it wrong.

So I climbed into bed next to Lydia and fell fast asleep.

* * *

It was dark—darker than dark. Suddenly, a light sprang to life. A single flame, bridging the gloom.

I recoiled at the sight of it, backing up quickly until I hit something. Jumping, I whirled around and found myself face-to-face with a pale man with bright green eyes. Instantly, I recognized them as they bore into me.

Taking several steps back, I was mindful to avoid getting too close to the candle. I had no weapon on me, and no clue where we were. We were alone.

"Hello, Ellie."

Nervous, I hugged my arms and kept my eyes trained on the king. "What do you want?" I spat.

Kromer smiled, his features relaxed as he stood with his hands casually in his pockets. He was somewhat disarming in a white, loose-fitting shirt and blue slacks. Quite different from the formal black attire he'd worn when I first saw him. I didn't trust this change.

"I was about to ask you the same thing. You're in my dream, after all."

I frowned. "No, you're in mine!"

He nodded toward the candle. "So, you have a habit of dreaming about that, do you?"

Narrowing my eyes, I watched him stroll around the light's perimeter. He eyed me with amusement, only infuriating me further. I began to calculate how easy it would be to snap his neck.

"No, I don't."

"But you *have* dreamed of it, haven't you?" I didn't respond. "I can see it in your eyes. I had that same look at first, too. Like a frightened little fawn."

"What makes you think I'm frightened?" I was trying to sound menacing, but my voice cracked.

He paused and stared. I averted my gaze to the ground. It was like he was reading me.

"You know, you're not what I expected," he remarked calmly.

"I don't know what you mean."

"When I came to your world, I was expecting to find some old hag bent over a cauldron. Not… you."

"You're destroying my world. Killing my people. You killed my panne!" I screamed at him. "I don't give a single damn what you think of me!"

I launched at Kromer with a screech, hands outstretched. The moment I came into contact with him, a blinding light erupted that sent me sprawling back to the ground. When I looked up, he still stood there, hands in his pockets. I scrambled to my feet and took several steps back, trying to catch my breath.

"H-how? You're, you're not a—"

"Celestial? No, I'm not." He strolled closer to me, and I clenched my fists, ready to strike. This only made him laugh. "Save your energy, dear. You can't hurt me here."

"Oh, you'd better believe I'll be hurting you the moment I can!" I spat on him. It hit a shield of light and slid to the ground.

Frustrated, I cursed and slammed my fist on my thigh. I was shocked to feel pain. "I thought you said—"

"I said *you* couldn't hurt *me*. Might want to cool your heels a bit though."

"Don't tell me what to do!"

Kromer laughed. "You are a spitfire, I'll give you that."

My anger was bubbling over, but I had no outlet, which frustrated me even more. Marching across the circle of light toward the dark void, I muttered curses and envisioned how I would gut him with the steak knife the moment I saw him in—

Suddenly I hit a wall, smashing my face. My hand flew to my nose as blood instantly flowed. Tears leaped to my eyes as I cried out in pain.

Instantly, Kromer was at my side. He grabbed my free hand, which sent a burst of light erupting from the point of contact. I tried to wrench it away, but he firmly held on as he tugged me toward the candle.

"It's all right," he said calmly. "I'm not going to hurt you, remember?"

My head swam, and I was too dazed to fight him. If this was a dream, then he was correct. I still had every intention of killing him, however.

Reluctantly, I allowed him to pull me along until we were standing in front of the cursed candle. Its light blazed steadily, holding back the evils of the universe. I could feel the thrum of power rising in my chest. My stomach roiled... but it drew me in.

Kromer was at my back, his hand over mine as he stretched it toward the light. I was becoming entranced.

"Just touch the wax, right below the flame," he instructed quietly in my ear.

My volition was impaired. I did as instructed, under his glowing, guiding hand. The moment my finger touched the warm wax, a wave of heat rushed through me. Startled, I snatched my hand away. Kromer held my shoulders firmly.

"Easy now, just give it a moment."

Slowly, the heat worked its way through before dissipating. The pain went with it. Gasping, my hand flew to my nose and found all the blood had disappeared.

Whirling around, I found Kromer smiling proudly. He side-stepped me and circled the candle. "You're welcome."

"I don't understand. What just happened?"

"You just harnessed the candle's power for the first time. Only remotely, of course. We're not really here."

A chill washed over me as my eyes danced back and forth between him and the candle. "You're lying. This is just a dream! I wasn't even really hurt!"

He stopped as his eyes snapped to mine. "You know this is no ordinary dream, Ellie. In dreams, you could've done whatever you wanted to me by now. I would be dead and mangled on the floor. Is that right?"

I stared him down with menace and counter-circled the candle. "No. Not dead."

His brows raised. "Really now? Enlighten me."

"All right, then. First, I'd cut your throat. But not deep enough to bleed you out entirely."

"Interesting," he mused, "go on."

"Next, I would slowly crush your leg in a vise. I'd listen to the sounds of your garbled screams as your bones creak before they finally snap and crunch."

Kromer cocked an eyebrow. "Just one leg?"

"Oh, the other will be ripped off soon enough."

He nodded. "Got it. So, my throat is cut and I'm legless. What comes next?"

My eyes drag him up and down, thinking of ways to torture him, to exact my revenge. "Your fingers. I'd snap them off, one by one. Feed them to the wildions."

"Or perhaps… a pantheour?"

I froze, my heart speeding up. Did he know? *How* could he know?

Kromer took advantage of my panicking and backtracked until he was standing before me, hands still casually in his pockets.

"Tell me, dear, have you noticed anything strange about your auras as of late? Any changing kinship with the natural world around you, hmm?"

My throat felt thick. I couldn't respond through the anxiety that was suddenly surging. I had to get out of there.

Wake up, wake up, wake up!

"You know what you are, Ellie." His voice was gentle, free from malice. He stepped even closer until we were nearly toe-to-toe. I found I couldn't move, so I stood there, shaking. His fingertips gently lifted my chin until our eyes met. "I can help you. We can help *each other*. I'm the only one that understands."

A wave of energy surged through me the moment he touched me. I gasped and took several steps back. "Don't touch me!"

Kromer smiled tightly and averted his gaze. "As you wish."

I scowled. "Oh, so now you're mocking me, too?"

He sighed in frustration. "You know, you're *really* trying my patience."

"I don't give a damn about your patience!"

His hardened eyes slithered back to mine as he quickly crossed the room and backed me into the wall. "I *will* find you. And when I do, you'll be ready for me. You will *beg* me to take you away."

I opened my mouth to argue when suddenly he clapped his hands right in front of my face.

With a gasp, I opened my eyes and bolted up in bed.

Chapter 19

It took me a while, sitting there, eyes frantically darting around in the dark, to be reassured that he was not there. Lydia stirred next to me in the bed.

"Are you all right?" she asked groggily.

"Yes, I'm fine. Um, just go back to sleep."

It took only half a moment before she was out again. Taking deep breaths, I buried my face in my shaking hands. There was no way I could sleep like this. Not with his face still blazing in my mind's eye and the clap still ringing in my ears.

Slipping from the bed, I took a deep breath and crossed the room to the adjoining door. Just as I was raising my knuckles to knock, there was a soft knock at the other door. I paused, staring across the room. Whoever was there was waiting patiently.

My heart flipped. Gil. We hadn't had any time alone for a while. No time to discuss our next move. As tired as I was, and as tired as he was, I couldn't blame him for choosing such an awful hour of the set to do it.

I tucked a stray lock of hair behind my ear and tip-toed to the other door, mindful of Lydia. The moment I cracked the door open, I was confused. There was no one there. Odd. I was sure there was a knock.

Slowly, I opened the door wider and stepped out, peering down the empty hallway. Gil's door was still closed.

Click.

The door closed behind me. I turned to grasp the knob, only to come face-to-face with Hunter. His hand was over my mouth before I could scream.

"Shhh! Don't be frightened. I only want to talk with you." His voice was calm. Slowly, he lowered his hand.

I narrowed my eyes. "We have nothing to talk about!" I hissed. "Especially not mid-set!"

"If it would make you feel better…" he pulled a silver dagger from his boot. I flinched, but then he turned it over and offered the handle to me.

My eyes darted from the dagger to his unreadable face. I was afraid. Those dark eyes could be hiding a million intentions. Especially with the way he had behaved earlier.

"What do you need to talk to me about?"

"Not here. Too many ears. Believe me when I say you'll want to hear it, though."

I stared at him, waiting for a wink or flirty grin. But he was steadfast. With a frustrated sigh, I took the knife. He reached for my arm, but I immediately pointed the dagger at his throat with a venomous expression.

"Do not touch me."

Raising his palms, Hunter shrugged and backed away before side-stepping me. Keeping the dagger firmly in my palm, I lowered it and followed him at a respectable distance, casting a long look back at the pair of doors. The door to my and Lydia's room was now unlocked, and I whispered a silent prayer that she would be safe until I got back.

We went down the stairs and through a series of turns until we arrived at a dark, polished wood door at a dead end. Hunter paused, staring back down the hall for a few moments with his finger to his lips before opening the door and admitting us.

A fire crackled in a fireplace in the small study. A red desk sat to the left, with a red couch to the right in front of the balcony doors. Books and rolled documents filled a shelf behind the desk, a juxtaposition to the wall of weapons to the right.

The door clicked shut behind me, and the room suddenly felt small. Hunter brushed past me to the desk and began pouring a pair of drinks from a dark decanter.

"Have a seat."

I eyed the couch warily. "I'd rather stand, thank you."

He rolled his eyes and smiled tightly as he came over and offered me a goblet. "Have it your way, although I really think you should sit down for this."

Reluctantly, I accepted the silver goblet. "What is this?"

"Wine." He tipped back a generous gulp and watched me, waiting.

It smelled like ordinary red wine. Fruity. Gingerly, I took a small sip. Tasted like it as well.

Satisfied that I had accepted his offering, Hunter took his goblet and sat in the chair on the other side of the desk. It felt like I was in one of Panne's meetings. But I was glad he was not on the couch or near me anymore.

"So," I began, still gripping the knife, "what do you want to talk to me about?"

Dark eyes pierced me from across the room. "I want you to know, first, that at this moment, you are safe. As are your companions. My people are under strict instructions not to touch you."

These words did not sit well with me. I was silent and waited patiently for him to continue, trying to calculate in my mind how long it would take me to run back to my room. It was a bit of a confusing path back, but as long as I hit the main hallways, it shouldn't be too difficult.

"Are you all right, Ellette?"

"Yes, I'm…"

My blood ran cold when it finally registered what he'd called me. What I'd responded to. My back hit the door, knife upraised as my heart pounded. "Who… how did…"

Steepling his fingers below his chin, Hunter made no move to get up. "We intercepted some interesting communication this rise. Apparently, there's a bounty out for a certain Ellette Humett, to be captured alive. And a Gillion Braxton, dead. Curiously enough, fitting your description exactly."

Now, I was shaking. But I could not move. My feet remained rooted to the spot, staring at him. The stones in my stomach piled up.

We'd been discovered.

"Are you sure you don't want to sit down? You look pale." He made a small move, about to get up, but I only flinched and raised the knife higher.

"Don't come any closer!"

He immediately settled again. "I can see that you're afraid. But you needn't be."

"Why should I trust anything you say?"

"I gave you the knife, didn't I? Although, I guess you could've just gone back into your room and got that dinner knife you stole earlier."

My face blazed. "Well, when are you collecting your bounty? Now, or will you at least be generous and wait until rise?"

To my surprise, Hunter started laughing. I was unamused. He shook his head and took another gulp of his wine, wiping his mouth with his sleeve.

"We don't do business with the king—*any* king. No amount of money would make us give up our location to the authorities. And we aren't hurting for it either. And, hell! Half of us have bounties on our own heads!"

I narrowed my eyes. "So then, why bring me here to tell me?"

His laughter died down. "Because, from one outlaw to another, I thought you should know. And also, because I'm curious."

The stones in my stomach eased a bit, and I finally allowed myself to take a drink of the wine, desperate for the fortification. "Curious about what?"

"Why the bounty is so damn high?"

My voice shook. "H-how high?"

There was a long pause. "Ten million crysts."

The goblet slipped from my fingers and clattered on the floorboards. "*What?*"

Hunter quickly rushed to my side and caught me by the elbow, walking me toward the couch. "Okay, this is why I wanted you to sit."

I plopped down on the couch and dropped the knife to the floor before burying my face in my hands. "This can't be happening..."

A hand laid on my shoulder, and I didn't have the wherewithal to shove it off. The cool metal rim of a goblet brushed my fingertips. I lowered my hands and immediately snatched it up, gulping down the whole thing.

Never one to drink, I knew it probably wouldn't settle well later, but I didn't care.

"How long have you been running?"

"Several rises. It feels like forever now."

"You know they'll never stop?"

I brushed my finger around the edge of the goblet. There was truth to his words, but not truth I wanted to hear. Squaring my jaw, I stuffed the emotion back down.

"Then we'll never stop."

"*Or...*" He rose, gently relieving me of the goblet. "...you could just stay here."

My eyes were on his back as he refilled my drink. "To the top, please."

Hunter laughed and obliged, returning it carefully. "You're going to have one hell of a headache in the morning if you don't slow down."

Rolling my eyes, I took a generous gulp. "What else is new?"

Taking a seat next to me, he stared at my cheek as I watched the flames dance in the hearth. It made me uncomfortable. Everything made me uncomfortable.

"I'm serious, though. You could stay here. This is probably the best place you'll ever find if you don't want to be found."

I scoffed in a half-hearted attempt to be cynical. "You don't even know us."

He grew quiet. "That could change."

Agitation was thinning my patience. "Look, if you're trying to flirt with me, you might as well save your breath."

"Ah, so you *are* married!"

"I didn't say that—"

"Then you're in an attachment with him?"

Now it was my turn to grow quiet. I wanted to say yes, but I honestly could not confirm. Despite our moments, Gil had yet to formally, or even *in*formally, declare anything to me. For all I knew, I could just be another Agatha, there as a distraction when it served a purpose.

"I... didn't say that either."

I caught his smile from the corner of my eye. "Good. Then there's nothing to prevent you from getting to know me."

My cheeks flushed crimson, a mingling of the wine and flattery. "Look, I don't mean to be rude here, but I'm really not in a good place to, um, get to know anyone. Like that."

Hunter rose and strolled over to the desk. His eyes were on me as he casually leaned back against the desk, hands in his pockets.

"I can see that I made an extremely poor first impression earlier. I want to apologize for that. Sometimes I get a bit carried away with myself."

Studying him from across the room, I gauged his sincerity. He sounded sincere enough, but the way he was looking at me told me there was a certain amount of urgency. Perhaps desire.

My head suddenly swam. I haphazardly set my wine on the side table and steadied myself. The room felt warmer.

"I'm sorry. I think I need to go back to bed. Too much wine…" Then it hit me. My eyes widened as I looked from the goblet and slowly back to Hunter. "Did you…"

"Did I… what?"

In an instant, the dagger was back in my hand, pointed his direction. "Did you give me bells?" My words came out thick.

His brows furrowed. "Bells? No! I would never do that without your… " Suddenly, he froze, and then slowly turned around and picked up the decanter. After briefly waving it under his nose, he slammed it back down onto the desk with wide eyes. "Oh, holy hellfire!"

He took three large steps before he was at my side, terrified. "I'm so sorry, I grabbed the wrong bottle!"

I swung the knife at him, but it ended up clattering to the ground as my grip relaxed. Everything was feeling relaxed and wound up at the same time. My vision was dancing between clarity and doubles.

"But you drank the same wine?"

In one swift movement, Hunter swept me up in his arms, heading for the door.

"I'm just about immune to the stuff. It's strongest when you first have it."

"What are you doing? Where are we going?" His arms were surprisingly warm and strong.

"I'm taking you back now. You need to be with someone you can trust when you're coming down from it."

We were rushing down the hallway, my arms looped around his neck. He smelled nice. "And I suppose I can't trust you?"

"We'll talk about it in the morning when you kill me."

I laughed loudly, and he shushed me, eyes darting around. It seemed like only seconds before we were back at our rooms. To my surprise, he knocked on Gil's door.

"Oh, wrong room!" I whispered loudly, slurring my words.

Hunter ignored me and shifted me in his arms before knocking again. When a sleepy, shirtless Gil opened the door, my heart started pounding. I grinned.

Gil's eyes flitted between us and hardened instantly. "What's going? What are you doing with my wife?"

Hunter rolled his eyes and practically shoved me into his arms. I yelped with a laugh and threw my arms around Gil's neck. "Gil!"

"Save your breath, Braxton. I know who you are. Now, listen: she's had bells, it was an accident, I—"

"She what?" Gil turned and flung me on the bed before charging out into the hallway and slamming Hunter up against the wall with his forearm against his throat. "What the hell did you do to her?"

Hunter gagged and pulled at Gil's shackle-like arm. "I didn't touch her! I swear!"

I was getting frustrated. One minute I was in Gil's arms, and the next I was cold and lonely on the bed. And all their fighting was giving me a headache. And why was it so hot in there?

Finally, Gil released him, only to rear back and punch him in the nose. Hunter slid to the floor, cradling it and groaning in pain. Gil glowered over him. "Never touch her again!"

With that, Gil stormed back into the room and slammed the door. I sat on the bed, wide-eyed, staring in admiration. I'd never seen him defend my honor that way before. But he looked less than pleased.

Catching his breath, Gil glared at me. Even when he was angry, his eyes were still striking. My heart flipped.

"What happened, Ellie?"

I shrugged. "He wanted to talk. We talked. I had wine." I slowly drew circles on the blanket with my fingertips as my heavy-lidded eyes met his. "Wrong wine."

Cursing, Gil ran his hand down the side of his face and came to sit on the edge of the bed. The moment he did, I crawled over and kneeled behind him. He seemed way too tense. After rubbing warmth into my hands, I began massaging his shoulders.

"Ellie, what are you doing?" he asked dryly.

I smiled and leaned around to kiss his cheek. "Trying to get you to relax."

His hand reached up and caught mine. "Please stop."

Disappointment crept in. "Okay." I pulled away, but his hand kept hold of mine as he turned around to face me. Stars, he was gorgeous...

I couldn't help it. He was so close. My lips crashed into his as my free hand wrapped around the back of his head. He still tasted like heaven. It brought back memories of his own time on the root.

"I dream about us too, Gil," I confessed in a fevered whisper when I finally broke the kiss.

Gil's lips hovered over mine, his warm breath rushing over. I knew he wanted me too. I could see it in his eyes. His lips found mine again a moment later. A thrilling spark swept through me. This was it. Our moment had come.

My hands flew to the buttons on my shirt and swiftly unfastened them. I longed to feel his touch, so I lifted his hand and put it to my left breast, only the thin fabric of my brassiere separating us.

I moaned behind our kiss. The moment I did, Gil snatched his hand back and broke away. "No, no!" He scrambled off the bed and paced the room, hands running through his hair as his chest rose and fell deeply.

Pouting, I tried to follow him but ended up stumbling back onto the bed. "What's wrong? Don't you want me?"

"Ellie, we can't do this. You're not in your right mind right now."

I opened my mouth to argue, but Gil shot me a stern look and I snapped it shut. He stopped his pacing at the foot of the bed and turned to me.

"Look, I'm responsible for you right now. And I'm not about to violate that trust. You might not even remember anything I'm saying in the morning, but I hope you know I would never do anything to hurt you or what we have."

I stared at him. "And just what do we have, Gil?"

He stared back. I waited for a reply that never came. A wave of dizziness came over me and everything faded to black.

Chapter 20

My head throbbed something awful. A ceiling faded into view as my eyes fluttered open. Starlight shone through the window. I lay on a bed, alone. As I shifted, soft sheets rubbed against my bare skin.

I was naked.

With a gasp, I bolted upright, clutching the blankets to my chest. This wasn't my room. Eyes darting around, they finally rested on Gil's sleeping form, on the floor under the window. He was fully clothed, facing the wall.

Panic set in. How did I end up in this state? The previous set was a dizzying blur. I remembered Hunter... and Gil's lips...

My hand flew to my mouth. *Bells.* I peeked at myself underneath the sheets to confirm that I was completely without a stitch of clothing. My cheeks burned. I had to find my clothes.

Wrapping the top blanket around me, I quietly slipped from the bed and went on the hunt. My clothing was scattered to the four corners of the room. I was just bending over to pick up my shirt when I heard Gil yawn. I looked over just in time to see him sit up and look at me. His eyebrows raised, and he quickly stood, averting his eyes.

"Oh, um, you're up."

Anger flooded in. I pursed my lips. "Damn right, I'm up!" Shuffling quickly around the room, I snatched up my clothes. I smacked him upside the head with my pants as I passed by.

"Whoa, Ellie, calm down! We need to talk about this."

"We don't need to talk about *anything* until I'm no longer *stark naked*, Gil!"

I stormed into the bathroom and slammed the door. Furiously, I threw my things on the counter and dropped the blanket. When I caught my reflection in the mirror with my insanely messy hair, I grew even angrier. Further evidence of what had occurred last set.

Muttering curses to myself, I shoved my clothing on as Gil pleaded with me from the other side of the door.

"Ellie, come on! It's not what it looks like, I promise!"

"I'm not stupid, Gil! Quit treating me like it!"

"I never said you were stupid. I just want to clarify that—"

"That what? It was good? Or was it bad, since I was drugged out of my mind? Huh? Which is it, Gil?"

"It was neither! There was no 'it'!"

I narrowed my eyes at the door. "Don't you dare lie to me, Gil! I know how you got when you were on the root, the way you wanted me, and how…" My accusation trailed off. The way he wanted me, *but I resisted.*

"Ellie, you were a wildion last set. You threw yourself at me. But I swear to you, we didn't do anything. I mean, we kissed, but that's it. And I'm sorry about that." I heard his forehead bump the door. "Please. You've got to believe me, El…"

He sounded downright despondent. I sighed and rubbed my aching temples. It stood to reason that he was probably right. After all, I didn't…*feel* different. Everything was such a blur. But if there was one thing I knew, it's that I would trust Gil with my life.

Upon opening the door, I met his watery eyes. My heart instantly melted, and the anger fled. I slipped my arms around his neck.

"You really didn't—"

"I would never." His arms wrapped around me.

Stroking his hair, I breathed in his scent and let my eyes slide shut. "I believe you. I'm sorry."

We stood there for some time, just holding each other. I felt… safe. And reconnected with the one constant thing in my life.

"I'm sorry you had to go through that, and I'm sure you feel like hell right now. We're going to get out of here."

He released me at last and began rummaging through the rucksack. I stood in the bathroom doorway, watching him for a moment. He looked exhausted. Dark circles had formed under his eyes. I thought about Hunter's words.

"Gil, let's stay one more rise."

He glanced at me incredulously. "Stay? After what he did to you last night? I don't think so."

"That was an accident! You should've seen his face when he realized what he'd done."

"Oh, sure. I bet it was an 'accident.'"

I frowned. "Yes, actually, it was."

Gil scoffed. "Ellie, the man wanted in your pants the moment he laid eyes on you. I know you don't have much experience with men, but trust me, I know what he was about."

"So? Maybe he wants me? That doesn't mean he tried to drug me on purpose!"

Gil growled in frustration. "You know, why are you defending him? You don't even know him."

"Oh, and you do?"

"I know I don't trust him. That's enough."

The more I watched his aggravation, the more I realized. "You're jealous... aren't you?"

He paused, not looking me in the eye. His tone was cold. "Don't make this into something it's not."

My heart pinched. I was expecting an entirely different response. *Hoping* for a different one.

"So, all these kisses we've shared meant nothing to you?"

Gil groaned and rolled his eyes. "Ellie, come on—"

"No!" I snapped. "I'm tired of you playing around with me, Gil!"

"*Playing?* How have I been playing with you?"

I narrowed my eyes and crossed my arms. "You know how."

Gil's burning gaze snapped to mine as he threw the rucksack to the ground.

"What do you want me to say? Hmm?" He strolled toward me. "You want me to tell you I'm head over heels for you? Or that every time I hold your hand, I die a little inside?" My eyes widened, but he continued his pursuit as his stare pierced mine. "O-or that every time you walk into the room, I feel like the breath is stolen from my lungs?" I backed up into the door frame, and we were soon toe-to-toe, with his arm posted above my head. "Or that last set, it took every ounce of strength I had not to make love to you." I was trapped by his gaze like a fawn in the clutches of a wildion. "Which is it, Ellie?"

The moment I opened my mouth to speak, there was a knock at the adjoining door. Gil bit his lip and flicked his eyes to the ceiling. I shared his frustration. We were on the edge of something, only to be yanked back to reality.

His words still swelled in the back of my mind as I reluctantly traipsed over to the door. I found a very concerned Lydia on the other side.

"Is everything okay? I heard shouting."

Glancing at Gil, who was back to organizing the rucksack, I pasted on a smile. "Yes, everything's fine. Just getting ready to leave."

She didn't look quite convinced, but slowly nodded. "All right, then. Well, do I have time to bathe before we go?"

"Of course," I assured pleasantly. Her eyes were continually wandering over my shoulder to Gil and back again.

"Okay. See you soon."

Once the door shut again, I heard the lock click on the other side. I sat on the bed with a huff. I wasn't sure how much of our conversation she heard, but I was embarrassed. Swinging my braid around the front, I began unraveling it, desperate to keep myself busy and not focused on a now-very-quiet Gil.

The atmosphere felt shifted in a way I couldn't quite describe. Words had been spoken that couldn't be taken back. One thing was clear: we were more than best friends. And it felt suddenly awkward and exhilarating at the same time. Yet, something was hanging in the midst of it all that gave me pause. Something about the expression he wore now that made me wonder if he regretted it.

Carefully, I began untangling my hair with my fingers, wishing I had grabbed a comb in the middle of the chaos before we left Silis. Before we fled all that we knew. Even the thought of our home hurt. I missed it. I missed *them*.

Visions of the buildings collapsing began flooding back in, replaying themselves over and over in my mind. The screams... the explosions... I was wide awake, and yet I heard them as clearly as if it were a suffocating dream.

I yanked at my hair, struggling with a knot as the chaos in my mind grew. Gil... death... love... pain...

It was all too much at once. Tears leaped to my eyes as I struggled with the knot, wishing I had a blade to cut off my hair. Why was this so difficult? Why couldn't things just go back to the way they were?

"Ellie..."

Why did Panne have to die? He was a good man!

"Ellie, what's wrong?"

Gil laid a hand on my shoulder, and I shoved him away. "This knot in my hair! And... just..." A dam broke, and I sobbed so hard I thought I would die. I wanted to die.

Burying my face in my hands, I slid to the floor and wailed. All the pent-up fear and pain came pouring out in a torrent. There was no switch to stop it. Every pore in my body felt like it would explode.

The room faded away as the violet glow returned. I was losing control again. That's when the shaking began.

Rumblings in the ground sent bits of plaster raining down from the ceiling. I hardly noticed them beyond my wavering vision. Gil's voice called in an echo as the destruction exploded around me. Everything shook violently as the walls fell and the floor gave way. I felt myself falling, screaming...

Then I stopped, hitting the hard ground. Pulling myself to my feet, I was immediately greeted with icy air. The shaking had ceased, and I was no longer in rubble, but up high on a dark mountain.

Rushing to the edge of the precipice, I looked down into a valley below to see the desert and Stone City far below. A flood of black dots was rushing in from ships as the town collapsed under explosions.

"Gil!"

I was trapped, too far away to do anything. The man I loved was dying, and I was helpless to save him. The icy wind whipped through my hair as I fell to my knees and clung to the black rock. Again and again, I screamed his name.

Eventually, my voice grew hoarse, and I collapsed, sobbing hysterically. The scene below was horrific, with gunfire and distant screams carried on the breeze. I covered my ears to shut out the sounds of the massacre.

A rush of clouds blotted out the stars above. It was dark as set and raining. Suddenly, a light caught my eye. Peering across the plateau, I saw it glowing steadily in the torrential downpour. The candle stood center upon its dark pillar, waiting patiently for me. Beyond the candle stood the silhouette of a figure... *him.*

In a fury, I pulled myself to standing and charged across the rock. "Make it stop! Now!"

The moment I passed the candle, I hit an invisible wall and flew back to the ground with a cry. My body sang with pain as I shook off the stun. I was back up on my feet within moments.

He peered back at me beyond the barrier. Kromer stood calmly, his hands folded in front of him. Wearing black from head to toe, dressed for the role of the dark authority he held.

"Hello again, Ellie."

His calmness did nothing to quench the rage and desperation I felt. "Stop this! Stop this now, Kromer! You've got me! Let them go!"

He tilted his head. "You think I brought you here?"

"Look, I don't want to play your stupid mind games! If you don't stop the attack, I'll—"

"You'll do *what,* precisely?" His words were like glass shards, and his expression stony. "Bound over here and kill me with your bare hands? Ha! You're out of control, Humett! Can't even keep your light under wraps!"

Ice crept under my skin. "H-how do you—"

"Every time..." He slowly stepped closer to me, eyes drilling into mine. "Every time you lose it, you call out to me. Whether or not you like it, I hear you. I *feel* you." He paused, just beyond the barrier. "It's getting rather exhausting, honestly."

"Then why don't you just kill me?" I half-pleaded. "Stop all of this!"

His mouth twisted in a wry grin. "What if I told you that *you* can stop all of this?"

Turning, I stumbled back to the edge. The city was largely in flames now, with screams still echoing into the dark. I could hardly see through my tears. "How? How do I stop it? I'll do anything!"

"Call to it."

"What?"

"You know what, Ellie."

When I looked back, Kromer was standing next to the candle, gazing into the flame. He wore a strange look of admiration, bordering on obsession. Then his eyes turned to mine, the light reflecting off the intense, inky pools in the center.

A shiver ran down my spine and I took a step back, stumbling at the edge. I felt myself begin to teeter and fall. In half an instant, Kromer was before me, grasping my arm and yanking me back. Crashing into him, we nearly fell back in the other direction. I quickly righted myself and shoved his hand away with a shriek. Mindful of my position, I backed away from him with wild eyes.

After we were once again at odds, I noticed he looked slightly rattled. But he continued to pursue me. I found myself backed into the rock face, fists clenched.

"They're dying, Ellie. Time is running short," he insisted. "You can hear them. I know you can."

My eyes continually darted toward the edge, where the orange glow was barely reaching the line of darkness. Tears were streaking down my face, mingling with the rain. If Gil wasn't dead already, he would be soon. I felt the pull of desperation in my spirit. I felt the pain and the terror increasing like a vise. A red aura was slowly lifting from my skin and growing brighter.

"Tell me what to do." I could barely speak.

Kromer came and took both my hands in his. I was too overwhelmed to resist. The instant he touched me, the light leaped to him and enveloped both of us. A strong thrum of power surged through me, unlike anything I'd ever felt before. I screamed and tried to let go, but he held fast.

"Look at me!" he shouted, squeezing my hands. "Look at me. Just focus."

Fighting the hyperventilation, I forced myself to look at him. His gaze was intense. I wanted to hide. Slowly, he backed us toward the candle, until he nearly bumped into it. He then lifted our arms and repositioned us so that we stood on either side of it, still holding hands.

Eyes still holding mine above the steady flame, he spoke to me, though I felt as if words were not needed. There was a strange connection brewing, and I could *feel* his words.

"Call to it. Tell it what you want."

I want you dead.

His brow flinched as if my thought had filtered straight into his mind. But he simply reiterated his instructions. "Call to it, Ellie."

My eyes slid to the flame. With every fiber of my being, I threw my focus and energy toward it.

Save Gil... Stop this...

The flame flickered as our glow brightened. Power grew, like a tingling wave. I felt its warmth, despite the cold. The exhilaration. It was nearly intoxicating.

"Don't stop."

Save Gil... Stop the destruction...

"Come on, Ellie, you can do better than that!"

"S-save Gil. Stop the destruction," I dared speak aloud.

"You can't be timid about this!"

"Save Gil! Stop the destruction!" The flame flickered and flared.

"Come on—"

"Stop this!" I screamed my words, and suddenly a wall of fire leaped from the candle and came rushing at my face. I had no time to react before everything went white.

Chapter 21

When the world came back into view, I was sitting on the bed again. Not a stone or a beam was out of place. Gil was standing nearby, still re-packing the rucksack.

Leaping to my feet, I ran to him and threw my arms around him. Gil dropped the bag and stumbled, nearly falling to the ground as he caught me in his arms.

"Whoa! Hey! Ellie! What are you doing?"

I hugged him as tightly as I could, as if he'd fade away. And then I felt it: the rumbling. Immediately, I released him and ran to the adjoining door.

"Lydia!"

Gil grabbed me by my arm, but I refused to move.

"Ellie, what's going on?" His eyes were darting around the room as the rumbling continued.

Whirling around, I grabbed him by the shoulders. "They're coming!"

Gil's eyes widened. He flew to the window just as shouts arose from the streets below and the bells began to toll.

"Blazing hell!" He ran to the adjoining door and pushed me aside as he began pounding with all his strength. "Lydia!"

I shoved the rest of the contents into the rucksack and threw it over my back. The adjoining door finally flew open and a very frightened, wet-haired Lydia was given no time to speak before Gil picked her up and threw her over his shoulder.

"Go!" he hollered at me as I ran for the door.

We crashed into the hallway and took off full speed ahead. Down, down, and around, until we were in the tavern, Lydia screaming all along the way. Once we hit open air, it was utter chaos. Explosions were rocking the city as guns and cannons fired from both sides of the wall.

Taking off in the direction of the carriage, we watched as a flood of outlaws rushed and bounded toward the front gates, armed to the teeth. Others were climbing up the towers to their posts, where they fired relentlessly on the encroaching enemy. Judging by the number of explosions and the smoke pouring above, we were not on the winning side.

When we reached our carriage, I cried out in disbelief. It was in flames. Utterly engulfed. Gil cursed.

"What do we do now?" cried a hysterical Lydia.

I scanned our surroundings and noticed a portion of the crowd was heading in the opposite direction of the front gates. It clicked: all cities have an emergency exit. This wasn't a normal city with normal people, but it was a chance we'd have to take.

"Follow me!" I bounded high above the crowd, barely missing people as I landed next to an outbuilding. After ensuring that Gil was following suit, I bounded again, and again, watching the flow of escapees.

Again and again, we leaped through the city, moving steadily toward the rear side of the wall that butted up against the hills. It was not far now. Mostly residential quarters surrounded us.

I reared up and bounded again, intent on clearing the entire street. An explosion jolted the world. I was flying one direction, and then suddenly knocked another.

The ground brutally rose to meet me. Stars burst into my vision as pain immediately seized my entire body. I vaguely heard Gil's voice calling my name over the ringing in my ears.

As I rolled onto my back, I felt a warm stream running from my nose, and tasted the viscous iron on my tongue. There was a weight on my body. It was quickly lifted off before Gil's face appeared in my line of sight, etched with concern.

I reached out to him, and he grasped my hand.

"Come on, try to get up!"

Pushing aside the pain and confusion, I pulled with all my might and got to a sitting position. My head swam and lolled back as I nearly fell again. Someone caught me from behind and I looked up to see Lydia.

"Oh, no you don't!" She grasped me under the shoulders, and with Gil's help, hauled me to my feet.

There was no time. No time to stop. I fought off the pain and started moving my feet in the intended direction. We moved slower, dodging the destruction. I ignored all further offers of help, hellbent on getting them both out of town. Hellbent on getting *me* out of town. I was the cause of this. I would be the salvation.

At last, I saw it— half-torn open, smaller, and more discreet than the front gates. "There!"

We wasted no time in hauling tail to the waiting gate. People were leaping over the rubble to get through it. Following suit, we mounted over fallen rocks and twisted metal, sliding down a large panel to freedom.

Our freedom was short-lived. The pile of bodies at the bottom was still warm.

"There!" Hands wrapped around my arms and yanked me forward, beyond the dead. I was too shocked to fight the armed men in the shielded helmets as they roughly dragged me across the grass.

"Ellie!"

I turned in time to see Gil and Lydia being apprehended by more soldiers with weapons drawn to their heads. A cry erupted from somewhere deep within at the sight. My light burst forth in a blaze of red.

"There's no need for dramatics now." Whipping my head around, I saw Kromer standing at the bottom of the ship's gangway. His smug smile faltered the moment I locked eyes with him. I could only hope I instilled as much fear in him as the rage I felt. He strolled closer but paused when I growled and the light flared.

"Let them go!"

Kromer's eyes flitted to Gil and Lydia, his jaw set harshly. "No. No, I don't think I will."

"You have no reason to hurt them! Just take me and let them go!" My voice broke with my resolve. I tried to turn and look back at Gil, but one soldier grabbed me roughly by the hair and forced me to face my abductor. He looked at me as if I were some pathetic child, begging her way out of a punishment.

"And why should I do that?"

My eyes drilled into his. "If you want my help, you'll let them go. Or should I ask the candle instead?" Immediately, my light flared, and I felt its rising heat. My captors cried out in pain and dropped me to the ground as they clutched their arms. Quickly, I turned and snatched one of their guns. As I rose to my feet, Kromer just smirked.

"You won't shoot me. You know the moment you pull the trigger, they're dead anyway."

I shoved the barrel of the gun under my chin, eliciting a collective cry of shock. Keeping my eyes on Kromer, I slowly backed away. "Tell them to back off! Now!"

Waving his men away from me, Kromer looked exponentially nervous. He hadn't planned for this outcome. I relished in the feeling of power I finally had over him, even though I shook with fear at the thought of what I was doing.

"Ellie let's not be rash about this—"

"Don't tell me what to do!" I screamed back, infuriated. "Tell them to let them go, and call off this attack, or I swear I will blow myself to hellfire!"

We stared each other down. The wheels were turning behind those intense eyes. I could sense the rising frustration. And the panic. I had him backed into a corner with a single gun.

It was an eternity before he finally gave the order. "Release them."

I heard shuffling behind me, followed by rapid footsteps. Glancing over my shoulder, I found Gil rushing toward me. I pivoted and held my hand out.

"Stop!"

Gil came to an immediate halt, wide-eyed in confusion. I kept a firm hand on the gun, eyes continuously dancing between him and Kromer.

"El?"

Though my eyes moistened, I kept my face stony. "Run."

He dared to take a step closer. "I'm not leaving here without you."

"Don't come any closer!"

Gil stopped and stared at me. "Ellie... what are you doing?"

"Run!" He opened his mouth to reply, but I shouted again. "Run! Get out of here! Now!"

The sound of an engine piqued our ears. A large, red carriage cruiser came speeding over the hill and halted abruptly nearby. The door flew open, and to my shock stood Hunter, aiming a large gun straight at Kromer.

"You guys need a ride?"

Lydia immediately ran and hopped in the carriage. Gil lingered, despite my ferocity. He held out his shaking hand.

"You're coming with me right now. Just give me the gun."

"No." I shook my head. "Get in the carriage, Gil."

Determined, he took a step forward, eyes locked on mine. "I won't leave you, Ellie."

"Gil—"

"I said I'm not leaving you!"

"Get in the damn carriage!" I screamed at him, flipping the gun from myself to aim at his head. Taken aback, Gil retreated a few steps. The betrayal in his eyes nearly broke me. I was on the verge of throwing the gun on the ground and running to him. But I kept myself hardened and spit as much venom as I could. I could no longer put him at risk. "Now."

Tears spilled down his cheeks. "You might as well shoot me."

My heart broke. Why wouldn't he just listen? Just as I was about to plead with him, panicked shouting erupted from the soldiers around us. When I turned to see what was happening, Gil quickly snatched the gun from my hands, shoving me to the ground in the process. Instantly, a black wall of fur was standing between us.

Gil stumbled backward, away from the bared teeth and the rumbled growling that marked him as a target. I clambered to my feet with a gasp. "Shade?" Her yellow eyes barely acknowledged me as she stood between Gil and me.

Viciously, she hissed at Gil and stalked toward him. His face paled as he slowly backed away. My heart thrashed in my chest. She looked as if he was genuinely on her menu.

"Shade, easy girl," I coaxed as I gingerly reached out and laid a hand on the back of her neck. Our light rose at the point of contact and she paused. "That's it… he's all right… we're all right…" A gruff escaped her lips, and at last, she nuzzled her head at my hip. Somehow, I'd gotten through.

"Now, since we've all wasted a lot of time," Kromer piped up behind us, "it's time for us to be going now, Ms. Humett."

I turned and scowled. "Go where, exactly?"

The corner of his mouth lifted. "You'll just have to find out, won't you?"

Gil aimed the gun at Kromer. Immediately, dozens of guns snapped into place, aiming at Gil. "She's not going anywhere with you, Kromer."

He sneered at Gil as if he were a piece of dust. "You will address me as 'Your Majesty'. And she's already made it quite clear she has no intention of going with *you*."

"I'd call your men off if I were you!" shouted Hunter, still aiming his gun at Kromer. "I'm probably a much better shot than they are."

Things were not going as planned. I had to think fast. Stepping close to Gil, I pretended to kiss him on the cheek. "Put the gun to my head."

"No! Are you crazy?" he whispered back.

"Trust me."

After a brief hesitation, Gil wrapped his arm around my neck and put the gun to my temple, glaring furiously at those around him. I cried out in disbelief. "What are you doing?"

"Tell your men to back down or I'll shoot!" barked Gil.

Kromer's eyes blazed, but he did as instructed. "You don't know what you're doing, Braxton."

Gil backed us up toward Hunter's carriage. "You take one step toward us, and I will end her!" He shoved the gun barrel harder against my temple, bringing out a genuine wince of pain. Shade growled, but one look from me calmed her down. She continued to follow us.

I let tears roll down my cheek. "Please, Gil, just let me go!"

"Shut up!"

This was getting a little too convincing. I could feel the rock-hard tension in his muscles. Our glow was barely visible. It scared me.

By now, Kromer was absolutely seething. "Let her go. *Now.*"

"And let go of my collateral? Ha!"

"You're bluffing."

We were almost to the carriage now. Gil stopped, glaring daggers at the king. "Bluffing, am I? Would you like to me to demonstrate?" His grip tightened around my neck, causing me to gag. Desperately, I clung to his arm, trying to pull it away. Gil subtly relaxed a bit, but I kept on gasping for air.

Kromer's eyes widened in panic. "Stop! Just… stop! You would harm your own lover?"

At last, we reached our destination. Gil sneered. "Just because I know how to get what I want doesn't mean I won't take care of myself. She means nothing to me."

My heart crumbled at the viciousness with which he spoke those words. Genuine hurt flashed across my face. Kromer must've picked up on it because I sensed a surge in his anger.

"You won't get away with this, Braxton. I will hunt you down and skin you alive!"

"Yeah, well, that makes two of us."

Suddenly, Gil flung me into the carriage and rushed in after. Shade leaped in behind us, momentarily rocking the entire rig. Hunter cursed and slammed the door before squeezing his way around the crush of new passengers and hopping into the driver's seat. Gunfire was already hitting the outer armor.

"Hold on to your asses!" he called before swinging us around and slamming us into gear. We shot forward like lightning.

I picked myself up off the floor and found a wall of Shade between me and the others. The carriage was large, but she still took up a generous portion. And she was in full protective mode.

Gil hopped into the passenger seat next to Hunter and began searching through visuals surrounding us. Stone City was quickly disappearing, as were the black ships.

"I don't understand," he said, eyebrows twisting, "they're not following us."

Hunter was grim as he kept us going full speed. "They'll find us. Don't make any mistake about that. This vehicle is signal-jammed, so it's not going to be easy, but if they found Stone City, they can find anything."

"What are we going to do?" asked Lydia, barely visible over Shade.

"Run like hell and then get off this godsforsaken planet."

Gil pivoted in his seat with wide eyes. "I'm sorry, do *what?*"

"There's nowhere to hide here," continued Hunter. "It's not common knowledge, but I know of a place with ships that can fly to other worlds. Just like they can."

"W-what kinds of worlds?" I asked, pushing my way to the front. Shade relented and laid down.

Hunter sighed. "I'm not sure. I've never left this one. But I know where we have to go."

"Where?"

"Basillian."

Chapter 22

Gil and I looked at each other in shock. *Basillian*. It looked like we'd be ending up at our destination after all.

"Now," Hunter glanced at me darkly, "I'd *really* like to know why they're after you, and why the hell there is a pantheour in my carriage?"

With a long sigh, I launched into the long, complicated tale behind our endeavors. Manne... soul pavers... Silis... the candle... and me. Hunter listened without judgment but cursed under his breath when it was all said and done. Overwhelming guilt lanced me. "I'm so sorry we got you involved. I understand if you don't want to take me any further. It's probably best if you leave, like you said."

"Whoa! Hey, I'm not just going to drop a lady off in the middle of nowhere. Just calm down."

Gil laid a hand on my arm. "Ellie, let's just—"

I shoved him off and stepped away. "Don't." The phantom feeling of his arm around my neck still lingered, as did the pain of his words. I felt his stare burning into me now as I pretended to focus on the screen.

He was persistent. "What's wrong?"

"Nothing. I'm fine."

Hunter whistled. I narrowed my eyes at him. He shrugged.

Gil started to say something else, but I walked away, carefully stepping around Shade and making my way for the narrow door at the back of the carriage. When I opened it, I was thankful to find a small utility room to sulk in. It was only a moment later, however, that the door opened and Gil slipped inside. It wasn't a large space, but I pressed my shoulder against the opposite wall and stared at the floor with pursed lips.

"Ellie, please talk to me," he whispered. Thankfully, he kept his hands to himself.

Taking a deep breath, I debated on filling him in on my feelings. *I* barely understood how I was feeling at the moment. It was hard to put a pin on it. We'd been so close to death at each other's hands.

"I'm... I don't know."

There was a long silence. I half-expected Gil to turn and walk out of the room. Instead, he waited it out with me.

"I hurt you, didn't I?" he said at last.

Sighing, I hugged my arms. "Yes."

"I'm sorry. What happened back there won't happen again. And what I said..." his words trailed off into the heavy atmosphere.

I bit the inside of my cheek and nodded. "Okay."

"I know you're not."

Glancing over, I met his eyes. They were full of regret. Pain. I'd hurt him as much as he hurt me.

"Neither are you."

Gil swallowed hard. "I'll be all right. But we have to stick together, Ellie."

"Even if it means your senseless death?" I blurted out.

"Oh, come on, El!" he groaned. "Have you not figured it out yet? I'm not leaving you! So don't you go leaving me either!"

The possessiveness with which he spoke those words was both flattering and annoying. I turned to him with crossed arms. "Well, I still get to make decisions about my own life, you know?"

Gil peered at me under weighted brows. "So you *want* to leave, then? Go our separate ways?"

"And what if I did?"

He scoffed. "What are you saying?"

I leaned back against the wall and averted my gaze. "I'm saying it's probably best I do this alone."

Silence filled the room like a wet blanket. I felt his heart drop in sync with my own. But I couldn't take the words back. I *shouldn't* take them back.

"Why?"

I flinched at how much pain was in that question. "This is all *my* fault, Gil," I replied quietly. "All this death… is on my hands."

He ran his hand down the side of his face. "Stars alive, Ellie! Is that what you think?"

My eyes snapped to his. "That's what I *know!*"

"Ellie, none of this is your fault. *None.* The king is a madman—"

"A very *powerful* madman! Gil, do you not realize what's at stake here?"

"I know exactly what's at stake. Which is why we should stay together."

"Stick together so I can watch you die? I don't think so."

"Stick together so we can be *successful!*"

"Really? And just how are you going to help with that? Are you going to become best friends with Kromer and convince him not to kill you on sight?"

Gil growled. "You are seriously frustrating me right now, Ellette!"

"Oh, *Ellette* now, is it? And if I'm frustrating you so much, then why do you want to stick around, anyway?"

"Because I love you!"

My eyes widened. Rendered speechless at last, I just blinked at him. Choked with emotion, Gil stared me down. He was shaking. We both were. At last, I opened my mouth to speak, but found I had no words to say. Not when he was gazing at me so intensely. The space was getting smaller.

"*You* are worth every risk," he continued.

When his hand reached up to touch my cheek, my breath hitched in my throat. The blazing blue of his eyes arrested me as they peered deeply into mine. Escape was no longer plausible.

"I love you, Ellie."

His quiet words fell on me like drops of rain in a scorching desert, cooling any animosity. My heart wanted to tumble right out of my chest. A lump rose in my throat. "I—"

A sudden sharp jolt that cut my words off sent us barreling into the shelves on the wall. Boxes and supplies came raining down on our heads. As quickly as it started, it was over. I could hear Shade whimpering and Hunter cursing loudly from the next room.

Groaning, I pushed my way out of the pile and found my footing. Shuffling around the mess of supplies, I helped Gil free himself from under the partially collapsed shelf. He stood, leaning on me for support as he hissed and clutched his shoulder.

"Are you okay?" he asked.

"Yes, are you?"

"I'm all right. I think we've stopped."

Gil was already kicking things out of the way and opening the door. I swallowed my silent frustration and tried to focus on the new situation at hand. *Why did he have to make such a confession at the most inconvenient time?* I wanted to slam that door shut and launch into his arms, come what may.

The outer door was already open and Hunter had moved his foul-mouthed diatribe outside. Shade was waiting patiently for me, her eyes large with concern as they darted between me and the door. She nudged my hip as I reached out to ruffle her ear.

Gil gently sidestepped us. I noticed the subtle way in which his hands lingered on my waist as he did. A wave of warmth flashed through me.

"What happened?"

"I think we hit something," said Lydia, poking her head out the door.

Soon we were all outside, with the carriage propped up on jacks. Something was smoking and blood was sprayed across the front. Hunter and Lydia lay underneath the vehicle, while Gil handed them tools.

"Capacitor wrench!" called Lydia.

Gil dug through the box and produced said wrench. "When did you learn how to fix carriages?"

She shot him a sharp look. "When did you learn to underestimate women? I haven't always been a damsel in distress, you know."

I bit back a snort. Gil's cheeks reddened as he passed the tool. It was thoroughly enjoyable watching the both of them getting showed up by her. She was working fast, her concentration like iron as her nimble fingers could reach spots Hunter deemed impossible. I knew little about repairs on carriages, so I simply watched in admiration as I hosed off the woolly cow remnants. It was not a pleasant task by a long shot, but I stopped now and then and let Shade drink from the hose.

The rise was cool and the stars bright. There was no sign of anyone following us, so for now, we were out of immediate danger. Still, my eyes continually tracked over the horizon. We were in the rolling hills now, with turquoise shrubs and sparse, white trees. It was so different from home. My heart ached for the broad field, the towering rocks, and even the fire forest.

The herd we'd hit was wild. I could tell by Shade's flaring nostrils she regretted the fact that we'd scared off the rest of them. Tame or not, I knew she needed to eat. And come set, the urge would be even stronger.

At last, Hunter and Lydia finished with their tinkering. They were covered in dirt and oil smudges, but entirely confident. When the blocks retracted, Gil fired up the engine and the carriage sprang to life… for a moment. It made an awful clunking sound before plopping back to the ground. Hunter cursed and kicked the wall, and then cursed again because he hurt his foot. Lydia rolled her eyes and clapped him on the shoulder. "Calm down, will you? We'll get it up and running!"

"We'd better. This is my best carriage! My *only* carriage now…" Hunter went on grumbling as they raised the jacks again.

"Well, your *best carriage* is overheated, so I wouldn't get back under there if I were you," cautioned Gil as he stepped outside again. "Give it a few hours."

Lydia crossed her arms and arched a brow at Hunter. "Did you remember to put the coolant cap on like I told you to?"

"I… um… no?"

They broke into bickering. Biting back an amused grin, I replaced the hose in its receptacle. This was going to be an interesting trip.

"I think they like each other."

I was startled to find Gil behind me. He was watching the scene with raised brows. Especially when Lydia started laying out point-for-point how his blessed carriage was inadequate. Hunter's jaw dropped in offense, and they took their argument inside.

"I don't know. They seem at odds."

"Appearances can be deceiving." Gil chuckled, "He wants her."

Whirling around, I found Gil's arm posted above my head. He was close—*very* close. As his attention turned back to me, his lips tipped upward. Warmth flooded me as my heart fluttered.

"Does he, now? And how do you know that?"

His eyes were too intense. I had to tear mine away, but made the mistake of looking at his lips. Stars, I wanted to kiss those lips…

"I see the way he looks at her when she thinks he isn't looking."

"And how is that?"

He paused, his smile fading. "Not quite the way I look at you, if that's what you're thinking."

Blinking in surprise, I didn't know whether to be offended or intrigued. Before I could answer, he took my hand in his and tugged me along. He paused at the doorway. "We'll be back in a while. Going for a walk."

Hunter and Lydia barely acknowledged us as they continued their heated conversation. My eyes lingered on Hunter's, trying to gather any mysterious clue as to how he felt about Lydia. I got no insight before Gil led me over the hill with Shade in tow.

Chapter 23

Once out of sight from the others, Gil let go of my hand. With a mischievous grin, he reared up before bounding high and long to the top of the next hill. When he looked back at me across the distance, I could see his beaming smile, and my heart lifted. It'd been so long since we simply bounded together, with no danger at our heels.

The moment my feet left the ground, I felt free. Soaring... the wind fluttered my hair behind me. Air filled my lungs. When I landed, it was beyond Gil.

"No fair!" he pouted before bounding again. I tried to catch his heel as he sailed overhead, but he was too fast.

We bounded over and over until we were a good distance away from the carriage. Soon, we came to a sparse line of trees with deep blue leaves that stood sentinel over a small river. Shade caught up and immediately began lapping at the clear water before swiping out fish onto the bank with her paw.

"She's hungry."

"I doubt fish will be enough to sustain her, though."

Gil was still wary of her. I could understand why, but I hated that I could not reconcile my affection for Shade with the risk I knew we were taking. For now, I watched her like a proud manne.

"She followed us all the way to Stone City."

"And nearly took my head off."

I rolled my eyes. "You know she was just protecting me."

"Clearly." Gil wrapped his arms around me from behind and interlaced our fingers. His breath grazed my temple before he pressed his soft lips there. "And do you still want protection from me?" His voice was quiet, husky. It sent lightning shooting through the core of me. Our glow was brightening as he planted whispering kisses down my cheek, making his way toward my neck.

I didn't answer. I couldn't. I was putty in his arms. My chest was rising and falling deeply as quiet desire spilled in like a flood. Clouds hazed my thoughts. What was the question again?

When his lips found my neck, his kisses became fuller. I felt hints of his teeth and tongue on my skin. So quietly, he kissed me. I felt like a mouse caught in his trap. I *wanted* to be trapped. Badly.

He reached the crook of my neck, and a long sigh escaped me as I tightened my hold on his hand. Slow torture was what it was amounting to. But his muscular arms held me firmly from behind, so I was unable to turn and kiss him back. I could feel how much he wanted me, pressing on my backside, yet he was content to take his sweet time.

Just when he'd begun laying open-mouth kisses and sucking on my neck, Gil released me and switched my hand to his other. He walked upstream along the bank, leading me along with a roguish smile. Still half-numb with desire, I followed him easily, silently hoping our journey would be short.

We walked at a decent pace, Gil looking back to smile quietly at me every several steps. I wanted to yank him to a stop and leap on him. He'd never looked so handsome as he did just now—with his hair haphazardly thrown into a braid, strands slipping down over his shimmering temples. I'd never seen him so… radiant. So strong.

At last, we reached a place where the stream widened into a clear, bluish pool that butted up against a wall of black rock. White pebbles lined the shores.

"What is this place?"

Gil smiled as he let go of my hand and began removing his boots. "It's a spring. I noticed it on the map."

"It's beautiful."

"It's also cold."

My eyes widened when Gil pulled off his shirt. "You're going in there?"

He tossed the shirt on his boots. "Yes."

We looked at each other for a moment. He was dead serious. Especially when his fingers traveled to the hem of his pants and began unbuttoning them. Eyes holding mine the entire time, he undressed fully and stood before me in all his glory.

My pulse quickened as my heart practically banged against my rib cage. I'd seen Gil undressed before in different situations, but never like… this.

Pleased at my reaction, Gil stepped away and entered the water. When it was up to his ribs, he turned and crooked a finger for me to join him.

His gaze was burning into mine as I removed my boots with shaking hands. Embarrassed, I wanted to find a tree or something to undress behind. I felt so… on display. But we were utterly alone. Even Shade hadn't followed us.

Be brave, Ellie!

Keeping my eyes trained on his, I slowly unbuttoned my shirt. *His* shirt. Just the thought that I'd been wearing something that belonged to him brought out a sigh.

Layer by layer, I peeled off my clothing in a slow ritual. I wanted to savor the growing fire in his eyes. The way he looked at me now was enough to turn my insides to mush.

At last, I stepped into the water to join him. The shock of cold had me gasping and nearly turning back. Gil laughed and grabbed me by the wrist. He yanked me into his arms, and we fell backward under the surface as our light flashed brightly.

When we righted ourselves, Gil was laughing. I lightly shoved his shoulder. "Gillion Braxton, you are the worst!"

His arms wrapped around my waist and pressed me close to his still-warm body. Color burst into my cheeks. He felt… amazing. Firm and soft all at the same time.

His laugh faded to a smile. "The *absolute* worst, thank you very much."

I lightly traced his collarbone with my fingers and winked. "You're welcome."

Sliding his eyes shut, Gil hummed under my touch. My eyebrows raised a little, but I enjoyed the fact that I was having an effect. Slowly, I slid my hands up his chest and slipped them around the back of his neck. My fingers gently twisted in and out of his hair, massaging his scalp.

"Stars, El…" he breathed. "That feels nice."

"You're so tense."

"So are you."

His fingers dragged lazily up and down the line of my back. Each pass sent heat coursing through me. I pressed myself even closer, chest fully to chest.

Gil's eyes blazed into mine before he dipped his head down and kissed me deeply. I reciprocated with fervor, drinking in every moment and sensation.

When his hands traveled down, exploring my curves, I broke the kiss. Holding his forehead to mine, I tried to catch my breath enough to get the words out.

"Before we go any further, I just wanted you to know that I love you."

His hand rose to my face and tipped it upward. Gil smiled, eyes misting up. "I've waited our whole lives to hear you say that."

"You have?"

His thumb grazed my lower lip. "I've loved you for ages, Ellie."

My brow lowered. "But I thought—what about Agatha?"

Gil shook his head. "It was never Agatha."

My heart fluttered. "Why didn't you tell me?"

"I didn't think you felt the same way. You turned down the marriage offer time and time again until I'd all but given up hope."

"*Gil!*" I grabbed the sides of his face and looked him square in the eye. "I said no because *you* never asked!"

As understanding dawned in his eyes, Gil's lips crashed into mine. Again and again, they sought me, moving from my lips to my jaw, down my neck, and dragging back up my throat. All the while, his hand gripped the back of my thigh and hitched my leg up to wrap around his waist. The feel of his hard cock pressing on me had me on the verge of something inexplicable.

"Marry me, Ellie," he breathed huskily into my neck. "Be my wife."

I didn't have to think twice. "Yes... yes, Gil... yes..."

With that sealed, Gil gripped me under my backside, lifted me, and carefully, slowly lowered me back down as he slid inside me at last. I clung to his shoulders, gasping as he hissed with pleasure. We sat there for a moment, adjusting, savoring the new feel of each other. Our light lit up the entire pool, reflecting even off the black rock.

"You feel so good, El..."

Gil moved his hips, pulling me gently into a rhythm against him. My hands traveled over his shoulders and his back, feeling every muscle as they contracted with each movement. I wanted to know him. Every blessed inch.

I couldn't hold back the sounds that escaped from deep within. The fire in me grew with each aching moment. I'd waited so long to be with him—to be with the man I *loved*. And love him, I did.

Our lovemaking grew more and more passionate until Gil was suddenly walking us out of the water. He carried me over the beach and laid me down on the grass, his body covering mine.

"I can't do everything I want to do to you in the water," he explained darkly in my ear. "And I've had a long time to think about what I want to do..."

I was instantly liquid.

With the added gravity, things went to a whole new level. I dug my nails into his shoulders as he made good on his word. I felt him in places I never dreamed that I would or could. The way he worshiped me was... magical.

When he rained kisses down my breasts, over my stomach, and came to rest between my thighs, I thought I would die of desire. The first stroke of his tongue up my center had me curling up with a gasp as I grasped his hair.

"Oh, Gil..."

He growled and feasted on me with a hunger that sent me to a new plane of existence. Just the sight of him and what he was doing drove me mad. When he added his fingers to the mix, I became a puddle under his touch.

I thought I would die from it when he left his ministrations to kiss me on the lips, burying himself inside me once again. I whimpered at the lightning-like shock of pleasure that ripped through me. The taste of us on his deep kiss was nothing short of delicious.

Gil was on me, in me, part of me. I never wanted it to end. I loved him. I loved him so much it hurt. And at the moment, the hurt felt good.

Things escalated chaotically. As we had our way with each other, I felt like I was winding up tightly. More… more… *more…* I just wanted more. I wanted it harder… faster…

Gil picked up on my cues and gladly obliged until we were both moaning loudly behind our kisses. The light was getting brighter and brighter with every thrust inside me. He was hitting my limit, taking my breath away.

"Gil…"

"Just let it happen."

Suddenly, the world burst forth into ribbons of color. I was floating or flying. Gil's body stilled on mine as we met our wild end. Light rippled around us in waves—warm and ethereal. It was like being surrounded by a sea of stars.

When at last Gil collapsed on top of me, the light slowly dimmed down to a strong glow that reflected off his glistening skin. He was shuddering as we both breathed heavily. I held his head to my chest, enjoying the lingering light.

For a long time, we just lay there wordlessly. What was there to say after an experience like that? I felt like I'd suddenly just bridged some unnamable gap I never knew I needed to cross.

At last, Gil lifted his head and smiled down at me, eyes beaming. His palms gently grasped the sides of my head as his fingers laced in my hair. Quiet words slipped into the trance he held me in. "How do you feel?"

My lips mirrored his. "Wonderful."

A gentle kiss captured those lips. "My Ellie is satisfied?"

His Ellie.

"For now," I teased.

Gil laughed and kissed me again before finally rolling off me. Immediately, I was chilly. Thankfully, I was welcomed into open arms. Snuggling in the crook of his shoulder, I hugged his chest and sighed in contentment.

"I wish we could just stay out here forever."

Gil traced down my upper arm with his fingers. "Me too."

We were lost in our thoughts for a bit. As much as I tried to think only about the utter bliss we'd just been brought to, I couldn't forget the candle. It was there—lurking on the edges of my mind. Images of monsters and fire were not far from it. And Kromer...

"Were you serious when you asked me to marry you?"

"Very."

I propped myself up on my elbow and looked him in the eye. "I don't want to wait. Whenever we reach Basillian, let's find a priest."

Gil's eyes widened, and he sat up. "Really? I mean, a-are you sure? I know I asked you sort of suddenly, but I'm not trying to rush you or anything—"

"I'm sure."

A bright smile slashed his cheeks. It melted my heart all over again. His warm hand covered mine. "All right, then. Basillian it is."

As his knuckle caressed my cheeks, I caught them and pressed them to my lips. I never wanted to stop kissing him. Not now that he was mine.

Gil's eyes flashed with desire, but he quickly stood. A pang of disappointment struck me as he reached for his pants. I was certainly *not* ready to head back yet!

He stood, rummaging around in the pockets for a moment before discarding them once more and returning to my side.

"Close your eyes."

Confused, I obeyed. I felt him shift behind me. Slowly, he lifted my hair off my neck and laid it over my shoulder. A soft kiss was planted on my bare skin of the exposed one, sending warm shivers running through me. I was happy to play this game.

Suddenly, something hard and cool settled on my chest before a whisper of chains brushed my neck. I knew exactly what was happening. My heart sped up and my smile evaporated.

"Open."

I opened my eyes wide and sure enough, a shining, teardrop amethyst lay on my chest. Carefully, I lifted it, turning to gape at Gil. "Gil! No, Gil, I can't! I can't take this!"

His smile faltered. "Why not?"

Tears leaped to my eyes. "This was your *manne's!* I know how much this means to you."

"I know. Which is exactly why it's the perfect gift for *you.*" He tapped my nose and winked before rising and heading toward the spring.

Exasperated, I stood and stalked after him, stopping at the water's edge. "Gil! I'm serious!"

Ignoring me, Gil swam out to the middle of the spring before diving below the surface. Rolling my eyes, I waited with crossed arms and a tapping foot.

He resurfaced and crooked a finger, a sly expression on his face. I arched an eyebrow and sighed before marching through the water to him.

"We're not done talking about this, Gil. You can't just…"

Pain seared behind my eyes. Grasping the sides of my head, I felt everything begin to shift. Gil's voice became a distant echo, as did my own when I weakly called out for him. A red light lifted from my bare skin, encasing me like a tomb.

Chapter 24

It stood there, stark against the darkness. Taunting me, *daring* me to come closer. To touch its steady flame with even a single fingertip.

Floating freely, I was not on a mountaintop. I was nowhere. It was an all-consuming void. Only me... and the candle. I sensed words swelling deep in my subconscious—a gentle, female voice not so different from my own.

Come...

"No. No!"

Come, Ellie. Here is where you belong.

"You are evil. I will destroy you! I will find a way!"

Destroy me, you destroy yourself. We are one, child.

"Why are you doing this to me?"

I am revealing you.

"What are you talking about? Who are you?"

There was no further reply. Only a deep, thrumming pulse that beat in my chest, in time with my heart. It grew stronger and stronger until it was slamming in my ears. I cried out in terror, but there was no escaping it.

"Stop! Make it stop!"

Come to me, Ellie. Draw your strength.

"I... will... not..." Even as I said those words, I sensed myself drawing nearer toward the light. It was a beacon, pulling me in with its ethereal beauty, one I could not resist even with all the dwindling strength I had left.

Closer... closer... an intoxicating warmth slipped over my skin like a deep bath. It prickled with an overwhelming rush, something I could only describe as a sense of power— all-consuming strength. It both terrified and intrigued me. I was torn between giving in and fighting with what little willpower I had remaining. Old strength was slipping away and being replaced by this otherworldly version. All the while, I continuously drew nearer to the flame of damnation.

Just as my fingertip was brushing the outer edges of the blaze, something latched onto my ankles and I was yanked downward. Falling rapidly, I screamed, reaching desperately for the light. It faded away into the distance. Suddenly, I hit a wall of shocking cold and was pulled down into a watery tomb.

"Ellie!"

I screamed and kicked against my captor until the world faded into view and I realized air was in my lungs once more. Gil had his arms wrapped tightly around my waist and we were standing in the cold spring. It took me a while to realize that I was, in fact, awake and in the real world again. Gil was staring down at me with wild, fearful eyes. I ceased my struggle and burst into tears. Immediately, I was tucked into his chest.

"It's all right now."

"I don't know what's happening to me, Gil."

"I don't either, but we'll figure this out together. I promise."

Breathing deeply, I brought myself back from the brink of complete panic. I concentrated on our shared warmth in the chill; concentrated on our light. When at last I felt somewhat centered, we left the spring and lied down on the grass again to dry. There were only another two hours at most before set, but I wasn't ready to go back and face the others yet— not when the candle was blazing so brightly in my mind. I clenched my fists in the grass blades and stared up at the tree above us.

"I saw it again," I confessed quietly.

Gil was silent for a few moments. "I know."

I rolled my head to the side and rested my eyes on his concerned profile. "It was even stronger this time. Pulling me in."

"You were floating. Far above my head."

My eyes widened. "I... what?"

He nodded, burying his eyes in his palms with a sigh. "I had to bound out of the water to reach you."

Sitting up suddenly, my head swam. I braced myself on the ground and shook my head. "You mean I was... flying?"

"I think flying is something more consciously done."

I narrowed my eyes at the hint of sarcasm in his tone. "I'm serious, Gil."

At last, he looked at me. All jest disappeared. "Ellie, you scared me."

My heart pricked at the expression he bore. He looked genuinely... afraid. Was I really that intimidating? The last thing I ever wanted to do was hurt anyone, beyond Kromer. And Gil? I never wanted to harm a hair on his beautiful head. Reaching out, I took his hand in mine. "I'm sorry, Gil. I really would never knowingly hurt you, though. You know that... right?"

His face twisted in confusion. "Hurt me? No! Ellie, I was afraid I was going to *lose* you. Literally. You were floating higher and higher— I thought you were going to end up in the stars!"

My cheeks burned. "I see. I'm sorry, things are just... things are so upside down right now. It feels like the life has been sucked out of the world, and maybe out of me too. Everything feels like it's on the verge of some sort of darkness. Every corner hides something."

Gil regarded me gravely. "We can't lose hope, El. We lose hope, then we might as well give up and let Kromer destroy everything."

Guilt pinched me. "I know. We've just lost so much already. Our world has lost too much. I just can't make sense of it all."

"The faster we get to Basillian, the better. If there's anywhere we'll find answers, it has to be there. And we *will* find them." He brought my fingers to his lips and kissed them softly.

My heart swelled. I could only hope and pray he was correct. The determination and sincerity in his voice lead me to believe he would do anything in his power to fight the darkness at my side. And I loved him more for it.

We lay there for a little while longer and finally re-dressed when dry. Just as I finished braiding my damp hair, Shade came lumbering into the grove.

Sleep hung in her eyes. Giving her ears a scratch, a smile crept across my lips.

"I hope you've had your fill of fish."

Gil rolled his eyes. "I still don't think she should be in the carriage with us this set."

"Well, what else do you expect? Is she supposed to ride on the roof?"

He slung the rucksack over his shoulders and threw a sidelong glance at the affectionate pantheour. "It would be better than being shut up with her."

I scowled. "You still don't trust her. After all that she's done to protect me."

His response was a shrug. I decided to save my energy and argue the point when we got back to the carriage. It was hard to argue at all with Gil after everything we'd just experienced together. His eyes were still like bright blue crystals as he stepped over and offered his hand. Irritated or not, I gladly accepted it.

"We'd better get back before the stars are gone."

Even the steady timbre of his voice still sent a wave of warmth through me. My hand subconsciously moved to touch the smooth stone hanging above my bosom as I nodded. A promise—etched in crystal. Gil noticed the gesture and his lips twitched up into a smile. He kissed me softly before we set off on our way.

* * *

We made it back to the carriage just as the last stars were dwindling above us. A chill was settling in the air. Something wasn't settling in my nerves and I couldn't quite pinpoint it. The roar in my stomach wasn't helping. I couldn't remember the last time we'd actually eaten. My time with Gil had infused me with new and strange energy, but something pervasive lay just beneath my skin.

Shrugging off the sensation, I stepped into the carriage behind Gil. When

I turned to call Shade, she was sitting with her back turned.

"Shade?"

Her ears barely twitched in acknowledgment. I stroked her head, but she was still as stone, nostrils flaring as her eyes scanned the horizon. That feeling in my gut flared again. I gingerly petted her neck, only to snatch my hand back again when I felt the low rumbling of a growl. She hadn't moved, but I could sense her tension.

A hand latched onto my elbow. Hunter firmly pulled me back into the carriage, his hardened eyes on Shade. "The stars are about gone. You need to be inside." It was an order, not a suggestion. I wanted to argue, but the door was quickly closed and locked. My heart fell.

Gil was at the controls. "Is everything up and running?"

"Appears to be. No thanks to Red over here," said Lydia.

Hunter sneered at Lydia before taking the driver's seat. I plopped down on one of the benches and hugged my stomach. An ache was growing. Lydia's hand rested on my shoulder.

"Hey, are you all right?" she asked quietly. "You're looking kind of pale."

Forcing a brief smile, I tried to pull myself together. "I'm okay. Just tired."

A twinkle found her eye. "You two *were* gone quite a while."

My cheeks burned, and my hand moved to cover the necklace. Was it so obvious? Sneaking a glance at Gil, I found him entirely engrossed in conversation with Hunter as they performed system checks. Flashes of the spring pricked my mind, and it took all my concentration to drag myself back to the present.

"We went for a walk."

Lydia nodded slowly. Nothing more was said about it. Had I not been so uneasy, I would've breathed a sigh of relief. But things were far from easy.

The carriage sprang to life and lifted from the ground. Lydia was exceedingly pleased. "This thing would be scrap metal if it weren't for me. Did you know that I actually—"

"Brace yourselves!"

Hunter's voice barely split the cabin air before a roaring blasted into the wall behind us. A massive force knocked into the carriage, sending us in a brief spin. Too shocked to scream, I picked myself up off the floor and climbed onto the opposite bench. The wall held without so much as a dent, but the roaring continued. *Several* roars. Immediately, my heart thrashed in my chest. I recognized Shade among them. I could feel her energy, fiery and feral.

We lurched forward as Hunter slammed the carriage into gear. Lydia climbed into the passenger seat as Gil pulled down the ladder to the gunnery turret. Panic seized me.

"Gil! Don't hurt her!"

"He doesn't have a choice!" snapped Hunter harshly over his shoulder. He glanced down at the side view screens and cursed. "They're everywhere, dammit! If we don't lose them, this armor won't hold forever!"

Wild growling and roaring filled the air, intercepted by the occasional cry of pain. We were being continually hit from the sides. The gun fired up top. I wanted to curl up in a ball and slam my hands over my ears. Shade could be killed at any moment, if she hadn't been already. Seething with anxious fury, I clambered to my feet and latched onto the turret ladder. Looking upward through the hatch, I saw it was a double-seater—each chair shooting an independent gun at one-hundred-eighty degrees. He needed my help. It sickened me, but I scurried up the ladder and strapped in the seat at his back.

"Ellie—"

"I'm not here to argue! Shut up and shoot!"

As I whirled my seat around and peered into the rim of light, my eyes widened. Enormous beasts with shaggy, glittering silver fur, luminous red eyes, and white teeth kept up in a pack of at least fifteen. I'd seen them only in books of myths and bedtime stories of heroes and voyagers. Claws the length of a man's hand, stomachs that could digest iron…

"Clypane wolves…"

"Big ones at that!" Gil fired off another shot, sending a wolf rolling into the night.

Between the wolves and the right side of the carriage, keeping pace, was Shade. Every time one would come close, she'd snap her head around with her mighty teeth bared and take it down. They'd fall behind the pack as she disabled her prey, but she'd catch back up within moments. She still dwarfed them in size, but with the sheer number of them, her odds were not favorable.

"Rotate ninety degrees! I'll take the right and you take the left!" I boomed.

Without argument, Gil hit the gear and rotated the whole turret. We pivoted our seats until we were nearly side by side and began firing into the halo of light with pinpoint precision. One by one, the wolves fell. Some merely shook off the flesh wounds that glanced over them and increased their furious pace. I'd never seen creatures so beautifully terrifying. All angles and muscled limbs, with tails flowing behind them in their wake. Had it not been for their determination to kill us, I would've been hesitant to so much as touch the trigger. As it was, I had to shake off my fascination and take them out.

Two more. Four. The fifth one fell with ease. My heart twisted with each kill. Shade kept up like a machine. I could see the sheen of foamy sweat on her coat and at the corners of her mouth. If she was tiring, she didn't let it show. I was careful not to shoot her, but I clenched my teeth every time I pulled the trigger.

At last, it came down to one—running directly behind Shade. It stared daggers at her tail, paying not even an iota of attention to the carriage containing an abundance of meals. The savage severity in those red eyes told the story of the one thing sought… revenge. The rest of the beautiful pack had fallen, and a perpetrator was within grasp. I could feel the seething fury coming from it in waves. The pounding heartbeat was in time with the paws on the ground.

Shade was growing tired. Her eyes were frightened. Wild, focused, but weary. For a moment, I thought I saw her glance up at me. A coldness was seeping into my skin, permeating my bones. Fear, deep and sharp.

"Shoot it!"

I hesitated. "It's too close! It's right on her tail! I-I don't think I can!"

"It's going to kill her or us if you don't!"

"What's going on up there?" shouted Hunter from below.

"One left!" called Gil as he shot me a wild-eyed stare.

I aimed the gun, my hand shaking on the trigger. Looking into the eyes of both animals, I knew it could be the end for one or both. This had to be done. Shoving aside my emotions, I focused on my target and took a deep breath.

Steady, Shade. Hold it steady...

With mechanical motions, I pulled the trigger and let the energy blast explode out of the gun barrel. To my horror, both animals cried out and tumbled out of the light. A blood-curdling scream tore from my throat.

"No, no, no! Shade!"

Pressing my palms over my eyes, I dissolved into screaming sobs, the image of her fall playing over and over behind my eyelids. I'd failed. I'd killed her.

Instantly, Gil was unstrapped from his seat and perched over me, a hand braced on the back of my head. Nothing he could say could make it okay, and he knew it.

Lydia was at the foot of the ladder. "What happened?"

Gil's reply was somber. "We're clear."

The carriage immediately dropped to a slower pace. I couldn't catch my breath. Frantically, I struggled with the buckles on my harness and sobbed. Gil took over, and I was freed within moments.

"I-I need to go down. I need to go down!" I insisted, hyperventilating. My head felt full of air.

In a flash, Gil was down the ladder, and I quickly followed. The moment I was on the ground, I fell into a heap and rested my forehead on the floor. "I killed her... I killed..." The words kept recycling themselves.

Lydia's arms wrapped around me as she laid her cheek on my back. "Just breathe, Ellie. Just take some deep breaths..."

"Might want to back away, Lydia. She's flaring again," warned Gil. Through my tears, I noticed the glow of violet, which only spurred them on.

Not now!

"You hush! She's just upset!" Turning her attention back to me, Lydia

182

spoke in soothing tones. "I'm right here, dear. You don't have to be afraid. Just breathe, focus on my voice, and we'll talk about it when you're ready, okay? That's it..."

My fingers found Lydia's sleeve, and I pulled myself up into her arms, letting my tears flow onto her shoulder. The light gradually receded, though my heart was still splintered into pieces. She helped me over to a bench and Gil fetched me a canteen of water from the receptacle on the back wall. After several slow sips, with them on either side of me, I pulled my wits together and wiped my eyes on the back of my sleeve before recounting my sins.

I found comfort among my companions, but exhaustion dragged my bones. Hunter and Gil agreed to take shifts driving through the set, with Hunter continuing for now. As tempting as it was to stop and rest, the evidence of beasts remained in gouges sliced in the outer hull.

We were all traumatized after the destruction of Stone City and everything else that had occurred in between. Hunter was like a stone himself, staring ahead into the darkness. Now that things were quiet, everyone had time to settle... and time to reflect.

The cabin lights were turned low, and we settled into our positions: Lydia on the bench, and Gil and I curled up on the floor. Not the most comfortable place to sleep, but I wouldn't have it any other way. I was afraid to sleep. Afraid to see the candle. Afraid to see... *him* again. Settling fully into Gil's arms, my back to his chest, I tried to concentrate on the feeling of safety and security, and not on how wrong everything was going. With all my willpower, I focused on Basillian—on being a bride. Something bright in the darkness. But inevitably, I fell asleep, and my dreams drifted into familiar, very much unwanted territory.

Chapter 25

"Did he hurt you?"

Scarcely had the light faded into view when Kromer rushed toward me, his face flooded with panic. I recoiled with a scowl, and he ceased his pursuit. Indifference slammed over his features once more before he pivoted toward the candle with his arms crossed.

I watched him for a moment, entirely confused by his behavior, but thankful for the distance between us. His hair was more disheveled than usual, and dark circles hung under his eyes. Not quite the hardened madman murderer he normally presented as. Part of me rejoiced in his discomfort. If it meant that he was suffering in the slightest, then I ought to be satisfied. Yet, it was… unpredicted, and that had my guard up even higher.

My reply was bitterly cold. "It's none of your business."

Kromer shrugged. "Suit yourself."

Keeping my distance, I circled the candle until I stood opposite my enemy. With blazing eyes, I spat my accusations. "You murdered another city full of people. Why?"

He kept his eyes reverently on the flame. "They were in our way."

Filled with disgust, I fought to keep down the bile touching the back of my throat. "You're a monster."

Pale green eyes snapped to mine. "And you're not?"

Pained roars echoed in my head. Shade, disappearing into the darkness. No. *No.* I wasn't.

"Don't evade the truth, Kromer! You—"

"Maximus."

I blinked. "What?"

"You keep calling me my surname. Call me Maximus. Or Max, for short."

His sudden casual demeanor only filled me with rage. "I'll call you whatever I damn well please! You deserve no respect from me or anyone!"

He returned his attention to the flame. "It's what *she* calls me. She respects me enough to use it."

I glared at him. "It's not a 'she'. It's an 'it', and *it* is nothing but a flame of damnation."

"Tell me, Ellie, would you blow it out if you could? Hmm? Douse it with a bucket of water? Watch it peter out until it's nothing but a curling thread of smoke?" He side-stepped the candle and stalked toward me. I backed up until I met the rock. Kromer ceased his pursuit when he was close enough that I could reach out to strike him if I wanted to. But the intensity of his gaze frightened me to a standstill.

"Would you unleash all the horrors of the universe with a single puff of air? How does it feel, knowing that you have that kind of power? Tell me, Ellie, how does it feel, knowing that she chose *you*?"

Straightening my spine, I faced him boldly. "And you would see life as you know it fall?"

Kromer's lips twitched upward as he met my stare, unblinking. "Life is temporary. I'm interested in things more... eternal."

"And if there's nothing after life? If you're wrong?"

"Oh, my dear, do you really believe that?" His finger brushed the side of my cheek. I jerked my head away with a scowl. He chuckled. "Still skittish, I see."

With a growl, I roughly shoved him and stomped to the other end of the clearing. "Don't touch me! You murdered my panne, in case you've forgotten!"

"Are you sure about that?"

I froze. "What are you talking about? You know what you did—"

"Oh, do I? Who told you that?"

My heart began thumping in my chest. The memory of the world plunging from beneath my feet when Gil delivered the news still haunted me. "Don't try to play games with my head. I'm not falling for it."

"What if I told you that your panne still breathes?"

Spinning around, I found him staring at me without a hint of jest. I jabbed an accusatory finger in his direction. "Y-You lie! Gil saw him—"

"What he thinks he saw and what happened are two different things."

I stood, eyes locked on his, as my heart pounded. "Why are you doing this to me?"

He shook his head. "I am not lying, Ellie."

Narrowing my eyes, I clenched my fists at my side, feeling a veil of heat envelop me. My crimson aura made its appearance. "I hate you. You liar!" Flying across the rock, with outstretched arms, I broke through the wall of air he tried to erect and tackled him to the ground. Straddling him, my hands wrapped around his throat. I felt his skin under my fingertips, but no matter how hard I squeezed, I couldn't contract it.

Staring at me with wide eyes and flaring nostrils, Kromer made no move to get up.

"You cannot hurt me here, remember?"

Screeching, I pounded on his chest and went to stand. Kromer grabbed me by the wrists.

"Do you want to see him?"

I struggled against him, but he held tighter. "Let me go!"

Repeating his question, he gritted his teeth. *"Do you want to see him?"*

"Why? So you can show me some fake image and try to manipulate me? I don't think so!"

"Ask the candle."

I stopped struggling. "What?"

He finally let go of my wrists and nodded toward the candle. "Ask the candle. It'll show you."

My gaze followed his, and the candle flickered slightly. The same female voice whispered in my ear.

Come, Ellie...

I felt a powerful draw. Rising slowly to my feet, I stepped over to the flame and gazed into it.

"If this is a trick…" All ferocity had leaked out of my voice.

"It's not. Just ask."

Taking a deep breath, I was careful not to release it too suddenly toward the flame. "Please show me my panne."

I stared into the white-hot center of the fire. Suddenly, it blazed higher, turning blue, and then black, and settling on white. A scene took form: a dim room… a bed… an older man with blue skin, sleeping soundly—chains around his ankles. Bruises and lacerations covered his face, but I knew him anywhere.

A strangled cry escaped my throat. Without thinking, I reached out to the flame, only to snatch my hand back when it burned. Immediately, it shrank back down to its normal state, the scene disappearing. I sank to the ground in utter shock, clutching my burned hand. The pain was searing, but not as excruciating as the knowledge that my panne could be alive, and I was not there to save him.

"Come to me," Kromer said quietly. "I will set you both up to live comfortable lives. No harm will come to you. I promise."

"And why should I trust you?"

"Because I could've killed you by now, but I haven't, have I?"

Dragging myself to my feet, I showed my full contempt. "You took my panne from me and destroyed my home. You think I care only about my own life? That I'm small-minded, like you?"

"I think all that you care about will be your downfall. You know what you are, Ellie. And you are not like them—like *any* of them."

"Your twisting will not work on me. I will never, *ever* join you."

"And you believe that you'll live happily ever after with Braxton? How long do you think it will be before you fully lose control of your little light show and kill him?"

I felt like I'd been punched in the gut. "How dare you! I would never—"

"Maybe not now, but who knows how long it will be until one little spat sends you over the edge and lover-boy meets his end."

"You know what? We're done talking now." I stalked away.

"Wherever you're going, you won't find answers there, Ellie. Only I can help you. Only the candle can help both of us."

"There is no 'us'!" I hissed over my shoulder.

Loud, pounding footsteps caught up to me as he snatched my wrist in an iron grip. I fought against him, but he held on with ferocity as I spewed a string of screaming curses. Suddenly, he pressed his fingers into my burned hand and dragged it firmly from palm to fingertip. I howled in pain. He held my glare, unflinching.

Within moments, the pain disappeared. I looked down to see the remnants of dried candle wax on my hand. Silently, I stared at it as the grip on my wrist relaxed.

"If I wanted to hurt you, would I have helped you now?"

"I don't understand you at all. You don't even know me—"

"That could change."

Briefly, I allowed my eyes to link with his and found them soft. His thumb brushed the inner part of my wrist, sending a curious alarm clanging through me. When his other hand slowly reached toward my face, I yanked myself free and took several steps backward. Hurt flashed in his features. Averting my gaze, I held my hand to my chest protectively.

"Thank you for healing my burn, but do not touch me. *Ever again.*" My words did not come out as harsh as I'd intended, but I hoped he got the message, regardless. I was not ready to deal with this other vein of madness from my enemy.

"You're welcome." He was suddenly cold and biting. I glared at his retreating form just as he disappeared into the darkness beyond the candle's glow.

* * *

When I awoke, it was nearing rise already. Everyone was sleeping except for Gil, who now sat in the driver's seat, yawning. I felt rested and exhausted concurrently. Grief over what I'd done to Shade seeped back into my mind the more alert I became. My right hand also had a lingering ache. I shuddered and pushed aside all thoughts of last set's dream.

Rubbing the sleep from my eyes, I plopped down in the passenger seat. Gil threw me a tired smile.

"Good rise, sleepyhead."

The display showed us driving through broad grasslands. "Where are we?"

"Almost to Basillian."

My hand moved to the smooth stone resting on my chest. A flutter in my stomach reminded me of what lay in wait there. It was exciting and terrifying at the same time. A marriage, a search for answers, the potential of another enemy invasion… all our hopes and fears boiled down to this one city.

Gil's hand found mine and gave it a gentle squeeze. Soon, he would be my husband; mine forever. Gratitude blossomed, and I brought his hand to my lips. He was my rock when everything was going wrong, and always had been. There was nothing I wanted more than for the universe to be righted again, and for us to simply be together—and start a family of our own someday to rebuild that which was lost. But what was lost? Images of Panne—unconscious, injured in a place far from reach bubbled to the surface. Was it true? Or simply a trick?

"What's wrong?"

I found Gil's eyes darting to me as he manned the controls. My thoughts felt on display. Buttoning them up with a tired smile, I reassured him. "I'm all right. Just waking up."

His weighted brow told me he was unconvinced. "You're worried."

"I've been worried since the day you left Silis." The mention of our home made him flinch. It would forever be a weight on us. I sighed, slumping back in the seat.

"It was one of the hardest days of my life; leaving you," he said quietly. "I had a bad feeling from the start, but Panne wouldn't listen. I suppose he thought Agatha would be some sort of consolation prize. Foolish man…"

It was hard not to agree with him. His panne was one of the few who had any pull with Premier Diltron, who should've known something was amiss. "I can't understand how the message arrived from King Wendil if it was Kromer who'd taken over?"

His jaw muscle feathered. "I didn't see it myself, but they have some sort of technology we don't. It was trickery and a damn good one at that. Premier Diltron would've never taken the risk if he didn't believe it was from the king."

"Unless Diltron was paid off." We both turned to find Hunter rising to his feet. "Not every leader on this rock is above lining their pockets at the expense of their people."

I shot him an incredulous look. "His own family was in Silis. I highly doubt—"

Hunter yanked his shirt up, revealing a dark, bulged scar just underneath his ribs. "It didn't stop my father from sacrificing me when Wendil took power."

Shock was not the word. "What do you... what happened?"

He glanced back at Lydia's sleeping form and stepped closer, lowering his voice as he righted his shirt. "When Wendil took power, it was a coupe. Not many people in the outer lands are privy to it, but his father did not die of natural causes. My father was the premier of Basillian, and he was part of the group that deposed him. I overheard their plans as a child. They caught me hiding behind the curtain. I ran and hid behind my mother's skirts. When my mother pleaded with him to reconsider his plan, my own father turned us over to the king for a reward. The guards took my mother's head, but I got a blade to the stomach."

Gil brought the carriage to a halt and gaped at him. "You're saying King Wendil *stole* his throne?"

Hunter scoffed. "He stole everything."

A sick feeling sat in my stomach. My panne had faithfully served under Wendil's rule my entire life. He would've died for him in a heartbeat. It may kill him yet to learn the truth of our revered leader. My view of Hunter was clearing.

We serve no king.

Outlaws who rebelled against the corruption so few knew… And now they'd fallen to a new pretender king. The fire within me flared. It would only stoke higher until at last I had my own revenge. Our people had been mercilessly slaughtered with equal callousness. Catching Gil's hardened eyes, he was having the same thoughts.

Kromer must die.

Chapter 26

An ancient city of beautiful colors crowned a hill. Basillian came into view just as the rise was fully reaching its peak. Red brick still faithfully held to red brick in the high walls surrounding the vibrant jewel that was my family's ancestral home.

Jewel-toned buildings of wood and stone flanked the winding streets. In the western part of the city was the hill's peak. A great, tiered, rusty-stoned edifice dominated the rise, its spire kissing the sky.

As we entered the city's gates, I climbed to the gun turret and took in the bustling sights below me. Vibrant carriages, families shopping, and people riding on the backs of lumbering, silver-coated torselhares made up the spindly river that flowed in opposing directions on the cobblework. Stars shone a little brighter here, casting their glow upon the pale tiled roofs as they soaked up the light, rendering them glittering diamonds.

"It's really something," I remarked to Gil as he joined me. His still-bleary eyes took in the beauty around us and widened.

"That it is."

"Was Star City like this?"

"No. It is—*was* bigger; *much* bigger. All golden and gleaming like a statue rising out of the flats. Their walls were twice as high as Silis."

I scoffed bitterly. "A beautiful prison, then."

"What do you mean?" I found his eyebrows drawn together, his attention no longer on the city sights.

The dream of the previous set came flooding back to me in a series of cold waves. I hesitated, unsure of how to explain it. My nerves crawled.

"When I sleep at night, I don't just see the candle, Gil... *He* is also there."

"Who? Your panne?"

Drawing myself up smaller, I buried my forehead in my palm. "No."

It took a moment for the realization to dawn on him. The air felt a little chillier. Why was my stomach turning so much?

"You dream of... Kromer?" The hint of disappointment in his voice was hard to miss. I cringed.

"Not voluntarily, believe me. He's just... there. It's like it's not even a dream."

He grew quiet. "I see."

"Something happened last night. He showed me something, in the candle—"

The carriage ground to a halt.

"All right! We're here!" called Hunter with a yawn.

"Good! We can get out of this stinky old rust bucket," said Lydia. They began arguing their way out the door.

Gil smiled down the hatch. "I really do think they like each other."

"If you say so."

His attention returned to me. "Now, what were you saying?"

"I saw—"

"Hey!" Hunter poked his head back in the doorway below. "If you're going to get all mushy with each other, it'll have to wait. I need you two to get out so I can lock the door."

Rolling his eyes, Gil headed down the ladder. "We're coming."

The opportunity to confess what ate at the forefront of my mind would have to wait. I followed him down and we stepped into the bustling street. Hunter closed the door and punched the key code in the outer panel. When the door was properly bolted, we followed him into a nearby teal three-story building with a swinging sign over the door that read, "The White Roof Inn".

Inside, the small, brightly decorated lobby was uncrowded, with only a few lingering patrons and a young, blue-skinned man behind the front desk.

He looked up from his task at hand and smiled warmly as we entered.

"Welcome to the White Roof," he greeted cheerfully when Hunter stepped up to the desk. "Weary travelers, I see."

"That's an understatement," muttered Lydia.

"We'll need three rooms, please." Hunter glanced at Gil and me, and my cheeks burned. Gil's hand slipped into mine, reminding me of our commitment. A smile stole across my face.

Nodding, the man swiped his fingers over the glass display before him. "And how long will you be staying with us?"

Hunter sighed. "Long term, for now, I'm afraid."

The man only briefly raised a brow, but then continued his work. "We can certainly accommodate you…" As he launched into pricing and policies, I lost focus as I noticed his violet eyes: cool, clear, and vaguely familiar. Perhaps it was rude of me to stare, but I couldn't look away. They reminded me of someone. Someone very, *very* dear.

At last, when Hunter paid and took the keys, I placed my palms on the counter. "Excuse me, sir?"

He looked at me directly, furthering my suspicions. "Yes?"

"Did you by chance know a Starla Hum—I mean—*Torril*?"

Though there was no grand brightening of his features, his dark brows lifted slightly. "I don't believe so, but I recognize the surname. There are many Torrils in Basillian. I'm distantly related to them."

My heart fluttered. I desperately clenched the edge of the white marble counter. "Do you know where I can find any,"—My eyes flitted to his name tag— "*Raphael?*"

Raphael's face tinged with pity. I knew vaguely that I looked like absolute hell: sleep-deprived, filthy clothing, and now on the verge of tears. Without a home, traumatized, and hunted— if he only knew the whole of it. Perhaps a look could somehow convey all of that, but looks didn't concern me as much as finally getting the answers I'd so desperately been seeking.

"If you want to find someone in Basillian, the best place to look is in the community records at the monastery. Births, deaths, marriages—it's all kept there in the vaults."

"Where can I find this place?"

He nodded toward the door. "You can't miss it. It's the enormous building atop the hill— hey! Wait!" I was already bolting toward the door. "You'll have to pay them a security deposit first!"

Without pausing, I spilled into the busy street, calculated the uphill slope, and bounded high and long above the crowds. Eyes craned upward as I soared, nearly knocking people over as I landed. Whistles split the air. When I dared to look back, I saw men in red, official-looking uniforms dashing up the street toward me. My stomach dropped at the sight. Bounding in city streets was forbidden in Silis, as well. I should've known.

A voice above caught my attention. "Ellie!"

Craning my neck, I looked up to see Gil on the sloped roof of the adjacent brick building, his foot braced on the gutter. His eyes darted between me and the rapidly approaching guards. Taking a step back, he jerked his head toward an alley. I crouched down and wove in between the clusters of pedestrians until I ducked into the opening. It was blessedly empty.

"Gil?"

"Up here!"

I looked up to find him peering down at me with a grin. He was already on the other side of the ridgepole, away from the eyes of the crowds. The commotion from my pursuers was drawing closer beyond the alley opening. Taking a deep breath, I reared up as best I could, and bounded in a zig-zag pattern between the walls until I finally landed at Gil's side. Below, we saw the men in red just passing by the alley, still searching for my rebellious, bounding self.

"I think Panne would have my hide right now, running from guards," I remarked with a nervous smile.

Linking his arm around the small of my back, Gil pulled me close to his warm body as he grinned roguishly. "I think your panne would know that you are completely untamable." His lips heatedly locked with mine, sending a rush of fire shooting through my veins. Our glow melted with that of the roof beneath our feet. For a moment, I forgot why I was there at all.

When at last our lips separated, I was left breathless. Gil gazed at me, bright-eyed, as he slipped his hand around mine. "Come on. This way."

"What?"

Gil laughed and sought my lips one more time. We had barely parted when he quietly reminded me, "The monastery?"

Redness bloomed in my cheeks. "Oh."

"Hey." He gently lifted my chin to meet my eyes. "We're going to find our answers here. And then..." Slowly, he trailed his fingertips down my neck... and chest... before resting on the necklace. I shuddered under his touch. It was tempting to postpone our trip to the monastery.

Gil turned and bounded long—to the next rooftop. Shaking my head clear of maddening thoughts, I followed suit. Again and again we bounded, working our way uphill. The roof tiles were like a blanket of strewn stars below our feet as I followed my love. Working deftly, we avoided the busiest streets to evade attention.

The red brick monastery loomed high and bright before us, tiered with many pillared, open-air passageways and glowing, pointed turrets. Unlike the shining metal of our tower home in Silis, all smoothness and sharp angles, this was an edifice more ancient and revered. Like an old soul pulled together in a perfect hewing of stone. There was something of immortal character there, watching us leap from roof to roof like insignificant insects. I felt keenly more aware of it the closer we got.

At last, we landed in the courtyard in front of our destination. Large inscribed, green doors stood weathered and waiting for us. A black sentry box stood adjacent to the door on the right, occupied by a dark-robed figure with a tall, shining silver spear. When our feet crunched the gravel, their head raised, bright emerald eyes met mine from a distance. I was surprised to find a solemn, feminine, green face staring back at me. A young one, at that.

"How may we assist you?" she half-demanded in an authoritative tone, squaring her shoulders as if attempting to broaden her petite frame.

Slipping on a congenial smile, I did my best to use the years of diplomacy I'd witnessed Panne use when he wasn't trying to kill Advisor Braxton. "Yes, hello, we would like to request access to the community records, please."

The sentry was nonplussed. Keeping her eyes glued to mine, she pulled a suspended rope hanging at her side, and a compartment slid from the outside wall of the box. "Fifty crysts. You can pick it up on your way out after you've been searched."

My eyes widened to the size of tea saucers. "Fifty crysts? Why so much?"

Only coldness met me. "No deposit, no passage."

I turned to Gil. He was already digging through his pocket. When he opened his hand, there were only two green, twenty-cryst pieces. His face bloomed in humiliation. "I'm... I'm sorry, I don't have it on me. I lost the rucksack. But if we get back, maybe Hunter can—"

"I'll take that."

My necklace. Her eyes and extended finger zeroed in on the amethyst. The starlight was glinting from its cut angles in a breathtaking dance. I snatched it protectively and looked to Gil for help. He wrapped an arm around my shoulders.

"Is there nothing else we could work out? Perhaps if I stay outside and she goes in?"

She rolled her eyes. "We're not going to keep it. We've no need for jewelry here. You'll get it back when you leave, same as money."

Hesitantly, I slipped my hands behind my neck and unhooked the clasp. Gil offered no argument as I carefully dropped the necklace into the receptacle. With another pull of the rope, it snapped back into the wall, stowing away my precious jewel. I fought the moisture building in my eyes and took a steeling breath.

Satisfied at last, the sentry pulled another rope and a bell rang beyond the doors. Patiently, we waited a few moments until the inner latch turned and one of them swung open. An old violet man in a brown hooded robe stepped out with a smile.

"Records request?"

I felt like I was going to spill into tears at any moment. Fortunately, Gil took the lead. "Yes, that's right."

"I'm Cyril, the archivist. If you'll follow me..." He admitted us through the massive, wooden door and shut us away from the world with an echoing thud.

Inside, a world of enormous flying buttresses held by massive stone pillars greeted us. Stained glass windows portrayed a colorful galaxy of legends and old gods. Ancient stone walls were covered with well-maintained tapestries of silver and gold, depicting fields of green under skies of stars, and beasts living in harmony with people. I wondered at the unusual scenes. We were prey and had long since been. With the fast clip at which were walking, I didn't have a chance to ask about it.

"It's quite a trek to the vaults, I'm afraid. Most people come early in the morning to give themselves more time for browsing," explained Cyril, not the least bit out of breath. "We'd bound, but it's forbidden now as there has been too much damage done to the ceilings where it lowers ahead. Well, and injuries, of course. But some of these murals above us are thousands of years old. Our abbess put a stop to it ages ago."

Craning my neck, I caught glimpses of deep crimson and purple hues, too far above to make out clear details. "You say you have an abbess?" I asked absently.

"Oh, yes. We do not discriminate here. From all walks of life, we are. Living in harmony under the heavens…"

Cyril gave us a rambling history lesson as we walked from hall to hall. Eventually, we came to a set of stairs in a darkened corridor that turned downward. Yellow light glowed from lanterns sparsely placed high on the walls. The crackling shuffle of stone beneath our boots echoed in the ever-turning chamber. It felt like a tomb.

When at last the stairs ended at a platform, it opened up into a cavernous drop beyond the rail. A rim of glowing lights stretching far beyond the barrier revealed the circular well. Above, the ceiling stretched into blackness, and below, only distant lights hinted at a bottom. To our right, the stairs continued—hugging the wall and gradually descending. My shoulders sagged. Our journey would drag on.

It took ages, and by the time we reached the bottom, my legs were aching something fierce. Even a full day of bounding didn't compare to taking the sheer number of stairs in a constant downward direction. I was *not* looking forward to the trek back up.

There was more light here, and warmth from several large hearths inset into the dark stone walls. They had positioned chairs and couches in front of each, presumably to recover from the journey. Ahead, soaring arches between mighty pillars opened the way into another chamber in which I could see tall bookcases and redwood desks for study, some already occupied. As much as I wanted to run in there and begin my search, I yielded to Cyril's insistence that we sit and relax while he fetched us tea and refreshments.

Gil stretched his long legs toward the crackling fire as he sank into the crimson couch. I plopped next to him and followed suit. So far below the starlight, I felt more tired than I had in some time. My muscles craved the rejuvenating glow.

"I never want to see another stair again," I groaned, sliding my eyes shut.

"I don't know how the old man does it," whispered Gil. "He didn't even break a sweat!"

Rolling my head to look the direction in which Cyril had trotted off, I couldn't help but laugh. "I sure don't envy his job."

"Maybe he'll take my forty crysts and let us bound back up to the top?"

I shot him a sarcastic glare. "Bribing a monk? My, my, Gillion Braxton, how scandalous!"

We teased back and forth until, at last, Cyril reappeared, pushing a wooden cart of promised refreshments.

"I hope blineberry tea and thumbprint cakes will suffice. And I'm afraid we're out of sugar down here. I'd offer to go up and fetch some, but well..." he shrugged apologetically as his eyes swung upward into the void.

"This is more than all right," assured Gil with a warm smile. "Thank you."

Cyril poured our tea and passed out the cakes. I noticed the first hints of weariness in his amber eyes. "Will you sit with us?"

"No, I'm all right. I've got other patrons to attend to. Thank you, though... Now, if you want to tell me what it is you're searching for, I can have the volumes pulled and ready for you?"

Straight to business, then. I gingerly set my tea down on the small table in front of us.

"Well, I'm looking for records pertaining to a family. *Torril.*"

His eyes widened. "Torril? Well, that's going to be quite the record! Loads of Torrils in these parts. Any particular century?"

"I, um... this one?"

Cyril laughed and nodded as he walked away. "I'll come to fetch you."

* * *

Hours later, after the rest of the patrons had gone, Gil and I were still poring over leather-bound volumes, some nearly the size of the desks which we hunched over. Births, marriages, deaths... so many lines, branches, and offshoots beyond that. It would seem that every Torril had an enormous family, which then bequeathed an even larger one. The Humetts were a tidy bunch in comparison—many only children, mostly male.

Groaning, I slumped back into the chair, my hand on the aching small of my back. "This would be so much easier if Manne had given me names and details! I feel like I'm grasping at the wind here."

Warm hands slipped over my shoulders and began to work at the tension in my muscles. "We can take a break if we need to."

I slid my eyes shut and sighed, relishing the massage. Gil always knew just the right amount of pressure to use. "Not too long of a break. I think our time's almost up."

"There's always tomorrow."

"I don't think I could sleep tonight without answers."

His lips brushed my cheek. "Who said anything about sleep?"

Laughing, I linked my arm around his neck and pulled him in for an upside-down kiss. "Behave yourself, Mr. Braxton."

"Behave? I always behave." His fingers shot to my ribs and began tickling me mercilessly in my most vulnerable spots that only he knew. I howled and squirmed in the chair, trying to escape. Gil held me fast between his long arms.

"Gil!" I bellowed, my laughter still echoing off the high stone walls.

The tickling quickly ceased, and Gil stood me up and whirled me around until we were face to face. Wearing a sly grin, he wrapped his arm around my waist and the minute space between us disappeared. Flooded with warmth, I glowed brightly.

His hot lips crashed into mine as the chilly surroundings faded away. My hands embraced the back of his neck, lacing my fingers through his silken, starlight hair. I loved the feel of it against my skin.

We sought each other until I felt his hands slide downward as our kisses grew more passionate. Suddenly, he gripped the backs of my thighs and lifted me, wrapping my legs around his waist. I whimpered in surprise when I felt the edge of the desk pressing against my backside. Gil's lips devoured mine as he firmly leaned into me.

"Gil," I gasped, breaking the kiss. He simply moved to my neck, driving me even further into a state of drifting. "Gil, we're... we're in... a monastery..."

He laughed into my skin. "We're alone."

I wanted to think of a thousand excuses, but I had no intention of voicing any of them when I felt his fingers creep over my shirt to the top buttons. My mind spun into a whirlwind of anticipation. Arching my back to give him better access, my hand shot behind me to the surface of the desk. Pages of the book hindered my traction, and I ended up sweeping it to the floor with a loud thud. The moment the book hit the ground, a bright vision flashed behind my eyelids.

Page 240. I saw her name in neatly printed letters. With a gasp, I broke away from Gil and pushed him off me. Immediately, I fell to the floor, my knees smarting on the hard stone, and began sifting through the book pages.

"Ellie, what is it? What's going on?" Gil kneeled next to me, confused.

Ignoring him, I desperately flipped through pages until I reached 240, and then scanned down with a shaking fingertip and razor-edged focus. At last, I saw it; I saw *her.* I could hardly believe my eyes.

"Starla Torril..."

Gil leaned over the book, and his eyes widened. "You found it! But how? How did you know?"

"I saw it." This did little to allay his confusion, but there was no time for that. "Look! It's a birth record. Born to Mariola and Caulin Torril, stardate 2317. It's the right year and everything!" My excitement was bubbling.

"Look over on this line." Gil pointed across the column on the massive page. "It has an address."

My vision zeroed in on the precious information. "Do you think they could still be there?"

"It's a good place to start. I'll find something to write with."

The more I stared at the precious letters, the more hope rose. I was going to find my family. I was going to find answers.

Everything was going to be all right.

Chapter 27

My hands were shaking as we strolled up to the large, deep-auburn house near the northern edge of town. It was nearly set, but there in the confines of the soaring walls, we were safe from the prowling of wild animals. I wish I had Shade at my side now, to pet her soft head and bolster my nerves. As it was, I grasped the necklace, which was safely back in my possession, and leaned into Gil's warm shoulder.

"Do you want me to knock?" he whispered. I nodded, too affected to speak. He left me at the bottom of the broad stone steps and made his way to the sandy wood door with the iron latch.

A small black carriage was parked out front. Everyone in that town had carriages. It was more sprawling than Silis and getting to the house took ages. I could only hope a vehicle meant *someone* was home.

Gil knocked a second time. He looked back with a reassuring smile I couldn't reciprocate. At least I wasn't alone.

There was the sound of shifting metal against wood, and the door slowly swung open. A small, deep blue woman with silver hair, weary violet eyes, and a bent back peered up at Gil.

"May I help you, sir?" she asked in a familiar, gravelly voice.

My heart leaped in my throat. I recognized it instantly. But... how? It couldn't possibly be...

"Mara?"

She poked her head past Gil and blinked at me with big eyes. "How do you know that name, dear?"

"I…" Shaking off my shock, I tried again, "I'm sorry, I'm being rude. My name is Ellette Humett, and this is Gillion Braxton. We're looking for a Mariola Torril."

Recognition, followed by sadness, registered in the woman's eyes. "I'm afraid you won't find her here. She passed on some time ago. I'm her sister, Nola."

The world shifted under my feet and I steadied myself on the rail post. Gil was at my side in a flash. I tried to reassure him I was fine, but it was a lie.

"Come in and rest awhile, dear. You look as if you could use it," said Nola.

She ushered us inside and took us to a small sitting room with faded floral wallpaper. It smelled of the rich, sweet spices filtering in from the kitchen. An array of plush emerald sofas and armchairs sat in a conversational square around a low, blond-wood table with curvy legs. The fireplace behind us sprang to life when Nola flipped the nearby switch on the wall. She smiled in satisfaction.

"Just had it installed last month. Getting too old to tote wood back and forth." She shuffled toward the doorway. "Have a seat. I'll fetch tea for us."

"Can I assist you?" Gil offered immediately.

Nola turned to him with a teasing, stern eye. "You most certainly cannot. You are my guest, and I insist you rest."

Gil nodded in surrender, and Nola disappeared down the hall. We sank down onto the love seat with a relieved sigh. It was like being cradled by a cloud after a long day of stairs and bounding. I immediately fought sleep. Every aching muscle wanted to unwind.

"This couch is so comfortable." I yawned, leaning into Gil's shoulder.

"Beats a carriage bench."

"Or a gun turret," I said with a chuckle.

We were silent for a moment, soaking up the warmth from the fire that was flooding around us. Distantly, I could hear Nola working with dishes in the kitchen. Potentially my last blood relative, and we were in her sitting room at last.

Gil's fingers laced through mine. "Are you all right?"

Nodding, I let my eyes wander the room. "Just a bit nervous. I can't believe we're finally here." A quaint little room was the destination we'd risked our lives for. Or so I hoped. I was tired of fighting. Tired of searching, and running, and grieving without end. If there were no answers there, then it was very possible that there were no answers *anywhere*.

After a short time, Nola reappeared with a wooden tray bearing a tea set and pastries. My stomach growled at the sight. I waited politely until she'd daintily poured the steaming drink from the round floral teapot. Immediately, I fixated on the teacup that was passed to me. Purple, crystal… utterly familiar. For a moment, I was back in the black pit, kept company only by a stranger I could not see. Raising my eyes to meet Nola's, I found her watching me with a curious twinkle in her eye.

"Who are you?" she asked, our hands on either side of the saucer.

"I'm the only child of Starla Torril."

Shock stole across her features. She quickly released the saucer, sending hot liquid splashing over the side onto my hands. When my face twisted with pain, Nola immediately bumbled apologies as she snatched the tea towel and attended to me.

"Oh, dear! I'm so sorry! Here, let me take that for you."

When we'd settled again, she carefully refilled my tea and took the chair adjacent. Her eyes swept over me with wonder. "You're… forgive me for staring, but I just had no idea you…" A rush of air escaped her. "Existed."

Disappointment pinched me. Was I some sort of awful secret? "I'm afraid Manne didn't give me many details about her side of the family. We lived in Silis."

"And you traveled all this way?"

A lump formed in my throat. It took every bit of self-control not to fall apart. Thankfully, Gil rescued me.

"I assume news has not yet reached Basillian."

Nola's brows drew together. "News? What news?"

Heaviness hung in the air.

"King Wendil was deposed. There have been attacks all over the kingdom—"

"Silis has fallen," I finished numbly. "And it's because of me." Silence followed. Nola's eyes rested on me patiently. I picked my wits off the floor and continued. "We won't be staying long here either. I'm being..." The word felt like poison slipping from my tongue. "...pursued."

"Your kind never have it easy, I'm afraid."

I gaped at her. "What did you say?"

A sympathetic smile lifted her lips. "I know what you are, dear. Your grandmanne was a paver too. And her grandpanne before her."

Shock hit me. Gil took the teacup as I absently passed it his way. To hear it confirmed from someone I had reason to trust was overwhelming. "A-are you...?"

She shook her head. "No. It skips a generation, but it chooses only one. Mara—that's what we called her—was my twin sister. She was special from the day she was born. Panne said he knew it from the moment he laid eyes on her."

The tears came out of nowhere. No sooner had I wiped them away when another wave came. Nola rose from her chair and fetched me a handkerchief. *Mara.* Deep in the black pit, she sustained me. My own grandmanne. A piece of my own spirit, wandering back to this plane to help me in my time of need.

"You look like you could use a hot meal and some rest," said Nola, gently grasping my elbow. "Why don't you come with me and I'll set you up in one of my guest rooms?" She cast a doubtful glance at Gil. "Are you matched?"

I sniffled. "Not yet."

"Well, no matter. I have another room to spare. I wouldn't dream of sending you both anywhere this time of dark."

Her kindness washed over me like a warm blanket. And she was *family*. I saw it in her eyes—hints of Manne. I wondered if she could see hints of her in me, too.

Accepting her hospitality, we were taken to her kitchen for a bowl of sweetmeat stew before being ushered up to the second floor to our rooms. My legs smarted on the stairs, but the sight of the bed with the white down duvet was worth every step. Green and gold-striped wallpaper and a slight smell of must covered the walls, but I wouldn't have complained for all the crysts in the world.

After taking Gil to his room down the hall, Nola returned to assist me. A small wardrobe near the head of the bed contained old dresses, with the drawer underneath holding nightgowns and underthings. She smiled wistfully as she laid out a long, soft blue nightgown with a tiny, green floral print.

"This was your grandmanne's when she was young. It's outdated now, but I've tried to keep everything in good condition. Might be a hair short on you. You're a great deal taller than she was."

I fingered the ruffles at the neckline. "What was she like?"

"Well." She walked over to a painting on the wall. Two little girls with long, violet hair and eyes, deep blue skin, and matching yellow dresses sat side-by-side with their hands folded demurely in their laps. "She was a bit wild, I suppose you could say. Never quite fit in with the other children. Bounding here and there, keeping Manne up at night. We might've looked the same, but we were as different as could be. It kept us balanced, though." As she reminisced, her fingers gently ran over the image of the girl on the right, a soft smile lighting her lips.

A small chord of jealousy struck me. All I had left of my childhood were memories. Everything else was lying in the burned rubble of my home. If there was even a chance that Panne was truly alive, I would have him too. But like everything else, I didn't know what to think or believe anymore.

"Her husband has passed too?"

Nola grew uncomfortable. "Yes. Although he wasn't your grandpanne by blood. She was very tight-lipped about that."

Another missing piece to the puzzle that is me. I hid my disappointment with a nonchalant bob of my head.

"I'll show you some more family mementos on the next rise. Let's get you ready for bed, shall we?" Light returned to her face, bunching up the sweet wrinkles around her eyes.

"All right. Oh! I do have one other question to ask you."

"Ask anything you like, dear. I'm sure you have many."

Wringing my hands, my eyes danced around my feet. "Do you know of a priest that can perform a... wedding?"

A sly half-smile split her cheek. "Feeling anxious, are we?"

I blushed furiously. "I-I, um—"

"It's all right," she said with a laugh. "I was young once too, you know. I know of one who is a friend of the family. But for now—*rest*. Would you like a bath first?"

"A bath would be *heavenly*."

Nola shuffled toward the door. "It's occupied by your beau right now, but I'll come to fetch you when it's ready for you." She paused, turning to eye me thoughtfully. "You really do look like her, you know."

"Mara?"

She smiled. "Your manne."

When I was left alone at last, I found myself filled with gratitude. There was a small mirror hanging on the wall across from the foot of the bed. My hands went to my cheeks as I gazed into it. Did I really take after her so much? A sigh escaped me. I would've given anything to see her again, if only for one last time. Her sage advice would be monumental. Gil aside, Manne was the only one that understood me. Or... was she?

The painting hung across the room, the bright eyes of the two little girls watching me. Mara's was slightly brighter. It was awe-striking to think that we'd met in the most unusual of circumstances. She might have been there with me now, watching from beyond the veil of life and death, however thin that may be. Was it she who had shown me the location in the book? Did a soul paver's power live on long after their life had ceased?

So many questions swam around in my head. My temples ached. Sleep beckoned me from the cozy bed. Without Gil, it may be a restless night, but at least we would close our eyes under the same roof. And the next rise... a smile lit my face as my fingers brushed the cool stone at my chest. He would be mine forever, for however long that may be.

No sooner had those sweet thoughts danced through my mind that they flew away. Upon returning my attention to the mirror, I stifled a horrified cry. A dark scene had replaced my reflection. In the center stood the candle.

Cold seeped into the room, and the lamps flickered. The bedpost met my back as my chest heaved frantically. *I'm awake! No no no no, this can't be happening!*

"*Come...*"

The voice was like a soothing stream, beckoning me to cross the space between us. A pull within my spirit wanted to guide me there—to the place where the light was gone, save for one singular source. I could feel the gentle, whispering wind graze my cheek.

When the lights cut out entirely, only the small glow from the candle leaked across the hardwood floor. My feet barely touched the warm edge of the light. All life had been sucked away and fed to the monster in the mirror. I was still in the room, but it was cold as ice. Surrounded only by darkness and death, the source of life was before me.

Slowly, I stepped forward, eager for warmth, despite my rattled nerves and all-encompassing fear. As I did, the calm voice returned.

"*Come, young one. You needn't be afraid.*"

Quaking all over, I took yet another step. My volition was weakening. The warmth was drawing me in. A gentle dance of fear and longing swayed me forward. Shimmering light lifted from my skin and mingled with that of the candle. I could feel the irresistible, prickling thrum of power surging through my veins, finding its way outward, pulling me along with it.

I could no longer pull my eyes from the brilliance. The more I gazed, the more it beckoned. Light shifted into a loving caress. Hard ground slowly fell away from my feet, and the light grew closer as the tips of my toes lightly dragged the floor. Like a child being coaxed in for an embrace, the glow surrounded me, filled me, drawing me across the room.

No more resistance.

"*That's it, come home. Come dance among the stars.*"

The blackness surrounding me burst forth into infinite colors of light. I was no longer in a room, but in a sea of stars that gently rotated around me and the steady flame of the candle. My hair floated in wispy, radiant locks. I *was* light.

I floated closer and closer to the candle. My fingertips stretched out before me—to the source of power and of life. I couldn't be afraid anymore. Not here among the universe. Not when I was where my home awaited. Warmth flooded me like a soothing bath; like Manne's arms, wrapped around me as she told me the story of our origin. The story of *this*.

Just as I grazed the edges of the candle's heat, the stars and the blessed light were ripped away from me. I was falling. *Screaming.* The hard floor smacked against my body. As the darkness receded, the room came back into view. I lay among shards of glass.

Withered hands cupped my face and then looped under my arm just as the room lights flickered back to life. Nola's fearful eyes gazed down at me. "Are you all right?"

In utter shock, I let her help me to my feet. The mirror lay shattered on the floor, among pieces of a broken clock. "I... I-I don't know..."

The bedroom door flew open, and Gil frantically rushed in, a white towel wrapped around his waist. "What happened? Are you okay?"

Nola faced Gil with darkened eyes. "The Pandemonium Candle beckons her strongly."

Once out of the glass, I sank down onto the bed, trying to grasp what had just happened. "I don't understand. I was awake this time. And in the mirror..." My gaze danced to the space on the wall where the round mirror once hung, a faded spot on the wallpaper the only evidence that it was ever there. Even now, my spirit reached out for the ghost of light. A shudder ran through me.

Warm hands grasped the sides of my face, gently drawing back to Gil. He inspected me closely, face twisted in concern. "You're safe now. It's all right."

Nola huffed. "She's not safe *anywhere!*"

Gil scowled at her. "What do you mean by that?"

"I *mean* her time is running short. Once it starts calling, it doesn't stop. Though she's young enough that she may be able to fight it a while longer than most."

"What? What happens when her time runs out?" asked Gil, more demanding.

I snapped, shoving Gil's hands away as I stood. "Stop talking about me like I'm not in the room!" He floundered as I stalked across the room toward the door.

As my hand touched the knob, Nola spoke firmly. "You shouldn't be alone, Ellette. Not now."

Clenching my eyes shut, I touched my forehead to the door. "I just want to take a bath, please. *Alone.*" Before they could protest any further, I slipped from the room and found my way to the bathroom, locking myself away to marinate in my sorrows.

* * *

It was sometime later that I exited the bathroom to find a now-fully clothed Gil sitting directly across the hall, just snapping his eyes back open. He threw me a sleepy smile and rose from the floor. I gripped the towel around me and peeked around.

"She just went to bed," he said quietly. "I'm to keep an eye on you."

Nodding, I went back to my room, Gil in tow. I didn't argue when he shut the door behind us. Truth be told, I knew I wouldn't catch a wink of sleep without him, anyway.

The floor had been swept clean of debris, and the room was back to being an ordinary one. I still got strange chills when I looked at the wall where the mirror had been. Thankfully, it had been the only such portal in the space.

Gil lay on the bed, hands tucked behind his head, eyes on the ceiling as I found underwear and then quickly changed into the nightgown laid out for me. I could see the weariness dragging his features. Too many long rises and sleepless sets. He looked thinner than he used to be.

I dug through a small bureau in the corner and found a comb. Wordlessly, I climbed onto the bed, sat cross-legged next to him, and began raking through my damp hair. It was comforting to feel the warmth of his thigh next to mine and to see the gentle glow it caused.

"I have something for you." He reached into his nightshirt pocket and extended his hand. In his palm lay a golden ring with a large, white, oval stone. I accepted it with confusion.

"Where did you get this?"

"Nola asked me to give it to you. She said it was your grandmanne's."

I ran my fingertip over the smooth coolness of the stone before slipping it on. "It's beautiful."

He ran his knuckle down my bare arm. "Are you all right?"

My eyes flicked to the ceiling. "You ask me that a lot."

"Well, I'm genuinely interested."

"I…" Pausing, I considered telling him the truth—that I was far from it, that I was scared out of my mind, and part of me still felt the haunting pull of the light. Instead, I managed a half-grin and lied. "I'm all right. *Exhausted.* But all right."

With a gentle tug, Gil pulled me back and wrapped me in his arms. He placed a soft kiss on the top of my head.

"I love you, Ellie."

I responded through a yawn. "I love you, too."

Surrounded by the security of the warm glow, we drifted off to sleep. I was so exhausted, I didn't have a single dream.

Chapter 28

Starlight shone through the lace curtains, gently pulling me out of my deep slumber. I was warm, tucked in Gil's arms under the soft sheets and heavy duvet. It'd been forever since we'd had such a restful set. I never wanted to leave our little haven.

Gil shifted behind me, stretching his legs with a yawn before curling up again and pulling me closer. As much as I relished in his embrace, the smell of something savory hit my nose. My stomach roared.

"I think Nola's cooking breakfast."

"Mmm-hmm."

"It would be rude to keep her waiting."

Moving the curtain of my hair, Gil's lips found the dip of my neck. "It would." He began planting nipping kisses along my shoulder, gently pulling down the sleeve of my nightgown. "It would be terrible…"

Giggling, I yanked my nightgown to its original position and wriggled free of his grasp. "You are still the worst!"

In a flash, Gil whipped me down and had me pinned to the bed by my wrists. That sly grin of his made its appearance once more as he peered down at me in victory. I saw him eying my ribs and knew another tickling session was about to begin. Thinking quickly, I suddenly remembered something.

"Nola knows of a priest."

His eyes snapped back to mine, losing their jest. "She what?"

Smiling broadly, I shifted under him. "We could be matched this rise."

The grip on my wrists softened as Gil stared blankly. *"This* rise?"

It was not the reaction I was expecting. "Well, yes… is that all right?"

In the blink of an eye, his smile had returned. "Of course! Sorry, I just… hadn't realized it would be so soon."

Something burned in my gut. My face fell. "Gil… are you having second thoughts?"

He froze.

The time that crept by without a response only confirmed the answer. Disappointment washed over me. I tried to hide it behind a smile, but it only faltered. "I guess that's a 'yes'…"

Gil sat up, still straddling my legs, and buried his face in his hands with a deep sigh. "Ellie, I—"

"It's okay," I said, not even convincing myself. "I guess we *are* being kind of impulsive." Sitting up, I shifted until Gil got off me and sat on the edge of the bed, his focus a million miles away. When he didn't respond, my heart sped up. Yet another confirmation. With my anxiety rising, I slipped out of bed and went to the wardrobe to go through the motions of getting dressed. A dowdy, green, calf-length dress with long sleeves and a high collar would have to suffice. I yanked my nightgown off and threw it to the floor.

"Listen, I don't mean to say that I don't want to marry you, it's just that—"

"I get it, Gil." I was snappy, but my irritation was surging. "You don't want to do it now."

"You're angry with me."

I paused, fingering the buttons on the dress in my hands. "I don't know what I am right now."

"Ellie…" He came to my side, gently laying a hand on my shoulder. "You know I love you, right? Nothing will ever change that."

"Then why wait? After all, *you* asked *me?*"

He was silent, which only increased my agitation. I shrugged his hand off my shoulder and pulled on my dress. I briefly swept my eyes over him. "You'd better get dressed or we'll be late for breakfast."

Just when I thought he would open his mouth to respond, there was a knock at the door.

"I've made you some breakfast," called Nola sweetly.

"We'll be right down," I replied, careful not to betray my fouling mood. Quickly, I braided my hair as I listened to her retreating footsteps. Gil stood there, silently watching me. I wanted to shake his eyes off my cheek, but I simply ignored him, not ready for the fight I knew was bubbling under the surface.

At last, he sighed in frustration and stalked from the room. I watched the door close firmly behind him with a pinch of regret. We'd quarreled plenty of times over the years, but this was different. This time, our hearts were lying raw on the line. And time was not on our side.

Nola's words floated through my mind. *"...her time is running short..."* I could feel the pull underneath the beats of my heart. My eyes fell. The glow in my chest was now noticeable, even in the starlight. I clutched my hand over it. Would they notice it too? Through my dress? Gil hadn't said anything. Maybe only I saw it?

Panicking, I swished through the hanging garments of the wardrobe, looking for anything to cover it. *A sweater. That'll do.* It was purple, missing a button in the middle, but at least it was another layer. Stuffing my arms into the sleeves, my fingers shook as I quickly worked the buttons. There was no mirror to check myself with, and I was too afraid to gaze into one anyhow. Gripping the edge of the wardrobe, I rested my forehead on my wrist and sighed. It would've been more convenient to hide away and give in to the swirl of emotion, but Nola was waiting patiently, and I was starving.

After finding a pair of brown slip-on shoes that were only slightly snug, I made my way downstairs to the kitchen, where steaming plates of eggs, thin steak, and porridge awaited. Nola snapped her book closed and smiled.

"Good rise, dear!" The smile faltered. "Where is Gillion?"

"He's getting dressed. He'll be down shortly, I'm sure." I cheerfully took the seat beside her.

Her eyes remained on the stairway. "He's not supposed to leave you alone."

My hand hovered over the spoon as I followed her gaze. "Oh... Well, I'm not alone now. You're with me."

"I am." Shaking her head, Nola returned to her usual cheerfulness. "You'd better eat before it gets cold."

Obediently, I spooned the sticky, sweet porridge into my mouth, which now felt dry. It was delicious, with bits of dried fruit and nuts mixed in. Better than Teli's ever was, though I felt guilty for even daring to think so. I missed her terribly. I missed them all. Thoughts of Silis encroached on my already-spinning mind. Thoughts of Panne, possibly alive. I still hadn't told Gil about my vision. There were a lot of things I still needed to tell him, and I had a feeling he had things on his chest as well. Yet I'd just shut him out.

Even my empty stomach couldn't settle with all the delicious food. I kept waiting and waiting for Gil to appear. Nola attempted to chat about the local news, keeping the conversation light. My responses were robotic. I was eager to see his face. Was he purposely avoiding me now? Had I been too harsh? A million scenarios spun through my mind.

I was so caught up in my thoughts that when he finally appeared on the stairs, it took me by surprise and I dropped my fork, quickly standing to my feet. He was breathtakingly handsome in a black button-down shirt with the sleeves rolled up to mid-forearm, exposing his strong muscles. Black trousers that seemed nearly tailored to him graced his powerful legs. Even his hair was braided back in the way most becoming. That familiar old flutter tickled my chest, and I smiled like a schoolgirl again.

When his eyes met mine, however, they did not reciprocate the same joy. Quickly, he avoided my gaze again.

"Good rise! Come eat, there's plenty left," said Nola.

With a nod, Gil came to the table, glancing back down the hall toward the door. After thanking Nola, he ate in silence, never once acknowledging my presence. I toyed with my food, attempting to keep my composure.

"I'm so glad to see my panne's clothes fit you. They've been going to waste in that wardrobe. He was tall like you, you know." Nola went on, talking about my great grandpanne. I tried to listen and soak in the precious tidbits the best I could. My family history was important to me. But so was the man at my side. My nerves were unsettled.

Subtly, I went to rest my hand on Gil's knee, but he stood the moment I touched him.

"I need to head back to the inn. We never made it back last set, and I'm sure our companions are worried," he explained to Nola as he stepped from the table. "Thank you for breakfast."

Immediately, I stood and followed him, smiling back at Nola. "We will be back later—" I ran into Gil.

"No," he said sternly, "stay here."

I frowned. "What? Why?"

Though his icy eyes bore into mine, they looked straight through me. "Stay with Nola."

Before I could argue, he turned on his heel and stalked toward the door. I pursued in a panic. "Gil? Wait! Just stop for a moment?" Just as he reached the door, I caught up to him and wrapped a hand around his elbow. At last, he stopped and rolled his eyes.

"Ellie, please let go of my arm?" he said through clenched teeth.

My brows rose as I stepped around to his side. "Wow, I got a 'please' out of you. That's progress, at least."

He opened the door and pulled me out to the front porch, glancing back to ensure we weren't followed. Fire was in his eyes, and not the kind of desire. "What? What is it? Am I not allowed to go anywhere without your permission now?"

Taken aback by his biting tone, my jaw slackened. "Without my—Gil, what the hellfire are you talking about?"

"This! This is what I'm talking about!"

"Okay, you're not making any sense, I'm afraid."

He groaned and ran a hand down his face. "Ellie, we've been together our whole lives. But we've only been *together* a short amount of time. And I want to be with you forever. But with everything that's happened, I'm just... overwhelmed."

I crossed my arms in a huff. "Then why did you ask me to marry you?"

"Because it's all I've ever wanted! To be your husband, to have a family with you, and live long happy lives! And we were just... in the moment, and I was so happy that you loved me back..." He stepped the edge of the porch and pressed his shoulder into the post, gazing across the city.

"But now you're worried we wouldn't have any of that," I finished. "You're worried I'm a poor investment because of—" My hand went to my chest as a lump formed in my throat. "—because of what I am."

"Ellie, I didn't say—"

"But that's what you *mean.* It's okay to admit it, Gil. I'd rather have your brutal honesty than a false bubble of hope."

Gil abandoned his stance, brows knitted over watery eyes. "You want my brutal honesty?" We slowly counter-stepped across the porch.

"Yes," I replied boldly.

"*My brutal truth* is that I am scared."

My eyes widened as my back hit the wall. "Scared of me?"

He paused, stopping just shy of reaching me. "I'm scared that—" Gingerly, he reached a hand out to brush my flushed cheek. "When the time comes, I won't be able to save you. I don't want to fail you. Not as a husband, especially."

Hearing the emotion strangling him, it took every ounce of strength I had to keep my wits. I caught his hand and cuddled it to my chest. "I don't care what you call yourself. What we call each other." I bit my lower lip to stop it from quivering. "But I don't need you to fix anything. I don't need you to save me."

Gil posted his arm next to my head, eyes drilling deeply into mine. "Then what is it you need, Ellie? My hands are empty. I have nothing I can give you. I can't even give you a wedding," he said bitterly.

We stood there, staring intensely at each other. There was no way I could possibly convey how much he meant to me. Not in a way that he would believe. His pain ran deep and was pouring out in a molten river. I could see it in his eyes. We'd been through so much in such a short amount of time. So much robbed from us.

"All I ask," I placed my free palm on his chest, over his wildly beating heart. Light spread around my fingertips. "Is for *this.*"

"Ellie—"

"It's *all* I ask for, Gil. Because you are more than enough for me. As you are. Even the broken parts." When his eyes fell, I gripped his chin and forced them back to mine. "And regardless of how much time we may or may not have, I have no intention of being anything but yours."

I pulled him in and met his lips with my own, still holding his hand to my chest. Finally, his resistance melted away, and he pressed into me. Driving a slow, deep passion, we sought each other. With tears running down his cheeks, Gil kissed me like it was the first time and the last. I held nothing back, brushing the salty streams away with my thumb. If there were any way I could give him the beating heart from my chest to mend the cracked one in his own, I would've done it that very moment. As it was, all I could do was pull him close and let our light mingle.

At last, Gil broke the kiss and tucked me to his chest. We stood there on the front porch, holding each other. I breathed in his scent and memorized every point at which we touched.

"Come back to the inn with me," he breathed into my hair. "Just for a while." His lips dropped to my ear. "I want to make love to you." The heavy way in which he uttered those words sent tingles chasing through me. His lips grazed my cheek as I nodded. "I'll let Nola know we'll be gone."

He disappeared through the door with a smile.

Chapter 29

Hours later, I awoke with a start. We'd been in the throes of heated passion from the moment we reached our room and eventually fell asleep when all energy was spent. My pure bliss, however, had been robbed from me the moment I closed my eyes.

The candle had spoken to me again, this time ripping me from Gil's arms. The universe was thrown into ugly chaos, swallowing up all that was good. None of the beauty of the stars was there to greet me, only the darkness. It ripped the air from my lungs and cracked me into something monstrous. All of my light, stolen.

Sitting up in bed, I ran my fingers through my tangled hair and tried to stop shaking. It was futile. I was thoroughly unsettled. Gil still peacefully slept at my side. A flash of jealousy seized me. He was so… normal. I was glad of it, but it also meant that he couldn't understand what I was going through.

I slipped from the bed and got dressed. As I did, I saw how brightly my chest was glowing, catching the cut prisms of the jewel hanging from my neck. If Gil had noticed, he hadn't breathed a word. Surely he must have? Our light of passion had been blinding, but this one was different. Even with the sweater, it still shined. Ached, even. My hand covered it, only for the veins to be illuminated through my skin.

A hand touched my shoulder. "Are you all right?"

I jumped. *How long has he been standing there?*

"Of course. Just getting dressed. We're all supposed to head back to Nola's soon, remember?" My smile was tight.

His arms linked around my waist from behind. "Ah, that's right. We get to introduce Hunter to decent cooking."

Hugging my chest, I tried to cover my divergent glow. It was nearly impossible to conceal. Gil's chin rested in the crook of my shoulder.

"You don't have to hide it from me, Ellie." Gently, he grasped my arms and lowered them, folding them in with his instead.

Wiggling uncomfortably, I left his embrace for the bathroom. "I know." Gil sighed and began dressing without further argument.

I bent over the sink, splashing cool water on my face. *Anything* to get the dreamlike fog to dissipate. It was disorienting. When I finished, I dried myself off with the soft white hand towel… and then made a mistake.

I looked into the mirror.

I didn't see the candle. I saw *him*. Staring back at me from another room, just as shocked to see me. The ache in my chest immediately grew into a throb.

Kromer slowly reached out to me, his fingers brushing the glass on the other side. I recoiled, my hand clamping over my mouth. And then my eyes fell to his bare chest, where a light pulsated brightly beneath his skin in perfect time with mine.

"No…"

Horrified, I backed away until the back of my knees hit the bathtub, sending me flailing backward with a screech. Gil was in there instantly.

"Ellie!"

He assisted me out of the basin, and I immediately turned my back to the mirror, panicking. "Is he gone?"

"Is who gone? There's no one here but you and me."

I dared to turn and peek over my shoulder. The reflection was back to normal. Breathing a shuddered sigh of relief, I pressed my palm to my forehead.

"Ellie, what's going on?"

I exited the bathroom, not wanting to press my luck. "I want to get out of here."

Gil eyed me in concern as I re-braided my hair. "What happened?"

Reluctantly, I confessed, unable to look him in the eye. "I saw Kromer."

"Wait, you what?"

"In the mirror. He was there, looking back at me through some other mirror. I think."

Gil's eyes widened. "You're saying you saw our mortal enemy through a *mirror*… And you've been dreaming about him, too?"

There was a slight hint of jealousy in his tone that drove a flash of anger through me. Red light immediately flared over my skin as my eyes snapped to his. "I have *no* control over this, Gil!"

His eyes hardened. "Clearly."

"You know what? You can ride with Hunter back to Nola's." I shoved past him toward the door, causing him to hiss in pain as our light collided at the shoulder.

"Where do you think you're going?"

I whirled around and glared. "I'm *walking*!"

"Not alone, you're not—"

"Oh yes, I am! You don't like being told what to do? Well, neither do I."

Gil crossed his arms and narrowed his eyes. "*Fine.* Don't blame me when you turn into a damned candle!"

I froze, gaping at him. Hurt lanced through me like a knife. And he showed no signs of apologizing, only seething frustration.

With a resentful nod, I turned and left the room, slamming the door behind me. I heard Gil curse loudly, but he didn't pursue. That hurt most of all.

By the time I reached the lobby, I was fighting hot tears. I was so distraught that I failed to notice Lydia until I ran into her upon exiting. She stumbled into the doorjamb, and I caught her by the arm, apologizing profusely.

"I'm so sorry!" I said as I righted her.

She smiled, though her eyes shone with concern. "It's all right. No harm done." We stepped back into the lobby and Lydia pulled me into an obscured corner, away from the curious eyes of the other guests. "Ellie, what's happening?"

Self-consciously, I hugged my arms over my glowing chest, but the red light still lingered elsewhere. Closing my eyes, I attempted to slow my breathing. Lydia waited patiently at my side for a response. It came out in a hush. "I don't know how to explain it, but I think I'm in trouble."

"I can see... here." I heard the rustle of fabric and opened my eyes to find her removing the over-sized black coat she was wearing.

"What are you doing?"

Lydia wrapped the coat around my shoulders. "Put this on and try to calm down."

I obeyed with furrowed brows. The coat swamped me, falling almost to my ankles, with the sleeves already rolled up multiple times. But it dampened the light. Slowly, the red aura faded. "Where did you get this?"

"It's Hunter's."

"Hunter's? Why do you have..." When I saw the color fill her cheeks, I had my answer. Gil's hunch was correct. I noted her new purple silk tunic and black trousers, and the shopping bag at her feet. On her neck, partially covered by her long hair, was a mark of passion. It surprised me at first, but I decided not to press her. "Oh."

"So, where were you going?" She swept her eyes back across the lobby. "Where's Gil?"

"I, um, I'm going to my great aunt's. Walking, that is. Alone."

Alone. The word hit me in the chest. Violet light immediately flared out to encase me.

"Oh, honey." Lydia gingerly reached her arm around my shoulders. "It sounds like a walk will do you good. How about I walk with you?"

Just then, I caught sight of Gil coming down the stairs. Our eyes met across the lobby. He was still sour, but headed toward us immediately. Before he reached me, Lydia intercepted and shoved the shopping bag at his chest with a tight smile.

"Be a dear and see that Hunter gets this?"

Gil frowned and started to protest, but Lydia whirled around, grabbed my arm, and hauled me toward the door, waving behind her. "Thanks, Gil!"

We were out the door before he could raise a single word of protest. I glanced back over my shoulder and caught his hardened stare and pursed lips. Rolling my eyes, I stuck my nose in the air and marched ahead into the crowded street.

Lydia squeezed my arm. "That's it. You just let him pout. Men can be such children sometimes."

I resisted the urge to look back. "Yes, they most certainly can."

"Now..." We came to an intersection and turned right. "What's going on with your lights?"

"Well, it's complicated."

She cracked a grin. "*Well*, we've got plenty of time, and I've got an open ear."

As we walked, I spilled all the fears and frustrations I'd been bottling up. I told her about seeing Kromer, my loss of control, even my spats with Gil. To my relief, she quietly listened without judgment.

We meandered through the city streets for what felt like hours. At last, we came to where things were quieter, heading uphill toward the sparser areas.

Lydia smiled. "Well, we're almost there."

I looked around. I'd been so caught up in my jabbering that I hadn't paid an iota of attention to where we were actually going. Sure enough, however, Nola's house was looming ahead at the top of the hill. Confused, I slowed to a stop.

"How did we..."

Lydia wouldn't look me in the eye, and her smile faltered. "What's wrong? It's right there." She motioned toward the house.

Slowly, I let go of her arm and stepped away, a growing sense of foreboding washing over me. "Lydia, how did you know the way here?"

"You led us here, silly!" she laughed. It was a nervous laugh.

Instinct took over the longer I looked at her. She was lying. And I'd just made the biggest mistake of my life. Out of the corner of my eye, I saw them—closing in like insects. Figures in black uniform, ducking in and out of the shadows, around corners, hiding in the foliage.

"No..." They were coming from every direction now. "No!" My molten eyes snapped to hers. "You! *You!* This whole time! It was *you* leading them to me!"

Lydia gave no response. Her solemn expression said it all. I'd finally figured out the cold, hard truth about someone I thought was a friend.

"ELLIE!"

I whipped my head toward Gil's echoing voice as he came bounding up the hill, fast and furious. My heart leaped with hope. Rearing up, I readied to bound, when suddenly a sharp pain lanced my neck. All the feeling rapidly fled my body, and I collapsed into the arms of a strange man. As my vision swam, Lydia stood over me, giving rushed instructions to the guard. She looked down at me one last time before the world faded to black, and I felt the full brunt of her betrayal.

Chapter 30

It was cold. Shivering uncontrollably, I shifted under the blankets as the surrounding blurs slowly resolved. A soft pillow cradled my head. Every muscle ached, even lying on a plush surface. I groaned and squeezed my eyes as a shock of pain went through my temple.

A warm hand covered mine. An echoey male voice spoke. "It'll pass. It's just a side effect of the tranquilizer."

"Gil?" There was no response beyond a thumb brushing the side of mine. The warmth from the glow wrapped around us. It was a familiar, comforting gesture. As hellish as I felt, I relished in his presence. We'd parted on soured terms, and after everything that happened…

The blurs disappeared as I opened my eyes again. A stark white ceiling stared back at me. White walls with no decoration… and two square windows filled with stars. Sparse furniture. A strange ring of pressure clamped around my ankle. I moved my leg and heard the clanking of metal.

"Would you like another blanket?"

The voice was clearer now. I whipped my head to the side and found Kromer staring back at me, patiently awaiting a response. He sat in a chair at my bedside, hand still resting gently on top of mine. With a sharp gasp, I ripped my hand away and tried to retreat across the bed, only to find I was still too dizzy and nearly passed out again.

Kromer rose and fetched a thick blanket from the bottom drawer of the polished steel armoire. Before I could protest, he flicked it through the air and carefully tucked it around me. I watched him with wild eyes.

226

"Where am I?"

He smiled. "My ship."

"What?" This time I scrambled back toward the headboard of the bed, the shackle around my ankle pulling the chain taut. I was a captive. "No! Let me go!" Repeatedly, I yanked my leg away, but it held fast. There was nothing within reach that could serve as a weapon. Gathering up the blankets in my arms, I hugged them to my chest and glared daggers at Kromer. He hardly flinched, standing across the room with his hands casually in his pockets. Light pulsed through the fabric of his black button-down shirt. Intrusive memories of his bare chest and the brilliance of the glow that shone through it speared my mind. Angry, I forced my eyes elsewhere.

"You'd better calm yourself, Ellie. You're going to turn red." Throwing me a wink, Kromer grabbed the chair and moved it out of arm's reach before sitting again.

If he sought to provoke me, it was working. Red immediately flared. Still shaking, I only attempted to calm myself because it hurt my muscles. "I don't advise you to come anywhere near me," I spat.

This amused him. "That's the strongest chain on this ship. You're not going anywhere. Not unless I say so."

"So I'm your prisoner now? Is that it?"

"That's really up to you."

"Then I choose to leave. *Now*."

"Go ahead then. Leave."

I wanted to leap across the room and claw his eyes out. "You're mocking me."

Kromer rose from the chair and fished something small from his pocket. He strolled over to the bed and flicked back the blanket covering my ankle. My stomach lurched when I saw the size of the silver shackle. Redness was already forming around the edges from my fidgeting.

Without another word, he slid the key into the padlock and clicked it open, freeing me. I immediately flew from the opposite side of the bed, poised to run, but the ground met me with a smack. I was still weak. Shaking like a leaf, I squeezed my eyes shut to shove down the roiling nausea. Whatever it was they gave me, it was far too strong.

"Let me help you." Arms scooped me up like a child and I was powerless to do much more than squirm and spit curses through chattering teeth. He brought me to a window, and immediately I ceased my protests.

Gone were the stars I knew, replaced by a vast blackness in which they sparsely stretched on for eternity. No trees, no grass, no ground. Only darkness. My fingers brushed the cold glass.

"We're... the heavens..."

"Your homeworld is that little blue speck below and to the right."

Tears leaped to my eyes. It was so small, barely noticeable as more than a piece of blue dust on the window, perhaps. *This can't be real!* A ragged cry tore from my throat.

"No, no, no, no! Take me back!"

Kromer returned me to the bed, where I drew my knees to my chest and clamped my hands over my eyes, desperate to awaken from the nightmare. "Take me home!"

"This is your home for now. Or it could be your prison. Your choice."

"I don't know what you mean!"

He paused. "I'll explain later—*after* you've had your rest. You're getting too worked up—"

"Too worked up?" I glared fire at him, the red glow intensely flaring around me. *"Too worked up?* You stole me from my home!"

"I—"

"Where's Gil?"

My question bounced off deaf ears. His eyes hardened. "You need rest." Before I could interrogate him further, he turned and stalked from the room, the lock clicking from the outside. Mumbled instructions beyond the door told me he did not leave me unguarded, either.

Had I not been so physically drained, I would've flung myself at the door. As it was, I was fortunate to be left unchained, but it was a cruel twist of fate that the chain was unneeded. Curling up on the bed, I gathered up the blankets to the best of my ability and soaked them with my tears until I fell asleep.

* * *

Something shook my shoulder. I awoke with a start. A pair of brown eyes peered down at me. The woman smiled, bright white teeth slashing her brown cheeks.

"Good evening, Ellie," she greeted cheerfully. Her black jumpsuit gave me pause. One of Kromer's people, of course. I recoiled into the blankets.

"I'm sorry?"

"I know. Time is disorienting when you're in space." She reached her hand out and gently touched my shoulder. "I'm Wanda. I'm going to be helping you from now on."

I bolted upright, my strength having returned at last. "Can you take me home?"

Her gaze averted uncomfortably. "I, um, I'm afraid I won't be able to help you there. But I can get you ready for dinner?" A smile returned to her face.

"Can I just eat here?"

She laughed and walked to the armoire. "Here? When His Majesty wants to dine with you? No, you'll be eating in his private dining quarters."

I froze and watched as she pulled out a long, deep-green cut of swishy fabric on a hanger. Eying it in admiration, she held it up for me to see. It hardly looked like a complete dress. A split sash with some jewels around the neckline and at what I guessed was the waist. My eyes widened.

"What is that?"

Wanda crooked her mouth to one side and arched a brow. "It's your dress, silly! Chosen for you by the king himself."

I wanted to be sick. "I'm not wearing that."

"Well, I'm afraid you don't have much of a choice. He said either you wear that, or the guards will strip you naked and drag you to dinner in the buff."

Horrified, I hugged the blankets. Another choice taken from me. I would've much preferred the dowdy dress and sweater. Perhaps with a sash of blades across my chest.

With a lot of coaxing, Wanda got me unbundled and into the scandalous dress. It connected at the back of my neck and plunged down the front, loosely covering my breasts before meeting the wide ruched waistband. Though the skirt was long, the fabric was so light I felt naked. Cool air caressed the surface of my excessively exposed skin. I fingered the glittering jewels strung like necklaces between the chest panels. They danced in the bright glow.

My hair was curled, and cosmetics applied. My feet were too large for the dainty shoes so I was allowed to go barefoot, with a shackle and long chain my only adornment. When Wanda tried to lead me to the tall mirror to look at her hard work, I vehemently opposed. I knew what I would see there, and it wasn't a young woman in a green dress. When hurt flashed across her face, I felt terrible, but it wasn't something easily explained in the few moments we had left before the dreaded dinner.

The guards were called in. Shackles were attached to my wrists and all my chains joined into one so that they could parade me like a well-dressed wildion through the halls. We passed many people, none of them Celestials. All of them eyed me with curiosity. Some with high-browed desire. I was to be a *thing*. My cheeks burned with humiliation, but I held my head high and kept my eyes trained ahead.

At last, we arrived at a pair of nondescript gray doors with two guards posted outside. The doors opened with a flourish, and they led me in to my demise. It surprised me to find it would be in a long, ornate room with a table that stretched nearly the length of it. A white tablecloth, silver candlesticks, and seating for two dozen stood before me.

At the other end of the table, Kromer waited patiently, standing with his hands gently grasping the back of the head chair. His suit was black with a starched white shirt underneath; less authoritarian and more formal. The moment our eyes met, a soft smile stretched across his face. Then his gazed dragged slowly down, drinking in every inch of me. I wanted to wrap the chains around his throat and watch those eyes bulge from their sockets.

He slowly crossed the room until he stood before me, a smug smirk still on his face. "So happy for you to join me this evening. You look lovely in that dress."

I raised my shackled hands to cover my chest, but he grabbed the bar and gently pulled them back down. "No hiding tonight."

Narrowing my eyes, I ripped my hands back. "And how am I supposed to eat with chains?"

"I'll feed you. Bite by bite." Indignation rose within me and I was about to start loudly protesting when he laughed. "We'll unchain a hand."

"Both hands."

His brow arched. "Pardon?"

"*Both hands.* Or I don't eat."

The idea was rolling around behind those green eyes of his as we stared each other down. At last, he spoke to the guards. "Unchain her hands."

"But, your majesty—"

Kromer's fiery glare snapped to the guard who'd dared to raise a word. "I said unchain her hands!"

His sudden blasting volume caused my ears to ring. I curled my head toward my shoulder and flinched. It served as another reminder of the type of person I was dealing with.

Quickly, they unshackled my wrists and attached my ankle chain to a notch drilled into the floor. I was to be on a short leash at the near the end of the table, closest to the guards. Satisfied, Kromer took the seat adjacent to my left side and nodded to his men, who disappeared from the room. The moment they were gone, a parade of servants filed in, bearing rolling carts of steaming dishes and wine.

I noticed my place setting was curiously absent of a knife, and my food was pre-cut into bite-sized portions. Smart, but disappointing. Annoyed, I picked up my fork and speared steamed greens into my mouth. "I see I'm to be treated like a child this set."

"I wouldn't move my seat at the table for a child."

Unimpressed, I motioned with my fork toward the empty end of the room. "Then why don't you just move back down there? I'm feeling a bit crowded."

Shrugging, Kromer sipped his wine. "It's my table. I'll sit where I want."

"Oh, that's right. I forgot. You're a 'king'." The word felt like vomit on my tongue.

"I am many things."

Many things. I leaned across the table and drilled my glare into his cheek. "You are a *murderer.*"

He paused, fork mid-air, and swiveled his head in my direction. "I am a *conqueror.* Every conquest involves sacrifice."

My blood boiled. "Is that what I am, then? Just another one of your 'conquests'?"

We stare each other down, my heart racing with pent up fury. Thoughts of stabbing him with the fork became more and more prevalent. He never considered the sharp tines of a fork. Just when I was gathering the courage to act on my impulse, the door behind me opened.

"I'm so sorry I'm late."

Immediately, my rage redirected. Lydia, dressed in a simple, deep blue evening gown, strolled into the dining room with servants at her heel. She smiled at Kromer and took the seat at the opposite end of the table. Her meal was quickly served, and the servants retreated once more.

Kromer smiled tightly. "It's quite all right. We were just chatting."

I gripped my fork with white knuckles and stood. *"You!"*

Lydia flinched but would not meet my eyes. "Good evening, Ellie," she greeted quietly before cutting into her meat.

"Ellie, I believe you've met my sister, Rodina."

Eyes flitting between them, my fury only increased. "Your sister? So, you've lied about *everything?*"

She demurred. "Now, Ellie—"

I picked up my plate and launched it across the room, sending it crashing into the wall by her head. She screamed and ducked.

"You betrayed me, *Rodina!* You betrayed Gil! And Hunter! Where are they now, hmm? Did you sacrifice them for your little *conquest* with your brother?"

Rodina locked her pleading eyes on Kromer. "Max! Do something!"

I was thoroughly encased in red. The floor rumbled beneath my feet. Power flooded my veins in molten streams.

"I can take you to your panne, Ellie."

Immediately, my focus snapped back to Kromer, who was now on his feet. "What?"

He held my gaze. "Come with me. I'll take you to him now."

"You're lying—"

"You know I'm not."

My chest heaved. *Panne.* Just the thought of seeing him again nearly sent me barreling from the room. As it was, I was still a prisoner to the whims of the man in front of me. He could be lying. Another trick. But I had little to lose.

Reluctantly, I nodded. The guards were called, my wrist shackles replaced, and Kromer himself led me through a disorienting maze of halls and lifts. I hardly had the presence of mind to track them, anyway. All I could think about was the possibility that I was going to see Panne's face at the end of our journey.

Kromer was quiet as we walked. Only two guards accompanied us, but kept their distance, as if that would somehow put me more at ease when the clanking of chains followed us everywhere we went. The gray ceilings were too low for me to bound, even if I wanted to. Everything was just stark white and gray. Lifeless. It was only there if it served a purpose. The walls felt like a tomb.

At last, we came to a short, nondescript hall. Another pair of guards stood outside a door. With a nod from Kromer, one unlocked the door and admitted us.

The room was dim and sparsely furnished, much like mine. At once, my eyes found the bed across the room, where a large lump lay under the blankets. I saw the slight movement of a rising and falling chest. With a cry, I flew across the room, nearly tripping over my chains. Kromer let them go, and I made it to Panne's bedside.

He lay there, pale and worn, healing bruises on his cheek and forehead. But it was my panne. I'd know him anywhere. The moment I touched his face, his eyes fluttered open and then widened.

"Ellie?"

I burst into tears and touched my cheek to his. Panne's arms wrapped around me, pulling me as close as his weakness would allow.

"Oh, my girl…"

It was so overwhelming to be in his arms—to know he was there, and this was real. I couldn't speak. All I could do was cry and cling to him like a frightened child.

At last, Panne sat me back and swept his eyes over me. They bounced back and forth continuously between the shackles and the brilliant glow in my chest. Heartbreak overshadowed him. I wanted to find something to hide with, but there was no concealing the truth any longer.

"I'll give you two a moment."

As Kromer turned and left the room with guards in tow, I glared at him. Had he not left so abruptly, I would've had the chains around his throat.

"Let it go, Ellie," Panne cautioned.

"I will kill him for what he's done, Panne," I gritted out through clenched teeth.

Panne grasped my hand and retrieved my attention. He was stern. "You will not sully your hands impulsively. I will not see you become a murderess out of spite!"

My jaw dropped. "Spite? Panne, he's destroyed cities and killed our people! He hurt you! Advisor Braxton is dead! And—"

"Justice will be served, my dear. Don't mistake me. The stars will mete out judgment in their time. But you must take extreme caution. You do not know what you are dealing with."

Frustrated, I buried my face in my palm. I knew what I was dealing with. And he wasn't omnipotent. "I'll fight him to the death if I have to."

"I don't think he wants to fight you, my dear."

I felt sick again. I knew what he meant. I wasn't blind to the way Kromer looked at me. Or the reason I was dressed the way I was. My only hope was that it was all a farce and I could expose his trickery.

"I'm supposed to marry Gil," I blurted out, my grief rearing its ugliness. "We… I…" I choked on a sob. "I don't know where he is now."

Panne launched into a coughing fit. I panicked, grasping his hand. "Panne? Panne?" He continued to cough, gasping for air. "I'll get help!" I started to let go, but he gripped my hand firmly and pulled me close.

"No, stay. I'm all right." He breathed heavily, but the coughing subsided.

"Panne, you're sick."

He shook his head. "I've been sick since before we left Silis."

My brows furrowed. "What?"

"I didn't want to worry you. So I hid it as best I could. The stress of all that's happened has..." He coughed again.

"Don't try to talk." Scanning the room, I found a pitcher and a glass. "Here..." Working as best I could around my shackles, I poured a messy glass of water and brought it back to Panne. He sat up just enough to take a few sips before collapsing again in exhaustion.

"Thank you... I'm so tired... all the time."

"Do they have doctors taking care of you?"

Panne nodded. "They've done what they can."

Not the reply I was hoping for. Such finality. I felt a spear in my chest. "Panne..."

He wiped a stream of tears from my cheek. "Don't. You need your strength, too."

"But... I can't lose you twice." Violet light surrounded me.

"So you *do* have the gift."

I sniffled and wiped my eyes. "What?"

Panne smiled. "Your manne talked about it, but I never believed her."

"She told you I was a soul paver?"

He flinched with recalled pain. "Your manne was a wise woman. So many things I took for granted. I'm so sorry, dear."

Manne's gentle face floated to the surface of my memory. We'd all taken her for granted. No one knew just how special she was until she was gone, having laid down her life for mine. For her wildion of a daughter. When she was descended from a soul paver herself, a precious jewel of the heavens.

"I miss her."

"So do I. Every day."

We were silent in our grief for a while, grasping hands. It was all we could do, being prisoners in the vastness of stars, our fate unknown. Hopelessness weighed on us, lurking in the corners. Without Manne, everything felt darker. She was always our strength and pillar. Now, I faced losing Panne too. It was nearly too much to bear.

"Ellie, I want you to listen to me. Whatever happens, you must trust your instincts. And don't let me be a factor."

"What? What are you talking about?" Just then, I heard the key in the lock.

Panne pulled me close and kissed me on the temple. "Be strong, my dear girl. I love you."

"I love you, too. But Panne—"

"Ellie."

I turned to see Kromer standing in the doorway, waiting patiently. My eyes narrowed. "I'm not done."

"Go on, Ellie." Panne coughed. "I need my rest, anyway."

"But—"

"*Go.*" He commanded me sternly, his eyes conveying a message beyond words. It was time to be strong. It was time to leave his side.

I gave him one last embrace and rose to meet my jailer. An overwhelming feeling sat on my chest. One I couldn't quite describe. But my instincts led me on, despite my heart staying behind.

Chapter 31

The journey took ages. At last, we arrived at a set of doors on the upper levels of the massive ship. Kromer dropped my chains. "Take them off."

Immediately, the guards unfastened my bonds, despite their confusion. A million scenarios ran quickly through my mind. I could escape. I could attack him. But backed by reinforcements, he stood a better chance of overpowering me. And I wouldn't get far in this giant maze. Inwardly, I cursed. I was thankful for the reprieve, at least.

Kromer opened the doors and motioned for me to enter. I hesitated. The room was pitch black. He rolled his eyes and grabbed my hand, pulling me in. The door shut behind us, and the cool darkness swallowed us whole.

Once inside, he released me, leaving me alone and disoriented in the dark. My voice echoed against the walls of the vast chamber. "Where are we?"

"You'll see."

A gentle hum filled the air before thousands of stars rushing into place suddenly permeated the darkness. I screamed and whirled around to find the door. An arm wrapped around my waist and pulled me back.

"It's okay! It's okay, it's just a hologram. They're images."

Clinging to his strong, glowing arm, I dared to turn around and face the brilliant sea of lights. They filled the space until I was only vaguely aware of the ground beneath my feet. Sprays of color danced throughout in beautiful ribbons. Gingerly, I reached my hand toward the closest star, only to find it went straight through without so much as a caress. It piqued my curiosity.

"What is this?"

"The known universe. Well, part of it."

I unwrapped myself from him and stepped deeper into the 'universe'. Solid ground met my feet. As I walked, the scene shifted around me, taking me deeper through the stars. At first, it startled me, but before long, I was raising my arms and spinning around, shocked by the sensation of floating in the heavens. For a few moments, I forgot where I was… and who I was with.

"This is amazing!"

Suddenly, soft, instrumental music filled the space. Upon turning, I found Kromer standing over a lit panel with buttons. He was pleased. My joy faded. I was still a prisoner, and this was only an illusion.

"I thought you might like it."

I hugged my arms and turned away, the magic tainted. How could I let my guard down? In the presence of my enemy? "Why did you bring me here?"

"So we could talk."

"You mean, 'negotiate'?"

Soft footsteps approached from behind. I turned and backed away, scowling. His chest glowed brightly, like a star. I hated it. He had no right to bear the mark of a Celestial, much less… what I was.

"You still see me as your enemy."

"Why would I possibly see you as anything else?" I spat.

Kromer held my gaze steadfastly. "Because we're the same. And we need each other."

I shook my head. "We are *not* the same! I don't do what you do! I would never—"

"Did you not kill my men without mercy?"

This took me by surprise. "I—what?"

"You've killed scores of them in our encounters. Did you think about their lives? Their families?"

Fuming, I clenched my fists. "Do *not* turn this around on me. Your murder hordes knew what they were getting into when they did your bidding."

He shrugged. "Fair enough. But we are the same in the most fundamental way. And I'm not talking about murder." His eyes fell to my chest. It was shining just as brightly as his. A rush of anxiety filled me, but I knew I could not hide the light. "You know what we are, Ellie."

I could not respond. It was impossible to deny it. And it was so unfair. I wanted to rip the light out of my chest and bleed there on the floor. What would happen if I did? Would it stop the candle from taking me? Would it stop *him?*

"I know this isn't easy for you," he continued, "but if you would listen to me, I can help."

"Where's Gil?" My eyes darkly flicked to his in time to see a flash of annoyance.

"It doesn't matter. He cannot help you anyway."

I exploded. "What makes you think I need anything from you?"

"Because you are one step from death!" A red aura burst from his skin as he stomped toward me. I scrambled back with a gasp, tripping on my skirt and falling to the floor. As quickly as the crimson light came, it dissipated, replaced by a look of shame. Kromer grasped his chin and planted a hand on his hip, breathing deeply.

"So you do mean to kill me," I observed quietly.

"Kill you?"

With a groan, I climbed to my feet, rubbing my smarting tail bone. "If you're going to do it, just make it quick, please. I think you've tortured me enough."

"You honestly think I've searched the universe for you just to kill you?"

I froze. "I don't understand."

"Ellie, you and I need each other to balance out our natures. To balance life itself. I've searched the whole universe, every soul paver, to find my match. To find *you.* If we don't have each other, then we disappear into the nether, like your grandmother. You are the strongest one I've ever found, which means your very existence keeps the candle in balance. If you are subsumed, the power tilts on an uneven keel, and pandemonium will be unleashed."

Monsters of hellish proportions screamed in the back of my mind. The dark mountain top... the opening of the depths... Horrid visions flashed before my eyes. I felt something warm on my forearm. When I re-focused, I saw red. I hadn't noticed the fact that I was clawing at my arm. Shaking, I held it with a hiss.

"Here..." Kromer took a handkerchief from his breast pocket and came to press it over the wounds. He covered my hand as I went to take over the pressure. I found him looking at me sincerely. "I'm not lying to you, Ellie."

That's what scares me.

"Please," I asked calmly, "where is Gil?" I was met with a hardened stare. Again, I pleaded, tears threatening to make an appearance. "Just tell me if he's alive or dead?"

Kromer's hands ripped from mine, and I clutched the handkerchief to my wounds.

"I have no idea, if you insist on knowing. Nor do I care."

His answer was unconvincing. Of course he wouldn't tell me the truth. Not about his greatest competition. I knew, however, that I'd find no answers without his help. And that grated on me most of all.

Suddenly, the stars shifted upward. A landscape appeared, with green grass beneath our feet, waving in a breeze I could not feel. Hills and trees dotted the distance. We stood in a broad field under a rise sky.

"What's happening?"

Kromer returned to my side and pointed ahead toward the hills. "I want to show you something. Keep watching."

Following his finger, I stared off into the distance. At first, I saw nothing—merely the dark rise above the treetops. Then, something strange happened. Slowly, the stars disappeared, replaced by a pale light that filled the horizon. The light grew and grew, taking on pink, orange, and golden hues as it ate away at the precious stars. Horrified, I backed away, only to meet Kromer behind me. He wrapped his hands around my upper arms.

"It's all right. Just watch. Remember, it's only an image."

More and more, the sky changed. I powered through the fear and kept my eyes trained forward.

It's not real, Ellie...

Then it happened.

An orb of golden light, brighter than the brightest star I've ever seen, peeked over the hills, big and beautiful. It rose slowly, chasing away the darkness and the glittering stars. The sky gradually transformed into a canvas of brilliant blue as it climbed higher.

"The sun..." I breathed, tears in my eyes.

He spoke quietly in my ear, his temple resting against my head. "I can give you the sunrise, Ellie." Speechless, I couldn't move. Even in the sun, our glow shined bright... and warm. Slowly, his hands slipped forward until his arms fully encased me. Caught like an animal in a trap, all I could do was breathe, wide-eyed.

"You're so beautiful in the light," he whispered. "You don't ever need to hide away in darkness again."

Glancing down at my arms, I was shocked to find them transformed. Beyond the contact glow, my skin was shimmering like diamonds. Gasping, I stepped from his arms and inspected myself. Every inch of me was glittering like a jewel.

"But... but it's just an image? It's not real!"

"It's a recording of a real sunrise. And when you're exposed to it in person, just think of how brilliant you'll be. How warm." He grasped my hands in his. "Ellie..." I met his bright eyes. "You are a being of the light. I've been waiting for you for so long... My soul's perfect half." Before I could speak, he wrapped a hand around the back of my head and pulled me in for a deep kiss. Gathered up in his arms, he kissed me in a way that sent whirlwinds of golden light wrapping around us, whipping my hair wildly about.

When his lips at last parted from mine, I clung to him, my knees feeling suddenly weak. Kromer smiled, hooking a stray lock of hair behind my ear. He planted another soft kiss on my forehead. I was too stunned to resist.

We were no longer in the sunlight, but back among the sea of stars. Music still wound softly in the background. I hardly noticed anything beyond the ground beneath my feet.

"What... just happened?"

"Our light combining. Just for a moment."

I craned my neck and looked around the starry space, mourning the sun. Golden light still burned in the back of mind. Its breathtaking beauty would never leave me.

"That was just a taste of what we are together." His knuckles caressed the side of my cheek. "Of how it's meant to be." I sensed his lips drawing minutely closer to mine once more. "I love you, Ellie."

These words snapped me back to reality. A flood of guilt came rushing in in the form of the memory of a certain silver man who held my heart. I recalled the way we bounded through the fields together… how he snuck up to my room every rise and many, many sets… the feeling of his long fingers interlaced with mine… the way he made love to me in the tall grass… and those very words spoken to me in fevered whispers over and over.

Kromer's lips had barely grazed mine when I pulled back and met his eyes. All the warmth left me. "Where is Gil?"

His brows furrowed with deep hurt. "What?"

Untangling myself from his arms, I backed away and firmly repeated my question. *"Where. Is. Gil?"*

Tension feathered his jaw as the look of love slid into one of anger. "This is your response? To *everything* that just happened?"

I crossed my arms and glowered. "Just answer the question, Kromer!"

He exploded with a sneer. "No!"

"Why? Why won't you just give me the truth? If you love me like you say you do, then you owe me that, at least!"

"It doesn't matter!"

"Why?"

"Because you're never going to see him again!"

My jaw dropped. "Why? What do you mean by that? What did you do?"

Growling in frustration, he marched over to me. "You know what? I think you just need some rest—" The moment he grasped my hand, a spearing beam of light shot out of my ring. Stars rushed past us in dizzying streaks. I tried to rip my hand away, but Kromer kept a firm grip.

"What's happening?"

Suddenly, they all stopped, and a single, bright white star stood out before us, connected to the beam. A beautiful corona of blues and purples danced around the edges. At once, I recognized the familiar pulling in my chest. My eyes snapped to Kromer's, and I knew he felt it too.

"Computer, send coordinates of the star to the main navigation queue."

There was a beep, and a voice spoke from all around us. "Confirmed."

"Is that…"

Kromer nodded, breaking into a broad smile.

"We just found the candle."

Chapter 32

Kromer rushed me back to my room, completely unchained. The whole time, he had a vise-like grip on my hand, and a crazed smile pasted on his face. Even the guards had to run to keep up. We received many confused stares as we bowled through passers-by.

When I was finally ushered through my door, Kromer paused only to pull me in for another passionate kiss. "Wait here, my love. I'll come later." With that, he fled the room, leaving the guards to lock me in.

Furiously, I wiped my lips to erase the phantom feeling of his. The madness in his eye told me I was merely a subset of his master plans, as if our argument had not just taken place minutes before. I made up my mind to sink my teeth into his lip the next time he even thought about kissing me again.

With nothing else to do, I paced the room, rubbing my arms. Anxiety was gripping me in a chokehold. Though I couldn't feel it, the ship was now careening through the stars, on its way to the singular source indicated by the ring. I avoided the windows, which now only showed dizzying streaks of white on a black canvas. We were getting farther and farther from my home. Farther from Gil. My heart cracked at the thought of a universe between us. Could I find my way back to him?

The ring on my finger was back to being a normal piece of jewelry. I was angry at its betrayal. As much as I wanted to remove it and throw it across the room, it was one of my only ties to my home. To my family.

Gil's mother's necklace lay under my pillow. I'd discreetly removed it before undressing, hoping to spare it from being stolen and discarded. I fished it out now, holding the cool, purple jewel in my palm. The memory of the precise moment I felt it drape over my neck surfaced. It was a promise of forever. His heart was in my hand, and mine in his, wherever he may be.

Curling up in the bed, I clutched it to my chest and emptied my tears into the pillow. I wished I could find Panne again, but I hadn't the slightest clue of where to look. Just knowing he was on the same ship was a sliver of comfort, at least. With any luck, I could beg my way into more visits, though I worried time was not on our side. I had not given him enough hugs. Not nearly enough.

My sorrow eventually drifted off when sleep found me. It was not a dreamless sleep. Instead, I stood back in the field of green grass, under a spray of stars. I looked to the hills, expecting to see the sunrise, but instead I found an obscure figure of black fur walking toward me.

It took time, but the closer it got, the clearer it became. A pantheour, large and beautiful. Familiar, glowing yellow eyes trained on me. A smile spread across my face.

"Shade?"

I stretched out my arms, ready to gather her up, but only a few paces away, she made a shocking transformation. At once, she stood on her hind legs and shrank down, fur disappearing like smoke. A violet-haired woman in a long, yellow dress walked in her place. Older, but not quite ancient. Her purple eyes seemed familiar. She smiled brightly as she approached me.

"Hello, Ellie."

Stupefied, I dragged my eyes up and down her new form. "I... Shade?"

She laughed. "I like that name. I have another though. *Mara.*"

It hit me like a boulder to the chest. "You're... the whole time you were..." Mara nodded. I stumbled forward and threw my arms around her. *Grandmanne.*

"It's all right, love. I know it's a shock." She soothed me with her words, running her hand over my hair. I sniffled and clung tightly to her, as if she were the only solid rock amid sinking sands.

"Why?"

"Someone needed to look after you. The pit would've driven you mad in your sorrow, and you needed protection on your journey. I thought my other form would be easier for you to accept."

I stood back and wiped my eyes. "But I thought you were…"

"Dead?" Grandmanne tilted her head thoughtfully. "I suppose, in a way, I am. But I had a little power left."

"And you used it on me?"

"I think it was well-vested." She winked.

Hugging my stomach, I tried to sort through my racing thoughts. "I don't know, Grandmanne. Everything is going so wrong now. I've failed. Badly."

"How so?"

"I think I've let my guard down, and now the man who's been wreaking havoc on our kingdom knows the location of the candle. I'm scared about what's going to happen. The candle—it wants me."

She nodded. "You've been found by your paver-match."

Looking at her in alarm, my heart raced. "What?"

Grandmanne sighed. "It's okay, dear. I know it's frightening. Unfortu-nately, it's a natural consequence of being… *what we are.*"

"What do you mean? I don't want to match with him!"

"Shhh, calm yourself, now! That's not quite what I meant." She placed a hand on my shoulder and sighed. "Soul pavers can only procreate with other soul pavers. Because of this, we are programmed to find our match. And unfortunately, some will stop at nothing to find them."

My heart stopped. "No. No, that can't be right. I don't want him, I want *Gil*. Gil is my intended." The hyperventilating came on quickly, and I lowered to my heels. "You're wrong."

Grandmanne sank to my level and brushed the hair from my face pitifully. "I wish I was. I wish to the heavens I was mistaken. When my match found me…" her words trailed off as she shook her head.

I looked at her desperately. "Please, tell me? I need to know."

There was a long pause. It brought her pain to speak of it. But I had to know the truth—no matter how ugly.

"When he found me, he was all flowers and poetry. Swept me clean off my feet. He came from a faraway place, made promises only a soul paver had any chance of keeping."

I grasped her hand. "What happened?"

Her gaze was far away. "I gave into him. The moment we found out I was expecting, it all changed. He thought only of finding the candle; gaining more power. What we had together wasn't enough. Something dark spoke to him. I would find him whispering into the mirror late at set. He became violent and angry all the time. When I finally wanted to tell my family about us, he threatened to slaughter them all."

"Oh, Grandmanne…"

She continued, pushing out the last bits of the awful truth with a shudder. "When I heard him speaking his awful plans to the mirror—plans to take the blood of innocents… and to blow out the candle, I knew the inevitable had come… I took my sharpest kitchen knife and took his life as he slept."

At last, it lay bare: the story of my manne's origin, and therefore mine. Tainted with the blood of violence and tragic murder. It gripped me by the throat as I watched Grandmanne's sorrow manifest. I took her hand in mine.

"You made the right decision."

"I know I did. The memory of the blood on my hands never goes away, though. Even in death." She straightened and looked me intently in the eye. "I told you this because I want you to know that you don't have to make the same choice I made. Candle or no candle, match or no match, your life is ultimately in your own hands."

I sighed. "I just want to destroy that candle and be free of it."

Grandmanne snatched my chin firmly between her fingers and forced me to look at her. "The candle cannot and *should not* be destroyed. *Ever.* Only kept in balance. It is the foundation of all we know. To destroy it would have consequences that reach far beyond a bad match."

"It's already destroying everything I know."

Her sternness melted, and she gathered me up in her arms. "Do not lose hope, child. This is not the end of things. If there's one thing that soul pavers do most powerfully, it's love. Your heart is stronger than most. I believe you will ultimately succeed. But you have to be prepared to do what it takes."

We sat there for a moment, melting into our thoughts. I relished in the comfort of her arms and the connection we had. But I knew it had to end. And when it did, we stood once again in the green grass, hands joined. Light was just rising over the hills. Grandmanne smiled.

"You look so much like your manne. She wasn't a soul paver, but I think she was braver than any soul paver that ever existed. You get that from her."

"I miss her."

"She misses you, too."

My heart leaped. "You've seen her?"

"We all become part of the heavens, eventually."

The golden light was peeking now, turning the sky a splash of warm color. Grandmanne linked her arm around my waist and we watched the rise, side-by-side. This time, I felt its warmth wash over me. It was more beautiful than any false image.

When I turned to smile at Grandmanne, she was gone.

Chapter 33

My fingers shook as I worked the buttons on my sweater. The moment I'd woken, I'd changed into my old clothes. Had there been a fireplace, I would've burned the other dress. I just wanted to protect myself; to *hide*.

When the necklace was around my neck once more, I kissed the jewel, silently reminding myself of the promise it held. I tucked it safely under the neckline of my sweater. I would fight to the death before I let them take it from me.

The lock on the door rattled and clicked. I backed to the opposite corner of the room, ready to stand my ground. Match or not, he would get nothing from me without a fight. My legs were strong. One well-timed kick in the wrong place could disable him long enough to escape. Or the dress; I could wrap the dress around his neck to cut off the air.

A thousand deaths were running through my mind in that moment before the door opened. At once, my plans shifted. In slipped Rodina. She was no longer in an evening gown, but a white top and form-fitting tan slacks with tall, black boots. And a look of utter shame.

"Hello," she greeted timidly, eyes trained to the floor.

Fury seized me and I clenched my fists. "Give me one good reason why I shouldn't snap your neck right now."

I got a fearful glance, but she did not flee. "I owe you an explanation."

"You owe me a hell of a lot more than that, *Lydia!* Do you have any idea what you've done?"

She tensed her jaw as a fat tear rolled down her cheek.

I sneered. "Spare me your tears. You insult me."

Rodina finally lifted her chin and looked me square in the eye. "All right then."

"Speak. And then leave."

She hesitated. I sensed her trepidation, but I wasn't about to give her the satisfaction of lying to me one more time, or worse, leaving without the explanation she truly did owe. It took every ounce of self-control not to unleash my rage. I crossed my arms tightly and glared at her. When she finally spoke, it was a quiet, solemn voice, not the bubbly, sweet Lydia I'd come to know. An entirely different woman stood before me.

"I am Rodina Kromer, sister of King Maximus Kromer. When you left Silis, you were being tracked. I was dropped off in the woods, directly in your path, with a tracker in the back of my neck. My role was to stay with you, relay information, and allow my brother to find you."

My eyes narrowed. "I gathered that already. Get Out."

Rodina raised a shaking palm. "Please. There's more."

"Really?" I strolled toward her, fully aware of the danger I was putting her in. "More lies to confess?" I swept my arm through the air. "By all means, confess them. Tell me just how *disgusting* you are." I stopped within arm's length.

"I lied about being in a breeding program… but I did not lie about my daughter."

This took me slightly by surprise. "Okay. So, you have a daughter. Where is she then? Running around the ship like a little princess—"

"Max took her from me!" Her outburst came with an onslaught of tears. I simply stared, waiting for her to continue. "He sent her away and won't let me see her. I wouldn't do his bidding, so this is how he has punished me." She was sobbing by now, grasping her hair. "He says she's safe for now, but if I don't obey, he'll… he'll…"

Rodina fell apart before me, sinking to the floor. I didn't know quite how to react. My anger still simmered, but it was dissipating as I watched her wounded heart lay bare. I was not a mother, but my own mother had laid her life down to protect me. An ugly scar on my back was proof that motherly love knew no bounds.

At last, she was reduced to sniffles. Red, watery eyes met mine. "I want you to put a stop to him."

My eyes widened, and I glanced toward the door before grabbing her arm and half-dragging her to the furthest corner of the room. "Rodina, I—"

She grasped my arms, fear permeating her grip. "Whatever he is, he's not my brother anymore. I accept that now. At one time, he was a good man, but the candle has poisoned his mind. He's obsessed with only two things: the candle... and *you*. He'll stop at nothing to gain the powers of the universe, even if that means slaughtering every other soul paver out there and absorbing their light."

"Wait, what? What do you mean?"

Rodina lowered her voice to a whisper. "You don't know? That's why he's been conquering worlds. He's been hunting out other pavers. When you kill another, you absorb their power, and any power they've gained."

I wanted to throw up. "You mean there were other pavers on my world? The whole time?"

She nodded. "He gained the power of discernment long ago, and ever since, he's used it for nothing but obtaining more power, and to find you. I've tried to stop him before, but he's too powerful. Once he gets to the candle with you, who knows what's going to happen."

"Rodina..." Now it was my turn to be weak-kneed. "I-I don't know how to stop him."

"You're his *match*. You've got a better chance than anyone on this ship. Hell, better than anyone in the universe!"

The pressure weighed down on me like a mountain. I wanted to send her away, curl up in a ball, and just give in. "I don't think I can do this alone."

She took my hand. "Come with me."

"Where?"

"We're getting reinforcements."

Rodina flung open the door with confidence and a smile. The guards eyed her in surprise. She approached one in particular—a broad-shouldered blond man with inky eyes.

"Hello, Toby. How are you today?" She bit her lower lip flirtatiously as she rested a hand on his shoulder.

Toby glanced at his partner and crooked a nervous smile. "Ro, I'm on duty."

She pouted. "Oh, come on. Aren't I part of your duty?"

"Your Highness, she's supposed to remain in her quarters," insisted the other guard dryly.

Rodina transferred her attentions to the red-haired man, who was just ripping a glare from his partner. She slinked over to him, standing toe-to-toe, staring up at him through her long lashes. "All right then. But…" a glance at Toby, "are we still on for later?"

A smug smile tugged at his lips, and he stood a bit taller. "Of course."

"Ro? What are you talking about?" Toby stepped to their side heatedly. "Why do you have plans with *him*?"

Red-hair arched a brow at his companion and shoved him back. "Back off, Toby! You don't own her."

"Neither do you, *Grady*! She had plans with me first!" Toby shoved Grady back, hard enough to nearly knock him off his feet.

Grady rebounded with a punch as Rodina yanked me across the hall just in time. As the men fought, she whispered in a rush, "I'll take out the one on the right. You get blondie." Before I had a chance to ask for clarification, Rodina ran at the wall, took a leaping step, and ended up straddling the shoulders of Grady. She squeezed his neck with her strong thighs as he desperately pulled at her knees and gasped for air. Toby pulled his gun and immediately began shouting, but they were a moving target, crashing between the narrow walls of the hallway.

I had no weapon beyond myself. For a moment I panicked, but then Panne's words came rushing back. *Trust your instincts.* The red light flared. I braced myself against the wall and took a deep breath. I waited for just the right moment and took a small bounce before flinging my legs ahead in a powerful thrust that hit Toby square in his side. There was a sickening crack of bones as he hit the wall and flopped to the ground like a sack of grain. A moment later, Grady fell, with Rodina still around his neck.

After unclamping her legs and righting herself, Rodina made quick work of removing their earpieces and guns. She tossed the earpieces on the floor. "Destroy those. They can track them."

I smashed them under my heel and then helped her drag the two unconscious men into my room. We shut and locked the door.

"Your brother will probably come soon," I noted nervously.

Rodina nodded. "We'll be quick. It'll buy us at least a little time. I've studied the maps. I know all the maintenance corridors. We'll stay out of the main halls."

"Why do you know all this stuff?" I asked suspiciously, as we quickly crept down the hall.

She barely glanced at me. "Ignorance is death."

I couldn't argue with that answer.

We ducked into a narrow door to the left and ended up in a stairwell with exposed pipes running along the ceiling and walls. Rodina took us down three levels before we stepped through a hatch into an even narrower, muggy space then followed a large red pipe.

"Stay to the right. The pipe is hot."

I took her word for it and hugged the wall as we ran and climbed carefully over welded sections and half-walls. It was claustrophobic, but I swallowed my nerves and pushed through.

Eventually, we came to a hatch in the floor that opened and revealed a drop ladder to another stairway. That stairway led to another hatch, which led to a crawlspace, and finally a normal hallway. By the time I was fully on my feet and breathing clear, cool air, I was damp with sweat and my back ached. But Rodina did not appear to care. She pulled me close and gave me the next set of instructions.

"Ahead, the hall turns left, and there will be a set of doors that lead to the prison. There will be two guards outside and at least one inside at a desk. We have to move quickly. Once the inside guard realizes what's happening, he can seal the doors and call for backup, and our chance is gone."

"Won't they just let you in? You're the princess, aren't you?"

She cast me a dry look. "You think they'll let me march back out with prisoners?

Blushing, I shook my head. "Good point."

"Follow my lead."

We hid our guns behind our backs and sauntered around the corner with sly smiles. Two male guards had just been in the middle of a conversation when Rodina interrupted with a pleasant greeting. I stood at her side and eyed them sweetly.

"Good evening, Your Highness."

"Who's your friend?"

Rodina crooked a finger suggestively. "We have a quick favor to ask of you, if you don't mind."

They looked at each other with confusion written all over their faces.

"Your Highness," said one of them, shifting uncomfortably, "with all due respect, we're not to leave our posts."

She dropped her act and pulled her gun. "Follow me, *now.*"

I followed suit and drew my weapon, casting a fiery glare at the men.

The guards raised their hands in the air and followed us as we backed around the corner. One moved his hand to press his earpiece, and I kicked him across the hall into the wall before it ever reached its destination. I repeated the action when I saw the other guard open his mouth.

We bolted to the doors, where Rodina quickly punched in a code and they swung open. The moment they opened, she shot a laser blast into the chest of the desk guard and stole a set of keys from his belt. I flinched when I saw the smoke rising from the scorched wound, but we had no time to stop and think of such things.

Our destination was deeper into the maze of cells, all of which stood empty.

"Where are all the prisoners?"

"My brother doesn't take prisoners. Not unless they can be of some use to him later."

It was a chilling thought.

At last, we came to the end of a hall, where a door capped the end. Rodina slid the panel open on the singular window and peeked in before hurriedly punching a series of numbers in the panel on the wall. Lights flicked on inside the room at the same time the lock clanged loudly. She flung the door open, and we rushed in.

A blindfolded man hung on the opposite wall, arms suspended wide by chains, with only a thin shelf for him to rest his feet on. His bare chest was covered in bruises and dried blood. At first, I recoiled in shock at the sight. He looked dead. Then he lifted his head.

Rodina ripped off the blindfold. I nearly fell over. His hair was shorn, and he looked like a shell of himself, but when his eyes met mine and focused, I knew him immediately.

"Gil!" I flew across the room as Rodina fished the keys out of her pocket.

"Ellie?" He was weary.

"You're taller; I need help!" said Rodina, holding the keys toward me. Immediately, I changed direction and took over, frantically unlocking the shackles.

The moment I freed him, he fell, groaning as his knees smacked the hard ground. I shoved the keys back into her hands and kneeled before Gil, gathering him up in my arms. "Oh, Gil, what have they done to you?"

Gil trembled violently and clung to me. "Are you real?" His hands found my hair, and he moved his cheek to press into mine. "Please tell me you're real this time?"

I shifted back and pressed my lips desperately to his. "I'm real, Gil. I'm here."

His eyes finally linked with mine. They were red-rimmed and his left eye was bruised. "You're real?" He then broke down in sobs and began kissing me over and over. I happily reciprocated. At last, he pulled away again and inspected me. "Did he hurt you? Are you okay?"

"I'm okay. I'm not hurt," I assured.

Gil was on the verge of breaking down again. "I'm so sorry! I should've never let you go without me! When I found Hunter unconscious on the floor—"

"Reunions will have to wait," interrupted Rodina. She was standing in the

255

doorway, continuously glancing down the hall. "We don't have much time."

Gil scowled. "What's *she* doing here?"

Rodina avoided his eyes. "Paying my dues and putting a stop to all of this."

We rose from the floor. Gil rotated his shoulders and stumbled. I reached out to steady him, but he shook his head. "I'll be all right."

"Kill me later if you want," Rodina offered as Gil cast her a murderous glare, "but we have to steer this ship away from the candle and kill my brother if any of us have a chance of living."

"The candle?" he asked, blanching.

"Go now, talk later!" she growled, rushing from the room. I grabbed Gil's hand and chased after her.

We came to a door just adjacent to his cell and Rodina punched in another code. The door swung open, and I was shocked to find Hunter sitting casually on the bench with an annoyed look on his face. Rodina didn't bother smiling.

"Hunter, look, I know I'm the last person you want to see right now, and there's a lot of explaining I owe you, but—"

"Save it." He rose to his full, towering height. "I have ears. What's the plan?"

She knitted her brows. "Aren't you mad at me?"

He laughed. "Oh, I'm beyond furious. But I trust *her*." He shoved a finger in my direction.

Rodina shrunk and nodded. "Fair enough." She motioned for us all to gather closer. "Now, what we need to do is manually disable the navigation systems and set off the shield alarms. That will cause enough chaos on deck and force them to halt the ship. And you—" She turned to me. "—need to go back to your room and wait for Max."

I frowned. "Me? Are you out of your mind? We left guards in there!"

"Take guns. And Gil."

Gil clenched his fist. "I won't need a gun."

She rolled her eyes. "Don't be a hero, lover boy. Or an idiot. He won't come alone."

"Okay, I think we've got it. Let's go!" urged Hunter.

Taking the lead, Rodina led us from the cell and back through the maze. We stopped at the entrance and relieved the dead desk guard of his gun. When we got to the outer hallway, however, we were dismayed to find only one guard on the floor. Rodina cursed.

"He escaped!"

Gil took the gun from the fallen guard and we took off running down the hall. We piled into the hatch and began our long trek through the bowels and walls of the ship. It was a tight squeeze in places for the men, but they pressed ahead without complaint. I was so thankful to have Gil with me, I didn't even mind it anymore.

We came to a crossroads. Ahead was the hatch that led to the final stairwell, and to the left was another passage. Rodina brought us to a stop.

"Ellie, ahead is the way back to your room. Do you think you can find it without me?"

I nodded. "I think so. Up three levels and right down the hall."

She smiled. "You're sharp, girl. All right, come with me, Red Cakes." Hunter wrinkled his nose but followed. Rodina stopped short and turned around, pushing past him to come throw her arms around me. She sighed. "I'm so sorry I got you into this."

Tears threatened my eyes, but I blinked them away. "I know."

She let me go and returned to Hunter's side, misty eyes flitting between Gil and me. "Good luck. We'll come find you soon and then we're getting the hell off this ship."

They disappeared down the passage, Hunter casting one last, long look back that seemed to convey a message of solidarity. I realized it could be the last time any of us saw each other if we failed. A shudder ran through me.

I looked poignantly at the hatch door and took a deep breath. "Let's go."

Gil grabbed my hand and brought me to a stop. His hand then slipped around my face as our gazes linked together. The warm glow washed over me.

"Before we go any further: I want you to know that no matter what happens, I love you… and if we die, I die as *your husband*."

Taken aback, I gaped at him. "A-are you sure?"

He nodded, brushing his thumb over my cheek. "I was a coward, Ellie. I'm so sorry. All I thought about in that prison cell was you. All the moments that were stolen from us."

"Oh, Gil..." my lips tugged upward. "But we don't have a—"

"We don't need one." He leaned his forehead against mine. His warm breath rushed over me. "Ellette Humett... Will you have me?"

I was the match of another soul paver. My life was fraught with danger. An instrument of life and death was slowly draining me away. But there was one sure thing in my life, and that was the man in front of me. I ran my hand over his cropped hair and brought my fingers under his jaw to lift his eyes to meet mine.

"I would have you and you only, Gillion Braxton."

He smiled briefly before I pulled him in for a long, sweet kiss. I wanted more time. More time to kiss him; more time to celebrate what just took place between us. But time was not ours to take.

We held each other for another long moment, knowing it could be the last time. And then we stepped through the hatch and rushed up the stairs.

Chapter 34

The hallway was eerily quiet. No alarms going off, or any signs of life. Glancing at each other ominously, we pressed on toward my room, guns firmly in hand.

When we reached my door, it was still locked. I pressed my ear against it and sighed in relief when I heard only silence. Gil slid the bolt over and we nodded to each other before swinging it open, pointing our guns. A dozen other gun barrels staring us down immediately met us.

"Drop your weapons! Show your hands!" one guard shouted as another radioed a message. We immediately complied and raised our palms. They rushed forward and grabbed us, slapping shackles on our wrists. Gil tried to kick at the guards, but received a violent blow to the jaw. He slumped forward, blood dripping from his mouth.

I screamed. "Leave him alone!"

A man with a menacing scowl gripped me by the chin and shoved me back against the wall, sending stars into my vision. "Quiet, you blue whore!"

A laser blast zipped through the air and the man's eyes widened before he crumpled to the floor. I whipped my head to the right and found a stone-faced Kromer standing just down the hall, an army of guards behind him. He wouldn't even look at me, only sweeping his eyes over his men.

"Anyone else want to say anything about my intended?" They silently stood at attention. He returned the gun to the guard next to him. "Bring them to the bridge."

They half-dragged Gil along as they marched us in the procession of black uniforms through the ship. Everyone we passed ducked into doorways that shuddered in Kromer's wake. Even I felt it—stirring in my chest. A thrum of power emanated from him, mixing with a rising sensation in my own veins. The air was charged with buzzing energy. When I glanced down, I noticed my chest light was pulsing brightly, taking on a purple hue. Something was happening.

I noticed Gil continuously glancing over at me with wide-eyed concern. He saw it too. I wished I could reassure him, but there was none to give. If we deigned to speak to each other, I knew Kromer wouldn't hesitate to use that gun again.

We came to a bank of lifts. Gil and I were separated, and I was brought into the same car as Kromer. He stood with his back to me, tall and proud. I wanted to leap and kick him—break his spine in two. But I was very aware of the other six armed men around us.

His calm voice cut the silence as the numbers rushed on the display. "You disappoint me, Ellie." I glared at his back without answering. "I thought you were far more intelligent than this."

I wanted to scream at him. Rip his throat out. Of all things, he insulted my intelligence?

Kromer shifted his head as if to glance over his shoulder, but not quite turning all the way. "No matter. You will be educated. Thoroughly."

A chill ran through me.

The doors opened, and we entered a cavernous room with a vast multitude of stations and displays, with people manning each one. A raised platform in the center held a singular chair, where a man in gray sat. All heads turned and people quickly stood at attention as we entered.

What took my breath away, however, was the massive window front and center, in which a bright orb nearly filled the display. My chest immediately ached and a blue glow lifted from my skin. I knew it; I knew it immediately. The dancing colors around the edges, the massive pull... it was like home calling to me.

My knees gave out. I was allowed to hit the floor, but I felt no pain. In fact, I didn't feel the floor at all. The shackles around my wrists busted open with a pop and fell to the ground. The guards around me reached out to take my arms but cried out in agony when they so much as brushed my light. I was encased.

A hand reached down to me. I hardly noticed as I took it and rose to my feet.

"Come."

I turned to see Kromer standing at my side with a smile, the same bright blue aura surrounding him and his eyes aglow. Everyone else kept a wide berth. Sweeping my eyes across the room, I found stunned and frightened faces. Gil, Hunter, Rodina—all in bonds, brought in to watch the spectacle. My heart pounded, my thoughts being continuously torn between them and the call of the candle. It whispered my name continuously, caressing the inside of my mind, coaxing me to come.

The lift across the room opened, and a woman pushed a wheeled chair into the room. I snatched my hand away and pushed past Kromer. "Panne!"

Panne weakly turned his head toward me. "Ellie?" His breathing was heavy.

I nearly made it over there before Kromer's words arrested me. "I wouldn't touch him if I were you." I stopped in my tracks, looking down at my hands. "You'll probably kill him."

In horror, I took a step back. Panne nodded sadly before launching into a coughing fit. The woman kneeled at his side and fixed a clear mask over his face, coaxing him to breathe slowly.

Clamping my hand over my mouth, I swallowed a sob. This was one of my greatest fears. And I couldn't care for him.

Gil stood nearby, eyes glued to me. All we could do was look at each other. There was nothing to say. I pulled the necklace from underneath my neckline and clasped my hand over the jewel before briefly bringing it to my lips. He noticed the gesture and nodded. *My husband.*

The familiar female voice whispered all around me. "Ellie..." I turned to the window, as if I had no control over my body. "Come," she said. The light of the star flared with the gently spoken word. A wave of warmth washed over every pore. It beckoned me like an embrace. An invisible

261

thread connected me to the light. Slowly, without heed to those around me, or the voices behind me begging me to stop, I stepped through the room toward the window.

I walked up the few steps and onto the long walkway that ran before the glass until I was standing before the display, enveloped by the light. It stood before me, radiant and lovely. The sea of stars that surrounded it paled in significance. A warm hand slipped in mine. I knew who it belonged to. There was only one who could touch me now. The beam of light shot out from the ring, confirming our destination.

"It's beautiful, isn't it?" he said in awe.

I nodded, barely able to speak. "Yes."

Again, I heard it speak in a gentle rush. "Ellie…" I shuddered.

"You don't have to be afraid." Kromer gently squeezed my hand. "Ever again."

Slowly, I tore my eyes from the star and found Kromer gazing at me intensely with glowing diamond eyes. "Will you come with me?"

Without a thought, the answer leaped from my lips. "Yes."

"No… no, Ellie! Don't do it!" Gil boomed across the room, joined by cries of alarm from Hunter and Rodina.

Just as I was turning my head to see what the commotion was about, Kromer snatched my chin and pressed his lips to mine.

The wind only lasted moments, rushing in my ears with such intensity that I thought they would burst. I screamed behind our kiss. When I finally freed myself from Kromer's hold, I fell to the ground. My eyes immediately ached. Surrounded by pure white in every direction, it was nearly blinding.

Then I saw it—there in the center of the endless space: the candle. It was no longer black, but white and brilliant. We were not on a dark mountaintop, but in the center of a beautiful star; a breathtaking haven of light.

As I stood to my feet, I looked down and found no floor, only the wavering, lightning-like contact of energy. I felt weightless, without pain or substance; one with the glow.

"How is this possible?"

"Anything is possible here." Kromer strolled past me toward the candle, mesmerized. "This is the center of all that is, all that has been, and all there will ever be." His words were full of reverence. "We're outside of time and space right now."

I took a few steps toward the candle and then stopped. The thrum of energy was overwhelming. Kromer himself remained a safe distance away. The longer I stared at its light, the more uneasy I became. I had to look away.

"It's... strong."

A rush of crackling footsteps brought him before me. He grasped my hands and caught me in a bright-eyed stare. "We're strong *together*. Ellie, think of all that we can do now! Even just standing here, we're soaking up more power than anyone in this entire universe has ever even imagined." His smile bordered on manic.

My heart started pounding. "Isn't this dangerous?"

He laughed. "You're worried about danger? Now? We were born for this, my love. We're to be feared by all."

Retrieving my hands, I stepped away. "I don't want to be feared by all."

This amused him. He cocked an eyebrow. "Oh, and I suppose you'd rather be *loved* by all? Pander to the masses? Be trampled under their feet? Is that it?" Turning from me, he breathed deeply, casting admiring gazes toward the candle. "No, dear, I won't have that. Not for me, or you. We're not destined for it."

The word 'destined' made me flinch. Here he talked about destiny when what I saw before me was simply a madman obsessed with power that could destroy all. My thoughts went to Silis... to Star City... to every other city on my planet that was decimated at his hand.

"Did you spare my great aunt?"

"Your what?"

I stepped past him, circling the candle at a distance. "Nola Torril. My great aunt, who lived at the house in Basillian. Or did you level that too?"

He looked at me strangely. "I must confess, I don't know."

Breathing deeply, I gripped my arms as I walked. "Oh, come now. I know you've done your research. You must know about her. You knew about my grandmanne, after all. Surely your sister filled you in?"

"Why do you care so much?" he scoffed. "It's not like you really knew her."

My eyes flicked to his as I approached and then passed him. "Ah, but I do care!"

"And why is that?"

I looked down at the white ring on my hand, recalling her kindness. "Because she's family." I glared at Kromer. "And family is important to me."

Kromer crossed his arms, agitation tainting his voice. "I spared your father, did I not?"

"My *panne*," I nodded. "Yes."

He smiled in satisfaction. "See? I have left you family."

Pausing, I pressed further. "And what of your family?"

"My family?" he asked in confusion. "What of them?"

"Yes. You have a sister… and a niece, do you not?"

Kromer did not answer immediately. When he did, it was with a tense jaw. "Why do you insist on talking about this pointless subject?" A forced smile spread across his lips. "You're my family now."

Now it was my turn to laugh. "Not yet, I'm not."

His face slackened. "What?"

"You haven't asked me to be your wife or even declared intent. Just went on and on about '*match, match, match!*'."

Suddenly speechless, Kromer just stared at me. It must've dawned on him that I was correct, because he suddenly marched over to me and fell to one knee. I was entirely confused when he grasped my hand and kissed it.

"Ellette Humett, my soulmate, will you be my wife?"

I smiled as brightly as I could manage, tracing my fingers lightly down the side of his face. "Maximus Kromer…" His eyes lit up in anticipation. "No."

At once, he dropped my hand and leaped to his feet, glowering. "Why not?"

I glowered right back. "I don't marry power-hungry tyrants."

"And who would you marry? Weak-minded men who can't protect you?"

My aura flashed from blue to red. "I don't need protecting."

264

The moment he tried to grab my shoulders, he flew backward with a howl of agony. I merely stood and smiled. He lay on the surface of light, red-faced, and hands clawed inward from the pain. I went back to circling the candle in satisfaction as he collected himself.

"Careful, Kromer. Don't let your feelings get the best of you. Not becoming of a conqueror."

"You..." He rose to his feet, seething with anger. "...would raise your power against your *match?* Destined by the candle it—"

"I decide my destiny!" I snapped, as we now counter-circled and stared each other down. "Not you, not a candle, nor anything else in this universe!"

Kromer jabbed a shaking finger in my direction. "I have destroyed worlds, traveled for years, turned this entire universe on its head—and I have done it all for *you!*"

"You did it for power!"

"I did it because I love you!"

I laughed darkly. "Love? *Love?* You don't know the first thing about love, Kromer! You don't know the first thing about me! You could've met me some other way, gotten to know me, romanced me like a normal person, but you took me by force like a-a—"

"A man in love!"

I froze in my tracks and glared over the candle flame. "You are no man."

We faced each other in a battle of wills. All tenderness had flown away. Kromer now looked at me with menace.

"You are my match, whether you like it or not."

"This candle holds no power over me. *You* hold no power over me. Not anymore."

His face crumpled with hurt. I'd finally found the mark and speared it head-on. But I couldn't resist one last jab. Slowly, I stepped up to the candle, no longer feeling the resistance, and briefly gazed into the flame.

"Gil is ten times the man you'll ever hope to be."

First, I saw the flash of red. Then I felt the shock of pain slamming into me. I didn't even have time to scream as I flew and landed on the ground. I lay there, my lungs furiously trying to expand and take a breath. The white around me wavered with shadows. When at last I sucked in air, the space righted itself.

I pushed myself to sitting and my eyes darted toward the candle. Kromer now stood just on the other side, gazing calmly at me. It scared me more than if I'd been the subject of an evil stare.

"You've tried my patience, my love."

The taste of iron coated my tongue. I coughed and spat it out, taking precious breaths. "Like I said… I'm not *your love*."

His upper lip twitched. "Then you will see just how much power I can hold."

Kromer bent forward…

My eyes widened…

And he blew out the candle.

Chapter 35

At once, the flame transformed, the white light disappearing, and a black flame springing up in its place. It washed downward, bathing everything in its path with soulless obsidian ink. All around us, bursts of red and blue lightning crackled as the star's beautiful light turned to darkness. Rumblings from the deep echoed in my chest as the surface below me flashed and cracked like glass. Looking down, I could see the writhing of scaled beasts and plumes of smoke rising.

Kromer still stood as a red-glowing silhouette beyond the black candle. His heart had gone dark. Glowing green eyes pierced mine. Scrambling to my feet, I took in the utter chaos around me. Shadows were shooting through the floor, out of the candle itself, swooping overhead—transforming into terrifying beasts with teeth and wings and fire. They shot off in every direction of the universe. What was once an endless plane of white was now a dome of swirling gray and black.

The noise was horrendous. Roaring and screeching—everything a child could ever imagine in their worst dreams come to life. Clamping my hands over my ears, I screamed. Every time I closed my eyes, I had only visions of my home, of beasts breaking out of the depths of the mountains and the oceans; of shadows descending from the sky to rain death. I had visions of other worlds, with monsters rising from the muds to consume flesh... stars consumed by shadow, no more to rise again.

"Stop this!" I screamed at the man who stood calmly by the very instrument of the destruction.

His voice cut through the chaos. "Do you not see? This is what you have chosen."

I ducked as a snake-like spirit came shooting at my head. It missed me by a hair's breadth. Kromer didn't flinch. I sensed his satisfaction pulsing across the plane. Stumbling my way toward the candle, I attempted to appeal once again. "You don't understand! You'll destroy everything! Everyone!"

In the blink of an eye, he was in front of me. Only an ice-cold stare bore into my pleading eyes. My voice shook. "Kromer… please…"

He spoke with malice. "You beg too late. Although I enjoy hearing it."

No sooner had my mouth opened when he pinned my chest and back between his hands. A horrific pulling sensation filled the area where my light lay. My ribs strained outward under the pressure. Screaming in pain, I clutched at his wrist.

Grimacing at the effort, a wild look filled his eyes as my inner light flickered chaotically. It was then that I realized he meant to rip it right out of my chest. Death was staring me in the face. And it would not be a pleasant one.

My back slammed into the ground before he straddled me and continued his efforts to rip my life away. Pain was rendering me weaker by the moment, unable to focus on anything else. I closed my eyes and tried to pull my wits together.

Trust your instincts.

I had to make a move and make one now. Snapping my eyes opening, I released my hands from his wrist, grabbed his shirt collar, and yanked him down. It caught him off guard enough that I could headbutt and shove him off. The world was teetering, but I managed to quickly find my feet and bound a large distance away.

Clutching my chest, I breathed deeply, recovering from the agony. My light was still safely inside, regaining its strength. An aura of red surrounded me. It was deeper—the color of my fear.

I swept my eyes over the dome. Kromer was nowhere to be found in the din. Shadows were continuously shooting through in a never-ending spectacle of monstrous births. At any moment, there could be another round of assault. I had to protect myself.

Forcing myself to focus, I funneled my anxiety into a new emotion: anger. There I was, prey to a man who'd taken everything from me. He'd hurt Gil and Panne and toyed with my emotions. But I was *not* helpless.

A brighter shade of red bloomed. The fatigue in my muscles leaked away, and I stood a little taller. I bounced on my heels. Still strong.

"Where are you hiding?" I shouted, my voice echoing all around.

Another voice whispered in response, "Here."

I lashed out toward his voice. He caught my fist in his hand. Our eyes met. He started to twist my arm. Overcoming the pain, I grunted and kicked him hard in the stomach, sending him flying back.

Before he could hit the ground, I was bounding again. Landing in front of the candle, I desperately wracked my brain for a way to stop this.

"Please! I don't know what to do!" I whispered to the pillar. The only response I got was a rush of whispers I couldn't decipher. A thousand voices speaking at once. Furrowing my brows, I reached out toward the flame and spoke again. "Tell me."

Just as my fingers brushed the dark fire, a force ripped me away and threw me through the air. This time, I tucked and landed on my feet, sliding across the ground to a stop. Kromer stood between me and the candle, fists clenched at his side.

"You are no longer worthy of touching the flame. It speaks only to me now."

I seethed. "You hear only what you want to hear. You've gone mad with power."

"On the contrary, my power has elevated me above all existence."

"This isn't elevation, Kromer, it's evil! Some part of you must know that!"

He tilted his head as he took slow steps toward me. "Evil? Such a small-minded concept. What is good? What is evil? There is only knowledge and ignorance, my dear; to rule or be ruled. I have chosen the former on either account."

As I back-stepped from his advances, I tried to keep my emotions in check, but part of me desperately needed to find the part of him that still had any speck of light. "Kromer—"

"Say my name."

"I-"

"Say my name!" he shouted with sudden red-faced ire.

I startled, but then swallowed my nerves and replied calmly. "Max."

He paused, the sound of it having a visible effect. "I have always afforded you the dignity of your name, but you never reciprocated. And yet you call me evil."

This set my blood simmering. I wanted to lash out, but wisdom told me otherwise. "You still make this about us?"

"Is it not? Am I not turning the entire universe on end for you?"

I couldn't believe what I was hearing. He truly was mad. "You're trying to kill me!"

For a moment, his eyes left mine. I hoped it was a sign of reflection. "I offered to make you my queen. You have chosen death. I'm merely giving you what you have asked for."

Speechless, I gaped at him. I could see his aura subtly flash from red to violet, and back again. He was wrestling. Good.

"You told me I was your match, Max."

Another flash.

"You were," he spat bitterly.

"Were? Did the candle tell you we're no longer matched?"

He sneered. "Of course not! The candle itself decided we were matched long before our births—"

"Aha!" I pointed at him. "Then I'm still your match. And you're trying to destroy what the candle has destined."

Max stopped, still a good distance away, and stared at me blankly. It was making me nervous. I subtly poised myself to bound if needed, but he didn't move.

"You don't care about that."

His words were quiet, losing their hostility. I knew I'd hit a mark when I saw another color change, this time longer than last. There was a faint, ever-so-slight glow flickering in his chest. I hated what I was doing. I should've been killing him, but there was more than one way to murder someone. For all the power I could feel coursing through my veins, the strongest one I had to go on was instinct. And I knew his weakest point.

Knitting my brows, I shook my head. "I never said I didn't."

There it was—another flicker in his chest.

He caught me looking at it and turned his back. I could've bounded, attacked him from behind, but something was telling me to have patience. This was a test.

I could see him swiveling his head in distress, as if fighting an oncoming headache. Pressure arose in my chest. When I looked down, my inner light was pulsing, trying to re-establish a connection.

"You tire me with your games." His fists clenched once more, red flaring. A sign of danger.

"I'm tired too, Max."

The redness ebbed. He pivoted and glanced at me. "Tired of mocking me, is that it?"

Boldly, I took a step toward him. "I've never set out to mock you. Disagree with you, fight you, but never that." Another step. "All I have ever given you is my honesty."

Suddenly, his hardened gaze snapped to mine. "What are you doing?"

I froze in my tracks. My throat bobbed. But I kept my eyes linked with his. I couldn't think of a response. "Max, I—"

"You think I'm a fool, don't you?"

Tread carefully, Ellie...

"I think you're in pain."

He laughed, but not jovially. "Pain?" Turning to face me, Max raised his arms, and to my shock, his feet slowly left the ground. "Do I look like I'm in *pain* to you? I'm dripping with power!"

"Say my name."

Confusion clouded him. "What?"

"Say my name," I repeated calmly.

In a rush, he flew forward, landing a few paces away, and stalked over to me, stone-faced. I stood my ground, and in a flash, we were standing

271

toe-to-toe. He glared down at me. I repeated my request once more, quieter.

"Say my name."

"Why?"

My jaw tensed. "Just say it, Max."

His red light flared. "Why?"

"Because if you're going to kill me, I want to hear you say my name one last time!"

"Why do you care?"

"Because maybe I like hearing it from your lips!" I shouted back, shoving him away. He went flying, landing on the ground and skidding to a long stop. Gasping, I clamped my hand over my mouth. It'd been so easy to push him… and so easy to utter those words.

When Max recovered, I knew I'd made a mistake. Murder was in his eyes. Before I could plot my next move, he was speeding through the air, and he knocked me off my feet.

My back hit the ground with a smack, taking the air from my lungs. Flashes of light and shadow filled my vision. My wrists were pinned together above my head by one of his vise-like hands, while the other pressed into my chest. His face was red with rage or pain, or a mixture of both.

"You are a liar!" he screamed.

Involuntary tears rolled down my cheeks as I shook my head and choked out words. "Just say it…"

He shook, gritting his teeth. The light around him rapidly flickering through an array of colors. I could feel the beginnings of the painful pulling on my chest. I had failed.

As the pressure increased, I screamed and arched my back. The shaking of his hands increased. We were on the precipice of life and death, love and hate.

Max yelled in agony, and suddenly, the pressure disappeared. He collapsed, his forehead resting on my chest. His back heaved with heavy breathing as his entire body shook. It was then that I heard the pained sound of my name, barely above a whisper.

"Ellie…"

I stared down at him, my eyes clouded with remnants of tears. I was alive... and held captive by a broken man. When he lifted his head, his eyes were rimmed with red. The grip on my wrists disappeared as he raised himself to hover over me, face-to-face. His tears dripped, mingling with mine.

"Ellie."

The red light was completely gone, glowing a bright violet, the same as mine. Slowly, his hand slid up from my chest to hold the side of my face. Again, my name softly leaped from his lips as they lowered to mine. A golden light immediately blossomed from the point of contact.

Everything else slipped away. All my plans, my past, my future. Even my hate. Every rational thought dissipated like smoke as we lay there amid horrors, his body covering mine, wrapped in a brilliant glow. I could feel the most exuberant energy washing through me in warm waves. It was nearly overwhelming.

The longer he kissed me, the more my pain lessened, and I felt my strength returning. And yet I was powerless to move. We both were.

When at last his lips parted mine, Max looked deeply into my eyes. I expected to see the look of love, but I found only sorrow and shame. He stroked the hair from my face.

"What have I done?"

I couldn't respond. I was more broken than he was.

He pushed himself from me and stood, reaching a hand down to help me up. The light in his chest had returned and was glowing brilliantly. In awe, I accepted his hand. When I was on my feet, he immediately rushed over to the candle. I followed close behind.

"What are you doing?"

"I have to stop this." Max began circling the candle, inspecting the carvings. "How?"

He shook his head. "I'm not sure, exactly, but there must be a way."

"What do you mean 'you're not sure'?"

"I wasn't exactly thinking straight, okay!" he snapped, briefly flaring red. He sighed and ran a hand down his face after I recoiled. "I'm sorry."

Upon scrutinizing the black candle, all I found were strange shapes. Some looked like stars, but I couldn't make out the rest. "None of this makes any sense."

Suddenly, he straightened, staring into the flame. I started to speak, but he held up a finger. For a long time, he simply stared. So long, that I was fearing he had fallen into another trance. My heart pounded. I had no idea how to escape that place—to get to safety—should he turn on me again.

Just as I was getting ready to retreat, Max reached for my hand. He took a deep breath and blew on the flame. For a moment, everything stopped: the monsters, the whispers, my heart. The flame disappeared into a trail of smoke. Then the ground shook. *Violently.* We were knocked off our feet and scrambled backward.

"Max! What have you done?"

"What the candle told me to do!" he shouted over the din.

"What?"

"It said that matched light combined could renew the flame!"

"Well, it sure as hell doesn't look renewed!"

Spidery, glowing cracks formed all around us— in the floor, in the walls. Sections of the dome began to fall away, revealing chunks of starry heavens. Panic seized me as I clung to Max. The star was falling apart.

"We weren't strong enough! I-I don't understand!"

I fought the rocking below us and climbed to my feet, pulling Max along with me. "We've got to get back to the ship!"

His eyes drew back to the dark candle. "But the candle—"

I grasped him by the shirt and forced his eyes back to mine. "We will die here if we don't go!"

Max nodded and grabbed my hand. "Hold on tight!"

Suddenly, he leaped, and we were in the air. Higher and higher we rose, gaining speed. I clung to his hand with every ounce of strength in me.

We flew out through one of the collapsed sections, straight into the open universe. I screamed, sure we'd be killed the instant we left the confines of the candle sanctuary, but our auras flared out brightly, encasing the both of us in a single sphere. I dared to look back at the ball of garish white and black, which was quickly falling to pieces. I felt the chaos within myself, beating down with every section that disappeared into the pit of blackness that was forming in the center.

I looked ahead just as we were careening toward the ship, straight into the bridge window.

"Max! We're going to hit!"

"I know! Trust me!"

There was no time to argue. One moment we were flying through open space, and the next, we were tumbling across the floor of the bridge. I slammed into a low wall with a shriek.

Commotion was already breaking out around me, people running, shouting. My head sang with pain, but I climbed to my feet and whirled around. The glass was miraculously intact, and I had not shredded to ribbons.

Max was shouting instructions to his crew to turn the ship around. I stood in a daze, watching out the window at the collapsing star. The precious candle extinguished. It felt as if my own heart was slowly dying with it. When I looked down, my inner light was weakening and flickering.

"Ellie!"

I turned to find a very frightened Rodina hovered over Gil, who was curled up on the ground, eyes flickering. Instantly, I stumbled through the room, my strength quickly waning.

"No, no, no!"

I collapsed at his side. He was flitting between consciousness and unconsciousness, his lips moving slightly with whispered murmurings. Bonds still held his wrists.

"Gil? Gil, can you hear me?" I turned to the guards, who were distracted by the frightening scene in the window. "Unchain him! Now!" They looked at me, wide-eyed and unsure, and I gathered enough energy to flare my light crimson. "I said now!" Without further delay, one fished the key from the key chain and unlocked his bonds. I motioned to Hunter and Rodina just as Hunter collapsed. Rodina cried out in alarm. I shouted at the guards, "Them too!"

I returned my attention to Gil, who slowly focused on me. His hand clutched his chest. "Ellie... what's... happening..."

Though I knew it was a risk, I gingerly reached for his other hand, relieved to find that it did not hurt him. I brought it to my lips. "It's the candle," I choked on a sob, "it's dying... *we're* dying, Gil."

My eyes left him and scanned the room, landing on the slumped figure in the wheelchair. "No!" I tried to rise and go to Panne's side, only to find my legs had lost their strength. I collapsed to the ground again, staring numbly at Panne's lifeless form. "Panne..."

"Your Majesty! The ship will not yield!" shouted the man in gray, above the pandemonium taking place. "We're caught in a gravitational field!"

Max now kneeled before the window, hand on the glass. "Keep... trying..."

"I don't understand what's happening!" cried Rodina. "Why are you dying?"

"Celestials are tied to the candle. Soul pavers... even more so." It was getting harder to breathe. "Max and I tried to fix things, but we... failed."

I turned to Gil, taking his face in my hands. He reached his hand up to cover one of mine, managing a weak smile. "You came back to me."

"Of course I did."

He brought my palm to his lips. "I'm glad you're here... If this... is the end, I wouldn't... want to be with anyone else." Gil coughed and weakened before my eyes. It frightened me to the core, but there was nothing anyone could do. We were completely helpless.

Tears broke their banks in torrents. I curled up on the floor and pulled myself close, wrapping my arms around him. Despite our dying bodies, our glow still sprang forth. It was warm and familiar, like an old blanket. I kissed him softly.

"I love you, Gillion Braxton."

Just as I finally decided to close my eyes and slip away with him, wherever we would go, I heard a thud behind me. My eyes fluttered back open. Max was on his knees, leaning over me, his face nearly as pale as Gil's. He snatched my hand away from Gil's face. I was too weak to resist.

"What are you doing?"

He then pressed my hand to his chest, above his weakening light. His eyes told of a solemn resignation. It was then that I realized what he was doing. I shook my head, eyes widening.

"Max... no!"

Max shook his head. "I'm just doing what I should've done a long time ago."

"But... but you'll die?"

His lips tugged up briefly. "I'm dying anyway. But this way... you might live." I tried to remove my hand, but he gripped it with a bout of strength that must've been his last. "Goodbye, Ellie."

Suddenly, hot, white light burst from the point where I touched his chest. He began pulling my hand outward, which was now fused firmly. A scream tore from his throat as his face contorted in agony. I shrieked, trying desperately to be free of the hold. No matter how hard I tried, my strength wasn't enough.

And then... it was over. I was released with ease, his grip relaxing entirely. Max sat there with a blank stare. One last rattling breath escaped him before he slumped to the floor. I was too shocked to move for a long moment.

Something fluttered in my upraised hand. When my eyes finally focused, I found I was holding a large, shimmering ball of light. *A small star.* It was warm and alive, its corona dancing around in beautiful colors.

He'd given me his heart.

"Max..."

I wanted to hug it to my chest, to feel its light and its warmth... but my instincts told me otherwise. I turned to Gil, who was now lying frighteningly still. His own light was barely perceptible under his skin. But he was still just as beautiful as the rise we met... as the moment he first laced his fingers through mine... as the moment we shared our first kiss... and as the moment we promised ourselves to each other. I wanted to remember his face forever; imprint it on my mind.

Pulling him close, I kissed him one last time... and pressed the light into his chest.

Chapter 36

Arms cradled me close to a warm chest. When I opened my eyes, a sea of stars greeted me. The glow enveloping me was bright... and golden. I looked up to find a transfigured Gil, focused on the distance. His eyes were illuminated brightly like stars, reminiscent of the strong glow that now resided in his chest.

We were flying through the heavens.

"Gil?"

He gave no response. I could feel the power coursing through him, leaking into my skin. Just being against him filled me with a small burst of strength. I couldn't believe my eyes.

When I turned my head, I saw only a large boulder, on top of which sat the dark candle. It was no longer surrounded by the beautiful dome of light or even the dark one. It sat floating, lifeless, and drifting. Yet somehow, I was still clinging to my own life.

My heart broke at the sight. All the stories Manne ever told me, the reverence of the soul pavers. Our legacy, now dying. Our people ceasing to exist.

We landed on the rock at the foot of the candle. Gil still had his eyes fixed on it.

"What are we doing here?" I asked weakly.

It was then that I heard it—that soft, familiar, female voice. "Ellie..."

I turned my head toward the candle. At first, it looked completely lifeless, but then I saw something— so small, it was easy to miss. *An ember.* On the very tip of the wick.

"I hear you."

Again, the voice spoke. "Come, Ellie." It was like a warm blanket over my soul. I was no longer afraid.

I reached out and touched the spark with a fingertip. The moment I did, there was a rush of wind. Suddenly, we were no longer standing on a dark rock, but in an endless white room. There was no candle to be seen.

Gil carefully stood me up, and I found that strength had returned to my legs. Mouth agape, I looked around, still clinging to Gil's hand. At first, we were alone. Then I heard the voice again, clear and gentle.

"Ellie."

I turned once more to find a shocking sight. There, dressed in a simple white gown, stood a tall, dark-haired woman. Her glowing silver skin was covered in tattoos—all the markings of the candle. A broad smile rested on her cheeks, underneath large, twinkling golden eyes.

"You're... you're..."

She nodded. "This is my humanoid form. I figured this would be easiest for you."

I fell to my knees, averting my eyes. The amount of power I felt in her presence was overwhelming. All the fear I had of the candle, all the horrors... how could it have come from the smiling woman that stood before us now? The one that had been continuously beckoning me all this time?

"Are we dead?" I dare ask.

"You are in the in-between, just as I am. But no, you are not dead." A hand reached down to me. I hesitantly accepted it and stood. She felt as corporeal as any other person.

When I was on my feet, I found her tattoos were all aglow. Immediately, I gasped and retracted my hand from hers. The symbols slowly faded back to black. She simply smiled.

"You're quite special, Ellie. I should be the one kneeling."

"Me?" I examined my hands. There was nothing untoward about them. My inner light was still somewhat weak, even. "I don't understand."

"You're the one who's going to save us all. You both are, in fact." Her gaze shifted to Gil.

He was still in some sort of daze. I slipped my hand in his, and he returned the grasp, but his eyes were gazing off into the distance. I frowned. "What's wrong with him?"

"His soul is newly transformed. He is still coming into consciousness."

This confused me. "But he brought me here?"

She stepped up to Gil. "He feels the call of the candle just as you do... and he feels you." Gently, she swiped her fingers across his forehead and down his temple before stepping back again.

Gil went completely rigid before blinking several times and taking a deep breath. My heart leaped when his eyes traveled from our joined hands up to find mine. They blazed with recognition once more. "Ellie?"

Nodding, I slipped my arms around his neck and pulled him in for a tight embrace, still in disbelief. Our light was once again golden and blazing like never before. Everything felt new and different, and yet entirely familiar. It felt like home. He was alive and in my arms.

Gil slipped his arms around me and held me close. We were beyond the point of tears. Only pure joy radiated between us. I never wanted to let go, but I had so many questions.

"What happened?" asked Gil, looking around us, his eyes resting on the woman. "I know you, don't I?"

She shrugged. "In a way."

My gaze continually drifted to the light in Gil's chest. At last, he noticed it and stood back, examining himself in confusion. "What's happened to me?"

"Gil, I think you're a..." I swallowed hard. "...a soul paver now."

"A strong one, at that," explained the woman. "Not only have you been gifted the light of another paver, but you have it in your lineage, Gillion Braxton."

"Lineage?" I swept my eyes over him. "But I thought it skipped a generation?"

"Yes," she said, "a one Phineas Braxton, your panne, was a child of the light, just as you are now. Your children will also be of the light."

Gil and I stared at each other in shock. The whole time, his grumpy panne was a soul paver? There was a flash of grief in his eyes. I grasped his hand.

"I know you have many, many questions. More than I can answer in the time we have left, I'm afraid."

"You said we're going to save everyone," I reminded her. "How? I thought you told Max that only the matched light could save you?"

"That is correct."

"But it didn't work?"

She smiled, staring at me with twinkling eyes. "Of all things soul pavers do powerfully, love is the most powerful of them all."

For a moment, I just blinked at her. Then, it slowly came to me. I turned to Gil with wide eyes. I reached out and placed my palm on his chest, feeling the warmth and the energy from his light. Tears leaped to my eyes. "It's you..."

"Always has been. Your path was simply a longer one," she said.

Gil smiled and covered my hand with his own. "Hey, I didn't need a candle woman to tell me that."

I laughed and was quickly gathered up in his arms. Gil tucked my head under his chin and breathed deeply. I loved to feel his chest rising and falling. It meant he was very much alive. We both were.

"Now," continued the woman, "I'm afraid our time here is at an end."

Disappointed, I frowned. "Already?" There was so much I wanted to know. So much I *needed* to know. But one look at her resigned face told me that this would be the way.

"I'm afraid so."

"How? How do we help?"

"It's simple..."

* * *

Before we knew it, we were whooshed back to the boulder, standing next to the candle. The calmness of the heavens surrounded us, with the ship still looming in the near distance. Gil had his arms looped around my waist, our light protecting us like a shell. He gazed into my eyes, his still illuminated brightly. I couldn't wipe the soft smile from my face.

"It's actually kind of peaceful out here," I noted.

He nodded, sweeping his eyes around the stars before returning them faithfully to mine. "It is."

"Do you think we'll dream of it? The candle, I mean?" I glanced at the dark pillar, remembering the woman's golden gaze.

Gil sighed. "I don't know. But no matter what happens, we'll get through it together now."

I caressed his cheek with my fingertips. "I couldn't have gotten through any of this without you."

"And you'll never have to." He captured my hand in his and planted a long, sweet kiss on my palm. My heart fluttered, just as it always did. I hoped he never stopped affecting me this way.

When I'd sufficiently re-gathered my thoughts, I took a deep breath. "All right, then... are you ready?"

He nodded, and together we reached our hands toward the candle, his atop of mine, as I gently lay one finger on the tip of the wick. *Step one...*

Step two... light.

Gil gazed at me with a smile on his face as his free arm pulled me even closer. "I love you, Ellie." He dipped his head, and our lips met in a deep embrace.

The moment we kissed, I felt the bolt of warmth burst from our chests and shoot down our arms like lightning. Beautiful, golden starlight whipped around us, followed by the sensation of floating.

When our lips parted, we were indeed floating, drifting high above the candle. Down below was an amazing sight. Bright light was bursting from the center of the candle, straight up into the heavens before branching out in all directions. The inkiness had melted away, and it stood as a white pillar once more.

An indescribable sensation of being whole filled my chest. My inner light beamed brighter than any sun, and every ounce of my strength was renewed and more.

And then the shadows came.

From every corner of the universe, every shadow, every creature that had spilled from the candle came back in a rush, pulled down into the light with a screeching velocity. The reversal had begun. I looked to the left and saw the ship shifting toward us.

"We have to get back to the ship!" I cried out in alarm, snatching Gil's hand and zooming ahead, using new instincts.

As we neared the window, sure enough, chaos had once again broken loose. We flew straight through the shield, and with a burst of light, entered the ship with ease.

Wild eyes flitted to us as people manned their stations, now under the command of Rodina, who'd unseated the captain himself. She stopped only for a moment to gape.

"Holy shit, you're alive! No wonder this thing's gone to hell again!"

I ran up the steps to her side. "Not hell; it's reversing. We reverted the candle."

"Well, whatever it is, it's trying to suck us in again!"

Watching out the window, the dome around the candle was rapidly rebuilding.

"We're too close!" shouted Gil.

"You think?" snapped Rodina, before shouting more orders. "We have to turn and jump to full hyperdrive!"

The former captain, who was poised over a station with a large star chart display in glowing red, shook his head. "Full? With the state we're in? Are you mad?"

Hunter stormed up behind him and grabbed him by the shirt collar, glaring. "The lady says jump, you jump!"

The man shrank and nodded. "How far?"

"I don't care, just go!" shouted Rodina. The ship vibrated. "Now!"

Suddenly, the ship banked sharply left.

"Hold on!"

I grasped the armrest of Rodina's chair and the window filled with streaking light rushing toward us. Screaming, I clenched my eyes shut and waited for it to finally be over. The pulling sensation on my stomach shot my anxiety levels sky-high.

Then, just as quickly as it started, it was over.

With a sigh of relief, I opened my eyes to find the candle no longer before us. Instead, we were floating before a large blue and green world. My heart leaped.

"That's not—"

"No," said Rodina regretfully. "It's not your home, I'm afraid. But…" She tapped on the display in front of her with furrowed brows. "This can't be right."

Gil and Hunter gathered around behind us.

"What is it?" asked Gil.

She tapped again, her eyes growing wider as she continuously looked up at the window. "It's Earth…"

One by one, the crew left their stations to stand before the window and behold the colorful sight.

I was entirely confused. "What's Earth?"

Rodina was transfixed. "It's a planet that hasn't been inhabited by humans for over two thousand years. It's supposed to be a wasteland…"

The captain returned to a station and rapidly tapped through settings before slumping down in a chair. "Scans are showing signs of life, Your Highness."

Rodina smiled and turned to me. "Feel like going on a detour?"

Chapter 37

It took ages of preparation, but at last, the small annex ship met the grounds of Earth. We were in one of five such ships, sent to investigate the renewed planet. I didn't quite understand the excitement of the humans, but I was glad at the prospect of finally being out of a mechanical fortress and on solid ground of some sort. Even if it wasn't the solid ground I was longing for.

It was only the four of us in our group: Rodina, Hunter, Gil, and I. I preferred it that way. My heart was still heavy over Panne. When all the excitement and chaos over our escape had died down, it was then that it hit me he was truly gone. Even the healing of the candle had not healed *him*. It was too late. He now rested in the large ship's mortuary, awaiting burial back on our homeworld, whenever that may be. Engine repairs were needed. The navigation systems were a mess. We were stuck for the time being.

"Are we ready?" asked Rodina, rotating around in the captain's seat and unbuckling her harness.

"Oh yeah." Hunter, who sat beside her, was looking pale, beads of sweat on his brow. She shoved him in the arm.

"Toughen up, Buttercup. We don't need you puking all over the planet too."

He threw her a weak scowl and began undoing his buckles, careful not to upset the bucket on the floor.

Her attention rested on me. "Are you all right?"

I bobbed my head. "I think so. Just…" I drew a shuddering breath. Gil's hand found my shoulder. Throwing him a weak smile of gratitude, I covered his hand with my own and squeezed it before I busied myself with unbuckling.

Soon, we were standing before the back hatch of the ship as it opened and lowered before us, touching green grass. Immediately, a cool breeze whipped in. Without delay, Rodina led the way down the gangplank and into the silvery light.

I hesitated behind, suddenly realizing this would be my first time on another world. What would I see? Would it be dangerous for someone like me? Would there be beasts? My hands shook at the thought.

A warm hand slipped into mine. Gil stood beside me, waiting patiently. He always knew.

Grateful for his support, I at last straightened my spine, and together, we marched down the gangplank and into the alien world.

What we found filled my heart with complete wonder. An enormous field of green grass stretched before us in either direction over rolling hills, flanked by groups of tall trees with green leaves rustling in the wind, and above… was a spray of stars. The wind tousled my hair and whipped gently over my skin. I breathed deeply and slid my eyes shut. It felt almost like home.

When I looked at Gil, he was filled with the same awestruck wonder. And he glowed magnificently. Even through the black uniform he now wore, I could see the blue-white lift from his skin, and the beam radiating from his chest. He caught me looking at him and a tint of pink filled his cheeks. I laughed and bumped my shoulder into his.

Rodina came jogging over to us, looking at the device on her wrist as she glanced continuously off in one direction. "Hey, I think we made it just in time!"

Hunter was close at her heels. "In time for what?"

I followed her gaze and saw something that brought a wide smile to my face. "I think you're right."

"Follow me. You guys are in for a treat!" said Rodina.

We all jogged after her through the fields, Hunter grumbling the whole way. At last, we found the tallest hill, and collapsed, resting our backs against the large boulder at the top. I wiped the glistening sweat from my brow, enjoying the familiar feeling of blood coursing through my pounding heart. Out of respect for Rodina and her tiny feet, we'd refrained from bounding, much to Hunter's disdain. I couldn't help but laugh at his grumpiness now.

"What are we here for?" asked Gil, rolling his head in Rodina's direction. She sat on the other side of me with an anticipatory grin.

"Just keep looking at the horizon. Straight ahead."

So we all rested our eyes ahead. We sat for quite a while in blissful silence, enjoying the rest and breeze. The ground beneath us was fragrant and welcoming.

At last, it started.

Little by little, the stars faded to a pale light. The pale light yielded to pinks and oranges, which then blossomed with gold. Gil's grip on my hand tightened slightly, and I could sense his heart was pounding a bit harder in his chest. I merely rested my head on his shoulder and smiled reassuringly.

When the first blaze of the orb appeared over the horizon, Hunter leaped to his feet and cursed.

"Don't stare directly into it," instructed Rodina with a laugh. "But keep watching."

The light rose higher and higher, bringing its glorious warmth and transforming the landscape with golden rays. Transforming *us*.

Gil sat up with a start, looking at his arms, examining me. We glowed and shimmered like jewels, rivaling the beauty of the star before us. Even Hunter glittered brightly. He desperately tried to brush it from his skin to no avail before cursing and slumping his shoulders in defeat. Rodina stared at him, mesmerized.

"What is this?" asked Gil, climbing to his feet.

I stood next to him, taking his hand in the golden light. With a smile, I turned my face into it and breathed deeply, soaking in the glory. Soaking in the fact that I was alive, and there with the man I loved, and that everything was going to be okay. We'd been through hellfire, the collapse of the universe, and so much darkness. Yet there we were, facing the light at last. And nothing would part us ever again.

"The sun."

The End

About the Author

Heather Carter is an independent fiction author who writes primarily adult fantasy and fantasy romance. She calls the St. Louis area home, and lives with her husband, two children and one extremely spoiled cat. (What writer doesn't?) When she's not writing, she loves to read fantasy novels, make music, and drinks way too much coffee.

You can connect with me on:
- https://heathercarter-author.com
- https://twitter.com/HLCarter_Author
- https://www.facebook.com/hlcarterauthor

Also by Heather Carter

Of Songs and Saltwater
A gender-swapped retelling of The Little Mermaid with a swoony male siren and a fiery Duke's daughter.

Meryn has always been drawn to the sea and the freedom it offers from her father's strict rule. But one day, after escaping her maid and guards, she steals a boat to enjoy a small taste of the waters—when an unnatural storm capsizes her ship and tosses her in the unruly waves.

Fivrial's heart has ached for Meryn ever since they were children, but he never expected their meeting to end in a memory wipe—saving her from the panic of seeing his tail. When he returns to the sea as a siren, his heart is torn, leading him to seek the aid of the sea witch who can grant him human legs. As he washes ashore, Meryn stumbles upon him, and his time begins: make her confess her love within three full moons or return to the sea forever.

Through battles, secrets, and ultimatums, Meryn and Fivrial must decide what they want to fight for. Is true love honestly worth the cost?

The Third Veil
Two halves, one soul... Can Seven find it within her battered heart and fractured soul to trust in love once more?

After working her life as a servant in her abusive mother's cathouse, Seven Ponds dares to dream of a future with the local farmer who stole her heart. But when her home is engulfed in flames, and the fire claims the life of her first love, she struggles against the grief consuming her.

When a strange mechanical device in the sky and terrifying shadow creatures appear, her town is thrust into an unnatural winter signaling the end of the world. Discovering secrets of an ancient past, Seven is thrown through a mysterious veil into a new world... a world full of magic.

Tasked with saving the world, and her mother, Seven stumbles along her fated path, finding it filled with monsters in beautiful disguise, passionate love from an unexpected soulmate, and bitter betrayal.

Can Seven work through her grief and anxiety to save Earth before it's devoured by the Aldaanians? Or will she crumble beneath the weight of the world sitting atop her shoulders?

The Curse of the Bloodwood
A witch's servant...
　　A forbidden love...
　　Until the hedge falls.

Lilia, a young fae lady from the Moonstone Court, stumbles upon a witch's dell and is trapped there by a giant, magical hedge.

Being forced to serve a grumpy old witch is terrible, but she finds companionship in the form of **Pandrus**, young man who's stone by day, handsome gardener by night. When the hedge falls, Lilia is faced with the choice between her freedom... or her heart.

www.ingramcontent.com/pod-product-compliance
Lightning Source LLC
Chambersburg PA
CBHW070726280626
47159CB00023B/2728